A PLUME BOOK

THE GIVING QUILT

Steven Garfinkel

JENNIFER CHIAVERINI is the author of the *New York Times* best-selling Elm Creek Quilts series, as well as five collections of quilt projects inspired by the novels, and the historical novel *Mrs. Lincoln's Dressmaker*. A graduate of the University of Notre Dame and the University of Chicago, she lives with her husband and sons in Madison, Wisconsin.

The Giving Quilt

• AN ELM CREEK QUILTS NOVEL •

JENNIFER CHIAVERINI

A PLUME BOOK

PLUME
Published by the Penguin Group
Penguin Group (USA) Inc., 375 Hudson Street,
New York, New York 10014, USA

USA | Canada | UK | Ireland | Australia
New Zealand | India | South Africa | China
Penguin Books Ltd., Registered Offices: 80 Strand, London WC2R 0RL, England
For more information about the Penguin Group visit penguin.com.

First published in the United States of America by Dutton,
a member of Penguin Group (USA) Inc., 2012
First Plume Printing, 2013

The Library of Congress has catalogued the Dutton edition as follows:

Chiaverini, Jennifer.
The giving quilt : an Elm Creek quilts novel / Jennifer Chiaverini.
p. cm.
ISBN 978-0-525-95360-9 (hc.)
ISBN 978-0-14-218024-2 (pbk.)
1. Compson, Sylvia (Fictitious character)—Fiction. 2. Quiltmakers—Fiction.
3. Quilting—Fiction. 4. Quilts—Fiction. 5. Domestic fiction. I. Title.
PS3553.H473G58 2012
813'.54—dc23   2012008405

Printed in the United States of America
1 3 5 7 9 10 8 6 4 2

Original hardcover design by Elke Sigal

To Marty, Nicholas, and Michael,
who give me love, joy, happiness, and hope every day.

Chapter One

Sylvia

An empty teacup in one hand and a folder of papers tucked under her other arm, Sylvia shut the library doors and strode briskly down the hall to the grand oak staircase of Elm Creek Manor, mulling over the many tasks she had yet to complete in the solitary hour before her guests were due to arrive.

She had descended only a few steps when she was drawn from her reverie by the uncanny sensation of eyes upon her.

She paused on the landing, her grasp firm upon the carved banister worn smooth from generations of Bergstroms who had inhabited the manor before her and the many friends and guests who had resided within its gray stone walls in the decades since. She glanced warily over her shoulder, but when she saw no one—not a soul on the second-floor balcony or on the stairs climbing to the third story high above—she continued her descent, the certainty that she was being watched increasing with every step. As she crossed the foyer and headed toward the older west wing of the manor, she sensed rather than heard soft footfalls on the black marble floor behind her. Turning quickly, she glimpsed a swirl of black fabric and upraised arms and sharp white fangs an instant before her stalker shouted, "Boo!"

"Oh, my heavens!" exclaimed Sylvia, clutching the folder to her chest. "What a frightening creature!"

Four-and-a-half-year-old James frowned around a mouthful of plastic vampire fangs, his arms falling to his sides. "You weren't scared."

"Indeed I was," Sylvia assured him. "Absolutely terrified."

"No, you weren't," James insisted glumly, his words muffled by the plastic teeth. "You didn't even drop your cup. It would have smashed into a hundred pieces."

Sylvia frowned briefly at the cup that had betrayed her. "I'm sorry to disappoint you, dear," she told the youngster. But she wasn't very sorry, considering that the teacup was one of the few precious pieces of her grandmother's wedding china that had not been broken or sold off long ago. She supposed she could have shrieked, thrown the folder into the air, and pretended not to enjoy James's triumphant grin as the pages fluttered to the black marble floor like blanched autumn leaves, but her knees and back were not up to the task of crawling around to gather up the scattered pages. There were limits to the amount of terror she was willing to feign for the boy's amusement. "You truly do make a most terrifying vampire."

"She would've been more scared if you hadn't yelled 'Boo,'" said James's twin sister, Caroline, stepping out from behind the draperies adorning one of the tall windows flanking the front entrance. "Vampires don't yell 'Boo.'"

"Zombies don't talk at all," James shot back, "so you should just be quiet."

"They do too talk," said Caroline, padding toward them in her pink ballet leotard and her mother's black leather coat. Sylvia eyed the hem as it skimmed the floor and wondered if Sarah was aware that her favorite autumn coat had apparently found its way into the twins' bin of dress-up clothes. "Zombies say, 'Braaaaiiinnssss.' Anyway, I can talk all I want because I'm not a zombie anymore."

"What are you, then?" Sylvia inquired. "A princess?"

Caroline looked mildly affronted. "No," she said emphatically, her blond curls bouncing as she shook her head. "I'm a vampire slayer."

"Of course. How foolish of me." Sylvia raised her eyebrows at James. "Well, it seems to me that if you're a vampire, and she's a vampire slayer—"

James yelped and bolted away, the black cape of his old Halloween costume streaming behind him as he raced up the stairs as fast as his little legs could go. With a shriek of delight, Caroline set off in pursuit. Smiling, Sylvia watched the twins hurtle up both flights of stairs and disappear down the third-floor hallway. The playroom door slammed, startling her so that she nearly dropped the teacup after all. Cradling it in her palms, she shook her head, sighed more in amusement than exasperation, and continued on to the kitchen, where several of her dearest friends awaited her.

Friends—such a simple word, defined differently by everyone who used it. No single word of any definition could encompass all that the Elm Creek Quilters meant to Sylvia. In the twelve years since she had returned to the small rural town of

Waterford, Pennsylvania, to accept responsibility for her family's estate upon her elder sister's death, the women gathered in the kitchen had become Sylvia's colleagues and confidantes, her apprentices and her advisers. But more than that—they had become her family.

The sound of their laughter and the aroma of cinnamon-roasted apples drifted down the hallway toward her, and she quickened her pace, eager to find out what amused them so. Surely they weren't laughing at poor, beleaguered Sarah, who had been engaged in a frenzy of cooking and baking since early that morning. In the spirit of Quiltsgiving, their annual winter camp session devoted to creating quilts for charity, Sarah had valiantly offered to take charge of preparing delicious meals befitting Elm Creek Quilt Camp's sterling reputation for themselves and their twenty-four guests. Her friends eagerly and gratefully allowed Sarah to take the lead, although they had assured her they would pitch in if needed.

When Sylvia entered the kitchen, she found her friends doing exactly that. Stout Gwen, her gray-streaked auburn hair falling in a heavy curtain down her back, briskly chopped vegetables and, with a dramatic swirl of long batik skirts and the clinking of beaded necklaces, turned to slide them from the cutting board into a large stockpot bubbling on the stovetop. She was a professor of American studies at nearby Waterford College and the mother of another founding Elm Creek Quilter, Summer, a graduate student at the University of Chicago.

"One of these years I'll join you for Quiltsgiving," Summer had said wistfully during her holiday phone call. "Maybe when I've finished my dissertation. I'll be with you in spirit."

Of course she would be, Summer and their other dear

friends who had left their circle of quilters but whose hearts remained at Elm Creek Manor—Bonnie, who had moved to Maui to run a quilter's retreat and was engaged to a handsome Hawaiian; Judy, who had moved away to accept her dream job as a professor of computer engineering at the University of Pennsylvania; and Anna, their former chef, who had once ruled over the kitchen with kindness, generosity, and impressive skill.

It had been at Anna's urging that Sylvia had agreed to install the dishwasher from which Maggie took clean plates and cups, her elegant hands graceful and assured. As she stacked the dishes in a nearby cupboard, a tortoiseshell barrette kept her long waves of light brown hair from falling into her oval face. At forty-three, Maggie was their newest teacher but not their youngest, although her coltish slenderness, the sprinkling of freckles across her nose and cheeks, and the shy cast to her soft hazel eyes often made her seem much younger. When Maggie glanced at the clock above the stove and sighed, Sylvia noted that it was almost time for Maggie's daily phone call from Russell, her long-distance boyfriend. He was coming to visit later that week, and Sylvia suspected that Maggie was already counting the hours until his arrival.

On the other side of the kitchen, Diane, tall and blond and admirably fit for a mother of two grown sons, poured banana bread batter into a series of small loaf pans, occasionally scraping the sides of the bowl with a spatula or pausing to sip from her favorite oversized pink cappuccino mug. She scowled as if she had been dragged unwillingly out of bed only moments before, but Sylvia knew for a fact that she had been up for hours, as every Sunday morning Diane attended a six o'clock kickboxing class as faithfully as she attended ten o'clock Mass.

Sylvia heard Gretchen and Joe rummaging around in the pantry before she saw them. Gretchen, the compassionate soul who had conceived of Quiltsgiving, stood on a stepstool and stretched to retrieve a sack of sugar from the top shelf while her husband steadied her and murmured warnings for her to take care. Gretchen wore a thick taupe cardigan buttoned over a crisp white blouse, but the formality of her navy wool skirt was offset by her comfortable fleece slippers, their size exaggerated by her thin ankles. She was in her early seventies, with steel-gray hair cut in a pageboy and a frame that seemed chiseled thin by hard times, but she had lost the careworn look she had brought with her when she had accepted the teaching position with Elm Creek Quilts and had moved into the manor with her husband five years before. Gretchen and Joe, an expert restorer of antique furniture, were the most contentedly married couple of Sylvia's acquaintance, with the exception of herself and her own dear Andrew.

At the thought of her husband, Sylvia glanced around the kitchen, not expecting to find him there but not entirely without hope that she might. He was probably outside helping Matt in the orchard or the barn, escaping the hustle and bustle of the kitchen for a few quiet moments of solitude before the quilt campers descended upon the manor.

Sarah turned away from one of the ovens, a steaming pan of apple-cranberry crisp in her oven-mitted hands, and her eyes met Sylvia's. "I don't know how Anna managed to feed fifty-plus quilt campers three meals a day five months straight year after year," she declared wearily as she set the hot pan on a cooling rack. Sighing, she tucked a loose strand of reddish-brown hair behind her ear and brushed a dusty smear of flour from her right cheek with the back of the oven mitt. The gesture nudged her wire-rimmed glasses out of place, and Sarah impatiently pushed them back upon the bridge of her nose. "And I *really* don't understand how she managed to be so cheerful doing it."

"Anna was a professional chef," Sylvia reminded her, then corrected herself. "*Is* a professional chef." After all, Anna had not abandoned her profession when she resigned from Elm Creek Quilts.

"I'd be thrilled to have her back even if she never cooked for us again," said Sarah glumly, taking a second pan of apple-cranberry crisp from the lower oven.

They all smiled at the improbability of that. On her all-too-rare visits to the manor, Anna reveled in whipping up delicious meals for her friends in the state-of-the-art kitchen she herself had designed. She was generous with her talents, as they all aspired to be, and she had regularly indulged them with their particular favorite dishes. Sylvia was partial to Anna's apple strudel, which reminded her so much of her great-great-aunt Gerda Bergstrom's celebrated recipe that with every bite, Sylvia imagined herself a child at Christmas again, surrounded by her parents and siblings and cousins, with snow falling softly against the windowpanes, a crackling fire in the hearth, and carols and laughter filling the air.

Snowy-haired Agnes's blue eyes, bright and cheerful behind oversized pink-tinted glasses, lit on the folder tucked beneath Sylvia's arm. "Are those for me?" she asked, setting aside her broom.

"Indeed they are," said Sylvia, handing her the folder of registration forms. Long ago, Agnes had been married to Sylvia's younger brother, although their romance had been cut tragically short when he had been killed in the service during the Second World War. Even though Agnes had remarried and had been widowed anew after many happy years, Sylvia would always consider Agnes her sister-in-law. "I made a few notes based upon the campers' interests and hometowns, but I'll leave the rest to you."

Agnes nodded eagerly, seated herself in one of the comfortable booths, and spread out the forms on the table before her. Agnes always took charge of room assignments, a task everyone agreed she handled best. Although Sarah tried to accommodate every camper's special requests as soon as their registration forms arrived in the mail or online, sometimes mistakes occurred, and other times the campers did not make their preferences known until they stood in the foyer. A quilter might need a first-floor room, only to discover that she had been given the key to a third-floor suite and that all first-floor rooms were booked. Two campers might decide on the way over from the airport that they wanted to room together, and roommate assignments would have to be shifted quickly and delicately, without hurting anyone's feelings. Agnes, with her perfect combination of diplomacy and amiable resolve, deftly spun solutions that made everyone feel as if they had received the best part of the compromise.

While Agnes worked on room assignments, Sylvia carefully washed and dried her teacup, and just as carefully put it away. Then she tied on an apron and joined in the preparations for the Welcome Banquet, a celebration that marked the commencement of each new quilt camp session—and would inaugurate the fifth annual Quiltsgiving as well, although it was no ordinary week of quilt camp.

Within months of joining the Elm Creek Quilters, Gretchen had come to Sylvia with an intriguing idea for a way they could use their creative gifts to give back to their community. She proposed that they hold a special session of winter camp devoted to making quilts for Project Linus, a national organization whose mission was to provide love, a sense of security, warmth, and comfort to children in need through the gifts of new, handmade blankets, quilts, and afghans. The participating quilters would enjoy a week at Elm Creek Manor absolutely free of charge, but rather than working on quilts for themselves, they would make soft, comforting children's quilts for Project Linus. Sylvia and the other Elm Creek Quilters found the idea absolutely ingenious. They quickly settled upon the week after Thanksgiving for their special camp session, and the season inspired the name.

In the months that followed, Gretchen founded a chapter of Project Linus in Waterford, which grew steadily over the winter and into spring as local quilting guilds spread the word and sounded the call for volunteers. Once a month the "Blanketeers" met at the manor to sew, knit, and crochet together, as well as to arrange the distribution of their handiwork. Elm Creek Manor became a drop-off site for donated quilts, afghans, and blankets, and every few weeks Gretchen would deliver them to the Elm Creek Valley Hospital, where they offered comfort to seriously ill children, and to the fire department, where they warmed youngsters rescued from fires and accidents.

The Elm Creek Quilters had hoped their ambitious project would result in many soft, bright, and beautiful quilts to warm and comfort mothers and children alike. But it was an untried experiment.

Only time would tell if it would succeed.

Before long, the time for planning and preparation ran out and Gretchen's ambitious experiment was under way. Unlike

Elm Creek Quilt Camp's summer sessions, where the days were packed with classes, lectures, and seminars and the evenings full of scheduled entertainment, the first Quiltsgiving was more akin to a glorified, weeklong quilting bee. Fifteen volunteers brought their own projects in various stages of completion and worked diligently upon them, alone or in pairs or in small groups, in whatever cozy nook or corner of the manor they preferred. Three times a day the entire group met for meals in the banquet hall. After nightfall, when the campers' eyes and fingers and backs had grown weary, Matt or Andrew would build a fire in the enormous ballroom fireplace and Gretchen would invite everyone to gather for a quiet, reflective hour before bed. They would sip tea or hot cider made from apples grown in the estate's orchards, munch cookies, and chat about the work they had accomplished that day and their goals for the next.

By the end of the week, the Quiltsgiving Blanketeers had completed an impressive number of quilts to donate to Project Linus, which they proudly displayed at the Farewell Breakfast that brought Quiltsgiving to a close. Sylvia thought that would be a fine high note to end upon, but perfectionist Sarah insisted upon distributing evaluation forms, just as she did at the end of each week of summer camp. "It's the only way to know if we're meeting our guests' expectations," Sarah explained as she gathered up the forms after the last campers had departed.

"They got a free week at Elm Creek Manor, enjoyed three of Anna's fabulous gourmet meals a day, and they made quilts for charity, exactly as advertised," Diane replied, eying the stack of forms warily. "What unmet expectations could they possibly have?"

Privately Sylvia agreed. Still, the following afternoon she joined Gretchen and Sarah in the library to review the forms.

To Sylvia's relief, the campers' comments were overwhelmingly positive. Yet a pair of wishes—for structure and instruction—did emerge. Several campers, most of them new quilters, expressed disappointment that they had not learned any new techniques or patterns that week. Although they had known that they would be working upon their own projects, they were unaccustomed to having so many unscheduled hours to fill and had expected to have more opportunity to benefit from the knowledge and experience of the Elm Creek Quilters. "I didn't think I'd have to stumble along on my own," one anonymous camper had written.

The remark stung, but Sylvia took a deep breath and reminded herself that they had solicited the campers' opinions and that constructive criticism would not benefit her if she became defensive.

Not so Gretchen. "We were always available to answer questions or offer help," she protested. "I wasn't aware that anyone was struggling."

"Perhaps they were too shy to ask for advice," remarked Sylvia. "We were hard at work on our own projects, except when we were preparing meals and such. Perhaps they were reluctant to interrupt."

"Maybe it's easier to ask us for help when we're standing at the front of a classroom," mused Sarah, returning her gaze to the evaluation forms. "We'll have to figure out a way to remind our campers that the Elm Creek Quilters are teachers, first and foremost, one and all."

"Would it be enough to tell them at breakfast each day?" asked Gretchen.

Sarah looked dubious. "Maybe."

"Perhaps we could designate one or two Elm Creek Quilters each hour to circulate among the campers and keep an eye on things rather than working on their own projects," said Sylvia.

"That couldn't hurt," said Sarah, but her slight frown and furrowed brow told Sylvia that she thought it wouldn't suffice. Sarah soon returned her attention to the evaluation forms, but Sylvia knew her younger friend's keen mind was already working on a solution.

That they would host a second winter camp for charity had never been in doubt; the abundance of warm, cozy quilts their campers had made for Project Linus the previous year was evidence enough that they should continue. The holiday season gave way to spring and National Quilting Day, followed by another busy summer of Elm Creek Quilt Camp, yet Sylvia, Sarah, and Gretchen never stopped thinking and talking together. By Labor Day and the end of the summer camp season, they finally concocted a solution to the problem that had bothered the novices among their Quiltsgiving guests: They would offer an optional, weeklong class, designed for beginners but suitable for anyone who wanted to learn a new, simple, attractive pattern that could be assembled with ease. Each morning they would tackle a different stage of the quiltmaking process, leaving the afternoons free for students to work on their projects individually and to seek extra help from their teachers. The Elm Creek Quilters would design quilts meant especially for giving— quick to put together but as beautiful and warm as any more complicated pattern. They could design a new Giving Quilt each Quiltsgiving to encourage volunteers to return year after year. Thus the most faithful volunteers would gradually build a repertoire of patterns they could draw upon whenever they needed to make a quilt on short notice or to make quilts to benefit their own local chapters of Project Linus.

Sylvia declared that Sarah's plan was inspired, and she asked for the honor of designing the first Giving Quilt. She chose the Bright Hopes block not only for its simple pattern—four rectangles framing a central square in the style of the popular Log Cabin block—but also for the rich symbolism of its name. All the Elm Creek Quilters had bright hopes for the second Quiltsgiving and for the many more winter camps they anticipated would follow.

Sylvia's Bright Hopes class proved to be an unqualified success, meeting with such high praise that Sarah readily volunteered to design the Giving Quilt the following year. She chose the Rail Fence block, a traditional pattern of four groups of four narrow rectangles sewed together lengthwise and arranged with the longest side alternately on the horizontal and the vertical. For the fourth Quiltsgiving, Gwen taught an improvisational version of the Stacked Coins pattern, which suited her eccentric nature. Later she confided to Sylvia that she had hoped to challenge her more rigid students, those who adhered to published patterns so strictly that they insisted upon matching the exact fabrics in the quilts shown in the accompanying photos. "If I don't push them to think outside the block," Gwen said, "I doubt they ever will." Afterward, the students' evaluations proved that Gwen had certainly accomplished her goal of challenging them, to the delight of many and the consternation of a few. Not every quilter, especially those who found comfort in tried-and-true patterns and methods, had appreciated being nudged none too gently out of her comfort zone.

For the fifth Quiltsgiving, Gretchen offered to create a more conventional Giving Quilt to appease the vocal minority of campers who had struggled unhappily the previous year. Sylvia knew Gretchen had stayed up well past midnight on the Saturday after Thanksgiving sewing the binding and a hanging sleeve to display her quilt, but when Sylvia had passed by the library on her way to breakfast early Sunday morning, she found a pajama-clad Gretchen seated before the office computer making a few last-minute changes to her instruction sheets. When she finally came down to breakfast, dressed and ready for the day, Gretchen reported that she had printed enough handouts for all of the students who had registered for the class, as well as a few extras. More campers were certain to enroll after they arrived for registration and saw the Giving Quilt hanging proudly from the second-floor balcony in the grand front foyer, given pride of place between the purple-and-green Broken Star quilt Sylvia had made as she was recovering from a stroke and a Round Robin medallion quilt the other Elm Creek Quilters had made for her around the same time. Enrollments would rise yet again after the Welcome Banquet, where conversation never failed to turn to that year's Giving Quilt and newcomers learned from veteran campers how popular the class was, how essential to a complete Quiltsgiving experience.

As midafternoon approached, Sarah and her friends completed as many of the preparations for the Welcome Banquet as could be accomplished ahead of time. Agnes cheerfully reported that she had made only a few minor adjustments to the room assignments, including giving a remote suite to a woman who warned on her registration form that she snored "like a thunderstorm rolling in" and reuniting two sisters who had asked to share a room but had been given suites on opposite sides of the manor. "They must be very fond of each other, to want to share a suite when they could have separate rooms for free," Agnes remarked with a sidelong glance at Sylvia, who had been locked in perpetual rivalry with her late sister, Claudia, and had only truly warmed to Agnes after they launched Elm Creek Quilts.

Sylvia gave Agnes a comical frown and shook her head to indicate that she was far too busy to rise to the teasing bait. At that moment, the three resident Elm Creek husbands arrived—Joe from his woodshop in the barn, Matt from his orchards, and Andrew from the banquet hall, where he had been setting tables for the Welcome Banquet. "Are we ready to get to work?" Sylvia asked, and everyone laughed, because they had already been working for hours.

Sylvia led the way to the front foyer, where they arranged two long tables on the black marble floor and placed several chairs on either side of them, a few for themselves and more for their arriving guests. Then they fell into their usual roles, the routine familiar and comfortable from years of practice. Gwen collated maps of the estate with daily schedules and descriptions of their evening programs, Maggie and Diane arranged fresh late-autumn flowers from Matt's greenhouse in each suite, and Agnes paired room keys with quilters' names and arranged them in alphabetical order in neat rows upon one of the tables. Sarah and Gretchen inspected the classroom to be sure that sewing machines, lights, and audiovisual equipment were in working order, while Sylvia supervised and lent a helping hand wherever she was needed. Matt, Andrew, and Joe stood by ready to park cars and assist with luggage, often peering out the tall double doors in case an early arrival surprised them. Over time the Elm Creek Quilters had learned that some campers anticipated the start of the fun-filled week so eagerly that they arrived well before the appointed hour. Once, years before, a camper had entered through the back door at nine o'clock in the morning and had sat alone in the kitchen, sewing a quilt block and helping herself from the pot of coffee left over from Sarah and Matt's breakfast. The Elm Creek Quilters didn't discover her there, perfectly content and comfortable and entirely unconcerned with her hostesses' astonishment and dismay, until lunchtime. Nowadays the more experienced, more mature Sarah wouldn't allow such a little thing to fluster her. Raising her bright, energetic, imaginative twins had taught her to take the unexpected in stride.

Whatever the hour of their return to Elm Creek Manor, a few veteran quilt campers preferred to take the fork in the road that wound through the forest and past Matt's orchards and the red banked barn Sylvia's great-grandfather had built in 1864, park their cars in the lot behind the manor, and enter through the back door as that notorious early arrival had done. On registration day, however, most guests preferred to use the front entrance and have Matt, Andrew, or Joe valet-park for them. Sylvia understood perfectly that the front approach to Elm Creek Manor bestowed upon their guests the sense that they had arrived at another, separate, sheltered and sheltering place, a haven from the chaos and disappointments of ordinary life. Although the lush, verdant greens of spring and summer had long since passed and even the brilliant colors of autumn were only a memory, the estate retained its beauty, a rustic elegance that befit any season.

After the campers turned off from the main road to Waterford onto the narrow, gravel drive to the manor, their cars and minivans would wind through the bare-limbed forest, rambling alongside the clear, rushing waters of Elm Creek until they reached the fork in the road, turned north, and emerged upon a sun-splashed clearing. There the gray stone manor would suddenly appear, steadfast and welcoming, surrounded by a broad, rolling lawn clinging proudly to the last of its fading summer green. Next visitors would see the wide, covered verandah, its tall white columns spanning the width of the manor, and as they approached, they would spot the twin arcs of the stone staircases descending to the driveway, which encircled a fountain in the shape of a rearing horse, the symbol of the Bergstrom family. Sylvia enjoyed watching campers as they climbed wide-eyed from their cars and took in the scene, awestruck and thrilled that they would be able to spend a week in such a grand place. Sometimes, especially upon returning from an extended trip, Sylvia still experienced that same thrill, even though Elm Creek Manor was as familiar to her as her own heartbeat, as the warmth of Andrew's hand in hers. Although she had forsaken Elm Creek Manor for fifty years, it had always been her true home, the home of her heart.

She was delighted yet again each time she welcomed new friends and old to it.

At ten minutes before two o'clock, a trifle early but not enough to catch the Elm Creek Quilters unprepared, the first guest arrived, lugging a suitcase and a tote bag stuffed with fabric, pattern books, and notions. Her thick, wiry mass of hair was tied in a knot at the nape of her neck, but its length still reached past her shoulder blades. Just inside the doorway at the foot of the four marble stairs that separated the tall double doors from the foyer proper, she stopped short and gave a little gasp at the sight of Gretchen's quilt, proudly displayed from the second-floor balcony. "Is that this year's Giving Quilt?" she asked in a voice flavored with a charming Southern drawl.

"It is indeed," replied Sylvia. "Our own Gretchen Hartley designed it."

The woman admired Gretchen's handiwork through thick, rectangular lenses with black plastic frames—but her gaze quickly turned doubtful. "It's so pretty, it's hard to believe most people could make it in a week."

"It's easier than it looks," said Gretchen, who had returned to the foyer from the ballroom at the sound of the front door, accompanied by her husband and Agnes, who promptly took her seat behind the registration table and smiled expectantly at the new arrival. "It's composed of easy-to-cut squares and rectangles, and I have lots of tricks to speed things along. You'll see."

Joe stepped forward to assist the newcomer with her luggage up the four marble stairs, and she trailed after him to the registration tables, her gaze lingering on the quilt. "I'll be in a front-row seat at class tomorrow," she promised Gretchen earnestly, her brows drawing together over green eyes as if to emphasize the significance of her vow. "If I really apply myself—and I intend to—I think I could make two Giving Quilts this week."

"That's the spirit," said Gretchen, smiling.

"I admire your ambition," remarked Sylvia.

The woman looked from one Elm Creek Quilter to the other, shaking her head. "Oh, I didn't mean to suggest that I wouldn't accomplish more than that. I brought a few UFOs from home to work on too. I intend to finish five quilts total this week."

Gretchen's eyebrows rose. "That's a quilt a day."

The woman shrugged. "Well, not really, not if you include

today and Saturday. I think I can squeeze in some sewing to-night and a few hours more before the Farewell Breakfast Saturday morning." She paused for a moment, thinking. "I'd like to make more but I think that might be pushing it."

"Please remember to take a few breaks to eat and sleep now and then, won't you?" said Sylvia, only partly in jest. When the woman nodded, utterly serious, Sylvia resolved to keep an eye on her throughout the week to make sure she set down her needle and enjoyed a walk by the creek or an evening program with new friends now and then. Sylvia wanted her guests to leave Elm Creek Manor refreshed, relaxed, and renewed, not utterly exhausted.

"What's your name, dear?" prompted Agnes.

"Pauline." The woman's gaze fell to the list on the table and she craned her neck to read the upside-down text. "Pauline Tucker from Sunset Ridge, Georgia."

"Welcome to Elm Creek Manor, Pauline," said Agnes warmly, handing her a room key and the various maps, schedules, and papers Gwen had sorted into neat packets. When Matt offered to valet-park her car, Pauline dug a set of keys attached to a jumble of souvenir key chains from her coat pocket, handed him the set, and jokingly asked him to fill up the gas tank while he was at it.

As Joe escorted Pauline upstairs, the double doors swung open again and in came three women in matching quilted coats worn over identical fuchsia sweatshirts. Sylvia smiled, recognizing the three inseparable summer campers immediately by their signature color and their companionship, although she didn't recall their names. In fact, if Sylvia ran into one of them alone on a street in downtown Waterford, clad in brown wool or navy tweed, she might think her a perfect stranger.

Fairly bursting with delight, Team Fuchsia—as Diane had privately nicknamed them—called out greetings to the Elm Creek Quilters and made their way to the registration table with rollaway suitcases in tow. Almost as soon as the door closed behind them, it opened again, and the president of the Waterford Quilt Guild entered. "Hello, Nancy," Sylvia said, welcoming her warmly as Andrew came forward to assist her with her bags. Sylvia linked her arm through Nancy's and escorted her to the registration table, inquiring about her husband, children, and various works in progress. Since Nancy had assumed leadership of the local guild, she and Sylvia had found many occasions to bring Elm Creek Quilters and Waterford Quilt Guild members together for socializing, advocacy for their mutually beloved art form, and, of course, quilting at the manor. At present the two groups were collaborating on the Waterford Winter Quilt Festival, a quilt show that would be held at the manor in February. Sylvia had the exhibit space and Nancy possessed the quilt show expertise, and together they were a formidable team. Sylvia hoped to find time during the busy Quiltsgiving week to take Nancy aside to review photos of several quilts recently submitted for entry into the show.

After Nancy collected her keys and paperwork and headed off to her room with a promise to see Sylvia later, Sylvia returned to welcoming other guests, sighing with contentment. She had so much to do, so many new challenges to tackle, so many good times with friends and family to anticipate. That, she believed, was the secret to her longevity.

The noise and activity brought James and Caroline running downstairs from the playroom, and they begged their mother to be allowed to help with registration. At first Sarah hesitated, but she soon relented and agreed that the twins could help hold the front doors open for the guests, welcome them to Elm Creek Manor, and direct them to the registration table—but they must not get in the way or try to lift any heavy suitcases. The youngsters took their jobs very seriously. Sylvia had to smile whenever she heard them greet newcomers with a sweet, enthusiastic, "Welcome to Elm Creek Manor!"

Throughout the busy afternoon, so many familiar campers passed through the doors of Elm Creek Manor that newcomers stood out. Soon after Nancy arrived, a woman with smooth skin the color of deep espresso entered clad in a knee-length charcoal-gray wool coat and sensible shoes. As well as Sylvia could ascertain from a distance, she appeared to be in her late thirties, with short, glossy curls and soft, dark eyes. She paused in the entranceway, and as she set down her tote bag to loosen a striking scarf of what appeared to be black cotton imprinted with geometric designs of white and rust, she ran a guarded, appraising gaze over the women enjoying refreshments and chatting and laughing and welcoming one another from the foyer to the second-floor balcony. Something in her carriage suggested sorrow and steel, and a determination that kept a soul-deep weariness in check, and Sylvia found herself suddenly, inexplicably moved. At that moment, Sarah approached the woman, and when she smiled and shook Sarah's hand, her face lit up with such warmth that Sylvia found herself smiling too.

Sarah directed her to the registration table, where Sylvia met her. "Welcome to Elm Creek Manor," she said, extending her hand. "I'm Sylvia Bergstrom Compson Cooper."

"Jocelyn Ames," the woman said, shaking Sylvia's hand. "It's a pleasure to meet you. I've heard a lot about you."

"Most of it good, I hope."

"All of it good, I'm sure," said Agnes stoutly.

"All of it good," Jocelyn assured them, and then, in a more confidential tone, added, "I signed up for the Giving Quilt course, but I wanted to verify that it *is* suitable for beginners?"

"It most certainly is," said Sylvia, indicating Gretchen's sample quilt hanging from the balcony. "We do assume that you've mastered some basic sewing skills first."

"Thanks to my high school home ec teacher, I have," said Jocelyn, accepting her key and information packet from Agnes. "The home ec teacher at the school where I teach gave me a re-fresher course last week too, just to make sure. Of course, we don't call it home ec anymore. It's Family Consumer Science."

Agnes's eyebrows rose. "Do you mean that all those years I called myself a homemaker, I should have said I was a scientist?"

Jocelyn smiled. "Apparently so."

"What do they call math class?" Sylvia inquired.

"For the sixth grade, it's Understanding Concepts of Everyday Mathematics."

"And what do you teach?" asked Agnes.

"Social studies."

Sylvia was surprised to hear it was still called social studies. name was ripe for revision if any a school subject was.

njoy all the topics I teach, but my passion is American Jocelyn said. "I saw on your website that one of your rograms later this week is a lecture on antique quilts ate. I'm very much looking forward to it."

" said Sylvia. "I confess it's pure self-indulgence on to show off my ancestors' quilts and brag about us of you and my other guests to humor me."

"Oh, Sylvia, that's nonsense," chided Agnes, but Jocelyn got the joke and promised Sylvia she would endure the program as best she could.

As soon as Matt appeared and offered to carry Jocelyn's bags upstairs to her room, a pair of quilters hesitantly approached Sylvia, pens in hand, and asked her to autograph their 1982 American Quilter's Society calendars, which featured her best-known work, *Sewickley Sunrise,* as the quilt for May. Thus she was preoccupied and witnessed only from across the room the reunion of the two sisters who had narrowly escaped being assigned to separate suites thanks to Agnes's intervention. They arrived separately but only minutes apart, so one sister, tall, blond, and sturdily built, had only just reached the top of the staircase when the other—blond, a trifle more slender, and a few inches shorter—crossed the threshold. "Linnea," the newcomer called out, and her sister promptly set down her suitcase and plastic sewing tote, raced down the stairs, and hustled across the foyer to embrace her sister. They laughed and rocked from side to side as they greeted each other, which told Sylvia that they did not live in the same town, or perhaps even the same state, and they saw each other far less frequently than they liked. Sylvia was well pleased that Elm Creek Manor could be the site for such a happy reunion, and she resolved to chat with the sisters later to find out if she had interpreted the joyful scene correctly.

After the initial cluster of arriving guests, the pace slowed, with one or two campers entering the manor every quarter hour or so. A few lingered near the refreshments table making the acquaintance of other guests over coffee and cookies, but otherwise the foyer was left to the Elm Creek Quilters. With too little activity to entertain them, the twins grew bored and ran outside to play on the front lawn under the watchful eyes of Matt, Joe, and Andrew, who had run out of registration work to occupy their time. For their part, the Elm Creek Quilters filled the lull with chat, and they were engrossed in conversation about their friend Bonnie's upcoming Maui wedding when a hesitant clearing of a throat caught their attention. Unnoticed, a guest had slipped in through the front double doors and had halted a discreet distance away from the registration table, as if she were reluctant to interrupt them or approach uninvited.

"Oh, hello," Sylvia said, greeting the newcomer brightly. "Here we are gabbing away when you want to register. Please forgive us for this poor welcome."

"It's really okay." The newcomer smiled shyly and shifted her backpack on her shoulders. She was of medium height, slender but somewhat pear shaped, and blue eyed, with chestnut-brown hair falling in a soft pageboy to her shoulders. "Who could ever feel unwelcome at Elm Creek Manor?"

The corners of her smile quivered as if she might be the rare individual who could, and something about her discomfiture struck Sylvia as familiar. "Karen?" she said as the name came to her unexpectedly, like a windfall apple rolling downhill and coming to rest at her feet. "Karen Wise?"

The woman's smile turned upward again in relief. "Yes, that's right. You actually remember me?"

"Of course I do." Sylvia glanced over her shoulder to Agnes, Sarah, Diane, and Gwen, who were nodding. Gretchen and Maggie, who stood some distance away helping a camper interpret the estate map, were unaware of the exchange and thus did not nod or even glance their way. Nevertheless, Sylvia added, "We all do."

"You made quite an impression on your last visit," said Diane.

Wryly, Karen replied, "So did you."

Diane winced at the memory. More than five years before, when the Elm Creek Quilters had sought new teachers to replace two founding members who intended to leave their circle to pursue other dreams, Karen had been one of the five applicants invited to interview at Elm Creek Manor. What the other Elm Creek Quilters did not figure out until later—and what Karen had probably never learned—was that Diane had tried to sabotage the interviews under the misguided hope that if suitable replacements couldn't be found, Judy and Summer would feel obliged to stay. Apparently Karen and her husband had miscommunicated about their child care arrangements, for she had arrived for the interview a few minutes late, harried and apologetic, pushing her youngest son in a stroller and desperately trying to persuade his older brother to sit quietly while she convinced the Elm Creek Quilters that she was the ideal candidate. Distracted by her children and caught off guard by Diane's belligerent grilling, Karen responded as well as she could have done—as well as *anyone* could have done under such circumstances—but she was given little opportunity to truly shine.

Despite those mishaps, which at the time had clearly bothered and embarrassed Karen much more than her interviewers, the Elm Creek Quilters had been quite impressed with her. No other applicant had so perfectly articulated the spirit of Elm Creek Quilts, which was why she had been invited to interview at the manor although she had never taught even so much as a single class at a quilt shop. Karen had taught undergraduate business courses in the chapter of her life before children, but she had never taught quilting, while the other four candidates had such experience in abundance. Elm Creek Quilt Camp students expected a great deal from their classes and workshops, and it would have been unfair to them—and to Karen—to give them a novice teacher.

Sylvia had volunteered to take on the unpleasant task of calling the eliminated candidates with the bad news, and when she had spoken to Karen, she had encouraged her to bolster her résumé by teaching at her local quilt shop, so that the next time Elm Creek Quilt Camp sought new faculty members, Karen would be a more viable candidate. Karen had agreed that this was sound advice, but whether she had followed through, Sylvia did not know. She did know that Karen had never returned for another session of quilt camp—until now.

Karen collected her keys and papers from Agnes, thanked her, and indicated Gretchen and Maggie with a self-conscious tilt of her head. "I see that you hired Gretchen Hartley and Maggie Flynn. I have Maggie's book. It's wonderful." She smiled, a little shakily, and Sylvia smiled sympathetically back, imagining how the younger woman must have felt running into the two people who had been selected for the job she had wanted so badly. "I was hoping you had hired the cookie lady."

Sylvia and Sarah exchanged a puzzled look, but it was Diane who asked, "The cookie lady?"

Karen nodded. "I met her on the day of my interview, but I never got her name. Ethan and Lucas—my sons, I'm sure you remember them—were a little wound up after napping in the car all the way from State College, and another finalist who was waiting to speak with you distracted them with homemade cookies." Her smile grew steadier as she remembered. "They were beautifully decorated like quilt blocks—and they were, without a doubt, the most delicious cookies I've ever tasted."

"Anna," said the chorus of Elm Creek Quilters around the registration table. "And I second your opinion about the cookies," added Sarah with a wistful sigh.

"Anna," echoed Karen, nodding. "She was so generous, and so helpful when Lucas got fussy. I'd hoped that all that good karma would ensure she got the job."

"Oh, but she did get the job," said Agnes, her blue eyes wide and earnest.

"Not the teaching job," Sarah clarified. "We hired her as our chef."

"But she doesn't work here anymore," said Diane, sighing. "Her husband found a job in Virginia and stole her away from us."

"I suppose that's one way to interpret events," said Gwen, shaking her head.

Karen's brow furrowed, and her cheeks flushed faintly pink. "Oh. That's too bad." With another quick glance at Gretchen and Maggie, still indicating important sites on the estate map for the other camper, she nodded to them all, smiled briefly, and carried her luggage upstairs.

"That makes eighteen and nineteen," Gwen remarked soon after another pair of quilters arrived together, a retired nurse from Waterford and her elderly mother, whom Agnes gave a quick, appraising glance and surreptitiously reassigned to one of the few accessible suites on the first floor. The room next door to it had been assigned to another camper who had not yet arrived, so Agnes quickly scanned her registration form, nodded to herself, and switched the sets of keys so the daughter and mother would be next-door neighbors.

Maggie peered over Agnes's shoulder to check the list. "Only five more to go, unless someone cancels."

"Who would dream of doing that?" scoffed Diane. "Unless they heard that Anna is no longer cooking for us. No offense, Sarah."

"None taken," said Sarah as she began tidying up the registration table before turning over her clipboard to Maggie and hurrying off to the kitchen. Gretchen inspected the refreshment table and reported that the plates of cookies and crudités had been fairly well depleted, but since the banquet would begin in little more than an hour, she would refill the coffeepot one last time but not worry about replenishing the sweets. Just then, Matt returned from the last scheduled shuttle run to the airport, where he had picked up three additional campers, women from small towns scattered across the Midwest who had never met before but had become fast friends on the ride over.

By that time, most of the campers had dispersed to settle into their rooms or to explore the estate's grounds, so some of the Elm Creek Quilters began packing up the registration materials while the others reported to the kitchen to assist Sarah. The penultimate camper arrived just as delicious aromas began to waft into the foyer from the west wing hallway. "I'm so glad I didn't miss the banquet," the quilter breathed, snatching up her keys and papers and hurrying upstairs with her luggage to freshen up before supper.

Five minutes passed, and then ten, and then the grandfather clock in the corner struck half past five. Alone in the foyer,

Sylvia and Agnes exchanged a look, a wordless question. Airline delays or traffic on the toll road could have delayed their last camper, but it was also possible that she had changed her mind and wouldn't be coming. Registration had officially ended a half hour before, and Sylvia and Agnes could be forgiven for abandoning their vigil and joining their friends in the kitchen to help prepare for the Welcome Banquet. But Sylvia was reluctant to let any guest, however overdue for whatever reason, arrive to an empty foyer, especially if she had never visited Elm Creek Manor before. Sarah always indicated new campers by placing an asterisk beside their names on the guest list, and when Sylvia scanned the page on the table in front of Agnes, she spotted the telltale mark.

That settled it. "You go on," Sylvia told Agnes. "I'll stay here to welcome our last arrival."

"Heavens, no," exclaimed Agnes. "Our friends can manage just fine without us. I'll keep you company."

Sylvia smiled her thanks and settled more comfortably in her chair. It would have been lonely to wait alone in the empty foyer knowing how much fun her friends and guests were having elsewhere in the manor.

The sisters-in-law agreed to wait until they had just enough time to hurry to the banquet hall before the feast began. Their other campers expected them to attend—Sarah always made the opening remarks, but it was Sylvia who led everyone from the banquet hall to the Candlelight welcoming ceremony, a revered Elm Creek Quilts tradition—and it wouldn't do to disappoint them because of one latecomer.

With five minutes to go, Sylvia and Agnes heard a strange thumping and scraping outside the front double doors. They exchanged a quick, puzzled glance before looking back just in time to see the door on the left open the barest of inches, then close again, then swing open a bit wider as if nudged by someone unseen, then slowly close again, coming to an abrupt stop on something thrust in the way at the last moment, a metal, rubber-tipped stick.

"Oh, my goodness," Sylvia murmured, bolting to her feet as she recognized the metal stick as the end of a crutch. "Just a moment," she called out as she hurried across the foyer. "I'm coming."

Before Sylvia could reach the entrance, a petite young woman wedged herself into the narrow opening between the door and the jamb and shoved it open wider with her shoulder, and wider still with her backpack. "Hi," she called back brightly, balancing carefully on her crutches as she scooted sideways through the narrow passage. She wore a flattering A-line red wool coat with six large black buttons in pairs down the front, black knit gloves, and a matching rolled-brim red hat over a profusion of long, blond curls. The coat flared just above her knee, revealing a knee-high black leather boot on her left leg and a cast on her right. A cold gust of wind followed her inside, and in the moment before the door closed behind her, Sylvia glimpsed a whirl of small, icy snowflakes in the darkening sky.

The girl—because to Sylvia she indeed seemed no more than that—frowned prettily at the closed door, then glanced hopefully back at Sylvia. "Could you do me a favor? Would you please hold the door open so I can go back for my suitcase?"

"I can do more than that," declared Sylvia, reaching to take the girl's overstuffed black, red, and white plaid backpack from her shoulders. Where on earth were the Elm Creek husbands, and why hadn't one of them helped the poor dear inside? "Did you drive yourself? Oh, never mind. What a foolish question. Of course you didn't."

"No, I did," the girl replied, balancing on a single crutch as she shrugged off her backpack. Expecting it to weigh half what it actually did, Sylvia took it from her, muffled a grunt, and set it on the marble floor with a solid thud. "I used my left foot. I'm not supposed to drive, so, um, don't tell anyone. Especially my mom. If she calls. I don't think she will, but, you know. She might. She's a mom."

"I understand perfectly, dear," said Sylvia, unable to disguise the faint alarm that crept into her voice at the thought of the girl driving along Pennsylvania's steep and winding country roads while inhibited by the cast.

"A nice old man offered to valet-park for me," the girl continued. "Should I tip him when he comes back?"

"Certainly not," said Sylvia, helping her out of her coat. "The service is complimentary."

Agnes hurried outside and returned pulling a black, red, and white plaid suitcase, a near-perfect match for the backpack. Matt followed closely behind, breathless. "Sorry," he said, panting, his cheeks and nose red from cold and exertion. "I was running around with the twins and I couldn't get here fast enough to help."

"Who's watching the twins now?" asked Agnes, offering the girl a quick, welcoming smile before hurrying back to resume her station at the registration table.

"Joe." Matt stooped to pick up the girl's backpack, suitcase, and coat and carried them to the foot of the grand oak staircase. "Andrew's parking the car."

"Are you sure I don't need to tip that nice old man?" Biting the inside of her lower lip, the girl made her way up the four marble steps by planting the crutches on a stair, hopping upon it with her good leg, and repeating the process, all with re-markable agility.

"That nice old man is my husband, and I assure you, you absolutely should not tip him." Sylvia followed the girl up the stairs, her arms outstretched to break her fall should she tumble, which, thankfully, she did not. "That would only embarrass him."

"You must be Michaela Phillips," said Agnes as they joined her at the table. Then she glanced at the remaining keys and shot Sylvia a look of utter dismay. Sylvia realized at once what the problem was: Agnes had given away the last first-floor suite to the daughter of the elderly woman who had arrived earlier that afternoon.

Sylvia's gaze automatically went to the grand oak staircase, and Michaela followed her line of sight. "No elevator?" she guessed.

"I'm sorry, dear, no, and we don't have any first-floor rooms left," said Sylvia. "Perhaps we could ask someone to switch with you."

"Oh, no, that's okay," Michaela assured her. "Everyone's probably already unpacked and stuff. I'll be fine. Leave the first-floor rooms for people who really need them."

It seemed to Sylvia that Michaela was certainly one of those people, but the young woman insisted that as long as some-one carried her bags for her, she could make it upstairs. "The staircase in my dorm is even steeper than that, and I've managed that when the elevator takes too long," she said cheerfully. "Stupid cast. I can't wait to get rid of it."

"I admire her pluck," said Agnes in an undertone as Michaela hobbled off with Matt trailing after carrying her luggage and coat.

Sylvia nodded. She did too, but she still wished Michaela had let them find a first-floor guest to trade rooms with her. She wasn't quite sure how the young woman was going to make it back downstairs again.

With all their guests successfully checked in, Sylvia and Agnes quickly gathered up the empty folders, collected the leftover maps and schedules, and cleared away the refreshment table. Matt, Joe, Andrew, and the twins came back inside as they were finishing up, bringing a cold gust of wind and a scattering of dried leaves in their wake. Matt took one glance at the clock and immediately steered the children upstairs to change clothes and wash up for supper, ignoring James's complaints about the shirt Sarah had chosen for him to wear, which, among other cruel torments, boasted a collar and buttons. Joe and Andrew folded up the registration tables and carried them to the storage room while Sylvia and Agnes trailed behind carrying the chairs. In the meantime, campers had emerged from their rooms and were knocking on doors to meet up with friends, while others milled about the foyer and parlor, admiring the photographs, quilts, and Bergstrom family heirlooms displayed there. The delicious aromas drifting down the hall from the kitchen had intensified, and as Sylvia hurried upstairs to freshen up and change for the banquet, she observed many a camper stealing longing glances in that direction, and at the banquet hall doors, which were still closed. Sylvia smiled, wishing she had time to assure them that it wouldn't be long now and the meal was sure to taste as delicious as it smelled. Chef Anna had left Elm Creek Manor, and they missed her terribly, but she had written down her most beloved recipes and had taught Sarah, Gwen, and Gretchen many useful tricks and techniques. The dishes might lack Anna's unique flair, but even so, Sylvia was certain that no one would leave the table disappointed.

She was putting on her favorite pearl earrings when Andrew entered their suite. "The ballroom's all set," he reported, snatching up a comb from the dresser and running it through his thinning white hair. "Chairs in place, quilts hanging just the way you wanted 'em."

"Thank you, dear," Sylvia said, adding a touch of lipstick. "And now I'm all dolled up and ready to go." She glanced at the clock on the nightstand. "With hardly a moment to spare."

"You look lovely, as always," Andrew said affectionately, kissing her on the cheek and offering her his arm. He escorted her downstairs to the banquet hall off the front foyer, where they found that nearly all of their guests had already seated themselves. The room had been transformed from its more casual lunchtime atmosphere by white tablecloths; centerpieces of colorful autumn leaves, mums, gourds, shiny ripe apples, and flickering tapers, and Sylvia's fine heirloom china, nearly translucent, with the Bergstrom rearing-stallion emblem in the center.

Voices were hushed yet full of anticipation. By tradition, the Elm Creek Quilters and resident husbands did not sit together at a remote head table but dispersed among their guests so that everyone would feel equally honored. Moments after Sylvia and Andrew seated themselves at one of the five round tables arranged in the center of the room, three young men and two young women bearing large, heavily laden trays emerged from the servants' door neatly attired in black slacks, white shirts, black ties, and white aprons. They looked so dignified and self-assured that Sylvia suspected the campers would never guess that they were students from Waterford College, part-time employees hired only for the week rather than career waiters.

To a murmur of appreciation, the young people set steaming bowls of sweet and savory carrot-ginger soup before the campers and their hosts, and from the first delicious taste Sylvia knew that Anna would have been proud of her apprentice chefs. The Caesar salad that followed was perfectly tasty, if neither as fancy as Anna's creations nor as embellished with obscure ingredients, and the main course—herbed roasted chicken, Parmesan and mushroom risotto, roasted autumn vegetables, and miniature leek, potato, and feta galettes—was simply divine. To her regret, Sylvia was obliged to set down her fork after two bites of Maggie's chocolate trifle—not because it wasn't delicious, but because she honestly couldn't eat another bite.

"I would weigh a thousand pounds if I ate like this every day," remarked one of her dinner companions, sighing as she licked the last rich chocolate morsel from her spoon.

"I would too, so it's just as well that we *don't* eat like this every day," said Sylvia, amused. "Not even during the summer, when camp is in session every week."

As they finished their desserts, the servers circled the room offering refills of coffee and tea. From a nearby table, Sarah caught Sylvia's eye and raised her eyebrows in a question. Sylvia nodded, squeezed Andrew's hand, and stood—and a sudden hush settled upon the banquet hall. The time had come. Evening had fallen; the floor-to-ceiling windows on the western wall framed a violet and rose sky in the distance beyond Elm Creek. Sylvia went to the door, where she paused, turned to smile at her guests, and in a clear voice that carried the length of the banquet hall, invited everyone to follow her for the second of their two first-night traditions.

Everyone, even those who were making their first visit to Elm Creek Manor, promptly rose. It was time for every Elm Creek Quilter's favorite part of quilt camp, regardless of the season, when the week still lay before them promising friendship and fun, and their eventual parting could be forgotten for a while.

Sylvia escorted the campers and faculty across the foyer to the ballroom, a relic of an earlier age when the manor's residents would regularly entertain hundreds of guests with lavish evenings of feasting, music, and dancing. During the summer, movable partitions divided the ballroom into multiple classrooms, but during Quiltsgiving, a single nook was set up in a discreet corner, awaiting Gretchen's Giving Quilt class the following day. A patterned carpet encircled a broad parquet dance floor, still smooth and glossy thanks to generations of careful tending, shining in the light of three chandeliers hanging high above from a ceiling framed with crown molding and decorated with a twining vine motif crafted from plaster. Rectangular windows topped by semicircular curves, narrow in proportion to their height, lined the south, east, and west walls. Along the far wall was an enormous stone fireplace, more than five feet tall and ten feet wide, and at the opposite end of the room was a raised dais, its furnishings concealed by a velvet theater curtain.

Sylvia led the way to a small set of stairs tucked away on one side of the dais and drew back the curtain to allow her companions to pass ahead of her. For a moment she worried about the perky young woman who had arrived on crutches, but the dark-haired quilter from Georgia quickly came forward to assist her up the steps. Sylvia followed the last quilter behind the curtain, which had concealed a dozen tall quilt stands arranged in a circle, an assortment of brightly colored quits hanging from them and facing the center.

Sylvia allowed the campers to walk about and admire the display for a while, but when their voices rose above a murmur, she raised her hands for their attention, slowly lowered her arms to evoke silence, and then, when all were still, she beckoned her guests to seat themselves in the circle of chairs arranged in the middle of the display. Murmuring, questioning, the campers took their places as Sarah stole away to dim the lights, and occasionally a nervous laugh broke the stillness. The quilters' voices fell silent again as Sylvia lit a candle, placed it in a crystal votive holder, and took her place at the center of the circle. As the dancing flame in her hands cast light and shadow on her features, she felt a tremor of excitement and nervousness run through those gathered around her, a sensation both familiar and new.

In the center of the circle, Sylvia turned slowly, gazing into the faces of her guests. "One of our traditions is to conclude the first evening of quilt camp with a ceremony we call Candlelight," she told them, as she had told hundreds of quilters before. "It began as a way for our guests to introduce themselves to us and to one other. Since we're going to be living and working together closely this week, we should feel as if we are among friends. But our ceremony has a secondary purpose. At its best, it helps you to know yourselves better too. It encourages you to focus on your goals and wishes, and helps prepare you for the challenges of the future and the unexpected paths you might set forth upon."

Sylvia allowed the expectant silence to swell before she explained the ceremony. The campers would pass the candle around the circle, and as each woman took her turn to hold the flickering light—

"I know," one eager camper broke in nervously. "You want us to explain why we came to Elm Creek Quilt Camp and what we hope to gain this week."

A few other campers stared at her, some startled, some annoyed by the interruption. Sylvia smiled indulgently. "I see you've visited us before." A ripple of laughter went up from the circle when the woman nodded vigorously. "You're right; that *is* the question we ask during our summer sessions, but for Quiltsgiving, we're more united in purpose than we are at any other time of the year, and so that question isn't particularly illuminating, is it?" She looked around the circle and found most of the quilters nodding and watching her expectantly. "It sheds less light on the workings of our hearts and imaginations than—well, than this candle." Sylvia studied the flickering light for a moment, allowing the curiosity to build. "We've gathered here to make quilts for Project Linus, to make quilts for children in need, to offer them a sense of love and comfort. We have come here to give. The question I would like each of you to answer—and to consider carefully before you answer—is why. Why do you give?"

This time the silence was absolute. Some campers held Sylvia's gaze as she looked around the circle at each of them in turn. Others quickly looked away, at the floor, at their hands clasped in their laps. Others turned uncertainly to the left or the right as if hoping to find an answer in a friend's eyes. Sylvia gave them time for contemplation before asking for a volunteer to speak first.

For a long moment, the only sounds were their own soft breaths, some shifting in chairs, the muffled clearing of a throat, the furnace kicking in as the night grew colder, the ever-present but usually unnoticed creaks and groans of the historic manor settling. Then, hesitantly, the dark-haired woman from Georgia raised her hand. With an encouraging smile, Sylvia passed her the candleholder and nodded for her to begin.

"My name's Pauline," the woman began, her accent soft and charming. "I'm from Sunset Ridge, Georgia, and I'm a 911 call center operator. I have a son and a daughter, both in middle school." Her listeners murmured a mixture of congratulations and sympathy, and Pauline nodded, seeming grateful for the pause in which to find the words for her response. "This is a difficult question, and I'm not sure if my answer is really what you're looking for . . ."

When her voice trailed off, Sylvia prompted, "The only answer I'm looking for is the truth of your own heart. It's really very simple."

"Easy for you to say," someone murmured anxiously, and the laughter she evoked seemed to dissolve the nervous tension somewhat.

Pauline took a deep breath. "I give because I'm needed," she said, her gaze fixed on the candle. "It breaks my heart to think of children sad or lonely or in pain, and if a quilt will offer them comfort—and maybe give their parents a little hope and encouragement too—then you'd better believe I want to make them a quilt." She offered Sylvia a quick, tentative smile and passed the candle on to the woman on her right.

"Oh, dear," she said, accepting the candle with a start. "I thought we were going clockwise. Okay. Let me think." She paused, biting the inside of her lower lip. "I'm Kathy. I'm from Harrisburg and I'm recently retired and enjoying every minute of it." Another long pause, and then she sighed and shook her head. "Oh, it'll take me too long to think up an impressive lie, so I'm going to be perfectly honest with you. It makes me feel good to help. My children are all grown up and on their own now, and sure, they still need me and probably always will—"

"You can count on it," murmured one of the oldest women in the group.

Kathy smiled. "Even so, they don't need my help in quite the same way as they did when they were younger. But these children do, and it makes me feel warm and happy in my heart to know that I'm able to do some good for them, to put a little love out into the world. Heaven knows the world could use it. I guess I'm just horribly selfish, giving to feel good about myself." She spoke with such comical despair that everyone laughed as she passed the candle on to the next camper.

The next camper, gray-haired and sitting tall in her seat with her ankles crossed, knew her answer well and spoke without hesitation. "I'm Miriam, and I'm a wife, mother, and grand-mother, and I was a stay-at-home mother long before the term was invented." She allowed a small smile as she peered around the circle over the rims of her glasses. "I give because it's an important tenet of my Christian faith. We're called to give, not from our surplus but to give all that we can. We're called to give to anyone who needs us, to comfort the least among us, because we are all brothers and sisters in the eyes of our Lord." Several other campers nodded their affirmation. "I've been given a talent and an interest in sewing, and I'm very happy and honored to use these gifts to help others, to keep them warm or to brighten their days. It's a privilege, and I'm thankful that the Elm Creek Quilters have provided us such a wonderful opportunity to give."

She passed on the candle to a woman with a long, dark French braid that reminded Sylvia, wistfully, of Anna's. "I can't believe I have to follow that," she exclaimed with mock shame in a heavy Brooklyn accent. "Okay. I'm gonna lay it on the line. I always make quilts for charity, and I just figured I might as well get a free week of quilt camp out of it!"

Everyone burst into laughter—except Miriam, who looked mildly scandalized. Gretchen spoke up. "I think everyone feels that way to some extent. The gifts of our hands are no less heartfelt or sincere or necessary if we enjoy ourselves while making them."

"For those of you who disagree and are convinced that giving has to hurt," Diane added, "we can find a hard pallet in the most cobwebby corner of the attic for you."

As the campers laughed, the candle moved along the circle to Michaela. "I'm Michaela, and I'm here for two reasons. I'm a student at St. Andrew's College but I'm really from Pheasant Branch—" She pointed, vaguely, over her shoulder as if to indicate a hamlet somewhere to the south, although Sylvia knew Pheasant Branch lay to the northwest. "I have to fulfill a community service requirement for graduation, and I thought this would be kinda cool. Also, most other community service jobs need you to be able to walk around a lot, and obviously that's not an option for me right now. But that's why I came here this week, not why I give. I guess I give because no matter how bad you think you have it"—she indicated her cast-bound leg with a gesture of humorous resignation—"there's always someone else who's worse off, you know? And at Quiltsgiving we get to help kids, sick in hospitals or burned out of their apartments or whatever. Who wouldn't want to help a kid? If they need a quilt"—she shrugged, and her blond curls bounced—"then I should make them a quilt. I mean, in my case, it's not like it would take time away from my marathon training."

"But, dear," asked a thin, silver-haired woman four decades her senior. "You're so young. Do you even know how to quilt?"

Almost imperceptibly, Michaela bristled. "Of course. My mom taught me. She's like the most awesome quilter ever. She came to summer quilt camp here two years ago, and she heard about Quiltsgiving, and she told me."

The older woman didn't seem reassured in the least. "You seem too young to be a quilter," she murmured as Michaela passed the candle along.

Karen Wise gave Michaela a sympathetic smile as she accepted the candle. "I give because I always have," she said simply. "I can't imagine not giving. My parents taught me to give and I want to set a good example of giving for my sons. I want them to know that giving is a joy, not a burden."

She passed the candle on to Jocelyn, who studied the candle for a long moment in silence before introducing herself, adding that she was a middle school history teacher from the outskirts of Detroit and the mother of two daughters. "I give because the need is so great," she said. "And while it's true that I could give on my own, closer to home, I think it's often important to gather together so that our acts of giving may have an even greater impact. 'Never doubt that a small group of thoughtful, committed citizens can change the world. Indeed, it is the only thing that ever has.'"

"Margaret Mead," said Pauline from Sunset Ridge, Georgia, promptly.

"Yes, that's right," said Jocelyn, offering Pauline a small, thoughtful smile before passing on the candle.

Around the circle went the flickering light, and each woman who held it shared her reasons for giving. Some were variations on what had been spoken before; others were wholly new or newly insightful. The sisters who had reunited in the foyer during registration were the last to speak, and when the younger of the pair took the candle, she confessed that she gave because people asked her to, and that she always felt like she ought to do more, or at least not need so much prompting to do it. "Mona's too hard on herself," said her elder sister, Linnea, when it was her turn to hold the candle. "She's just as busy as the rest of us with work and family, and she fills every other available moment with volunteer activities. I can't imagine how she could possibly do more unless she abandoned sleeping altogether." Linnea fell silent for a moment, thinking. "I suppose I give to balance the scales in life. I've been richly blessed throughout my life, with a wonderful family"—she gave her sister a little nudge and a smile—"work I enjoy—"

"Most days," her sister broke in.

"Most days," Linnea agreed. "Good health, wonderful children, a loving husband, a roof over my head. I have it all, or at least I have everything that truly matters. I look around at the world—actually, I don't even have to look much farther than my own neighborhood—and I see so many others who are struggling just to make ends meet from day to day. How could I not share what I have in abundance?"

Around the circle, the quilters nodded, their gazes faraway as they sank into private reverie, considering, perhaps, not only the anonymous children who would benefit from their Quiltsgiving project, but other people of all ages whom they knew, friends and neighbors and family, who were in need in those difficult times.

After a moment, Sylvia took the candle from Linnea and indicated the quilts surrounding them with color, beauty, and the promise of warmth. "All of the quilts you see here were made with giving in mind," she explained, walking around the circle. "Some are Giving Quilts from past Quiltsgivings. Others were made to express love or affection." She paused by the twelve-block sampler Sarah had made for Matt in honor of their first anniversary. "Others were made in memory of a loved one to comfort the grieving." Her voice caught in her throat as she paused by the Castle Wall memorial quilt her late sister, Claudia, and Agnes and had made for Sylvia from scraps of her first husband's clothing after his tragic death in the Second World War. "I hope that these quilts and the stories we've shared tonight will inspire you to give, this week and always."

And with that, the first day of Quiltsgiving came to an end.

Early the next morning, the real work would begin.

Chapter Two

✿

Pauline

Pauline woke before sunrise on Monday morning, but instead of anticipating the fun and potential new friendships awaiting her in Elm Creek Manor on that first full day of Quiltsgiving, her thoughts flew to the Château Élan on the outskirts of Atlanta and what the Cherokee Rose Quilters might be doing at that very moment.

They were probably still in bed as she was, but sound asleep, wiped out from a late night of talking and laughing and sewing and indulging in wine from the resort's own vineyards. A record ninety quilters had signed up for their annual benefit retreat, the most important of the guild's many significant charitable activities, which raised money for several homeless shelters and soup kitchens in impoverished Atlanta neighborhoods. Quilters would travel hundreds of miles and pay not-insignificant fees for an inspirational week of workshops, lectures, and trunk shows offered by the guild's renowned members, proud to know that the proceeds would support worthy causes. Pauline would bet her Bernina that not one of the Cherokee Rose Quilters had given her a second thought since setting foot on the resort's beautiful grounds. In such glorious surroundings among their most creative friends, they were surely too busy—and having too much fun—to waste a moment missing her.

She wished she could say she didn't miss them.

Dispirited, Pauline sat up, reached for her cell phone on the nightstand, and called home. Her husband answered on the third ring. "Good morning, sugar," he said. "Did you get any sleep or did you stay up all night quilting?"

The warmth in Ray's voice always made her smile. "This'll probably shock you, but I got a full night's sleep. Yesterday evening we had a banquet and a rather dramatic welcome ceremony, and then it was straight to bed." For Pauline, anyway. Judging by the sounds from the hallway that hadn't ceased entirely until after midnight, many campers had stayed up quite late, going from room to room to reunite with old friends and meet their neighbors. Someone had knocked softly on Pauline's door around ten o'clock, but by that time she had already brushed her teeth, put on her pajamas, and curled up in bed with a few quilting magazines, so she had ignored the friendly gesture. "The serious quilting starts after breakfast. Are the kids ready for school yet?"

"They're getting there," said Ray. They chatted for a bit about how Colton had overslept and Kori had eaten only half an orange for breakfast, again, but they were both more or less ready to head out for the bus. Then Ray, who knew her through and through, abruptly changed the subject. "Sugar, you'll have fun this week. Just push Brenda right out of your head. Don't let her miserly spirit ruin your vacation."

"You're right," said Pauline, raking a hand through her long, wiry hair, tangled and tousled even more than usual thanks to her restless night. "I shouldn't."

"Get out of bed, go for a walk, and put a smile on your face when you go down to breakfast. You're going to have just as much fun at Thanksquilting as you would've had at the guild retreat. You'll see."

She had to smile. "It's Quiltsgiving, not Thanksquilting."

"What's the difference?" They both laughed. "I love you, sugar, and I miss you. Take care of yourself."

She promised him she would, and she assured him she loved and missed him too, and then they said good-bye.

Ray was absolutely right. She was at Elm Creek Manor, for crying out loud. What was there to regret? Resolute, she flung back the pretty pink-and-yellow Friendship Knot quilt and climbed out of bed, vowing to have a wonderful Quiltsgiving from the get-go. And if she couldn't manage that, at the very least, she would stop wallowing in self-pity. She couldn't waste another second longing for the circle of friends that had broken and reformed without her—and imagining Brenda, self-satisfied and smug, privately gloating over Pauline's absence.

She changed into her sweats—the thickest, warmest she owned but untested against a northern climate—laced up her walking shoes, tugged on a knit hat and gloves, threw on her coat, and left her room, greeting the few other campers she passed along the way as she descended the grand oak staircase to the foyer. When she opened the front door, a cold gust of wind made her shiver, and when she stepped out onto the verandah, the sight of frost on the crisp green lawn gave her pause. As the heavy door closed behind her, she might have given in to the temptation to hasten back inside if she had not spotted two campers at the foot of one of the curved stone staircases, bundled up as she was for cold-weather exercise. Their heads were bent close together over a map of the estate, and when the taller of the pair straightened and pointed off to the north, Pauline recognized them as the two blond sisters she had met at the Candlelight ceremony the previous night. The taller, elder sister was Linnea—Linnea the librarian from Los Angeles, Pauline had noted when she introduced herself at the Candlelight ceremony, the better to remember her. She prided herself on her quick, sharp memory, and she didn't consider it cheating to resort to mnemonic devices from time to time.

The librarian must have felt Pauline's eyes upon her, for she glanced up. "You look like a woman who knows where she's going," she called. "Are there any walking trails around here?"

"I'm not sure," Pauline admitted as she descended the stairs. "I was going to walk through the north gardens and the orchard, trail or no trail."

"That sounds like a good idea," said the shorter sister, and with no further ado the three women fell into step as if they had planned to walk together all along, striding briskly along the circular driveway before stepping off onto the lawn.

"You're the 911 operator, right?" asked Linnea. Her thick, ash-blond hair was blunt-cut at the chin and held back from her face by a wide, black knit band that served as earmuffs. "From Georgia? Paula?"

"Pauline," she corrected with a smile. "And yes, I am, and I am."

"I'm Linnea." She indicated her sister with a casual wave of a mittened hand. "And this is my sister, Mona."

"Yes, I remember," said Pauline. "Mona the manager from Minnesota."

The sisters smiled at the alliteration, but then Mona's face turned rueful. "I am for now, anyway."

"Which are you planning?" asked Pauline, curious. "A name change or a new career?" Mona had mentioned a husband and children the previous evening, and she seemed too young to contemplate retirement.

"A career change, but not voluntarily."

"Same here," said Linnea, more grimly than her sister.

"Oh, you are not," scoffed Mona, nudging her as they walked along. "You love those kids. You wouldn't last a day without them, and the children's department wouldn't last a week without you."

"That's what I'm afraid of," said Linnea. "You're the only one of us with job security, Pauline. There will always be emergencies and people calling in to report them."

"Oh, I don't know about that. I'm sure I'll be replaced by a robot eventually. But you two . . ." She looked from one sister to the other, smiling encouragingly. "Offices will always need managers to keep them running smoothly, and where would we be without librarians?"

"Ignorant beyond any hope of redemption," declared Mona, throwing her sister a proud smile.

"Sometimes I think half the population is already there,"

Linnea said dryly. " 'A person who won't read has no advantage over one who can't read.' "

"Mark Twain," said Pauline automatically.

"Very good." Linnea nodded in approval. "If we play Trivial Pursuit at Games Night this evening, I want you on my team."

"It's a deal," said Pauline, delighted. In such a scenario, a librarian would be a formidable ally.

"I can only imagine how stressful your workdays are," Linnea remarked. "If I have a bad day on the job, I might shelve a book in the wrong place or recommend a novel that a kid just can't get into, but if you have a bad day . . ." She shook her head as if unable to give voice to the nightmare scenarios that might unfold.

"I try not to have too many bad days," said Pauline, smiling.

"But your job must be very rewarding too," said Mona.

"It's both, actually—rewarding and stressful—but quilting and exercise help me relieve a lot of the stress." Spending time with her small, invitation-only quilt guild had once helped too, but recently the Cherokee Rose Quilters had become a greater source of stress than her job.

"Quilting and chocolate are my two favorite stress relievers," Mona said with mock dismay. "Hence the need for long, vigorous walks, even on vacation."

Their laughter rang out merrily, and the frosted blades of grass crunched crisply beneath their running shoes. As they passed in front of the manor, they chatted about the previous night's Candlelight ceremony and the lovely quilts displayed on the dais. Pauline was pleased to learn that the sisters had signed up for the Giving Quilt class, and she resolved to grab a seat

beside them later that morning, even if it meant not sitting in the front row as she had promised the instructor.

At the corner of the manor, they passed a thicket of denuded lilac bushes surrounding a broad patio that appeared to be made of the same gray limestone as the manor. A pathway of similar stones continued into a stand of bare-limbed elms, oaks, and maples, and after a quick glance at Linnea's map, they followed the meandering path until it broadened and opened upon an oval clearing. At the near end of the garden, four round planters holding pruned rosebushes and frost-withered ivy were spaced evenly around a black marble statue of a mare prancing with two foals. It was a fountain, Pauline realized, though the water had been shut off, likely in deference to the temperatures, which in that season dipped well below freezing at night and didn't climb particularly high during the day. The lower halves of the planters were two feet thicker than at the top, forming smooth, polished seats where visitors could rest, but Pauline and her companions strode briskly past them without pausing. They circled a large, white wooden gazebo, passed several bare flower beds and terraces cut into a gently sloping hill, and followed another gray stone footpath to the west, nearly hidden amid a grove of evergreens. Before long the stone gave way to hard-packed earth, the smoothness broken every few paces by tree roots that seemed to reach for their ankles like gray, gnarled fingers. By unspoken agreement, the women slowed their pace and made their way more carefully. They were all breathing hard from exertion by then, and as they passed beneath the leafless canopy, Pauline felt the first rumblings of hunger and hoped they wouldn't return too late for breakfast.

Their conversation naturally turned to quilting and why they had come to Elm Creek Manor for Quiltsgiving. The sisters, lamenting the miles that usually separated them, explained that they reunited for a vacation every year, just the two of them, to spend time together before the whirlwind of the Christmas holidays set in and throngs of family and friends descended. Mona admitted that she was an inexperienced quilter, which was why she had enrolled in the Giving Quilt class rather than bringing any UFOs—Unfinished Fabric Objects—from home to work upon. "A simple and easy pattern, that's what the course description promised," Mona said, her breath coming in faint white puffs as she spoke. "And I'm going to hold them to it." Linnea, a longtime quilter, had signed up for the class to keep her sister company.

Both sisters were impressed when Pauline mentioned that she had recently celebrated her twentieth quilting anniversary, and they marveled when she explained her ambitious plan to complete five quilts before the week was over. She worried that they would think her an irritating show-off—an accusation she had once overheard Brenda make, when she may or may not have known Pauline was in earshot—but they seemed genuinely admiring. Even so, Pauline decided not to divulge her plans to anyone else, just in case.

After meandering through the forest for a mile or perhaps two, the path led them to a footbridge that crossed a narrow stream, which Linnea surmised aloud was probably a tributary of Elm Creek. Another forested mile set them to pondering the question of whether they had left the Bergstrom estate far behind and were trespassing on a neighboring farm, but eventually the path ended at the apple orchards, rows upon rows of trees bare of all but the most tenacious brown leaves, fluttering crisply in the chilly breeze that blew steadily from the southwest.

From the orchard, where they spotted several other campers who had sought exercise or quiet contemplation outdoors, it was but a short distance past the red banked barn, over the bridge across Elm Creek, and up the four stairs to the manor's rear entrance. Pauline was breathless from trying to match the taller women's long strides, and the tip of her nose and fingers felt numb from the cold, but she was sorry the excursion was over. She had enjoyed their tour of the estate, which had proved to be lovely even in the waning days of autumn, if not as ostentatiously glorious as Château Élan was in that season.

In the rear foyer, the manor's welcoming warmth enveloped them, carrying tantalizing aromas from the kitchen a few paces down the hall. "Showers before breakfast or breakfast first?" asked Mona, glancing first to her sister and then to Pauline as she stripped off her mittens.

"I'm fine either way," said Pauline, pleasantly surprised to be included in the sisters' plans.

"Showers first," said Linnea firmly, with as much implied necessity as if it were a muggy afternoon in mid-August and they had run a half marathon. Mona laughed indulgently, and they agreed to meet at the foot of the grand oak staircase in the foyer in a half hour. Pauline fairly sprinted off to get ready, but not without a fleeting twinge of worry that she might be intruding upon the sisters' reunion. She considered leaving them to themselves, but her reluctance to walk into the banquet hall alone won out. If she were at the Cherokee Rose Quilters' Benefit Retreat, she could have chosen from among a dozen longtime friends who would have been happy to have her take an empty seat at their table. Here, she knew no one.

Pauline was ready a full five minutes before the sisters descended the stairs, so she passed the time admiring the artwork displayed in the foyer. Stunning quilts hung from the second-floor balcony, and on the foyer walls were sepia-toned and black-and-white photographs of several generations of the Bergstrom family. Interspersed among them were several paintings of the manor and the surrounding estate. Although they had been created with considerable skill and reverence, the paintings were not dated, and Pauline could not make out the signature, a mere jumble of initials, one of which could have been a "B." She wondered who the artist was, whether he or she was one of Sylvia's ancestors or if the paintings were more recent, perhaps the gifts of a former camper who was as confident with a brush and paint as with needle and thread.

She was studying a curious painting, a landscape with what appeared to be the charred ruins of a log cabin in the middle distance, when Linnea and Mona arrived, tote bags full of fabric, notions, and tools slung over their shoulders. Pauline wished she had thought to bring her supplies along too. Now she would have to race upstairs for them between breakfast and the start of class. She hoped her poor planning wouldn't cost her a seat near the sisters.

In the banquet hall, Pauline, Linnea, and Mona marveled at the sight of a lavish buffet set out upon two long tables near the windows overlooking the rear of the manor. The campers had been promised a continental breakfast, but as they carried their trays of delicacies to an unoccupied table, Pauline and the sisters agreed that the offering of buttery pastries, fresh fruit, Greek yogurts, and cranberry walnut granola far exceeded their expectations.

"All this, an entire week of luxury and quilting fun, for free," sighed Mona happily, stirring cream into her coffee.

"All of this for the cost of our labor," Linnea corrected her. "There's no such thing as a free lunch, or a free breakfast either. But since our labor benefits Project Linus, it's a trade I'm very happy to make."

"Me too," Pauline chimed in. "I bet everyone here is."

As she looked around the room, Pauline saw women of all ages and races and backgrounds and demographics, united not only by their love of quilting but also in their eagerness to share their talents and time. She had no doubt that each of them would have been willing to make quilts for children in need even without the benefit of a week at Elm Creek Manor. Quilters were the most generous people she had ever known. Even Brenda, for all her faults, made quilts for charity—although she never volunteered to teach at the guild's benefit retreats, nor did she assist in anyone else's classes.

Thoughts of Brenda naturally led to thoughts of the other Cherokee Rose Quilters. "Every year, my quilting guild hosts a retreat at a resort near Atlanta to raise money for local charities," Pauline said, almost without meaning to. "It's in a similar spirit to Quiltsgiving, except we charge a fee for food and lodging, we donate the profits, and everyone keeps whatever quilts they make."

"Lucky you, to have two quilt retreats in the same year," said Mona.

"Well, actually—" A nervous, illogical impulse compelled

Pauline to glance at her watch. "My guild's retreat is going on right now."

"Then why are you here instead of there?" asked Linnea.

Why indeed. "It seemed . . . time for a change."

When the sisters regarded her with unmistakable curiosity, Pauline glanced away and changed the subject to the first thing her gaze lit upon—the young, blond college student on crutches, struggling to make her way from the buffet to a table with her breakfast in hand. "Oh, look at that poor girl. Someone should carry her plate for her."

She pushed back her chair, eager to be that person and thereby avoid more uncomfortable questions, but before she could stand, another camper—Jocelyn, the African-American middle school teacher from Michigan—appeared at the struggling girl's side. They exchanged a few words, and with a grateful smile and a nod, Michaela handed Jocelyn her plate and they made their way to a nearby table. Fortunately for Pauline, the distraction sufficed; Linnea and Mona had abandoned the subject of Pauline's strange absence from her guild's retreat in favor of possible color combinations for their Giving Quilts. Pauline left them to it, explaining that she had to retrieve her quilt supplies from her room before the start of class.

"Save me a seat?" she asked as she rose and cleared away her dishes. She waited for the sisters to nod before hurrying off.

The classroom turned out to be a small section of the ballroom set apart by moveable partitions, and Pauline arrived just in time to claim an empty seat beside Linnea. Gretchen Hartley, a thin, gray-haired, seventysomething Elm Creek Quilter clad in a dark brown corduroy skirt and a beige twinset, stood at the front of the room smiling a welcome to each student as she entered. Behind her hung that year's Giving Quilt—a charming confection of small red and larger purple squares set on point upon a light cream background framed by a double border, one narrow, one wide. The arrangement of blocks was simple and pleasing, reminding Pauline of bubbles rising from the bottom of an aquarium or colorful balloons floating up into a clear summer sky. Studying the quilt, she easily deduced which quick-piecing techniques Gretchen would likely employ so that the students would be able to assemble their tops within a matter of days. Pauline smiled as she arranged her supplies neatly on the table beside her sewing machine, confident that she would be able to achieve her quilt tally for the week.

At precisely one minute after nine o'clock—enough time to grant stragglers a grace period while still remaining within the realm of the punctual—Gretchen raised her hands for their attention. "Good morning," she said. "For those of you I didn't have the opportunity to meet at registration, I'm Gretchen Hartley, and it's no exaggeration to say that I'm thoroughly delighted to be leading the Giving Quilt class this year."

Pauline didn't doubt it. Gretchen fairly glowed with warmth and eagerness as she gestured to the quilt hanging upon the wall behind her. "This quilt may look complicated, especially if you're a beginner." Gretchen peered questioningly around the room over the tops of her glasses, and a handful of students, including Mona, raised their hands. "Well, never fear. Appearances can be deceiving, and in this case, they definitely are. These Resolution Square blocks are composed of simple squares and rectangles, joined with easy straight seams. It's the on-point arrangement of the blocks that lends the quilt its more complex appearance."

The campers studied the quilt and nodded thoughtfully.

"We'll begin by choosing our fabrics," Gretchen said. "Feel free to dig through the classroom stash if you can't find exactly what you want among the yardage you brought from home. For the pieced blocks, please choose one half yard of a dark print, one and a quarter yards of a medium, and one and a half yards for the background. You'll also need one and three-quarter yards for the inner border and two yards for the outer border. Those can be the same dark and medium fabrics you use for the blocks, or something else entirely. It's up to you. The quilt police aren't permitted on the premises."

A ripple of laughter passed through the room as the quilters dug into their tote bags and satchels, pulling out fabrics, draping them side by side upon the tables, and standing back to scrutinize them, heads to one side, glasses on or off as necessary. Some campers took Gretchen up on her offer and searched through the milk crates full of fabric at the back of the room until they found the exact shade of blue or the most cheerful novelty prints they needed. Others wandered through the rows peeking at their classmates' stashes and proposing trades.

Pauline had chosen a jewel-toned purple-and-red grape print for her borders and was weighing the merits of several different fabrics in complementary hues when someone in the row behind her said, "Excuse me—Pauline, isn't it?"

"Yes, that's me," she replied, glancing over her shoulder to find Jocelyn turning a hopeful look alternately upon her and her fabric stash. "What can I do for you?"

"Could I interest you in a swap?" Jocelyn gestured to one of Pauline's fabrics, an ocean-blue textured solid with a pattern like crumpled parchment paper. "Now that I've seen the sample quilt, I'd like to use lots of different fabrics to give mine a scrappy look, but I didn't bring enough blues from home. You're welcome to take anything I have in trade—except the blues and oranges, of course. I'll need those."

"Sure." Pauline admired Jocelyn's neatly folded yardage arranged in orderly stacks on the table beside her sewing machine. Her stash seemed to be composed entirely of nineteenth-century reproduction fabrics fresh from the store. Pauline compared several different reds and purples to her grapevine border fabric before she settled upon an exquisite red paisley. "Blue and orange, huh?" she said as they exchanged fabrics. "That'll be a bold combination."

"Those are our school colors," Jocelyn explained. "We're the proud Westfield Wildcats."

"Go, fight, win," replied Pauline, and Jocelyn smiled back.

"I'm using my school colors too," Michaela interjected. She sat at the workstation beside Jocelyn with her cast-bound foot stuck awkwardly into the aisle. "Red, black, and white for the St. Andrew's Crusaders."

"Very nice." Pauline nodded appreciatively as she studied the younger woman's fabrics. She would have considered that palette too strong and dynamic for a child's quilt, but the combination worked, perhaps because the Scottie dog print Michaela had set aside for the borders added a note of whimsy. "I feel like I lack imagination or school spirit or both," she added with mock dismay. "I could have chosen old gold and white for Georgia Tech, but instead I played it safe and went with purple, red, and cream, like the sample. I guess I'm just a copycat."

"But wouldn't you have still been a copycat if you had chosen school colors like Michaela and I did?" said Jocelyn, amused.

"I suppose I would have been, just in a different way," Pauline agreed, laughing at herself. She knew no one in that room would second-guess her choices. A glance around the room showed that she was not the only camper following Gretchen's lead. And why not? Gretchen's version was eye-catching and appealing, although Pauline had selected rich tone-on-tone fabrics rather than the small florals Gretchen favored.

"Hold on a sec." Michaela dug into her fabric stash and triumphantly pulled out a half yard of fabric badly in need of a hot iron, but even wrinkled, the white lacy pattern on a red-orange background was quite pretty. "Jocelyn, could you use this? I was going to, but it's not quite red enough for my quilt."

Jocelyn's eyes lit up. "Yes, thanks. It's perfect."

As Jocelyn and Michaela worked out a trade, Pauline finished selecting her own fabrics, admired Linnea's and Mona's, and awaited Gretchen's next instructions. When all the students were ready to proceed, Gretchen told them they would cut their background pieces first. Smiling, she added, "This will give you time to make sure you're happy with your focus fabrics before you cut them into pieces."

Next Gretchen gestured to the cutting tables set up along the perimeter of the classroom and instructed the students to cut three strips three and a half inches wide, selvage to selvage, and then to cut the strips into sixty-four two-by-three-and-a-half-inch rectangles. While waiting for a turn at a cutting table, Pauline took her cream background fabric to an ironing station at the back of the classroom, sprayed it generously with sizing, and pressed with a hot iron until the fabric was dry and stiff. She did the same when Gretchen told them to cut strips from their dark fabrics and make sixty-four three-and-a-half-inch squares.

Michaela eyed Pauline curiously as she returned to her sewing station with her stiffened red squares in hand. "Do you mind if I ask you a question?" Without waiting for a reply, she asked, "Why are you spraying your fabrics with that stuff?"

"Sizing stabilizes the pieces." Pauline handed Michaela a red fabric square, which now had the texture and rigidity of construction paper. "It requires a little extra time and trouble, but it makes the pieces easier to work with and less prone to stretching and distortion when I sew."

Michaela nodded thoughtfully and handed back the red square. "Cool. Mind if I copy you?"

Pauline laughed. "I think we've already established where I stand on copying. Go for it. Now, do you mind if I ask *you* a question?"

"Go right ahead."

"How did you hurt your foot?"

"Actually, it's my ankle, and I fell." Michaela hesitated. "Or I was dropped. Depends who you ask. Either way, it was a tragic cheerleading accident. Tragic for me, anyway. And possibly no accident."

Pauline couldn't remember any other time in her life when she had heard the words "tragic" and "cheerleading" in the same sentence. "I'm sorry. Does it hurt a lot?"

"Not so much anymore." Michaela sighed and frowned at her cast. "Although I won't be throwing any back handsprings any time soon."

Pauline shook her head regretfully. "Me neither."

Michaela stared at her in utter surprise for a moment until she realized Pauline was joking. "Don't rule it out," she teased, or perhaps it was a warning. "I could teach you."

"Oh, no. No thanks. I'd break my neck."

"You wouldn't," Michaela insisted. "I'm a very good coach."

"I'm sure you are, when you're working with someone with a certain bare minimum of athletic ability. That would rule me out."

Michaela shook her head. "Don't talk like that. You just need to pace yourself."

"Pace myself?"

"That's right. Pace: 'Positive Attitudes Change Everything.' "

"I'll keep that in mind," Pauline said, but she knew it wasn't only her attitude preventing her from turning back handsprings across the ballroom floor.

Just then, Gretchen called for the campers' attention, and after confirming that they were ready to move on, she instructed them to cut even more strips, this time two inches wide, selvage to selvage, from their dark and background fabrics. Cheerfully the campers set themselves to the task, taking turns at the cutting stations, chatting as they worked, and admiring one another's fabric combinations. When they had returned to their places with their carefully trimmed strips in hand, Gretchen seated herself at the sewing machine at the front of the room. With the help of a strategically placed mirror overhead, she demonstrated how to sew a dark strip to each background strip lengthwise to make a strip pair. After pressing the seam toward the dark fabric with a hot iron, she took up her acrylic ruler and rotary cutter and neatly sliced across the seam to make a pair of contrasting squares joined along one side. "You'll need sixty-four square pairs, two for each Resolution Square block," she told them as she deftly cut more from the strip until only a small scrap remained, trailing threads. "Be sure to square up the end if necessary so that your strips lie straight and true. We need perfect right angles, no slouching."

The students laughed, and a happy buzz filled the classroom as they measured and cut with care. Pauline made quick work of her fabric strips and soon had all of her square pairs arranged in neat piles beside her sewing machine. She glanced around the room, certain she would be the first to finish and preparing herself to assist anyone who seemed to be struggling. To her surprise, she spotted another quilter at the back of the room who must have accomplished the last step even more swiftly, because she was already tidying up her work area. Karen, Pauline quickly recalled, thinking back to the Candlelight ceremony. Karen Wise. She was carin' for two young sons and was wise in the ways of quilting because she worked in a quilt shop not far from the Elm Creek Valley.

Pauline felt a quick, unreasonable surge of competitiveness, and she quickly turned back around and began to studiously organize her cut block pieces. Karen Wise must have made that pattern before, Pauline told herself, although she knew that wasn't possible, since Gretchen had designed the quilt especially for that year's Quiltsgiving. She sighed and sat back in her chair, impatient with herself. What did it matter who finished first, who chose the most harmonious fabrics, whose quilt was the most meticulously sewn? There were quilting competitions aplenty, but this wasn't one of them. The object of the week was to learn, make new friends, and sew quilts for children in need, not to outperform her fellow campers.

Sometimes Pauline wondered whether she was too proud, whether the true spirit of quilting eluded her. Sometimes too, she feared that it was that same foolish pride rather than a noble sacrifice that had cost her a cherished place among the Cherokee Rose Quilters.

Pauline had known the Cherokee Rose Quilters by reputation long before she befriended any of them. The most exclusive guild in Georgia, they were admired and respected for their talents; their superb quilt museum in Savannah, founded decades earlier with a bequest from a wealthy member; their diligent efforts to preserve the state's quilting heritage; and their charitable works. As a group they had accumulated an impressive number of awards, ribbons, grants, and other recognitions, and every Best of Show prize at every state and county fair for the past forty-five years had gone to a Cherokee Rose Quilter unless no one from the guild had submitted an entry. It was perhaps inevitable that their success evoked a fair share of envy, especially since they capped their membership at twelve and filled rare vacancies only after a lengthy application and interview process. Through the years, some of the state's most gifted quiltmakers had been denied membership for reasons their admirers could not fathom, and occasionally rejection inspired some disgruntled candidates to create similarly small, exclusive guilds of their own. But none of the groups that emulated the Cherokee Rose Quilters could match their success or acquire equal fame, and most eventually disbanded.

No one, not even their harshest, most jealous critics, could deny that the Cherokee Rose Quilters were tireless champions of the quilting arts, respected ambassadors for the state of Georgia in the art world, and dedicated benefactors of numerous worthy causes. Their annual quilt retreat at the Château Élan was universally acknowledged to be worth every penny spent, every mile driven, and every seam ripped out and resewn in order to impress their perfectionist teachers.

Pauline had been quilting for about eight years when she and two friends attended a Cherokee Rose Quilters retreat at Château Élan, humorously dubbed "French Finishing School" for that year's emphasis on borders and bindings. She returned home utterly transformed, a traditional patchwork scrap quilter whose eyes had been opened to the glorious world of landscape quilts, abstract compositions, and embellishment. Even Ray noticed that her work improved dramatically in the months following the retreat, becoming more evocative, complex, rich, and technically precise. Best of all, the entire quiltmaking experience became more freeing, more fulfilling, and more engrossing than she had ever dreamed it could be. Considering how stressful her job was and how busy her life as a wife and mother, this was an unexpected blessing she rejoiced in every time she picked up her rotary cutter or sat down at her sewing machine.

Three years later, when Kori was in second grade and Colton was an eager kindergartener, Pauline met Jeanette, the mother of one of Colton's classmates, a towheaded boy who shared Colton's obsession with plastic dump trucks and pea gravel. Almost every day after school, Pauline and Jeanette let their children work off their pent-up energy on the playground before walking home. As the semester passed, the women became friends nearly as quickly as their sons did. They gossiped about the other mothers and commiserated over the usual parenting woes, scheduled playdates for the boys, and occasionally met for coffee on a rare weekday off. Even so, Pauline didn't discover that Jeanette was a quilter until the spring, when Jeanette mentioned that the president of the PTA had asked her to make a quilt in honor of their beloved principal, who would be retiring at the end of the semester after thirty years in the district.

"I adore her," said Jeanette, "and I'm happy to make the quilt. I just wish they'd given me more notice. Now I'll have to throw something together, and I'm sure that I won't be satisfied with the results."

"You have two months," Pauline reassured her. "That's plenty of time."

Jeanette shook her head, frowned, and said, almost to herself, "Not for one of my quilts it isn't."

Were her quilts especially complex, Pauline wondered, or was Jeanette exceptionally slow? "I'll help you," she said impulsively, adding modestly, "I quilt a little myself."

"Really?"

"Really, I quilt, and really, I'll help you," said Pauline, laughing and squeezing Jeanette's arm reassuringly.

Jeanette hesitated. "I don't usually . . . collaborate on my pieces. I have more of a . . . solitary vision. I know that sounds arrogant—"

"No, no, not at all," Pauline hastened to say. So Jeanette was an art quilter, or perhaps she thought of herself as a fiber artist. Either way, Pauline knew the type, and, admittedly, she had become something of an art quilter herself. She knew how to handle an artist's temperament. "Here's what we'll do. You can think of me as your assistant. I'll cut pieces, go shopping, thread needles—whatever you need. You focus on the big picture and dump the busywork on me. I can take it."

After a moment's pause, Jeanette smiled and agreed.

The following Saturday, Jeanette invited Pauline to her home and led her upstairs into a spacious room over the garage Pauline hadn't known existed. "This is my studio," Jeanette said with a grin, standing at the threshold and spreading her arms dramatically. "My sanctuary."

Pauline nodded, muffling a gasp of amazement and envy. The two longest walls were lined with cubbyhole shelves bursting with fabric bolts and flat folds of every color and hue imaginable. Upon the shorter wall to the right of the entrance hung a design wall covered in cream-colored flannel marked with a grid, to which several meticulously pieced blocks were affixed, signs of a different work in progress. A cutting table covered in mats and racks for rulers and rotary cutters stood in one corner opposite an ironing station with both a standard iron and a commercial steam press. Skylights flooded the room with warm, natural light, and on the far wall was a sewing table boasting all manner of drawers and containers for thread, tools, and notions—and a gleaming Bernina that Pauline knew cost nearly twelve thousand dollars.

"I don't know how you can get anything done in such a cramped space," Pauline managed to say. "And with so little fabric and such outdated tools."

Jeanette laughed. "Oh, I know. It's a luxury, and the commissions I earn barely pay for it. I always feel like I have to justify having a studio, which is why I rarely bring anyone up here except other members of my guild."

"An artist needs a workspace," said Pauline staunchly, turning slowly in place in the center of the room and taking it all in. "If you were a painter, and a man, no one would argue that you didn't need or deserve the tools of your trade and a place of your own in which to use them." Then her friend's last few words sank in. "You're a member of the guild? I've never seen you at the meetings."

"Not the Sunset Ridge Quilt Guild," said Jeanette. "I belong to a group called the Cherokee Rose Quilters."

"No kidding?" She should have known. "Wow."

Jeanette offered her a painful, uncomfortable smile. "Is that a good wow or a 'Now I hate you' wow?"

"That's a good, very impressed wow. I went to one of your retreats a few years ago, and it was a revelation." Pauline didn't remember seeing Jeanette there, but perhaps she hadn't joined the group yet. "Why the heck did you keep this a secret from me? I thought we were friends."

"Of course we're friends." Jeanette noticeably relaxed. "I didn't know you were a quilter. I didn't think you'd care about my quaint little hobby."

Pauline heard the ironic emphasis Jeanette put on the last three words and nodded sympathetically. Her own quilting had been dismissed many a time by the ignorant and the uninformed. "Even if I weren't a quilter, I'd still care. You should be proud to be a part of something so special."

"I am." Then Jeanette shook her head and waved a hand as if her remarkable accomplishments were the most boring subject imaginable. "I've made a few sketches for the principal's quilt. Want to see them?"

Naturally Pauline did, and they were as unique and

amazing as she had expected. Jeanette's design captured the most important events of the school year and the highlights of the principal's long career in a series of vignettes rendered in appliqués cut in the fashion of folded paper dolls or snowflakes. Pauline thought it was absolutely perfect, and she said so when Jeanette generously asked if she had any suggestions.

Throughout the spring, they met in Jeanette's studio every weekend to work on the quilt. Jeanette retained complete artistic control, altering the design as the spirit moved her and sewing every stitch, while Pauline took over the responsibilities of transferring Jeanette's meticulously crafted patterns from paper to fabric and cutting out the appliqués. Sometimes they chatted as they worked; sometimes Jeanette needed complete silence as she wrestled with a particularly intricate motif. But even then, their quiet companionship relaxed and invigorated them both.

Together they completed the quilt on time, and when it was unveiled to thunderous applause at the principal's retirement party, even Jeanette admitted that she wouldn't change a stitch—despite her confession to Pauline a few weeks before that she was never completely satisfied with any of her creations, that she never felt that any of them were entirely complete.

"My only regret is that the project's over," Jeanette said as they left the party. "I enjoyed working with you."

"The feeling's mutual," said Pauline, suspecting that she would miss their collaboration even more than Jeanette would. "I guess we can always hope that the new principal will retire in a year or two."

Fortunately, their newfound friendship endured even though another opportunity to sew together didn't immediately rise. At Jeanette's prompting, Pauline attended another Cherokee Rose Quilters charity retreat, and she was delighted to be invited to sit at the guild members' table at mealtimes. A few months later, an even more astonishing surprise arrived in the mail: a letter on thick paper embossed with the Cherokee Rose Quilters logo inviting her to apply for membership in the guild.

Safely alone in her kitchen when the invitation arrived, Pauline squealed and jumped up and down, alternately waving the letter triumphantly overhead and clutching it to her heart. But as the afternoon passed, and she awaited Ray's return home from work so she could share the good news, the sober realization sank in that her selection for the coveted place was far from certain. It was entirely possible that she had been invited only because she was Jeanette's friend and not because of her merits as a quilter. She had won a few awards and ribbons, and a few of her quilts had been juried into prominent national quilt shows, but surely every other quilter vying for the vacancy could boast of similar accomplishments. She knew she ought to content herself with the invitation, and she mentally rehearsed telling Jeanette that it had been an honor just to be considered.

But her rehearsals proved unnecessary when, after an interview and a second, follow-up interview, Pauline was invited to join the guild. As she reveled in the unexpected honor and celebrated at the initiation party held at the guild's Savannah museum, Pauline nonetheless harbored secret doubts that she was truly the most deserving. Did the other quilters really want her, or had Jeanette advocated for her so relentlessly that they had eventually surrendered and agreed to choose Pauline out of sheer exhaustion?

Ray urged her not to second-guess the guild's decision and to simply enjoy this wonderful reward for her hard work and talent, but it was nearly impossible to do so. In her first few months as a Cherokee Rose Quilter, Pauline found herself studying the other guild members for any sign that she was not truly wanted. Jeanette was obviously thrilled that she had joined the guild, and most of the other members were friendly, warm, and welcoming in various degrees depending upon their personalities, but one quilter stood apart, aloof, no matter how often Pauline tried to engage her in conversation. While all the other members of the guild had introduced themselves to Pauline at the party, Brenda Hughley had not. As the evening wound down and Pauline realized that she had made the acquaintance of all of the Cherokee Rose Quilters save one, she quickly put together two small plates with an assortment of treats from the dessert table and carried them over to the corner where Brenda stood, sipping a glass of sparkling water with lime.

"Hi." Pauline greeted her brightly, holding out one of the plates. "I noticed that you're the only one without dessert, so I brought you a little sampler before everything's gone."

Tall and lanky, with sandy blond hair cut boyishly short and angular features, Brenda waved the plate away. "Oh, no, thank you. I don't eat that sort of thing."

"Not even at a party?" Pauline set the extra plate on a nearby table, wishing she had chosen the fruit salad instead of cookies and brownies. "I guess I should have known, with a figure like yours."

"I do Pilates." Brenda glanced past Pauline's shoulder and nodded to someone behind her. "And I don't put junk in my body."

Pauline laughed weakly and set down her own plate, piled embarrassingly high with decadent goodness, next to the one she had prepared for Brenda. "I should follow your example."

"Oh, go ahead." Brenda waved a hand toward the plate. "Indulge. Why not, in your case?"

Pauline wasn't sure what Brenda meant and she didn't want to ask. "So, have you decided what class you're going to teach at the retreat?"

"Oh, I never teach unless I'm paid for it." Brenda sipped her sparkling water. "Besides, teaching would take away too much time from my quilting."

"The other Cherokee Rose Quilters seem to manage both just fine," Pauline remarked, immediately regretting it when Brenda's slight frown told her it was the wrong thing to say. "I guess you're probably busy with other things. Which committee are you in charge of?"

Brenda shook her head and shifted her weight. "None of them. I'm much too busy."

"Oh, I didn't realize you were one of the officers."

"I'm not, but that doesn't mean I'm not busy." Without meeting her gaze, Brenda edged away. "If you'll excuse me."

Puzzled, Pauline watched her go, feeling slighted and more than a little foolish. She picked up her dessert plate, nibbled a mocha brownie, and wished she had made a better first impression. She would make up for it later, she decided, taking both plates in hand and dumping them discreetly into the wastebasket.

But in the weeks that followed, that proved easier said than done. Brenda never smiled when Pauline greeted her at the start of a monthly meeting, nor did she reply with anything more than a nod when Pauline bade her good-bye afterward. When the group discussed upcoming plans and projects, Brenda usually acknowledged Pauline's suggestions with a shrug and a muffled sigh before asking if anyone else had any *good* ideas.

"She doesn't like me," Pauline told Ray. "I don't know why, but she doesn't."

Ray's brow furrowed in puzzlement as if he couldn't imagine how anyone wouldn't adore his wife as much as he did. "How does she treat everyone else?"

Pauline mulled it over. "She seems to get along fine with the others. Not that she's ever the most outgoing or bubbly person, but she at least talks to them."

"Maybe she's shy," Ray suggested. "Maybe once she gets to know you, she'll talk to you more."

Considering how forcefully Brenda voiced her opinions at the Cherokee Rose Quilters' roundtable discussions, Pauline doubted shyness was the problem. "I think I offended her at the initiation party," she reluctantly admitted. "I was just chatting, you know, asking questions like you do when you're trying to get to know someone, but maybe she thought I was criticizing her."

"Criticizing her how?"

"By implying she doesn't do enough for the guild. She doesn't teach at the retreats, she's not in charge of any committees, and she's not an officer." Pauline was struck by a sudden thought. "You know, I can't help wondering why she doesn't play a more significant role in the guild. Everyone else does. I've been a member for only a few months and I'm already leading the publicity committee and serving on two others."

"Well, sugar, giving doesn't come naturally to everyone."

"But the whole point of the guild is to give—our time, our labor, our expertise, our encouragement—to support the art and heritage of quilting throughout the state of Georgia."

"And you get a lot in return," said Ray. "Satisfaction in a job well done, good times with your friends, development of your own artistic talents, and not a small amount of fame and glory."

"Not to mention an annual free vacation at the Château Élan." Could Brenda have become a Cherokee Rose Quilter not because she wanted to give of her time and talents to support the guild's mission, but because of the fringe benefits—the admiration of other quilters impressed by her membership in such an exclusive group, the gratitude of the people served by the charities the guild supported, the development of her own artistic talents through guild critiques and workshops?

Pauline didn't want to believe it. "She can't be in it just for herself. She does participate, just maybe not as much as everyone else."

Ray frowned dubiously. "If you say so, sugar. I've never met the woman."

"I've known her for months and I can't figure her out either." Pauline sighed. "If I did offend her, I wish she'd just tell me so I could make it right."

But although Pauline tried and tried again to befriend Brenda, she remained as aloof as ever. Brenda did speak to her when they were obliged to work on projects together, but although she chatted about her job and family with veteran guild members, with Pauline she was strictly business.

Bemused, Pauline found reassurance in the friendships she had struck up with the other guild members, some of whom became as close to her as Jeanette. They admired her quilting, and their amazing talents inspired her to reach even greater heights. They seemed to appreciate her dedication to the guild and the energy she brought to their charitable works. Before long she felt perfectly at home in the guild she had once admired from a distance—comfortable with everyone except Brenda.

"Would you want to be friends with Brenda if you weren't members of the same quilt guild?" Ray asked her not long after her first anniversary with the guild passed, a milestone Pauline had hoped would lead to some softening of Brenda's standoffish manner.

"I really doubt it." After so many slights and rebuffs, Pauline would not have persisted in trying to win over Brenda except that her unfriendliness was the only flaw that kept the Cherokee Rose Quilters from being, for Pauline at least, absolutely perfect.

"Can you still work with her even if you'll never be best buds?" Ray asked.

"I've been able to all this time," Pauline replied. "I guess I can keep it up."

And so she decided to abandon her dogged quest to get Brenda to like her. Pauline had admired the Cherokee Rose Quilters for too long to let one person prevent her from enjoying a group that otherwise meant the world to her. It was her refuge from her demanding, stressful job and her cherished but often overwhelming role as a wife and mother. She could not let one disappointment, however glaring, ruin it for her.

She had almost resigned herself to Brenda's indifference by the time she took over the office of guild treasurer. Pauline relished the opportunity to contribute more to the success of the group that had given her so much pleasure and inspiration. In her first month in office, she overhauled their accounting system, entered all their paper records into the computer, and linked to their bank accounts online, earning praise and heartfelt thanks from the others, who had discussed the upgrade for years but had been reluctant to take on such an arduous task. She paid their bills on time and met with their portfolio manager to be sure their investments were on track. It was the sort of task-oriented, attention-to-detail work she excelled at, and she thoroughly enjoyed it, except for one important but nagging duty she was required to complete every few months: collecting fees from her fellow guild members.

Upon joining the guild, every member was informed of the various financial contributions that would be expected of her, from annual membership dues to donations to the president's thank-you gift fund. It was the treasurer's responsibility to announce upcoming deadlines, calculate the required fees, and collect payments. Most guild members paid promptly and without complaint within days of receiving Pauline's reminder e-mails, and a few paid ahead of time. Inevitably, some members forgot until the due date arrived, and Pauline would field a flurry of apologetic e-mails and phone calls assuring her they would send her a check the following morning.

And then there was Brenda.

She never paid on time—not her annual dues, not her nominal year-end donation to the museum endowment, not her contribution to the supplies fund, which they used to buy cones of thread and batting for their charity quilts. Pauline found herself nudging Brenda nearly every month for one outstanding bill or another. The first time Brenda missed a deadline, Pauline paid for her and sent her a cheerful e-mail assuring Brenda that she could reimburse her at their next meeting. Two weeks later,

Brenda instead mailed her a check, without a word of thanks or explanation. After a few more missed payments, Pauline began to wonder if Brenda and her husband had fallen upon hard times like so many other folks, and she considered offering to pay Brenda's guild debts until they got back on their feet. Fortunately, before she could figure out how to delicately propose an arrangement, she overheard Brenda discussing the new car she was buying with her husband's annual bonus, sparing Pauline from offending Brenda beyond redemption by offering unnecessary charity. If money wasn't the issue, Pauline wondered, why wouldn't Brenda just pay up on time like everyone else?

As the months passed and stretched into years, Pauline retained the position of treasurer, a time-consuming post that no one else especially wanted and everyone—except Brenda—agreed she handled with aplomb. She hoped she would become accustomed to Brenda's quirks and more patient in dealing with them, but instead she only became more practiced at concealing her annoyance. She vented to Ray, but she couldn't bring herself to complain to Jeanette, the guild president, or any of her other close friends in the guild. As far as she could tell, everyone else liked Brenda and considered her a valued member of their circle, whereas sometimes, even after five years in the guild, Pauline still felt as if she had to prove herself worthy. And so, in the interest of maintaining peace and harmony, she kept her frustrations to herself, gritting her teeth every time she sent Brenda one courteous e-mail reminder after another, paid Brenda's overdue fees, and awaited reimbursement rather than let the guild's accounts slip into the red.

She should have known that approach would work only so long.

Eight months before Quiltsgiving, when the Cherokee Rose Quilters had recovered from the previous year's charity fundraiser retreat but weren't quite ready to begin planning the next, the catering manager of the Château Élan phoned Pauline with an enticing offer. In appreciation for their longstanding relationship, the Château Élan offered to reduce their usual fees by 25 percent if the quilt guild would pay half up front at least six months before the date of their event.

The offer was enticing. The Cherokee Rose Quilters could contribute the money they saved on resort expenses to the homeless shelter, or the museum endowment fund, or additional supplies for their charity quilts, or scholarships to defray the costs of their retreats for quilters facing financial hardship, or any number of good works. But could they pay half up front as the Château Élan required? Usually the guild paid a nominal fee when they booked their reservation, followed by a larger percentage of the total cost after registration fees began coming in, about three months before the retreat. They had already paid that year's booking fee, but half up front would be a rather considerable sum, more than what remained of their annual budget.

Pauline promised to get back in touch with the catering manager as soon as she discussed his proposal with the rest of the guild.

First she examined their accounts to see what she had to work with. By taking a little from this fund and a little from that, and shifting some surplus from here to there, she figured they could scrape together enough cash if each guild member contributed an additional two hundred dollars. It could be considered an early payment of their annual membership dues, and when the retreat tuition checks began rolling in, they could replenish the guild's account. No one would have to pay a dime more than usual; they would simply have to pay earlier.

Pauline knew that some of the Cherokee Rose Quilters were quite well off; others, like herself, belonged to households that managed to get by fairly comfortably on two modest incomes. A few struggled, supporting themselves on their artist's commissions without the benefit of a spouse's salary. Pauline realized that especially for these few, an early payment of their annual dues might not fit within their tight budgets, and she was tempted to forget the whole plan rather than ask anyone to pay more than they could afford. But when she thought of all the good they could do with that 25 percent savings, she knew it was her responsibility to tell the guild about the Château Élan's offer and what they needed to do to accept it.

She outlined her proposal in an e-mail, which she sent out to the guild's mailing list. Within minutes, several members replied to the list, agreeing that the challenges of paying their dues earlier than usual were outweighed by the benefits of saving such a large sum. A casual vote conducted by e-mail a few days later was unanimously in favor of accepting the catering manager's offer. No one abstained from the vote, not even Brenda, who typically did not bother to respond to any of Pauline's messages.

The day after the vote, Pauline called the catering manager to confirm and sent out another e-mail to the guild asking them to pay her at the next meeting. Nearly everyone remembered, and of the three that forgot, two apologized and promised to put a check in the mail the next day. The third was Brenda, who looked past Pauline's shoulder, shrugged, and said, "Oh, I'll get it to you in time. Relax. You're fine."

Pauline felt her hackles rise, smiling through clenched teeth as Brenda turned and wandered off. Nothing was less likely to make her relax than Brenda's command that she do so, and she was definitely not fine. "In time" meant at that meeting, not some vague date of Brenda's choosing in the distant future. The resort had set a deadline, and if they didn't have all the money by then, they wouldn't receive their savings.

Checks from the other two forgetful members arrived within days, but Brenda sent nothing. A week after the meeting, Pauline e-mailed her a cheerful reminder, to which, not unexpectedly, she received no reply. Another week passed without a word, so Pauline sent another, considerably less cheerful e-mail. The third week brought more silence and yet another reminder, and before Pauline knew it, a month had gone by. Pauline had hoped that Brenda would slip her a check at the guild meeting, but Brenda didn't so much as glance in Pauline's direction by the time the evening wrapped up and the quilters headed out to their cars.

Pauline steeled herself and hurried to catch up with Brenda before she could drive away. "I guess you haven't been getting my e-mails," she began, managing what she hoped was a cordial smile.

"Oh, yes, those." Brenda shifted her purse on her shoulder and glanced at her watch. "I got them."

"Oh, good. I was worried. So, did you bring a check?"

"No, not tonight. I said I'd pay you in time and I will. Relax."

There was that word again. "Brenda, it's already past time to be 'in time.' Could you write me a check tonight so I can pay the resort, please?"

"I don't carry a checkbook. I do all my checks on my computer."

Or not at all, as it suited her. "Okay, then when can I expect to receive it?"

"Soon." Brenda's SUV chirped as she pressed a button on her key fob. Pauline stepped out of the way as she opened the door and climbed aboard. Without another glance in Pauline's direction, Brenda drove off, leaving Pauline dumbfounded and fuming in her wake.

Pauline could have paid Brenda's share as she had many times before, but Ray didn't like it and Pauline wasn't especially thrilled with shelling out so much money with no idea when she might be reimbursed. But it wasn't just about what Pauline could afford or couldn't. A principle was at stake. Brenda had voted in favor of the plan, she had agreed to pay, and her salary was at least twice Pauline's, so she could certainly afford it. She was just being stubborn. She just didn't like Pauline telling her what to do.

Pauline waited four days, long enough to be sure that if Brenda had mailed the check the day after the guild meeting, it would have arrived. And then, with the resort's deadline swiftly approaching, she composed an e-mail to the guild, the usual weekly summary of their accounts, income, and expenditures. In a postscript, she noted that the resort's deadline for securing their discount was only two weeks away. "Almost everyone has paid," she added, "so, Brenda, if you could please get that check to me immediately, I'd really appreciate it."

The first response was from the guild president addressed to the entire list, thanking Pauline for the detailed update.

The second response was from Brenda, and it was sent privately.

From: Brenda.Hughley@peachmail.com
To: pauline.e.tucker@monroecty.ga.gov
Subject: Your e-mail

Pauline:

Thanks for the oh-so-thoughtful reminders about the
payment. FYI, I already have a mother, but if you would like the
job I can definitely tell you where to go to apply.

I will tell you yet again to RELAX. I have been a Cherokee
Rose Quilter for much longer than you and have always paid my
fees. I told you I would take care of it and I will. If the treasurer
job has become too stressful for you, maybe it is time for you to
let someone else take over.

Brenda

Pauline felt as if the air had been squeezed from her lungs.
Hands shaking, she scrolled back to the top of the e-mail and
read it again. Taking a deep breath, she pushed herself out of
her chair, paced to the window, and forced herself to sit down
and read the message again.

It was no better on the third reading than it had been on
the first.

Pauline sat back in her chair, wondering what to do. She
wanted to call Ray, but she hated to bother him at work. She
wanted to call Jeanette, but she and her family were spending
the weekend at their cabin in the Chattahoochee National
Forest. So instead she forwarded the e-mail to Jeanette, adding
only a single word as preamble: "Wow."

She doubted that Jeanette would have e-mail access even on
her phone, so she wasn't really expecting a response. When Ray

came home from the office, she promptly dragged him off to the computer and showed him the e-mail. "Maybe you should apply for the mother job," he mused, peering at the screen. "You would have brought her up to take care of her responsibilities."

"For all we know, her mother tried her best, but Brenda wouldn't listen." Pauline paced back and forth. "What should I do? I have to respond somehow."

"Don't do anything yet." Ray wrapped her in a hug and pulled her close to his burly chest. "Sleep on it, and write back when you're calm and collected. You can't unsay something once it's said."

Wearily, Pauline agreed.

That night she slept poorly, and the next morning she felt far from calm and collected. She picked at her breakfast before realizing she had no appetite, so she sat down at the computer to compose a response before sending the kids out to the school bus and heading off to work. The words wouldn't come. She couldn't think of what she could possibly say to defend herself, to get Brenda to pay up, and to make peace between them. Perhaps that was too much to ask of a single e-mail. With time running out, she instead wrote to Daria, the previous guild treasurer.

From: pauline.e.tucker@monroecty.ga.gov
To: stitcherdaria@georgiapostal.com
Subject: Fwd: Your e-mail

Hi, Daria. I apologize for dragging you into this, but after discussing this upsetting e-mail from Brenda with Ray, I wanted to ask your advice as the person I inherited this job from. My only intention was to make sure we met the resort's deadline and secured the reduced rate, but Brenda has clearly taken offense. I'm willing to step down as treasurer if you think that's appropriate.

Thanks,

Pauline

She didn't realize she was considering resigning from office until she wrote the words.

She sent a similar e-mail to Jeanette, with apologies for interrupting her vacation with such ugliness, and then she left for work. When she returned home later that afternoon, she hoped to find supportive responses full of wisdom and sympathy in her in-box, but neither Daria nor Jeanette had replied, leaving her feeling more alone and lost than ever. Pauline was reluctant to write back to Brenda without first consulting another member of the guild, but she worried that Brenda would interpret silence as cowed acquiescence. So, with a little editorial help from Ray, she responded and hoped for the best.

From: pauline.e.tucker@monroecty.ga.gov

To: Brenda.Hughley@peachmail.com

Subject: Re: Your e-mail

Hi, Brenda.

I regret that my reminders offended you. All I wanted was to get us that discount and to save us some money that we could put to good use, but that's clearly not how you took it.

From my point of view, though, your response was unnecessarily hostile. If you think I've treated you inappropriately or unfairly, you should feel free to tell me in a frank, constructive manner.

I hope we can clear the air, since we may be working together as members of the Cherokee Rose Quilters for quite some time.

Thanks,

Pauline

The next day, Brenda wrote back.

From: Brenda.Hughley@peachmail.com
To: pauline.e.tucker@monroecty.ga.gov
Subject: Re: Your e-mail

Pauline:

I did not feel that you handled things in a nice, appropriate manner. Since you are not my mother, you did not need to repeatedly remind me after I told you in person that I would pay on time. If you couldn't resist, you should have (1) been nice about it and (2) told me privately instead of dragging the whole guild into it.

The way I see it, you started the snippy comments and when I called you on it, you did not like the results. What did you expect? You ought to know to treat others as you would like to be treated.

That said, I do not hold a grudge against you. I just did not feel that the snide comments were appreciated or necessary.

Brenda

Pauline read the message twice through before sitting back in her chair, utterly bewildered. Which of her comments, either spoken or written, could be construed as snide? How was it snippy to remind Brenda her payments were overdue? Pauline knew snide and snippy, and if she had wanted to be either she could have piled on the snide and snippy as thick and searing as a can of tar on an open fire in the Mojave.

"How big of her, not to hold a grudge against you for doing your job," Ray remarked later when she showed him Brenda's latest missive. "Sounds like she has some mother issues too."

"Yeah, I noticed that." Pauline sighed heavily. Her head ached and her heart hurt. "I also noticed that she seems completely unaware that she said anything wrong, she doesn't acknowledge that she should have paid up by the deadline, and—and this is key—she doesn't mention anything about finally getting me that stinking check."

Ray snorted. "I wouldn't count on getting one cent from her. She's dug in her heels, and now she's stalling just to spite you."

But it wasn't only Pauline she was spiting. If they didn't pay the resort on time, the Cherokee Rose Quilters would lose the reduced rate, and they wouldn't have that tidy sum of money to put toward other causes.

Later that night, Pauline received a response from Daria, her predecessor as treasurer.

From: stitcherdaria@georgiapostal.com
To: pauline.e.tucker@monroecty.ga.gov
Subject: Re: Fwd: Your e-mail

I'm so shocked I don't even know what to say. You didn't do anything to deserve this sort of response. I need to think this over carefully. I'll call you tomorrow, okay? In the meantime, try to get a good night's sleep. Thank you again for being treasurer. We all (well, almost all) appreciate it.

Daria

The next day was a Saturday. While Ray shuttled the kids back and forth to their weekend sports and clubs and activities, Pauline moped around the house, attending to neglected chores and waiting for the phone to ring. Before Daria could keep her promise to call, Jeanette showed up on her doorstep, unexpected but very much welcome.

Pauline invited her in, poured them each a tall glass of sweet tea, and led her outside to the back porch. When Pauline asked about her vacation, Jeanette offered a few brief, hasty anecdotes before jettisoning any pretense that this was an ordinary social visit.

"I can't believe what Brenda wrote to you," Jeanette said, fuming. "Well, I can believe it, since I know Brenda and I saw the e-mail, but still, I can't *believe* it."

"I know what you mean," said Pauline glumly. "I don't know if my response made things any worse, but it definitely didn't make them any better."

"Pauline . . ." Jeanette hesitated. "Is there some reason why you reminded her about her late payment in the weekly update sent to the entire guild rather than writing to her privately?"

"She never responds to the e-mails I send her privately." Pauline lifted her hands and let them fall into her lap, helpless. "And I do mean never. In all the time I've been treasurer, I've sent her what has to be hundreds of overdue-payment reminders, and she's never once replied. I'm never even sure that she receives them."

"Oh, she receives them, all right," said Jeanette grimly. "She never responded to Katie, either."

"Katie?"

"She was the treasurer before Daria. She moved to Texas

before you joined the guild." Jeanette picked up her glass, which was misty with condensation, but she didn't drink. "Okay. Here's what I think, for what it's worth. I think Brenda believes you wanted to publicly humiliate her, to get back at her for paying late."

"That wasn't my intention. I didn't want to punish her. I just wanted to get her to pay, and since she seemed to resent my reminder e-mails, I thought I would just add it to the weekly update as a casual, breezy aside." Pauline hesitated. "And okay, maybe I wanted everyone else to know how late she was, but only to put the pressure on so she would pay before we lost the discount." The way things were going, that outcome seemed inevitable. "I never intended to humiliate her. Honestly, I didn't think she was capable of being humiliated."

"I believe you," Jeanette said. "I'm just trying to explain how Brenda probably sees it."

"If this had been the only incident . . ." Pauline began, thinking aloud—and then the whole story came tumbling out of her: Brenda's perpetual tardiness, her unresponsiveness, the number of times Pauline had paid her way and had not always been reimbursed. As she spoke, Pauline realized for the first time just how long the unpleasant situation had been going on, and how many times she had forced a smile and dealt with it rather than encourage Brenda to dislike her even more than she already did. Why had she put up with it so long?

All at once, she was struck by the realization that she didn't want to anymore.

Jeanette took in the whole sorry tale, and when it was over, she took a deep breath, puffed out her cheeks as she exhaled, and said, "Look, you need to talk to Daria."

"I sent her an e-mail. She said she would call. But really, I think the damage has been done." Pauline steeled herself. "Brenda's right about one thing. I should step down as treasurer."

Jeanette put a hand on her arm. "Oh, no, Pauline, please don't make any rash decisions when you're upset. You're the best treasurer we've ever had. You're the most organized person I've ever met. I've never heard anything but praise for you and the job you're doing."

"You must not have included Brenda in your poll."

"Before you make any decisions, talk to Daria. I think you'll find she has similar stories to tell."

And Daria did.

After a few days of playing phone tag, Pauline learned that Daria's experience with Brenda mirrored her own. Brenda had paid all her fees late, if she paid at all; she had ignored Daria's increasingly tentative reminders; and she generally had made Daria's tenure as treasurer miserable, driving her to quit and pass the job, gratefully and guiltily, to Pauline. "I should have warned you what you'd be dealing with."

"It's okay," Pauline told her. "I would have thought you were exaggerating, and I would have accepted the job anyway." She had enjoyed being treasurer, and if not for Brenda, she would enjoy it still. She was good at the job and she liked making an important contribution to the guild.

Brenda had taken all that away.

Daria sighed. "I was in office three months before guilt got the better of Katie and she confessed that her husband had made her quit."

"What?"

"It's true. When Brenda's payments were overdue, Katie would charge them to her credit card, and she often didn't get reimbursed in time to pay off the bill. Her husband got so fed up with all the late fees that he finally put his foot down and said that if she wanted to stay in the guild, she couldn't be the treasurer anymore."

"Wow." Pauline tried to imagine Ray ever ordering her to do anything and failed. "I guess he's the boss of her?"

"He had good reason to be upset."

Pauline couldn't deny that.

Daria had more stories that echoed Pauline's own experiences, and she predicted that Brenda would pay the day before the Château Élan's deadline arrived. She would pay at the last minute and not a second sooner because she wanted to make a point, because she could, because it would drive Pauline crazy, and because it was as far as she could go without inflicting any lasting harm upon the guild and turning the others against her.

And so she did.

Pauline couldn't figure out how Brenda had been allowed to get away with her behavior so long. She had been the bane of many a guild treasurer, compelling two that Pauline knew of to step down, and yet no one had held her accountable. No one had been willing to confront her or tell her that her behavior was unacceptable—no one except Pauline. But Pauline didn't want to engage in pointless squabbling or browbeat Brenda into following the guild rules. Brenda was an adult; she ought to be able to do what was right and follow the guild rules just like everyone else.

Pauline hoped that resigning from the treasurer's position would alleviate the knot of tension that tightened in her gut every time she thought of Brenda and the Cherokee Rose Quilters, but it didn't. Tensions grew as Jeanette and Daria told other members about the conflict, forwarding e-mails and repeating conversations and sharing their own Brenda stories.

The growing divide in the guild dismayed Pauline, but she couldn't see any way to stop it from widening. She skipped the next monthly meeting, unwilling to go through the motions of the evening's business as if nothing had happened. She also doubted her ability to get through the meeting without telling Brenda, in front of God and the Cherokee Rose Quilters and any unfortunate passersby, exactly what she thought of her.

Daria agreed to take over the role of treasurer until Pauline wanted the job back, a qualifier Pauline tried to get her to drop since she had no intention of returning to office. She felt tired and sad, and she felt even worse when, after her third skipped meeting, Daria sent her an e-mail lamenting Pauline's absence, denouncing Brenda's behavior, and declaring her intention to call a vote and demand that Brenda be expelled from the Cherokee Rose Quilters so that Pauline could return.

Pauline's heart sank. If Brenda were expelled, her closest friends—because she surely had some—would likely go with her. Who knew how many others might follow them out of sheer disappointment that the guild had allowed personal conflicts to tear them apart? The Cherokee Rose Quilters might not survive the schism, and then all the good they had done—supporting those in need, introducing the art of quilting to schoolchildren, inspiring quilters to strive for greater mastery of their beloved craft, preserving and celebrating Georgia's rich quilting heritage—all of that would be over.

It never should have come to that. Why had no one in

Brenda's long history with the Cherokee Rose Quilters held her accountable for her behavior? Daria fired off angry e-mails about hypothetical votes, but throughout the whole sordid affair, no one—not Daria, not Jeanette, not the guild president—had sat Brenda down, told her that she had behaved badly, and asked her to make it right. Brenda would never do so without prompting—strong, insistent prompting. She still didn't believe she had done anything wrong, and unless and until she did, Pauline could count on more of the same bad behavior from her every day they both remained Cherokee Rose Quilters.

Eventually, reluctantly, Pauline realized that the only way to save the Cherokee Rose Quilters would be for either Pauline or Brenda to quit. And since Brenda was certain to stubbornly hold on to the guild as long as there was breath in her body, Pauline had to be the one to go.

Jeanette tried to talk her out of it. Daria tried even harder. Pauline's loyal daughter declared that Brenda ought to be the one to go and that Pauline ought to let Daria call for that vote. Her faithful son agreed.

"Don't throw yourself on your sword for her sake," Ray told her. He adamantly believed that she shouldn't let one nasty, mean-spirited person drive her out of the Cherokee Rose Quilters, a group she was so proud of and loved so dearly.

"Don't you understand?" Pauline choked out. "It's because I love the group and—almost—all the people in it that I have to quit. I can't see it fall apart all because of me."

"It's not all because of *you*," Ray corrected gently. "It's because of *her*."

"Well, she's not going to do what's necessary to hold it together, so I have to."

Ray took her in his arms and held her as her tears began to fall. "If you're sure this is the right thing to do, sugar, then do what you gotta do. Whatever you decide, I'm with you all the way."

Pauline was grateful for that, because she felt as if she were losing a part of herself. And although she knew it was for the greater good, she was as angry as she was sorrowful, because she had given up something very dear to her—and Brenda had won.

It seemed like she cried for a week, but then, drained and miserable, she resolved to pull herself together. She rejoined the Sunset Ridge Quilt Guild and signed up for a kickboxing class at the gym to fill the hours she had once spent balancing the guild's books. From time to time she and Jeanette got together for lunch or an afternoon of companionable quilting. At first Daria and the other guild members in the know pleaded with Pauline to come back, insisting that things just weren't the same without her. The few guild members who remained blissfully unaware of the conflict had somehow got it into their heads that she was too busy with work to attend guild meetings anymore, and they wrote to express sympathy and hopes that her workload would ease up soon.

Pauline was surprised that they hadn't learned the real reason for her departure through the grapevine and that they had seized upon her job as the explanation for her extended absence. The emergency call center was the one workplace in her long employment history that had never required her to take work home at the end of the day. Did her friends really believe that the operations center was so overwhelmed that it had begun routing emergency calls to its employees' cell phones after hours?

The very question exhausted her, so in a way it was a relief when the e-mails and phone calls stopped coming. "We'll keep your place vacant for a while," the guild president promised in her last message, but Pauline knew they wouldn't hold it for her forever. As long as Brenda remained in the guild, Pauline couldn't bring herself to return.

She tried to move on, but as November approached, Pauline's thoughts turned to the Château Élan retreat, which always fell on the first week after Thanksgiving. It pained her to think of all the work that went into running a successful retreat and how she could not pitch in to help. She thought of all the lovely quilts that would be made that week, and how much money they would raise for worthy and important causes.

The Cherokee Rose Quilters gave so much to their community, to their state, to the world of quilting. That had always been what Pauline admired most about them. And now, they continued their good works while Pauline stood on the sidelines, watching and missing them and wishing she could help.

Ray noticed her melancholy deepening, and he worried about her. He tried to cheer her up with flowers and candy and dinner dates and sweet notes tucked into her lunch sack, but although she appreciated them and adored him for trying, nothing worked.

Finally Ray pointed out something that should have been obvious. "You know, sugar, you don't have to be a Cherokee Rose Quilter to give."

And of course, he was right.

Pauline had heard about Elm Creek Quilt Camp and Quiltsgiving some time ago, although she couldn't remember where— perhaps from a feature in *Quiltmaker* magazine, perhaps from a quilter she had met at the Château Élan. She studied their website with Ray peering over her shoulder, barely able to contain his eagerness. This, he surely thought, would perk up his darling wife. This would do the trick.

And so it had, at least a little. Looking forward to her week away had lifted her spirits. Upon her arrival, she had discovered that Elm Creek Manor was lovely and safe, the quilters gathered within its gray stone walls kind and generous. The thought of making quilts to comfort children in need eased the pain in her heart and helped her see her own disappointment in a different light.

Her sacrifice had kept the Cherokee Rose Quilters together. Their good works would continue, and Pauline could do good works of her own, on her own.

But somehow she sensed that among the Elm Creek Quilters and their campers, she would never be entirely alone.

"Pauline?"

She started and turned toward the voice to find Linnea studying her worriedly. "Yes?"

"Are you all right?"

"Of course. I'm fine." Then Pauline noticed that Gretchen was watching her from the front of the classroom, her brows drawn together in concern. The other students had already packed up and were filing from the room. Quickly Pauline jumped up and began loading her things into her tote bag.

"You've been staring into space for quite some time," said Jocelyn.

"Waiting for inspiration to strike?" asked Michaela.

Pauline forced a laugh. "You guessed it. Sadly, my muse decided not to put in an appearance this morning."

From the back of the room came a laugh. They all turned to find Karen Wise smiling their way. "She'll turn up," Karen promised, slipping the straps of her tote over her shoulder. "This is Elm Creek Manor, after all. Inspiration is never far away."

Suddenly Pauline found herself smiling, her melancholy lifting.

She didn't doubt Karen for a moment.

Chapter Three

☙

Linnea

Over lunch—the campers had been offered a choice between a vegetable curry with basmati rice or a chicken and pesto panini, and Linnea had chosen the sandwich, grilled to perfection—Linnea, Mona, and Pauline discussed their first Giving Quilt class and concluded that the Resolution Square quilt was charming, Gretchen was a lively and encouraging instructor, and they were unanimously pleased that they had signed up for the course.

"After lunch, I think I'm going to go back and cut enough pieces for a second quilt," said Pauline thoughtfully as they cleared away their dishes and left the banquet hall. "Maybe even a third, each in a different color palette. How are you two going to spend the afternoon?"

"I brought a stack of Girl's Joy blocks from home," Linnea said. "They've been sitting in a box at the back of my closet for years, so I'm finally going to sew them together and give the finished quilt to Project Linus."

Mona declared her intention to curl up in a chair by the ballroom fireplace with a good book and read to her heart's content, a luxury usually denied her back home, where her four sons' cheerful, boisterous activity rarely gave her a moment of quiet solitude. Pauline seemed disappointed that the sisters wouldn't be joining her in the classroom, so Linnea quickly suggested that they meet in the lobby at five o'clock and have supper together. Brightening, Pauline agreed.

"I like her," Mona remarked to her sister after Pauline departed.

"So do I," said Linnea. Pauline was funny and endearingly eager to please, but she seemed rather lonesome. Linnea wondered why she had skipped her own guild's annual retreat in favor of Quiltsgiving at Elm Creek Manor, but it was obvious that Pauline didn't want to talk about it, so Linnea had to leave her insatiable curiosity unsatisfied. Perhaps by the end of the week, Pauline would open up and share her story with her newfound friends. In the meantime, Linnea would try to cultivate patience.

The sisters returned upstairs, Linnea for her quilt blocks and Mona for her book, and before long they found themselves back in the ballroom, where, from the sound of things, Pauline was not the only student hard at work behind the partitions that marked the walls of the classroom. While Mona settled down in her fireside chair with a contented sigh and turned to the first chapter of her novel, Linnea carried her blocks and tote bag full of supplies to one of the sewing stations set up on long tables near the tall windows that looked out upon the rear of the manor, where a few small, icy snow-flakes drifted lazily in the breeze. She exchanged brief, cordial smiles with the campers sewing industriously at the stations to her left and right, and then set herself to work, sewing Girl's Joy blocks into rows, pressing the seams, and sewing the rows together.

By midafternoon, she had completed the center of the quilt top and had only to add borders to finish it off, but her legs were stiff from sitting so long and the back of her neck ached from her tendency to draw her shoulders up to her ears when she concentrated. A break was definitely in order.

She gathered her things and tidied up in case another camper needed to use the sewing machine, and then joined her sister at the fireplace on the other side of the ballroom. Several chairs had been arranged in two concentric arcs around the hearth, where a lively blaze gave off warmth and light and a cheerful crackle of sparks. Nearly all of the chairs were occupied with a camper reading as Mona was, sewing quilt pieces together by hand, or dozing.

"I need to stretch my legs," Linnea said, resting a hand on the back of her sister's chair. "Want to go for a little walk?"

Mona read to the end of the line before pausing to smile up at her. "Another walk? You must not have noticed the snow flurries. Are you sure your Southern California constitution can handle it?"

Linnea shook her head, patiently exasperated. Sometimes Mona deliberately forgot that Linnea had grown up in Minnesota the same as she had and knew quite a lot about enduring winter weather. "Those few little flakes aren't much, and anyway, I'm staying indoors. I thought I might search out the library."

"Why am I not surprised?" Mona marked her place with a finger, closed her book, and rose, yawning and stretching. "You go on. I'm happy with the book I have right here."

"You don't want to explore?"

"I do, but not as much as I want to stay warm and cozy by the fire." Mona smiled an indolent apology, sat back down with her legs tucked to one side, and opened her book on her lap.

Mona did look much more relaxed, as if the cares and woes of her workplace had been forgotten, or at least tucked out of sight where they would not trouble her for a little while. For more than a year, ever since the new governor had been elected and had launched a merciless campaign to abolish all collective bargaining rights for state workers, Mona had been under tremendous stress—first because of the threat to her job as an office manager for the Minnesota Department of Transportation, and second because of her prominent position as vice president of her labor union. Not only did she have to worry about impending pay cuts and the loss of her own benefits, she had to worry on behalf of the thousands of other workers relying upon her to advocate for them. If spending less than twenty-four hours at Elm Creek Manor could work such miraculous cures, maybe Linnea and Mona should have booked two weeks. Maybe Linnea should have brought her husband along too.

With a sudden pang of longing, she bade Mona good-bye and hurried out to the foyer to call him. He answered on the second ring. "Hey, sweetheart," Kevin greeted her, forewarned by the caller ID that this was not the call from a potential employer he had been praying for. "How are you? How's your sister? How's quilt camp?"

Linnea smiled, warmed by the sound of his voice. "We're all

fine." She told Kevin about her day and asked about his. Although it was three hours earlier in Conejo Hills, California, he had already been quite productive. On his way to join the president of the Friends of the Library and a few other like-minded citizens for coffee, he had stopped by the post office and mailed ten updated résumés and two follow-up letters. Later that afternoon, he planned to meet a former coworker at the driving range. Kevin didn't know whether his former colleague was hiring, but if he wasn't, he might be aware of someone who was—and if he did, he would surely recommend Kevin. For five years they had worked together in the marketing department of a European luxury car manufacturer's West Coast division, but eighteen months earlier, the four branches spread throughout the Los Angeles region had been consolidated into one central office. Kevin's friend had been transferred there and promoted to assistant vice president. Kevin's job had been eliminated entirely.

"This is what I get for taking a job with a foreign car company," Kevin had said on that first demoralizing evening after the rumors that had been circulating for months were finally confirmed by an unceremonious summons to his supervisor's office and a terse dismissal. "My father probably rolled over in his grave the day I went to work for them. Maybe now he can rest in peace."

"That's ridiculous," Linnea had replied. "Your father would have done the same in your place."

"I'm not so sure."

Kevin's father had worked on the line for General Motors for more than forty years. He had bought a house in a modest Detroit suburb and had put three kids through college with his earnings, fair wages secured for him by his union. His favorite prank was to secretly paste BUY AMERICAN bumper stickers on his neighbors' Toyotas and Hondas. But for all his staunch pride, first and foremost he had been a loving father, and Linnea knew he wouldn't have blamed Kevin for taking a job with a foreign car company considering that General Motors had laid him off and no other American companies had hired him. Kevin's father had understood and respected a man's right to support his family through honest work—as long as that man didn't cross a picket line to take a loyal union man's job. He wouldn't have wanted Kevin to decline honest work just to make a point.

Ever since Kevin had become unemployed for the second time in twelve years, he had searched in vain for another position, but as the months dragged on, he had begun to suspect that often he was eliminated on paper before anyone bothered to meet him. At fifty-six, with decades of employment and countless successful marketing campaigns to his credit, he was usually more educated, experienced, and qualified than the people who were doing the hiring. Bewilderingly, these very factors had somehow become liabilities. Even when Kevin assured the interviewers that he was aware the position he had applied for was entry-level and absolutely did not expect anything remotely close to his former salary, they didn't believe him, and they rejected him as too expensive. Even when he assured them he was certain he would find the job fulfilling, rewarding, and challenging, they suspected that he would start looking for another, more interesting job the minute they hired him.

After far too many promising leads sent him careening headlong into brick walls of disappointment, Kevin, whom Linnea had once considered capable of selling ice to penguins, had ruefully remarked that he must not be cut out for marketing after all, since he apparently couldn't successfully market himself. Maybe his former employers had been right to lay him off.

"That's ridiculous," Linnea had retorted. "It's not you. It's them, and it's the economy. Things will turn around. Things will get better. They always have."

But even Linnea knew that that didn't mean they always would.

Kevin didn't usually need lots of reassurance. He was by nature optimistic, and even in the bleakest of times, he retained his sense of humor. Linnea's salary and benefits would keep them from losing their house, the kids' college funds, and their health care, and after years of wishing for more of it, he finally had ample time to spend with his family and to take care of the many home-repair chores he had been putting off indefinitely. He took over the housecleaning and the laundry, and he cooked supper almost every night, firing up the grill and learning to prepare just about anything on it. "We do have a stove, you know," Linnea reminded him with amusement when she came home from the library one evening to find him outside on the porch preparing Tex-Mex Four-Alarm Chili in a Dutch oven.

"The grill is more manly," Kevin pointed out, his mouth involuntarily quirking into a smile. Linnea smiled back, thankful beyond measure that she had married a resilient man. He would not slip into depression and insecurity as so many other men and women who had lost their jobs in the downturn of the economy had done. Kevin would never give up, and even in the midst of his struggles he would never lose sight of his many blessings.

Linnea tried to follow his example and keep a positive outlook on the future, but sometimes she felt as if they were precariously seated on a broken, teetering, three-legged chair. By working together they could keep their balance, but if something came along to knock one of the remaining legs out from beneath them, they would come crashing down.

Linnea felt that precarious uncertainty anew as she held the phone to her ear, yearning to offer her husband that one elusive, essential piece of advice that would help him find work. But when no wisdom came to mind, she instead told him again that she loved him, and she wished him good luck with his coffee shop gathering and at the driving range later. They both knew she wasn't referring to his stroke.

After they hung up, Linnea stood alone in the foyer, thinking of Kevin and wishing she could devise some ingenious plan to land him the job of his dreams—but lately it was all she could do to cling to her own job and to remember the dreams and hopes that had set her upon the path she had chosen.

Neither she, nor Kevin, nor Mona had expected their livelihoods to be on such shaky ground at that point in their careers. They had expected to be settled, stable, and working steadily toward the retirements they were carefully and frugally saving for. They had not counted on recessions or politics to throw everything into upheaval.

The sudden appearance of three quilt campers laughing and chatting as they descended the grand staircase roused Linnea from her reverie, and she needed a moment to remember why she had been standing alone in the foyer.

The library. Of course. She had heard that the manor

boasted a glorious library, but it was not included on the maps distributed at registration. Soon after her arrival the previous day, Linnea had wandered into the parlor and had found a small bookcase stuffed with well-read novels and paperbacks previous campers had left behind. A note card on the top shelf encouraged visitors to borrow books during their stay or take one and leave one of their own in trade. While this was a pleasant amenity, it could not possibly be the magnificent library full of antique treasures Kevin's distant cousin had raved about at the last Nelson family reunion.

Linnea pushed her worries about Kevin back into the far reaches of her mind and set off in search of the library. She passed guest suites and storage closets, the laundry room and the kitchen, and she even discovered an unlikely door that led outside to a gray stone patio, perhaps the one she, Mona, and Pauline had passed on their walk that morning. As she wandered, she began to suspect that the west wing of the manor was decades older than the elegantly appointed, expansive south wing. The rooms in the west wing were more modest in size, the ceilings lower, the windows smaller. Perhaps the west wing was the original residence built by Sylvia Bergstrom Compson Cooper's first ancestors to come to America, and their descendants had added the south wing after the family prospered. It did have a certain Gilded Age look about it.

But none of her speculation brought her any closer to finding the library. Eventually she concluded that the library, if it existed, could not be on the first floor. She decided to head upstairs to her suite for her registration packet and search the map of Elm Creek Manor for a library-sized blank portion, perhaps labeled "Here there be books."

She doubled back to the foyer and was about to set foot on the bottom step when suddenly two young children came bounding down the staircase, alternately shrieking with laughter and shushing each other. Instinctively Linnea stood fast, ready to break their fall if they should stumble. She was standing there yet when the children reached the bottom. The boy, faster and a few steps ahead, plowed into Linnea, while the girl had time and the presence of mind to seize the banister and bring herself to an abrupt halt. Linnea stumbled backward, trying to keep her feet and keep the boy on his so that neither of them would crash painfully to the cold marble floor.

"Are you okay?" she asked the boy as they steadied themselves.

He nodded and gulped, catching his breath. "I'm really, really sorry," he said. His thick, brown hair had glints of red and gold in it. Linnea would have trimmed it shorter were he her child, but she could understand his mother's reluctance.

"I'm perfectly fine," Linnea assured him, "although I don't think your parents would be happy to see you zooming down the stairs like that, do you?"

"You should be more careful," remarked the girl as she gracefully stepped down upon the marble floor, as if she had slowly and serenely descended the two dozen or so stairs instead of hurling herself down them as heedlessly as her brother had.

The boy scowled. "You were running too."

The girl's mouth fell upon in a wordless protest, but Linnea raised her hand. "I was here and I saw the whole thing. Both of you were running, and impressively fast too."

The girl's pretty features twisted in worry beneath her cap of tousled blond curls. "Are you going to tell on us?"

Linnea pretended to mull it over. "Well, no one was hurt, and I believe you'll be more careful in the future, right?" The children nodded vigorously. "In that case, I think we can keep this off your permanent record."

The boy heaved a sigh of relief, while the girl, who had straightened as if an electric shock had passed through her at the phrase "permanent record," murmured a soft, "Thank you."

"As a matter of fact," Linnea mused, going down on one knee to condense her generous height to something closer to their own, "I'm glad I ran into you."

"*I* ran into *you*," the boy corrected her.

"You're absolutely right, and as it turns out, I'm glad you did. I need a guide—actually, I think this job requires two guides, because it's quite challenging. I don't suppose you two know your way around Elm Creek Manor?"

"Of course we do," said the boy. "We live here."

"This is our house," the girl added, just in case Linnea required additional clarification. "Our mama is Sarah McClure and our daddy is Matt McClure."

"And Miss Sylvia is our great-grandma except not really," said the boy.

"Oh, of course," said Linnea. "Then you must be James, and you must be Caroline."

The twins nodded when she spoke their names, looking not the least bit surprised that she knew them.

"Excellent." Linnea clasped her hands and rubbed them together. "This must be my lucky day. I can't imagine any two guides more qualified to take me to the library."

The twins exchanged a look. "We can't drive," Caroline said carefully, as if she wasn't quite sure whether the strange lady before her was teasing her or was simply not very smart.

"No, no, honey, not the public library, although I'm sure it's very nice. I mean the library here in the manor. I've heard there's a wonderful library somewhere on the premises, and as a librarian myself, I would love to have a look at it."

Linnea waited while a swift, wordless exchange passed between the twins. Then James shrugged, and Caroline said, "We can show you where the best books are, if that's what you mean."

"That's exactly what I mean," said Linnea, holding out her hands for the twins to take. With James on her left and Caroline on her right, they made their way up both flights of stairs to the third floor, evoking smiles from the few quilt campers they passed along the way. They turned left and headed down the hallway, past closed doors that Linnea surmised led to other guest suites, which were probably unoccupied during the smaller Quiltsgiving session but full of quilt campers in the summer.

They came to a halt at a single door at the far end of the hallway. "Here it is," said Caroline grandly as she opened the door and led the way inside. Linnea followed the children into a spacious playroom bathed in afternoon sunshine. Snug nests of pillows and quilts had been carelessly fashioned upon the window seats, and toys and games were scattered about the room in happy, haphazard fashion.

James seized Linnea's hand and tugged her toward the southernmost wall, where two bookcases flanked an empty fireplace that looked as if it had not seen a pile of logs, burning or not, in ages. When James gazed proudly at the books upon the shelves, Linnea scanned the titles on the spines and saw that she was in the presence of all the childhood classics she had adored as a schoolgirl and many of the same wonderful new stories she loved to press into the hands of the children who visited her library. Then she understood. This was where the best books were, according to her guides—and could she really say they were wrong?

"I love this story," Linnea said, sitting cross-legged upon the braided rag rug and taking a battered copy of *Half Magic* from a shelf. "Have you read it?"

"Not yet," said James.

"He can't read," said Caroline, with all the pity of one who could and understood the deprivation he suffered better than he did.

James flushed. "I can too." He seized a copy of *Go, Dog, Go!* from the other bookcase and began to recite it from memory, the speed with which he turned the pages not quite keeping pace with his words.

"Very good," said Linnea, who understood that this was indeed reading of a sort, a very important precursor to what was more commonly understood as reading.

"Mama read *Half Magic* to us," James explained.

"I could read it all by myself if I wanted to," said Caroline, "but it's more fun when Mama reads to us."

"I know exactly what you mean." Linnea returned her gaze to the bookcases, admiring their collection. "I wonder if you have . . . I'm sure such a well-stocked library must—" Her gaze lit upon a familiar title on a well-worn spine, and she plucked down the book with delight. "Have you ever read—or heard—*Magic by the Lake*?" The twins shook their heads. "Then you're in for a treat. This story is by the same author who wrote *Half Magic*, Edward Eager, and it's about the same four children— Jane, Mark, Katherine, and Martha. Would you like me to read it to you?"

James and Caroline nodded so vigorously that Linnea almost feared they would injure themselves. She asked them to take her to their favorite reading spot and was not at all surprised when they led her to the most comfortably appointed window seat. She settled herself in the middle of the nest of quilts and pillows, and with one twin snuggled up to her on either side, she began reading the story of the children's magic-infused summer vacation on a northern Indiana lake. She had just reached the part where Mark encounters the talking turtle when someone appeared in the playroom doorway.

"There you two are," exclaimed Sarah, striding into the room. The twins, who had become so engrossed in the story that they had nearly climbed onto Linnea's lap in their eagerness for the next sentence, scrambled down from the window seat. "Why didn't you come when I called you?"

"We didn't hear you," said Caroline.

"We were listening to a story," explained James, indicating Linnea.

Sarah sighed. "I hope they weren't troubling you. They love books, and they love being read to."

"Believe me," declared Linnea, "nothing troubles me less than children who love books, and nothing troubles me more than people of any age who don't."

"This is a great story, Mama," said James. "You should read it."

Sarah glanced at the cover. "I have read that book, honey. It's one of my favorites." For Linnea's benefit, she indicated the bookshelves flanking the fireplace. "Many of these books are mine, books I loved and read over and over again as a child. My mother saved them for me." Sarah smiled as if touched anew by her mother's generous foresight. "The others were books beloved by the children of the Bergstrom family, going back generations. Sylvia decided that her childhood favorites belonged up here with mine rather than out of sight among the rest of her books. Now the twins can hold them and look at them and enjoy them whenever they wish."

"Sylvia is a sensible and wise woman." Linnea rose and handed the book to James. "As if we needed any additional proof."

"We're done reading?" James cried.

"I'll read you a little more tonight, and we'll finish the book together, bit by bit," Sarah quickly promised. "But Miss Linnea is here for quilt camp, and we ought to let her get back to it."

"Thank you for a charming diversion, children," said Linnea, shaking their hands. "I'm thoroughly delighted to have met such promising young readers."

The children beamed, and James piped up, "I'm really glad I *ran into you.*"

"I'm glad you did too." Linnea winked to assure him the collision would remain their little secret.

It wasn't until Linnea was back in the ballroom bent over the sewing machine again that she recalled Sarah's words and Sylvia's decision to put her books for younger readers with Sarah's rather than keeping them with the rest of her books.

So there *was* another library somewhere in Elm Creek Manor. Linnea had been diverted from her search, but she would try again, and she would find it.

She could ask one of the Elm Creek Quilters instead of searching on her own, but that would take all the fun out of her quest. She knew James and Caroline would understand.

Linnea had enough time before supper to sew the borders to her Girl's Joy quilt top but not enough time to press it, so she decided to save that task for another day. She packed up her supplies and scraps, left them in her suite, and met Mona and Pauline in the foyer. Supper was as tasty as every other meal had been—mini chicken potpies served in ramekins or tofu and vegetable stir-fry. When Linnea remarked aloud that the Elm Creek Quilters seemed to offer a vegetarian option with every meal, another quilter seated at their table said, "I bet that's Summer Sullivan's influence. She doesn't teach here anymore, but as a vegetarian herself, she probably taught her friends to make different options available."

"You don't have to be a vegetarian to love this," said Mona, who had chosen the stir-fry.

"Karen," asked Pauline, studying the other quilter intently, "how do you know so much about the faculty here?"

"I attended a week of summer quilt camp a few years ago, and I took Summer's Quick Piecing Shortcuts class," replied the other quilter, whom Linnea remembered as the woman from the Giving Quilt class who had encouraged Pauline not to abandon the search for inspiration. After a moment's hesitation, Karen added, "I also might have applied for a job here a few

years ago, and Summer might have been one of my interviewers."

"Might have?" echoed Linnea. "You don't remember?"

Karen laughed self-consciously and poked at her stir-fry
with her chopsticks. "Of course I remember. It's just not the
most pleasant of memories, since my interview was a disaster
and obviously I didn't get the job. I don't blame the Elm Creek
Quilters. The other candidates were far more qualified." With
two discreet nods, she indicated Gretchen and another Elm
Creek Quilter named Maggie, who were enjoying their chicken
potpies and lively conversation at two nearby tables.

Everyone murmured sympathetically, and Michaela, who
along with Jocelyn completed the group at their table, said,
"Tough competition."

"The toughest," Karen agreed, nodding.

"Something else will come along," said Mona, with a quick
glance for Linnea, who knew all too well that sometimes "something else" took its own sweet time in coming.

"Oh, it's okay. I mean, Sylvia was as nice as she possibly
could have been in such circumstances, and something else did
come along." Karen set down her chopsticks and drew her
hands into her lap, out of sight beneath the table. "A few months
later I found a job at a quilt shop, and I've been working there
ever since."

"That sounds like a dream job for a quilter," said Jocelyn.

"Do you have like an awesome employee discount or what?"
asked Michaela.

"Yes, it's quite nice, actually," said Karen, smiling. "Definitely the best perk they offer."

"Are they hiring?" asked Mona.

Karen looked pained. "No, I'm sorry, we're not, but if you send me your résumé—"

"She was just teasing you," Linnea broke in, shooting her sister a look of amused exasperation. "It's a long commute from Minnesota and she's heard me complain about the hassles of moving too many times through the years to even contemplate moving out of state."

"Ask me in February." Mona shivered as if imagining a blizzard swirling about her. "I might give you a different answer."

Everyone laughed.

After supper, the campers had an hour of free time to relax or, for the more ambitious, to sew a few more stitches before gathering once more in the ballroom for the evening program. The Candlelight Giving Quilt display on the dais had been dismantled, and in its place were six tables with four chairs pulled up to each. Sarah welcomed the campers and instructed them to break up into six teams of four. Immediately Linnea felt Mona seize her arm, and Pauline took a quick step toward them as if afraid they might be separated. Over the heads of the other campers, Linnea saw Michaela and Jocelyn pair up with a middle-aged woman and her elderly mother. Karen stood in the center of it all, glancing from one rapidly forming team to another uncertainly.

"Karen," Linnea called out, beckoning. "Come join us."

Karen smiled, relieved as she made her way to them. "Thanks," she said, and Linnea shrugged as if it were no big deal, but of course it was, because even among friendly quilters it was demoralizing to be the one left over, the one not chosen, the one not noticed but assigned by default to the group with the fewest members.

Karen proved to be a most welcome addition to their team. First Sarah led them in a game of Quilters' Trivial Pursuit that had them laughing so hard they had to wipe tears from their eyes. A game of Quilters' Pictionary followed, and after that came a raucous match of Quilters' Charades. The team of Linnea, Mona, Pauline, and Karen were declared the Games Night champions for winning two out of the three rounds, having sealed their victory in the closing seconds of charades with Karen's impossibly intuitive understanding of Linnea's frantic attempts to act out the phrase "lengthwise grain."

The other quilters cheerfully bemoaned their losses while applauding the winners, who were awarded Elm Creek Quilts pins as the grand prize. Pictured upon each pin was an elm tree, brilliant with the colors of autumn, growing tall and strong on the bank of a flowing creek with green hills rising in the background. Mona and Pauline kept their pins safe in their cellophane bags, but Linnea and Karen eagerly tore the plastic open and fastened their pins to their blouses for everyone to admire.

Linnea wore hers out of pride for their hard-fought and hard-won triumph in the games, but something in Karen's shy smile, flushed cheeks, and furtive glances to Sarah told her that Karen wore hers because it made her feel more like an official Elm Creek Quilter.

The next morning, Linnea and Mona woke shortly after sunrise, bundled up in their warmest workout clothes, and went down the hall to rap softly upon Pauline's door. It swung open immediately. "Ready to go?" Pauline whispered brightly. Linnea nodded, biting her lips together to keep from laughing at her new friend's eager excitement. It was just a walk, after all, and likely to be a cold one at that.

The morning was indeed chillier and more blustery than the previous day had been, and they saw fewer other campers out and about on the estate's frosty grounds. "We're diehards," Linnea puffed as they strode briskly through the north gardens, the better to reach the warmth of Elm Creek Manor sooner. "Hard-core."

"Hardheaded, maybe," Pauline replied, panting, prompting laughter from the sisters.

A lengthy stretch in the warmth of the back foyer, showers, and breakfast followed their workout, and before long they found themselves back in the partitioned classroom awaiting their second lesson in the making of a Giving Quilt. The room seemed warmer somehow, the students more cheerful and chattier, a result, Linnea suspected, of having broken the ice with the fun and friendly competition of Games Night. At the front of the room, Gretchen had to raise her hands as well as her voice to command their attention when she was ready to begin. "Good morning, everyone," she greeted them, smiling. "I'm glad to find you so energetic and eager to go, because we have a lot to accomplish today. Now that you have all of your pieces cut, it's time to begin assembling your blocks."

She held up a single Resolution Square block, tilted it on point, and held it against the display quilt so her students could better discern where one block blended into another. "Please study the block carefully and then pass it on to your neighbor," Gretchen said, handing the block to Pauline, who sat at one end of the front row. As the block made its slow progression around the classroom, Gretchen seated herself behind her sewing machine, glanced at the mirror overhead to be sure it was tilted at the proper angle, and sewed a small white rectangle to one of the purple-and-white square pairs she had made in her demonstration the previous day. "Match the corners carefully with right sides facing each other, align the edges, and pin if you prefer," she continued, selecting another rectangle and square pair and joining them in the same manner. "Color placement of the squares is very important, so be sure to sew the rectangle to the correct edge of the square pair. Finish one set, double-check to be sure it's correct, and then keep it on the table nearby as an example to follow."

Linnea joined her classmates in following Gretchen's instructions. Their voices rose above the whirring of their sewing machines as they worked and conversed. Those who finished first—Pauline and Karen—carried their sewn pieces to the ironing stations and pressed the seams, and other classmates soon followed suit. When Pauline finished, she bounded back to her place and began quickly repeating the process with the green-and-white pieces for her second Giving Quilt, while Karen left her pressed block segments at her place in the back row and hurried over to help a struggling classmate.

Pauline seemed not quite finished with the pieces for her second top by the time the rest of the class completed the step and Gretchen announced that it was time to move on. "Count your block segments," she advised. "You should have sixty-four. If not, please check on the floor around you or the pressing tables for those wayward pieces." Sure enough, someone gasped and exclaimed that she had only sixty-three, but another quilter quickly found the missing pieces mixed in with her own.

"Next we'll sew a large medium square to each segment

you just completed." Gretchen sat down at her sewing machine and sewed a medium square, which in her case was a red floral and in Linnea's was a bold blue solid, to the square-pair-and-rectangle piece. "Color placement is crucial in this step too, so be sure to use the display quilt or the sample block as a model."

The students did as they were told, making what could have been dull work a more pleasant task by chatting and joking with their neighbors and by taking time to admire their classmates' work. With a little help from Linnea, Mona proceeded slowly and cautiously along like the tortoise of the fable, assembling her blocks properly at her own steady pace. By all appearances, Pauline was her counterpart, the hare, although Linnea suspected Pauline would turn the tale on its head and finish her quilt top first and flawlessly rather than pausing for a nap along the way.

Linnea had finished sewing her block segments and was helping Mona when Gretchen glanced at the clock and announced that due to the time, she would demonstrate the next step even though not everyone had reached that point. Holding up one newly sewn, neatly pressed unit, she said, "This is one half of a Resolution Square block. To complete the block, all you need to do is sew two of them together. Abut facing seams where you can, and pin all along the edge to keep the halves from shifting." With that, she pieced two halves together on the front table so they could follow along in the overhead mirror, seated herself at her sewing machine, and stitched a quick, perfect seam, removing the pins as they approached the darting needle rather than sewing heedlessly over them. Linnea would do well to follow her example. She had broken many a needle and had sent shards of pins flying dangerously close to her face by neglecting that one important safety measure.

The students worked busily, but not even Pauline or Karen finished all thirty-two of their blocks before the end of class. Gretchen reminded them that they were welcome to use the classroom sewing machines and pressing tables or any of those set up outside the partitioned walls if they wanted to finish up their blocks during their afternoon free time. "I encourage you to do so," she added, "since tomorrow we'll be sewing the blocks into rows and assembling the tops."

"My book can wait," said Mona as she and Linnea packed up their things, placing their carefully pinned but not yet completed blocks at the top of their tote bags. "I want to stay on track. I'd hate to reach the end of the week without finishing a single quilt to donate to Project Linus."

"What do you suppose they do if a camper doesn't finish a single quilt?" mused Michaela, who apparently had been listening in from her seat in the row behind them. "Do they keep a running tab of our expenses, and then, if we don't have a quilt to show off at the Farewell Breakfast and donate to Project Linus, they hand us a bill?"

Linnea laughed, but Karen, who was passing by on her way to the front of the classroom to speak with Gretchen, came to a halt and said, "I really doubt it."

"But do you know for sure?" Michaela persisted.

Karen winced slightly. "No, but that doesn't sound like something the Elm Creek Quilters would do."

"I'm sure we're on the honor system," said Jocelyn, tugging the straps of her tote bag over her shoulder. "If we don't finish by Saturday, they'll probably ask us to finish our Giving Quilts at home and donate them to our local chapter of Project Linus."

Karen nodded, but Pauline looked pensive. "If we stay on schedule, we shouldn't have anything to worry about," she said. "But just in case, if any of you can't finish your Giving Quilts in time, I'll let you borrow one of mine for the show-and-tell."

"That's like so nice of you," said Michaela, and the others chimed in with their thanks—except for Karen, who merely nodded to show that she agreed that Pauline was very nice. She seemed the least likely of them to need to take Pauline up on her offer.

The quintet of quilters went to lunch together, Linnea carrying Michaela's quilting gear and Karen her lunch tray. The younger woman moved along exceptionally well on her crutches, but Linnea couldn't imagine how Michaela managed the stairs. Halfway through lunch—a hearty vegetarian four-bean chili or a Tex-Mex beef-and-pork version that reminded her wistfully of Kevin at the grill—Linnea's curiosity compelled her to ask.

"Someone carries my stuff for me, and I just scoot up on my bottom, one step at a time," said Michaela cheerfully, breaking off a piece of corn bread and dipping it into her vegetarian chili.

"That sounds time-consuming," remarked Jocelyn. "Not to mention labor-intensive."

"It is, but I don't need to go back to my room much. Just at the end of the day."

"But how do you get *down* the stairs?" Linnea asked, persisting.

"The same way she got up them, I suppose," said Karen, "but more carefully."

Everyone laughed, and the conversation turned to how Michaela managed to do any number of other things that her cast would make more difficult. It wasn't until later, after they had finished their lunches and made plans to meet in the ballroom in an hour to work on their Giving Quilt blocks, that Linnea realized Michaela hadn't really answered the question.

When Linnea, Mona, Pauline, Jocelyn, and Michaela reconvened an hour later, they decided to forgo the classroom for the sewing stations arranged on the long tables near the west windows, the better to enjoy the view. The windows looked out upon a decidedly more wintry scene than earlier that day; the blustery winds had subsided, but a snow shower had taken their place, and as best as Linnea could estimate, a little more than an inch had accumulated on the grass, the parking lot, and the campers' cars.

"If this keeps up," she remarked to her sister, "our morning walk will be a little more challenging tomorrow."

"I hope you brought your snowshoes," Mona replied.

Linnea shook her head. "They wouldn't fit in my carry-on."

"Check the closet in the back foyer," Karen advised, glancing up from her work. She had only a handful of unfinished Resolution Square blocks remaining, which made Linnea suspect she had taken a speed-sewing course at some point in her quilting career. "The Elm Creek Quilters always keep a few pairs in the back. I'm sure they'd let you borrow them."

Linnea and Mona exchanged amused glances. Apparently their humor was too deadpan, because no one else ever seemed to get it. "Thanks, but let's hope we won't need them," Linnea told Karen, and settled down to work.

She was about two-thirds of the way through her stack of

pinned blocks when the urge to get up, stretch, and explore began tugging her attention away from her work. "Can you watch my stuff?" she asked her sister. "I thought I'd take a walk."

"What if someone else needs the sewing machine?"

Linnea jerked her thumb toward the two vacant workstations at the far end of the table. "They can use those."

Mona folded her arms and regarded her sternly. "What if other quilters claim those places while you're gone, and this is the only free sewing machine left?"

"Including those in the classroom?" Linnea sighed goodnaturedly. "In that unlikely event, please move my blocks out of the way and tell this hypothetical quilter that she's welcome to work here."

That satisfied Mona, so Linnea rose and started to leave. Pauline looked up from her work. "You're finished already?"

"No, just taking a break. I never did like to sit still in one place for long."

"Tell me about it," said Michaela, frowning at her cast. "Before this stupid injury, I was a total exercise nut. Now I'm—"

"Just a nut?" Jocelyn offered.

Michaela grinned. "Exactly."

"Linnea heard an enticing rumor of a library somewhere in the manor," Mona explained to their new friends with a teasing glance at her sister. "She's determined to find it. No library shall escape her sight."

"I looked around yesterday, but I got led astray by the McClure twins," Linnea said. "It's not on the maps, either. I double-checked last night."

"Maybe we're not supposed to use the library," said Pauline. "That would explain why it's not on the map."

"Maybe they closed it down," said Michaela.

Linnea felt her heart lurch. "I sincerely hope not."

Immediately Mona reached for her hand and gave it a sympathetic squeeze. "Few things pain a librarian more than the thought of a library closing," she explained to the others.

"Books being tossed onto bonfires is one," said Linnea. "Shrill parents demanding the banishment of perfectly wonderful books they've never read but heard dire warnings about on talk radio is another."

Jocelyn frowned and shook her head. "I feel your pain. In our school district, there's been talk of cutting back library hours to one hour before and one hour after the school day. A school board member actually suggested firing all the librarians and staffing the library with parent volunteers."

"Oh, I'm sure they'd have a line out the door of qualified parents eager to sign up for that," said Pauline dryly.

"Naturally. If people know alphabetical order they can shelve books, and anyone can say, 'Shush,' and there's really not much more to the job than that, is there?" Linnea gripped the back of her chair and forced a smile. "Now I really need that walk. I'll see you all later."

As she turned to go, Karen called after her, "The Elm Creek Quilters haven't closed their library. They use it as their office, and it's—"

"Don't tell me," Linnea interrupted, smiling to soften the abruptness of her request. "I'd like to find it on my own."

She felt their curious gazes upon her as she turned and left the ballroom.

. . .

aela could not possibly know how close to the mark her
ds had struck Linnea, or how painfully deep.

Like so many other librarians she had known throughout
er life, Linnea had fallen in love with her neighborhood library
as a child, and in all the years since, libraries had not lost their
power to enthrall. She still remembered how awestruck she had
been on the day she first realized she could wander through the
stacks, choose any book that caught her eye, examine it at one of
the tables or upon the window seat in the children's section,
and, if she liked it well enough, take it home to read and to
savor. Her mother had brought her to Saturday Story Time since
before she could walk, and as she grew older and learned to
read on her own, her mother continued their weekly pilgrimages. Linnea would spend hours browsing the shelves of
the children's section, asking the librarian for recommenda-
tions, checking to see whether her favorite authors had written
anything new, and then, when her patient mother told her it was
time to go, she would check out as many books as she could
carry. "Are you sure you can read all of those in a week?" the
clerk at the circulation desk asked the first few times Linnea
proudly presented her library card, signed in ink in her best
cursive penmanship. She assured him she could, and would,
and eventually all the circ desk staff knew her well enough not
to ask. Instead they smiled indulgently and wished her happy
reading.

A voracious reader with insatiable curiosity and eclectic interests, Linnea explored not only novels and collections of short
stories but also nonfiction books on an endless variety of fasci-
nating subjects, records by musicians she had never before
heard of, magazines written especially for children and some-

times by children, and newspapers from far-off cities she longed
to visit. Sometimes she liked what she checked out and sometimes she didn't, but she always learned from them, and every
so often she would experience the thrill of discovering something new that she really, really liked. The poetry and drawings
of Shel Silverstein, for example, and New Orleans jazz, and *Jack
and Jill* magazine, and the magical stories of Edward Eager.

Over time, she learned that the only joy greater than having
a librarian offer her a book and confide, "I set this book aside for
you because I knew you would love it," was placing one of her
own recommended reads in a child's hands and watching a pair
of bright, eager eyes light up with happiness and anticipation.

Upon receiving her master of library science degree from
the University of Iowa, Linnea had worked for several years as
an elementary school librarian. Later, after marriage and children
and two cross-country moves as Kevin was transferred up the
corporate ladder, she accepted a position as the children's librarian of the Conejo Hills Public Library, in their new hometown
about forty-five miles north of Los Angeles.

She loved her work, and she loved her library. On any given
day, she could look up from the reference desk in the children's
department and see elementary school students browsing
through the nonfiction books in search of sources for class
projects, new mothers pushing strollers and perusing the bins
of board books, and harried parents keeping their active pre-
schoolers in sight as they scoured the shelves for rainy-day activity books. Over the low walls separating her department
from the rest of the library, Linnea might observe a book club
having an intense, quiet discussion around a table, teenagers
studying for exams and silently flirting, a silver-haired woman

researching her family tree, a middle-aged man in a suit and tie discreetly nibbling a contraband sandwich while paging through a bestselling thriller fresh from the "New Arrivals" shelf, a young couple nodding with relief as a reference librarian guided them through a bewildering maze of local government services and contacts, a shabbily dressed man leafing through the "Help Wanted" ads in the local newspaper and those from surrounding counties, a new immigrant proceeding haltingly through a lesson with encouragement from her ESL tutor, or an unshaven young fellow frantically studying for the LSATs. Later that evening, the library's meeting rooms could play host to a monthly gathering of the Conejo Hills Chess Club, a lecture by a local historian, a debate on the merits and drawbacks of a hotly contested ballot measure, or a reading by a nationally known author. Ancient Rome had its forum; Conejo Hills—and countless other communities across the nation—had its library.

The Conejo Hills Public Library expanded during the economic boom of the 1990s, investing in new technology, adding a climate-controlled storage area for less frequently circulated materials, and replacing the roof, which had been damaged in the Northridge earthquake. In cooperation with the acquisitions department staff, Linnea nearly doubled the library's young adult collection and successfully persuaded the Friends of the Library to add manga and graphic novels to lure in more reluctant readers. She hired two part-time assistants, coordinated an able staff of retiree volunteers, and initiated an after-school anime club. During the summer she directed the reading incentive program, and throughout the rest of the year, she collaborated with district teachers and school librarians to make sure resources would be available whenever their students had important term projects to complete.

Since all of the elementary schools in the district followed the same curriculum, by keeping in touch with a few teachers, Linnea learned what the upcoming units were and could change her displays in the children's department or schedule programming accordingly. Some themes occurred annually, such as the fourth-grade focus on California history or the sixth-grade concentration on the environment. One of Linnea's favorite units was the first graders' study of great artists that fell between spring break and the end of the school year. She would hang prints of famous, child-friendly works of art throughout the children's department, display picture books and beginning-reader biographies about artists both well-known and obscure, and invite an artist, usually someone local, for a Saturday morning demonstration and discussion of his or her work. Her greatest programming coup was booking Eric Carle. More than three hundred children and parents from throughout Southern California attended to hear him read from his most recent book and demonstrate his unique tissue-paper collage method of creating pictures. Later that day, thirty particularly fortunate students nominated by their teachers for their good grades and good citizenship attended a workshop where the artist and author taught them how to make their own Brown Bears or Hungry Caterpillars. Linnea cherished the rainbow-hued bear he had made for his demonstration and had autographed for her as a token of his thanks for the day. She kept the framed picture on the wall above her desk next to a photograph of herself with former president Bill Clinton, taken when he visited the library to promote his charitable foundation and read from his recently published book *Giving*.

Linnea loved her work, her colleagues, her young patrons, and her library. As she often told Mona, even her worst day at the Conejo Hills Public Library was better than her best day anywhere else. There seemed to be no reason why she shouldn't be able to continue pursuing her passion until sometime in the far distant future, when she and Kevin would decide to retire.

The recession changed everything.

It struck some of her friends like an incoming tide, slowly and inexorably washing away the solid ground beneath their feet and dragging them out to sea. Others it struck with the force of a tsunami, sudden and devastating. Friends and neighbors lost their jobs or saw their paychecks slashed. Families lost their homes to foreclosure. Almost two years to the day before Linnea came to Elm Creek Manor, the biggest employer in Conejo Hills had laid off nearly a third of its workforce. Those who still had jobs and homes feared losing them, and people everywhere turned inward, driven by a primal instinct to conserve what they had for them and theirs before thinking of people they had never met. As the months passed, more and more people sought assistance at the St. Vincent de Paul in the oldest section of town. Visitors to the food pantry sponsored by Linnea's church steadily increased in numbers even as donations dwindled and the shelves became sparsely stocked.

Linnea could see the strain in people's faces as they distractedly browsed the stacks at the library; she read it in alarmist letters to the editor in the *Conejo Hills Call*. Anxiety haunted even those who had thus far escaped the economic downturn relatively unscathed, and as everyone pared back to the essentials, Linnea began to fear that giving would become a luxury limited to more prosperous times. Whenever her family gathered around the supper table, she reminded them anew of her lifelong belief that it was important to remember the less fortunate even when one wasn't feeling particularly fortunate oneself. Perhaps it was even more important at such times.

Her beliefs were soon to be tested.

Rumors of office mergers and closures had hung ominously over Kevin and his coworkers for months before the storm finally broke. Kevin's boss had assured him that he would do everything in his power to retain him even if that meant a transfer, but ultimately even his support wasn't enough. Kevin was offered a modest severance package and career counseling, and after a week of shock and disbelief spent mostly in front of the television watching classic sports channels, he shaved, found a copy of his old résumé in a box of files they hadn't unpacked since their last move, and updated it on the computer. Then came months of sending it to prospective employers, searching the Internet for job postings, networking with friends and former colleagues, and making himself useful at home while Linnea was at work. They had tallied their income and expenses, and they calculated that as long as Linnea kept her job, they would get by. They could pay the mortgage and tuition; they could pay the utility bills and buy food. They would have nothing left over to splurge on luxuries, and Christmas would be a far more frugal affair than they were accustomed to, but they would manage. Their children offered to contribute their part-time after-school wages to the family budget, but Linnea and Kevin could not bear to accept. Their children were saving for college—their eldest was already a sophomore at UCLA—

and those plans mustn't change. They had worked too hard to earn good grades to let anything interfere with their educations.

When rumors began to circulate through the library about city budget cuts, Linnea felt the same anxiety seize her as when similar hushed whispers spread dire warnings through Kevin's office. The axe was lowered, not in one swift, merciful blow, but inch by inch, kindling more fear and worry as the days went by. First the library administrators were summoned to a closed-door meeting with the city budget committee. They returned to the library haggard and tense, and at an emergency meeting of the senior staff the following day, they exhorted everyone to cut their department budgets as much as possible. Linnea cut until it hurt, as did her colleagues, but it wasn't enough. First the most recently hired part-timers were let go. Then Sunday hours were cut in half. Then they opened an hour later on weekdays and closed an hour earlier. Then, at last, the whole truth came out on the front page of the *Conejo Hills Call*: Due to the disastrous performance of the stock market and a drastic reduction in assets, the city faced a budget shortfall of nearly four million dollars. For a community of that size, this was a shockingly large amount—enough, in fact, to bankrupt them.

The people of Conejo Hills, already stressed and anxious from job losses, foreclosures, and their uncertain future, reacted with anger and outrage. They demanded that the mayor and every member of the city council resign at once, but cooler, wiser heads prevailed. The city council's predecessors had created the current financial circumstances in a more optimistic era, and banishing the people most familiar with the mess they were mired in would make it even more difficult to pull themselves out. So the city leaders set themselves to the daunting task of slashing the budget without cutting any essential programs, raising taxes, or offending anyone. This quickly proved impossible, so they conferred with legal counsel, met with an advisory committee from the governor's office, and asked the public to submit suggestions for how to balance the budget.

Someone along the way proposed closing down the library.

The mayor promptly dismissed the suggestion, but it was leaked to the press and made its way online. Once bolstered with spurious data gleaned from an organization better known for their efforts to ban books from school libraries than for their accounting prowess, it caught fire. Closing the library would make up more than two-thirds of the budget shortfall, proponents argued. Libraries were not profitable. In the age of the Internet, they were not even necessary.

Aghast, Linnea, her colleagues, and the library's most loyal patrons promptly responded. They wrote clear, fact-based letters to the editor. They made impassioned speeches before the budget committee. They passed out bookmarks at the circulation desk listing the top twenty ways public libraries benefited their communities. They urged patrons to contact city hall to make their wishes known. If their opponents knew the facts, they assured one another, they wouldn't dream of closing the library.

The mayor and city council seemed firmly on their side until word of the conflict caught the attention of Ezra McNulty, a talk-radio firebrand Linnea and Kevin had always considered more of a showman than a journalist. On one slow news day, he read aloud a letter he had received from a member of the group Close the Book, California, an affiliation of parents and citizens dedicated to removing books they deemed offensive from school and public libraries. "After reading about the budget debate online, I infiltrated this seemingly wholesome small-town library and examined the shelves," the writer, known only as "Concerned Citizen," had said. "Within minutes I found nearly all of the books on the American Library Association's list of the one hundred most challenged books. More shocking yet, several of the most offensive books—*The Great Gatsby*, *The Catcher in the Rye*, *The Grapes of Wrath*, *To Kill a Mockingbird*, *The Color Purple*, *Beloved*, and *Lord of the Flies*—were protuberantly displayed in the middle of the children's department! It makes me absolutely sick to think that my tax dollars help pay the salaries of the subversive librarians who peddle this trash to children."

Ezra McNulty applauded Concerned Citizen's investigative reporting and urged his listeners to visit the Close the Book, California website to learn how to support their cause. "Think this couldn't happen in your town?" he asked, lowering his voice ominously. "How long has it been since you've visited your local public library? If it's public, shouldn't it represent your values? Do you know what's on those shelves? If you don't, you should. I tell you, folks, you'd be outraged."

Linnea didn't listen to the program as it was broadcast. She had been working at the time, and she never tuned her dial to that station anyway, preferring music and the far more rational and less strident news coverage found on public radio. She listened instead to an online, archived edition in the library director's office with Alicia Torres, the president of the Friends of the Library Foundation, and Gary Moore, a representative from the city department of human resources. The three watched Linnea pensively as she listened.

"We've received dozens of letters of complaint," the library director said when the program broke for a commercial. "More were sent to city hall."

Linnea took a deep, shaky breath, thankful beyond measure that Concerned Citizen had not mentioned her by name, otherwise the outraged listeners surely would have sent more letters directly to her home—or staged a protest in the public easement in front of her house.

"The books were *protuberantly* displayed," Alicia said acidly. "Someone's been abusing his thesaurus. And how clever of him to successfully navigate our defenses to infiltrate our library. Only a highly trained navy SEAL could read the sign on the door and know to pull instead of push."

"Alicia," the library director said, "I understand your anger—I share it—but let's focus on our next step. Linnea, do you have any response to this?"

Linnea managed a shaky laugh. "Other than shock, disgust, and dismay?"

The library director folded her hands upon the top of her desk. "If Ezra McNulty phoned the library today and asked why those books were set out on the shelves of the children's department, what would you tell him?"

"Well, first I'd clarify that they were in the young adult section, not on the shelves with the picture books and early readers. Then I'd explain that the books in question were part of a display about Banned Books Week." Linnea's explanation was for the human resources representative's benefit; Alicia and the library director already knew. "Those books are also included in the Conejo Hills High School curriculum and have been on the syllabus for years. We've never had a single complaint from a parent or library patron in all the time I've worked here." Suddenly her heart lurched. Were they going to tell her she no longer did?

The library director must have seen the alarm in her eyes. "We're on your side, Linnea. We know you've done nothing wrong."

With a glance Gary's way, Alicia added, "Our concern is that our opponents might use this completely fabricated controversy to justify closing the library."

Nodding, Linnea too turned her gaze upon Gary, who wouldn't necessarily be on the library's side as far as city budget cuts were concerned. "May I ask why you're here?"

"To meet you, and to witness that you've been apprised of the situation." He dug in the inside pocket of his suit jacket and handed her his card. "Close the Book, California has a history of suing cities, libraries, and individual librarians. If this should happen to you, I'll be your contact person within city hall. I can help you secure legal representation and advise you of your rights as a city employee."

Linnea felt the blood drain from her face as she accepted his card. "You're just giving me the worst-case scenario, right? This isn't likely to go to such extremes, is it?"

He thought carefully for a moment before replying. "It's best to be prepared."

"You will not be a scapegoat," the library director told her as soon as the meeting ended and Gary and Alicia left. "You aren't going to lose your job over this."

Linnea thanked her and took what little reassurance she could from her words. Perhaps she would not be fired straightaway, but eventually they might *all* lose their jobs over this.

Praying that Ezra McNulty would find a more interesting topic for his radio program and the whole contrived controversy would soon blow over, Linnea resumed the usual pattern of her workdays by sheer force of will. She refused to consider the likely opinions of Close the Book, California when she met with the director of acquisitions, and she did not flinch when her office phone rang. She wrote a column for the library newsletter and chose three new novels for the Tween Book Club. In anticipation of the upcoming annual "Great Artists" unit, she pulled appropriate books from the stacks and checked the events calendar for a suitable date to schedule the "Saturday with the Artists" program. It was then that she realized none of the first-grade teachers had contacted her about coordinating their efforts as they had always done before.

Bemused, she phoned the teacher she knew best, Theresa Salazar, and offered her assistance with coordinating resources for the children. Before Linnea could ask which of several local artists she might prefer the library to invite, Theresa broke in. "Oh, Linnea, I'm so sorry. With everything that's been going on around here with the budget, I completely forgot to tell you."

"Forgot to tell me what?"

"Did you know the district laid off most of our art teachers last summer?"

"No." Linnea felt a pang of remorse—and apprehension, as if a warning shot had whizzed past her ear. "I didn't."

"We've been left with only one teacher at the elementary level, and since she can spend only one day at each school, we had to cancel the 'Great Artists' unit."

"You're kidding," exclaimed Linnea. "It's one of the high-lights of the year." Her own children, now in high school and college, remembered the unit fondly, and Linnea and Kevin still displayed the artworks they had been inspired to create in the living room.

"I know. I know. For us teachers as well. The parents were upset too, but the furor's died down since the news came out last semester. I suppose people are worried about other things these days." Theresa sighed. "For a while I hoped that the budget would be restored and we could return the unit to the curriculum next year, but that's looking less likely now."

Linnea agreed wearily that none of them should expect anything but smaller budgets for the foreseeable future.

After they hung up, Linnea sat at her desk, heavyhearted. Her gaze fell upon the stack of "Great Artists" books she had pulled. She ought to reshelve them, now that the program was canceled.

She studied the books awhile longer before leaving them on her desk.

As far as she knew, Ezra McNulty did not mention the Conejo Hills Public Library on his program again, but a week after the unsettling conference in the library director's office, an ad appeared in the *Call* announcing the formation of a local chapter of Close the Book, California. All interested citizens were invited to the inaugural meeting at the food court at the mall, where they would organize and strategize.

Linnea's younger son offered to attend the meeting as a spy. Her daughter thought Linnea and her colleagues should crash the meeting wearing buttons identifying themselves as "sub-versive librarians." Linnea thanked them for their suggestions but decided to ignore the incipient group rather than dignify them with her attention. She wanted to believe that her community was sensible and tolerant and that so few of her neighbors would be interested in their mission that a local chapter of Close the Book, California would never form.

But form they did, and although their membership numbered only about two dozen, they were loud and relentless. They pressured the city council to hold a public hearing on the proposal to close the library, and eventually the council gave in and agreed to schedule a hearing as soon as possible. As it happened, the first open date on their calendar, taking into account various members' previously scheduled summer recesses, wouldn't come until early September.

The lengthy delay no doubt incensed the members of Close the Book, California, but the staff of the Conejo Hills Public Library cheered. Surely the city council could have cleared an earlier date in the calendar if they had wanted to, but instead they had imposed a cooling-off period in which fiery tempers could subside, certain radio personalities could grow bored and move on to other trumped-up outrages, and library supporters could come up with alternative solutions.

"The city still has to balance its budget," the library director cautioned the senior staff. "They have to cut spending somewhere, and if they don't cut our funding, they'll have to cut spending somewhere else. We are vulnerable."

Linnea mulled over the director's words long after the meeting ended. They carried truth relevant beyond the budget matter, truth she could not ignore.

Needs had to be met, and if what was essential couldn't come from one place, it had to come from another.

She stayed up late that night thinking and feverishly working up a plan. The next day, after receiving the go-ahead from the library director, she e-mailed Theresa Salazar and the other first-grade teachers to tell them of her intention to lead a "Great Artists" program at the library throughout the month of May. Young children needed to discover the wonder of art, and if the overworked, beleaguered art teacher couldn't do it that year, Linnea had to step in and give what she could—her time and talents—to make it happen.

Delighted, the teachers wrote back immediately to offer Linnea classroom materials and suggestions for programs and events. After hours, they helped Linnea decorate the children's department with materials borrowed from their classrooms as well as her favorite prints of famous works of art, and they lent her books of their own to enhance Linnea's displays. "I've never lent a book *to* a library before," Theresa remarked as she handed over a well-loved collection of coffee-table books full of enthralling photographs from the Louvre, the Met, the British Museum, and the Hermitage.

Every Saturday Story Time in May featured stories of artists, both famous and fictional: Tomie dePaola's *The Legend of the Indian Paintbrush*, W. Nikola-Lisa's *The Year with Grandma Moses*, Michael Garland's *Dinner at Magritte's*, and other enchanting tales. With donated supplies begged from an art supply warehouse in Los Angeles, Linnea covered the floor near the back wall of the children's department with drop cloths, placed canvases on easels arranged side by side, set out paints and brushes, propped up a *Starry Night* poster nearby, and encouraged children of all ages to contribute to the library's own version of the iconic Van Gogh evening scene.

Van Gogh also inspired Linnea's favorite activity of the entire "Great Artists" program. Moving the puppet theater out of the way and setting up a low table and child-sized chairs in its place, Linnea arranged cut sunflowers in a vase, set out paper and crayons, and encouraged children to draw a picture of the bouquet. Throughout the day, Linnea would glance up from her desk or the stacks to find a child or two, or perhaps more, seated at the table, brows furrowed in concentration as they colored. When the children finished, Linnea admired their drawings and invited them to follow her to her desk, where she showed them two laundry baskets, one filled with green fabric of all different hues, the other with brown and gold. She invited the children to select a green fabric for the centers of their sunflowers and a brown or gold for the petals. Then she photocopied the drawings, wrote the children's names on the back, and confided to them that they were now part of a very special, very secret art project that would astonish and delight all who beheld it.

In the evenings at home, Linnea would trace the features of the children's drawings onto freezer paper, creating ap-pliqué templates, which she used to cut flower centers and petals from the green and gold and brown fabrics the children had selected. As soon as she accumulated enough fabric sun-flowers, she arranged them on a piece of creamy, light beige background fabric three feet wide and four feet long, pinned the flower shapes carefully in place, and machine zigzag-stitched them to the background. She added stems and a vase based upon those in Van Gogh's paintings, and after framing the center still life with accenting borders, she delivered the top to one of several volunteers from her guild for machine quilting and binding. By then more children would have com-

pleted their sunflower drawings, and Linnea would begin ap-
pliquéing anew.

Every June, as soon as schools closed for the summer, the
Friends of the Library held a barbecue in a park adjacent to the
library to kick off the Summer Reading Program. That year, in
addition to food and games and music, partygoers were also
treated to a display of eight marvelous quilts created from the
children's drawings and fabric selections—their very own sunflower series. Children who knew that their favorite librarian
had been working on a top secret project dashed over to search
the quilts for their own familiar flowers, shouting or squealing
with delight when they discovered their artwork transformed
into quilts. They pointed out their flowers to their parents, their
teachers, their friends—even to Linnea, who knew each one by
heart and had written the young artists' first names by their
flowers with an indelible fabric pen.

Throughout the afternoon and evening, the quilts were offered up in a silent auction. Naturally every parent and grand-
parent wanted the quilt that their favorite young artist had
contributed to, and the bidding became fiercely competitive.
Linnea had hoped that the quilt auction would be a rousing
success, but even she was astonished when, after the auction
ended and the library director collected checks from the winners,
she discovered they had raised more than eight thousand dollars
for the local food pantry.

"This is what libraries do," Kevin said later that night as
they enjoyed a celebratory glass of wine on their patio. "They're
assets to the community. They *create* community."

"I know," said Linnea contentedly. Her "Great Artists"
program had succeeded beyond her fondest wishes, and fears

that she might be fired over the radio debacle had slipped to the back of her mind.

"*We* know, but I'm not so sure the community does." Kevin looked as if he anticipated the sudden flash of insight that always preceded the creation of a brilliant marketing plan. "We need to tell the city council what exactly the library contributes to Conejo Hills. Not just rosy, idealistic anecdotes of children falling in love with books and teenagers having a safe place to go after school and adults taking classes on how to use the Internet. Those are all worthwhile endeavors," he hastily added when Linnea was about to interrupt and tell him so. "But the city council and all your detractors need to see, in black and white terms too, what the library gives to the community."

"This sounds like a job for an expert in creative marketing," Linnea remarked.

Kevin nodded firmly. "My thoughts exactly."

Putting his lackluster job search on hold, Kevin met with the library director, the Friends of the Library board, and several patrons who volunteered their expertise in everything from accounting to finance to law to urban planning. They rallied public support for the library with editorials in the *Call*, a spirited web campaign, and a mailing drive in which library patrons, young and old, were invited to create postcards with an image of their favorite book on the front and a brief message explaining why they loved the library on the back. Linnea set up tables where the *Starry Night* canvases had been, replenishing them with trimmed card stock and art supplies nearly every other day. Before patrons mailed their postcards to city hall, Linnea photocopied the most moving, adorable, creative, and amusing creations and displayed them on bookshelf endcaps throughout the library. Nearly every patron who saw them wanted to make one too, and some who found it too difficult to choose only one favorite book or only one reason to love their library made many postcards. Linnea did not see every card or read all of their messages, but she hoped and prayed that the impact the postcards made upon the mayor and the city council would be at least half as powerful as it was for the library staff. In such times, it was profoundly gratifying to hear from their loyal patrons how much the library meant to them, how they sincerely believed it transformed their city into a community.

On the day the city council convened the special public hearing on the budget crisis and the future of the library, Linnea and Kevin walked into city hall surrounded by library staff, Friends, and patrons, and Linnea felt that they had prepared as well and as completely as anyone could have done.

The main room and even the gallery of the council chambers were filled with restless, eager citizens on both sides of the debate. People who wanted to speak had been required to register beforehand and were instructed to limit themselves to five minutes. The library director was the first to speak, and she listed the many tangible services the library provided to city residents, including services to the vision impaired, citizenship and English as a Second Language courses for new immigrants, computer and Internet access for those who could not afford it in their homes, and more, much more than could be described in five minutes.

The president of the Friends of the Library Foundation spoke next. She passionately evoked the democratic principles upon which the nation was founded, praising the egalitarian nature of the library, for anyone regardless of wealth, gender, age, color, religion, education, or status could pass through its doors and gain access to its wealth of information and resources. "Franklin Delano Roosevelt called libraries 'the great symbols of the freedom of the mind, essential to the functioning of a democratic society,'" Alicia declared. "Libraries and librarians are essential to a healthy democracy because they ensure that everyone— *everyone*, not merely the privileged and the powerful—can gain access to information and thereby become informed citizens and voters. Without this access, people may not know what their elected leaders are doing on their behalf, or what candidates are promising to do, or what the consequences of a proposed measure might be for themselves, their families, and their neighborhoods. This is especially important for the poorest among us, those who can't afford books or newspapers or home computers or high-speed cable Internet. A healthy democracy cannot endure if only the wealthy are aware of and engaged in the process of governance while the poor and powerless are left uninformed and uninvolved." Alicia's penetrating gaze traveled along the high bench where the city council members sat impassively, and then she turned to take in the entire gallery. "Believe me, my friends and *mis amigos*, we should all be wary of any powerful group that wants to keep the poor ignorant and disenfranchised."

A smattering of applause and cheers and a low rumble of disapproval greeted her as she stepped away from the microphone and returned to her seat—head held high, expression proud and defiant. The mayor banged the desk with his gavel and called for order, warning that any further outbursts would be grounds for expulsion.

Next the leader of the fledgling Conejo Hills chapter of Close the Book, California took the podium and used her five minutes to denounce the inclusion of "filthy, age-inappropriate" materials in the library's collections. "Libraries must be safe places for children and young adults, who make up a significant percentage of library users," she said, pounding a forefinger onto the podium for emphasis. "If offensive books cannot be kept out of the reach of patrons under eighteen, then we demand the librarians institute a warning-label system using the same codes that are used for television programs, movies, and video games. If warnings are considered essential for those media, why not for books?"

Linnea had a sudden vision of herself seated on the floor of the children's department surrounded by piles of books taller than her head, reading each one; evaluating the content for references to sex, violence, drugs, and swearing; and slapping each cover with a color-coded sticker—green for innocuous Sandra Boynton board books, fiery scarlet for *I Know Why the Caged Bird Sings*. Scarlet stickers would become a magnet for curious teens, whose rebellious streaks would guarantee heavy circulation for any scarlet-stickered book.

"Did she help us or hurt us?" one of the Conejo Hills reference librarians murmured. Linnea figured it was anyone's guess. The woman hadn't called for the library's closure, but she hadn't exactly championed it either.

A man who looked to be in his early forties took the podium next, and he spoke briefly and angrily about how high taxes were destroying the economy. "I don't use the library, so I shouldn't have to pay for it," he declared. "If people can't speak English, they shouldn't take a free class at the library—they should go back where they came from." Someone in the gallery above shouted out in agreement, and the mayor banged his gavel. "Libraries have become after-school day care centers for smart kids and hangouts for homeless people. I shouldn't have to pay for that. If people want to buy books or computers, they should get a job, save their money, and buy them. I don't work forty-plus hours a week to subsidize some other guy's access to free books."

Linnea sighed as the man returned to his seat, nodding and raising his hand to the gallery in acknowledgment of their support. She never understood how people like him failed to realize that everyone benefited when their neighbors were educated, informed, and involved. Some people just couldn't think beyond the walls of their own homes.

Another, calmer man followed, and before he ran out of time and was required to step down, he offered a lucid explanation of how much money would be saved, and how few jobs would be lost, if the library were closed. To her dismay, Linnea observed several of the council members leaning forward in interest as if to catch every crucial fact and figure. Two council members were so engrossed that they forgot to maintain a veneer of impartiality and nodded from time to time.

"His figures seem questionable," Kevin murmured close to her ear as he rose and joined the queue to speak. When it was his turn, he presented his own cost-and-benefits analysis of the library, clearly and objectively. The council listened attentively, and Linnea was proud and relieved to see just as many, if not more, minuscule nods in response to his presentation as the earlier speaker had received.

It would have served the library's cause well if the public

hearing had ended with Kevin, but a few more people spoke on both sides of the argument, most reiterating points that had already been made. The last to speak was a young man with dark, curly hair wearing black-rimmed, rectangular glasses and a UC Santa Barbara sweatshirt. Linnea straightened in her seat, expecting to hear the voice of youth advocating the library's cause, but the young man's appearance was sadly deceiving. "Libraries are obsolete," he began, spreading his hands as if stating a universally accepted fact. "Everything worth reading is on the Internet now. See this?" He reached into his back pocket and pulled out a smartphone. "I can get more classic novels and references on this than I could ever read in my entire lifetime. In twenty lifetimes." He paused to shake his head. "I've lived in Conejo Hills most of my life, and yeah, I came to Saturday Story Times when I was little, but the world has moved on. Conejo Hills is broke. The whole country is broke. We just can't afford obsolete information stores anymore. We shouldn't keep these dusty relics on life support for sentimental reasons or because it's tradition, especially when everything we could possibly want to read is online."

Linnea longed to interrupt him to correct his error-strewn remarks, and she felt the librarians and library supporters around her tensing as they fought the same impulse. Not everything was online—far from it—and not everyone had access to the Internet in their home. Oneself and one's friends never accurately represented a diverse community. Why were comfortable young adults always the first to overlook that?

"My generation is online and the generations coming after us will be too," the young man continued. "We're three generations removed from people who actually needed physical libraries. We learn and think and consume information different than people of the past. If you want children to be prepared for the new economy, you'll teach them to use e-readers and forget about obsolete paper technology."

"If he says 'obsolete' one more time," Alicia muttered, "I'm going to stand up and scream at him."

Linnea patted Alicia's arm to advise patience and restraint.

"Also, all this talk about libraries creating community misses the point of today's reality," the young man said. "Community doesn't happen in a big public building anymore. It all happens online. I have hundreds of friends, and I don't have to be with them in person to have community. People of my generation are the future, and we should have a big say in the budget because the consequences will affect us much longer than it will affect you."

Because the rest of us are old and creaky and teetering on the edge of our graves, Linnea finished for him silently. This young man had attended Saturday Story Times, perhaps during her tenure. Where had she gone wrong?

The young man leaned closer to the microphone as he glanced around the room. "Sorry to be so harsh, but that's the way I see it. Thank you."

He left the podium to a startling crash of applause.

"The blindness of the privileged," exclaimed Alicia, incredulous, her words barely audible in the din. "It will be generations, if ever, before everyone has their own personal access to the technology he takes for granted. How can a college student be so unaware of how most of the world lives?"

Linnea could only shake her head.

The mayor announced that the time allotted for the public to address the chamber had elapsed, but they would review all written remarks as long as they were submitted before five o'clock. Linnea, who had said all she intended to say, wanted nothing more than to go home, crawl under a quilt, and rest until the city council reached a judgment.

For a week the mayor and city council met in several lengthy sessions closed to the public. Rumors raced through the city like capricious winds, shifting, ephemeral, and ever changing. Linnea refused to heed any of them, doggedly going about her usual routine. They would know the library's fate soon enough.

Linnea was shelving young adult manga when one of the teenage pages dashed over and breathlessly told her that the mayor had called a press conference and the library director wanted senior staff to join her in her office. Linnea dumped her armful of books on a cart and hurried through the library, past contented patrons browsing the stacks or reading in comfortable chairs. Behind the scenes in the area restricted to staff, she passed coworkers grouped around computers watching the press conference stream live over the web, so intent they did not glance up as she raced by. She was the last of the senior staff to arrive in the library director's office. The computer screen had been turned to face them, and the mayor had already begun speaking.

The city council's decision was both more and less than what Linnea had hoped for, and nothing at all that she had expected.

The council had set aside the matter raised by Close the Book, California. Concerns about the library's collection, while certainly worth further scrutiny, were not relevant to the current budget crisis.

Linnea heaved a sigh of relief and closed her eyes. Someone patted her on the back. She had not cost her friends and colleagues their jobs after all.

The mayor continued reading from his prepared statement. Although in principle the city council was opposed to deficit spending, circumstances warranted emergency measures. The city had secured a loan sufficient to fund the library throughout the next fiscal year.

Linnea gasped and seized the arm of the person next to her. In the distance, they heard cheers erupting throughout the library. They were safe. They would not have to close. They had another year, an entire year to come up with a plan to keep their doors open forever.

But the mayor was not finished.

The city council had passed a measure to create a referendum on a dedicated millage to fund the Conejo Hills Public Library—.7 mills for five years. If the referendum passed, during that five-year period, a capital campaign would be launched to newly endow the library foundation to ensure that its operating expenses would be met for generations to come. The special election would be held in December, on the last business day before the holiday recess.

The sounds of jubilation subsided. Inside the director's office, some of the senior staff stared at the computer, while others exchanged looks of stricken dismay.

The city council's plan was sound—reasonable and pragmatic, both for the short term and the long. But who in such troubled economic times would vote to raise their own taxes?

"We have a few months," the library director said quietly, breaking the silence. "We have time to make our case to the public the way we made our case last week. We'll rally the support of the community. Too many people want us to keep our doors open for us to fail."

"Too many people won't miss us until we're gone," muttered the head of the reference department.

Linnea feared he was right.

Autumn found her dividing her time between the children's department and the Vote Yes for Libraries headquarters, better known as Alicia's dining room. Kevin soon became a leader of the movement. They labored ceaselessly to get the word out, to motivate potential voters, and to refute the false and frenzied reports of their opponents, who claimed that the small increase in taxes to preserve an important community asset would result in nothing short of the destruction of life as they knew it.

The holidays approached, but Linnea gave them hardly any thought until Kevin asked if she and Mona had discussed their annual sisters' reunion.

The question caught Linnea utterly by surprise. "I assumed we'd have to skip it this year." Their husbands always treated them to a getaway week shortly after Thanksgiving as an early Christmas gift, but between the upcoming ballot measure and their tight family budget, Linnea had assumed they couldn't afford to go.

"Of course you don't have to skip it," said Kevin, appalled. "It's tradition. You and Mona look forward to your week together all year around. You need that time together."

"I need to save the library."

"You'll be gone only a week. There will be plenty of saving

left for you to do when you come back." He placed his hands on her shoulders and regarded her earnestly. "I'll be here for the kids and to do my part for Vote Yes for Libraries. You know you'll be able to work better after some time away. You've been too stressed out. A week with Mona is just what you need—and I bet a week with *you* is just what *she* needs."

Linnea was well aware that Mona was under considerable pressure from her employer, the governor's new directives, and her union. They both needed time away from the stress and strain. So it was mostly for her sister's sake that she acquiesced, but she warned Kevin that he would have to agree to a very modest travel budget or she wouldn't go.

Kevin remembered hearing a distant cousin sing the praises of Elm Creek Quilt Camp at a Nelson family reunion a few summers earlier, and when he searched online and learned about Quiltsgiving, he decided it was meant to be. A week in a historic manor in beautiful rural central Pennsylvania, delicious meals, as much quilting as Linnea could possibly desire, the opportunity to support a worthy cause—all the husbands had to do was come up with airfare, and the sisters would be set.

And so Linnea found herself far from the strife and worry of home, spending precious time with her sister, quilting, making new friends—and resting up for what would surely be the fight of her life.

Instinct as much as reason drew Linnea toward the grand oak staircase in the foyer. She had already searched the first floor of Elm Creek Manor to no avail. The twins had led her up to the third story, where she had seen the playroom, guest suites, and a trapdoor in the ceiling that surely led to an attic, an unlikely setting for a library. Only the second floor remained unexplored, so that was where she would go.

On the second-floor landing, she glanced down the hall to her right and saw doors to guest rooms, including her own, and she suspected they continued around the corner. To her left, on the far side of the broad stairwell, were two French doors with filmy taupe curtains covering the windows on the inside. She peered at the ceiling and determined that the room was directly below the spacious playroom and likely the same size—large enough indeed for a family's library.

She knocked on one of the doors. "Come in," someone called to her in reply.

Linnea entered a room that spanned the entire width of the manor's south wing. Between tall, diamond-paned windows on the east and west walls stood dozens of high bookcases, their shelves bowing slightly under the weight of hundreds of volumes. A blaze crackled merrily in a large stone fireplace on the south wall, where an antique scrap Castle Wall quilt hung on the wall to the left of the mantel and what appeared to be unjoined sections of a Winding Ways quilt were displayed to the right. Two armchairs and footstools sat before the fire, and in the center of the room, the twins sat on the floor playing Candy Land, ignoring the coffee table and the chairs and sofas surrounding it nearby. Sarah was seated in a tall leather chair behind a broad oak desk cluttered with a computer, papers, and files; Sylvia sat, one leg crossed casually over the other, in a smaller leather chair on the other side of the desk. Both women looked inquiringly up at Linnea, but it took her a few moments to realize this, as she was transfixed by the books, the glorious collection of leather-bound, antique books among which, surely, several priceless first editions awaited discovery.

"I've been looking for this place," Linnea said, taking it all in.

"Well, it seems to me you've found it," Sylvia replied cheerfully. "Were you looking for something to read?"

Linnea laughed. "I'm always looking for something to read."

"This is the book lady," James informed Sylvia. "I told you, remember? We already showed her where the best books are." He turned to Linnea and added, "You can read any of them any time you want. You don't have to ask. It's already okay."

As one, the women smiled indulgently. "Thank you so much," Linnea told him. "I think I'd like to look around here too, though. I'm sure there are some wonderful books on these shelves."

James frowned slightly and shook his head. "Nope. They all have tiny little letters and no pictures."

"Some of them have pictures," Caroline said, and she took her brother's hand and led him off to find one.

"When I searched for the library earlier and couldn't find it," Linnea said, "I was afraid you had gotten rid of it, or that it never existed."

"Perish the thought," declared Sylvia. "Rest assured, my dear, this library will remain long as there's breath in my body."

"Or in mine," Sarah added.

"People need stories." With some effort, Sylvia pushed herself out of her chair and beckoned for Linnea to accompany her to one of the bookshelves. "We use stories to teach, to learn, to make sense of the world around us. As long as we need stories, we will need books, and as long as there are books, there will be libraries."

Linnea's gaze traveled from Sylvia's knowing eyes to the books upon the shelves, family heirlooms treasured by generations of readers. "I hope you're right," she said softly.

She had no doubt that private libraries like the Bergstrom family's would endure. What she feared for were the even more essential libraries—those that were open to all, those that offered the opportunity for learning and discovery to those who could not find them any other place, to those who needed them most. Their fate, like the fate of her own beloved Conejo Hills Public Library, was far less certain.

Chapter Four

✿

Michaela

Michaela was lying on the floor awkwardly working her way through a series of yoga poses when she heard the plaintive chords of a familiar Bob Dylan song. She lumbered over to the nightstand and snatched up her phone. "Morning, Mom," she said, flopping down on the unmade bed.

"Good morning, angel. How are you feeling today?"

"My foot and I are both fine, although we're not on speaking terms." Michaela scowled at the cast. "Why can't it heal faster? If I don't have a good aerobic workout complete with sweat and an elevated pulse soon, I think I'll go crazy."

"If you do your yoga properly, you'll get there. Have you been drinking the herbal teas I blended for you?"

"Faithfully." They tasted terrible, but most of her mother's remedies did, in direct proportion to how swiftly they worked. Michaela knew she'd have been in much worse shape without them.

"That's my girl. Keep it up, and think positive, healing thoughts." Her mother sighed. "I was hoping time away from school would help you relax and boost your immune system, but if you're stressed out and unhappy, it doesn't justify all those missed classes."

"Mom, relax," Michaela said, and she heard her mother immediately take a deep, cleansing breath. "I'm having a great time, really. Elm Creek Manor is as gorgeous as you promised, and the food is way better than at school."

"Have you made any friends? I'm guessing there isn't anyone else your age around."

Only rarely did Michaela find someone her own age within a gathering of quilters. "I've made a few friends," she said, thinking of Jocelyn, the sisters, and the other two quilters she'd kind of been hanging out with lately. They were funny and nice, and they didn't make any annoying, disparaging remarks about her age like that one lady at the Candlelight had.

Michaela told her mother about the previous night's program, knowing she would appreciate it. Sarah McClure had given the campers blank journals covered in plain canvas, which they had decorated as their hearts desired—some with fabric, others with paint, ink, dye, or decoupage or a fantastic mixture of techniques. When everyone had finished, they had set their gloriously transformed journals on a table to dry and admired one another's creations. Then Sarah had explained that these were Giving Journals, and that every night, they should describe five ways they had given of themselves to others that day and name five people for whom they were especially grateful.

"What if you can't think of five of each?" a quilter had asked.

Sarah had smiled. "Then tomorrow, think of how you could live differently—more consciously, deliberately, and aware—so that you'll have more than enough to write in your journal. Trust me, the more faithfully you keep your Giving Journal, the more abundant your life will be. The only problem you'll have with writing your nightly entries is paring down the possibilities to only five."

"I always did like Sarah McClure, and now I have another reason," Michaela's mom remarked. "I should start a Giving Journal of my own. Did you have any trouble coming up with your lists?"

"A little with the first one," Michaela admitted. "I've been so focused on making the Giving Quilt and studying at night that I wasn't thinking about giving to others. But today I will." The second list had been much easier. Michaela was most grateful for her parents, of course, that day and every day. She had also listed Jocelyn, Linnea, and Karen, who had carried dinner trays and quilting supplies for her as she maneuvered around the manor on her crutches. Last but definitely not least on her list was her college friend Emma, who had promised to share her English Lit notes for the week Michaela was missing class—and no one had been more supportive than Emma throughout the dismal months surrounding Michaela's accident.

" 'Incident' is a better word for it than 'accident,' " she muttered scathingly to herself after she and her mother hung up. Then she remembered her Giving Journal, heaved a sigh, and decided to give the two students who had injured her the benefit of the doubt. They wouldn't know she had done so, but maybe, somehow, through karma or a weight of guilt lifted off their shoulders, they would feel it.

Or maybe they wouldn't, if no guilt had weighed them down in the first place. Michaela would probably never know the truth, and it wouldn't change anything if she did.

She sighed again and hobbled off to get dressed for breakfast.

With help from Jocelyn and Pauline—two people for the second part of that evening's journal entry and it wasn't even nine o'clock—Michaela managed to get from the buffet to a table to the classroom without dropping anything, falling on her backside, or injuring anyone.

"You know what occurred to me?" she mused as they took their usual seats—Pauline, Linnea, and Mona in the front row, Michaela and Jocelyn seated a row behind. Karen had broken her two-day-old tradition of sitting in the back row and had moved up to take the seat next to Michaela.

"What's that?" asked Jocelyn with an encouraging, expectant look Michaela suspected she practiced a lot on her students.

"We're all involved in education," she said. "You're a teacher, Karen teaches quilting, Pauline runs an annual quilting retreat where I'm sure lots of teaching goes on—"

"Ran," said Pauline. "I *ran* retreats, past tense—and really, I only helped. I didn't do it all myself."

"That's good enough," said Michaela. "Linnea does a lot of work with literacy in her library, and I'm an education major. That's probably why we all get along so well."

"What about me?" said Mona.

"Well, you . . ." Michaela thought for a moment. "You're related to a librarian. That counts."

Everyone laughed—even Gretchen, who had caught the end of their conversation as she took her place at the front of the classroom. "I hope you did your homework and finished all thirty-two of your Resolution Square blocks," Gretchen said as soon as all the students had taken their seats, "because today we're sewing them together."

A soft, forlorn wail went up from the back row, evoking a few sympathetic chuckles from other students.

"You have time to catch up," Gretchen assured the student who was apparently trailing behind her classmates, and then she turned to Pauline. "May I please borrow a few of your blocks?"

"Take as many as you like," said Pauline, clearly thrilled to have been chosen.

Gretchen thanked her and gathered up a few of her red-and-purple blocks, which were arranged in an orderly stack next to a nearly identical pile of green-and-pink blocks. "You're awesome," whispered Michaela, impressed.

Muffling a laugh, Pauline gazed heavenward and waved off the praise.

Taking Pauline's blocks to the design wall, Gretchen turned one forty-five degrees and pressed it to the felt until it stuck. "This is called an on-point setting," she explained, arranging more blocks rotated to the same angle around it. "A straight, horizontal setting is more common, and a bit easier to assemble, but an on-point setting can often create new and interesting secondary patterns. That's the secret to this Giving Quilt's striking appearance."

Michaela nodded along with the other students and typed a few notes on her smartphone.

"We'll begin by sewing our blocks into rows—unequal rows," Gretchen continued. "You'll need two rows of three blocks each, two of five blocks each, and two of seven."

Mona's brow furrowed. "That leaves two blocks left over."

"No, that leaves two rows of one block each," Linnea said.

"Well, when you put it that way, it's obvious," replied Mona, tossing her sister a grin as she reached for her pile of purple-and-gold Resolution Square blocks.

The usual hum of conversation was more subdued that morning, as the campers concentrated on pinning their blocks together and joining them with quick, neat, quarter-inch seams. Some of her classmates pressed their blocks after every seam, and some pressed after completing a row, but Michaela decided to wait until she had assembled all of her rows and press the seams all at once to save herself trips to the ironing station.

As was her custom, Gretchen walked through the classroom while her students labored, offering a word of encouragement here and a helpful tip there. Michaela had just finished pressing her last seam when Gretchen returned to the front of the room and raised her hands for their attention. "I know some of you are still sewing your blocks into rows, but since class is half-over—" A few gasps and exclamations of astonishment interrupted her, and several quilters glanced sharply up at the clock on the side wall to see for themselves. "Time flies when you enjoy your work, doesn't it? Now, don't panic; you'll have all afternoon to finish up, but I do want to demonstrate the next step, especially for you beginners, before we run out of time."

She instructed them to cut four squares from their background fabrics, nine and three-quarters of an inch by nine and three-quarters of an inch, and then to cut each square on the diagonal twice from corner to corner. "These are your side setting triangles," she explained, demonstrating with her own rotary cutter, ruler, and background fabric. "You'll have two triangles left over, but unless you're running short of fabric, the time you save using this quick-cutting technique is worth the waste. Besides, extra fabric is never really wasted, is it? You can always use those leftover pieces in another project."

Her students nodded, watching in the overhead mirror as Gretchen deftly sliced the last of her side setting triangles. "Next you'll cut your four corner triangles," she said, giving them the proper measurements for two squares that they then cut in half along the diagonal. Borrowing Pauline's block rows, she arranged block rows and setting triangles on the design wall so that the students could see how the various segments were meant to fit together. Although a diagram appeared in the handouts Gretchen had distributed the first day, Michaela snapped a photo with her phone as a backup. Before putting away her phone, she e-mailed the photo to her mom. Almost immediately, her mom texted back a smiley face.

The campers set themselves to work, and after they had been pinning and sewing for a while, Gretchen put on some stirring orchestral music to inspire them. After one particularly vigorous piece almost had Michaela fired up enough to attempt a back handspring despite her cast, she asked anyone within earshot what it was.

"That's Dvořák's Symphony No. 9 in E Minor," said Jocelyn. "It's known as the *New World Symphony* because Dvořák composed it in 1893 during a visit to the United States."

"Oh. Classical stuff." Michaela had assumed it was from a

movie soundtrack. "Do you know that because you're a history teacher?"

Jocelyn smiled. "I know that because I love music. My husband plays—" She hesitated. "My late husband played the French horn. There are some achingly beautiful horn solos in this symphony, so he listened to it a lot at home." Her gaze turned inward. "His friends from the orchestra played an excerpt from the largo movement at his funeral."

Michaela held her breath for a moment, stunned by the sudden, naked pain on Jocelyn's face. Jocelyn had mentioned her husband a few times that week, but she had never called him her late husband, and she had not mentioned a funeral. Michaela definitely would have remembered that. "I thought you said your husband was a science teacher," Michaela asked faintly. She didn't know if she should say she was sorry Jocelyn's husband was dead—of course she *was*, but if he had died a long time ago, it might seem like a dumb thing to say. Suddenly she realized it didn't matter how much time had passed—Jocelyn was obviously still very sad and Michaela was truly very sorry for her grief. She should have said so right away, but she had asked that other lame question instead and now it would be too awkward.

"He was a teacher, and a very good one," Jocelyn replied. "The orchestra was a part-time gig, mostly for fun. He used to say his stipend barely paid for his sheet music."

Jocelyn smiled briefly, but her gaze was faraway, and Michaela felt as if she were intruding on a precious, private memory. As she looked away, her eyes met Linnea's, and from the shocked sympathy she saw there, she knew Linnea hadn't known about Jocelyn's grief either.

. . .

Before breaking for lunch, Gretchen demonstrated how to add a mitered double border to their quilt tops. Michaela had mastered that technique while she was in middle school, so she merely listened politely as she pinned her last two rows together instead of taking notes. She was not the only camper who was not quite ready for that last step; only Karen and Pauline had finished sewing all of their rows together.

"The classroom and the workstations throughout the ballroom will be available for the rest of the day," Gretchen reminded them. "I'll be around if you need my help, but if you can't find me, feel free to ask any of the Elm Creek Quilters, or seek help from one another. I'm sure none of you kind and generous ladies would need the extra incentive, but if you give another camper help with her quilt, that's something to list in your Giving Journal."

A light ripple of laughter went through the classroom, and then everyone got back to work. No one, not even Pauline and Karen, finished assembling her quilt top before the end of class, and nearly everyone left her supplies and works in progress at her place.

Jocelyn and Michaela headed off to lunch together as they had the previous two days, and this time, Karen fell in step beside them. "All I have to do is press my borders," she said, "and I'm done with my top."

"I'm nowhere near that point," said Jocelyn, shaking her head. "I have only half of my rows sewn together."

"After lunch I was going to work on some UFOs I brought from home, but I'd be happy to help you if you like," said Karen.

"That's kind of you, but I'd like to do this on my own," said Jocelyn. "I've wanted to learn to quilt for a very long time, and I think it will be more satisfying if I sew every stitch myself."

"You should have plenty of time," Karen assured her.

"Oh, I'm not worried. I'll skip the evening program if I have to."

They had reached the banquet hall, where Pauline stood holding open the door so that Michaela could swing through on her crutches. "You can't miss the evening program," she exclaimed. "The Waterford College Chamber Ensemble is coming to play for us. Sarah says they're marvelous."

"I've heard them before, and they're quite good," Karen added. "Sylvia said the program includes 'music for the season.'"

"Thanksgiving carols?" said Michaela, dubious. "I didn't think there were any."

Karen smiled. "I think she meant Christmas music, but you never know."

"I would hate to miss that," admitted Jocelyn.

"Just get as much done as you can between lunch and supper, and then take a break for some fun," said Mona, who stood just ahead of them in the lunch buffet queue with her sister. "That's what I'm going to do, and I'm even farther behind than you are."

"I don't think either of you is technically behind schedule," said Karen. "We don't really need to have our tops finished until tomorrow morning."

Linnea dug into her tote bag and pulled out the syllabus. "Tomorrow's agenda includes pressing our quilt tops and longarm machine-quilting them."

"That will be so awesome," said Michaela. "I've always

wanted to use one of those big machines. I keep trying to talk my mom into buying one, but she loves to quilt by hand. I would too, if it didn't take a million years to finish a single quilt."

The others chimed in with their agreement, all except for Jocelyn. "I was actually hoping we would learn to hand-quilt," she said, picking up a plate for herself and one for Michaela. "That's more my style. I was looking forward to learning a more traditional method."

"Must be the history teacher in you," Linnea remarked.

"I'm sure one of the Elm Creek Quilters would be happy to teach you during free time," Karen said. "Really, though, machine-quilting is the way to go if time is of the essence."

Jocelyn nodded. "In this case, it definitely is."

"I suppose the only solution is to come back for a week of Elm Creek Quilt Camp in the summer so you can take a hand-quilting workshop," said Linnea.

Jocelyn laughed. "I like that idea."

"I think we all do," said Pauline.

They found a vacant table and seated themselves around it. Michaela set her crutches aside and thanked Jocelyn for helping her carry her lunch. "I never would have guessed you were a beginning quilter," she added. "Your quilt is coming together so well."

"I've noticed a tremendous amount of progress between your first blocks and your last," Pauline chimed in, and then she made a sudden, pained face as if someone had kicked her beneath the table. "That came out wrong. I'm not saying your first blocks looked bad—"

"That's not how I took it," Jocelyn broke in, laughing. "Thank you. I think I've come a long way in a short time too."

"Doesn't it feel good to be quilting after wanting to for so long?" Mona asked her. "Linnea has been promising to teach me for years, but we live so far apart, it's been impossible to fit lessons into the schedule."

"Our visits are too few and too far between," Linnea lamented. "And whenever we're able to get together—"

"There's always so much to do," Mona broke in.

"And too many other people around," Linnea finished.

"I learned how to quilt here at Elm Creek Manor," Karen said. "A few years ago, when I was expecting our first child, my husband surprised me with a week at quilt camp after I mentioned that I had been seized by an irresistible compulsion to make a crib quilt. I can't really explain it. None of my friends or family quilted at the time, and I hadn't grown up with quilts around the house."

"You don't have to justify your obsession with quilts and quilting to us," Pauline assured her.

"I forgot I'm among people afflicted with the same condition," said Karen, smiling. "So, I didn't have anyone to teach me, and I was absolutely terrified of what might result if I tried on my own. Once I learned how, though, there was no holding me back. I think that week at quilt camp might have been the best gift my husband ever gave me."

"Other than your children, of course," Pauline said.

"No, that's the best gift *Karen* ever gave *him*," said Linnea, and everyone laughed.

"My mom taught me how to quilt," said Michaela, suddenly missing her very much. Her mother would have enjoyed Quilts-giving. Why hadn't they signed up together?

"I meant to take a class a couple of years ago," said Jocelyn.

"I had my tuition paid, my supplies purchased, and everything, but then—" She drew in a deep, shaky breath and after a moment, she managed a smile. "Well, things don't always go according to plan, do they?"

"No, they don't," said Linnea.

She spoke so firmly that Michaela knew, somehow, that she was referring to something else besides quilting.

"No," she agreed, frowning at her cast. "They definitely don't."

Michaela's favorite picture of herself as a child had been taken by her mother more than twelve years before. Her parents had brought her along to a football game at the local high school where her father was the principal. From their front-row bleacher she had watched, enthralled, as eight older girls in red and white sweaters and pleated skirts ran onto the sideline laughing and shouting, their hair pulled back into ribbon-tied ponytails, their smiles confident and bright. When they told the crowd to shout, even the grown-ups obeyed. When they danced, the audience clapped along. When they did cartwheels and kicks up and down the field, the audience responded with thunderous applause. They were pretty and admired and everyone did whatever they said. Michaela was transfixed. She left her seat and clung to the guardrail at the front of the bleachers, the only barrier that prevented her from running onto the field to join them.

"Do you see them, Mommy?" she called, turning around. "Aren't they awesome?" That was when her mother snapped the photo.

Anyone else viewing the picture saw a pretty girl frozen in

a moment of perfect childhood joy, her blue eyes wide with wonder, her blond curls tousled by the September wind. Michaela alone knew that the photo had captured so much more than that, for it had been taken at the very moment she realized for the first time exactly what she was going to do with the rest of her life.

When she grew up, she was going to be a cheerleader.

Fortunately, she only had to wait until junior high to begin fulfilling her dream. The first time she cheered with other girls instead of at home in front of the mirror was in seventh grade. In eighth grade she was chosen captain and learned how to do a round-off back handspring. When she moved to the high school the following year, she was the first freshman to make the varsity team in the history of the school. Her knees shook so badly when her new coach handed her the long-coveted red and white uniform that she almost sank to the floor weeping tears of relief and gratitude. Only her deeply ingrained cheerleader poise allowed her to keep her composure until she got home.

That year she added a standing back tuck to her repertoire; by the time she was a sophomore she could do as many back handsprings in a row as there was room to do them. Her team won the state cheerleading championship every year she was a member, and in her senior year they were invited to perform in the Rose Bowl Parade. As she danced behind the Bank of America float in the glorious New Year's Day sunshine of Southern California, Michaela knew that it was the most thoroughly fulfilling moment she had ever known, perhaps that she would ever know.

For all too soon high school came to an end, and Michaela was forced to move on.

By then she had realized that professional cheerleading was not for her. Those teams didn't want athletes; they wanted sexy Barbie dolls with perky breasts and tight buns, and although Michaela had them, she wasn't about to shake them in front of a national television audience when her grandparents could be watching. Instead she would become a coach. She would earn a college degree in secondary education, find a job in a nice high school like the one she had attended, and help future generations of young women achieve heights never before seen in the sport.

When the time came to select one of the five colleges that had accepted her, Michaela chose St. Andrew's College because it was within driving distance of home, but not so close that her parents would drop by unannounced; because it had a highly respected school of education; and although she would never admit it, because its school colors were red and white, just like her high school. Actually, its official school color was a red, white, and black plaid called Crusader Tartan, but that was close enough.

When autumn arrived, Michaela felt a strange hollowness that the excitement of starting college couldn't fill. For the first time in six years, she was watching the football games from the bleachers with the civilians instead of taking her proper place along the sidelines. But at that first game she ordered herself to stop mourning and start planning. Cheerleading experience at the college level would give her an edge when it came time to apply for coaching jobs, and if she were going to be a Crusader cheerleader, she needed a plan.

She embarked on a detailed program of study, attending every sporting event she could in order to see what skills she needed to learn and what dancing styles the team preferred. She saw at once that she would need to learn more difficult partner stunts, since the guys were always flinging the girls up in the air in ways that her all-female high school squad never could have done. Her tumbling was fine, but her dance style would need to become more daring. A surreptitious investigation of the current team members suggested that decent grades and a sorority membership wouldn't hurt. She was disappointed to learn that an archaic university policy forbade her from trying out until the following year, since all candidates had to have two consecutive semesters with a GPA of at least 3.0 before they could join the team. It wasn't fair, since no other sport had a similar requirement, but she decided to use the time to her advantage.

She enrolled in a dance class for her physical education elective and spent her evenings in the gym or in the library, knowing that if she started out with a solid GPA she could ease up once she made the team. Her dorm roommate had turned out to be a ghastly creature who dressed in baggy clothes, wore black lipstick, and wrote morbid poetry about death and despair, so at least she didn't distract Michaela with too much socializing.

The days fell into a routine that kept her busy but not overwhelmed. She had three classes on Mondays, Wednesdays, and Fridays; two on Tuesdays and Thursdays; dance or tumbling practice in the afternoons; and studying every evening. Her worst class was Basic Chemistry, which she managed to get through by reminding herself of the GPA requirement for cheerleading. College Writing—or Freshman English, as everyone but English department faculty and the registrar called it—was her favorite class, mostly because the professor encouraged them to choose their own topics. She earned an A for her personal narrative titled "Rose Bowl Bound: A Cheerleader's Journey to Southern California," and the professor had scrawled a note at the top of the page admitting that she had opened his eyes about the athleticism involved in cheerleading. His new awareness, and her 3.75 GPA, brought her first year of college to a satisfying end.

Summer passed. Michaela impatiently studied and danced and tumbled her way through the fall semester of her sophomore year. It seemed forever until February and the organizational meeting for cheerleading tryouts.

When the day at last arrived, Michaela attended to her hair and makeup with care, put several crisp sheets of paper into a thin binder with the St. Andrew's College emblem prominently displayed on the front, and carried her favorite lucky silver pen. When she brought out the supplies to take notes, she would make exactly the right impression: school spirited, motivated, prepared but not too bookish.

As she entered the library auditorium, she made a swift check of the competition. Most looked nervous, some looked frightened, but a few near the front looked relaxed and confident. Michaela recognized the last group as the younger members of the current squad. The senior cheerleaders sat at a long table on the stage with the coach. Michaela decided to take a seat in the center—behind the current cheerleaders to show respect, in the coach's line of vision but not in her face.

The coach began the meeting by welcoming the prospective cheerleaders and thanking them for their interest. Then she described the tryout process. Eight men and eight women would be selected from the approximately forty women and twelve men who were present that night, and that included the juniors on this year's team, who had to try out again like any other candidate. There was a murmur of satisfaction at this news, but Michaela knew better than to think all sixteen openings were truly open. Even if the coach managed to avoid favoring the current cheerleaders, their experience would all but guarantee that they would reclaim their spots.

Beginning in the middle of February, the coach continued, she and the graduating seniors would hold workouts every weekday in the auxiliary gym, where candidates would learn stunts, practice the Crusader Cheer, and receive individual help on any other elements they desired. The workouts would also give the coach a chance to get to know them, to learn about their work ethics and personalities.

A redhead in the back row raised her hand. "Are the workouts mandatory, I mean, if you don't need any help?"

Michaela sucked in a breath as the seniors and the coach exchanged glances and raised their eyebrows at one another. "No," said one of the male cheerleaders, with the barest trace of condescension in his voice. "We won't be taking attendance like in Freshman English."

Someone muffled a laugh. In her notebook Michaela wrote, "Attend absolutely all workouts." She underlined "all" so firmly that she almost tore the paper.

In the ninety minutes that followed, she filled several sheets with valuable information. The tryouts would be held on the last weekend in March. First cuts would be held on Saturday. That evening, female candidates would perform the Crusader Cheer, the Hell Dance, a tumbling run, and two stunts; the men would do everything but the Hell Dance. The judges would pick the twelve best men and twelve best women to go on to final cuts the following afternoon.

The twelve male candidates grinned when the number was revealed. A few exchanged high fives. Several of the women sank down into their seats in despair, but not Michaela. She was too busy writing "Find out what a Hell Dance is" and planning her tumbling run.

Final cuts would consist of a private interview with the coach and the athletic director, followed later that day by their final performances. The men would perform their original cheers and be evaluated on how well they motivated the audience, while the women would perform an original three-minute dance and stunt routine to their own music selections. "And then," the coach said, building up to a shout, "we will choose our new Crusader Cheerleaders!" It was clear that she expected an enthusiastic response, so they gave her one.

Before ending the meeting, the coach said she deeply regretted that not everyone who tried out would make the team. "There are other options, however," she said. "Men who don't make the cheerleading squad can still try out for mascot."

A scoffing snort came from behind them, and Michaela turned her head slightly to see who had made it. At least a dozen men stood just inside the door at the back of the auditorium, waiting, Michaela guessed, for the organizational meeting for mascot tryouts. She knew from her observations last year that it was considered far more prestigious to be the Tartan Crusader than a mere cheerleader. No other symbol of St. Andrew's College was as well-known or beloved as the Tartan Crusader. It was unthinkable that the role of Tartan Crusader would be anyone's second choice.

As if it were an afterthought, the coach said, "Women, if they like, can join the pompom squad."

A ripple of laughter eased the tension in the room, but Michaela didn't allow herself to join in. The pompom squad was such an easy target that it was cruel to make fun of them. It was a club rather than a sport, which meant that it had no coach and only the thinnest of ties to the athletic department. They didn't even hold tryouts, but they never had so many applicants that they had to turn anyone away. The pompom girls wore pretty costumes—which they paid for themselves—and danced during halftime at games the real cheerleaders were too busy for or didn't want to attend, like the intramural football games and the Harry Potter Society's Quidditch Campus Cup. They were earnest and happy and unintentionally funny. Michaela felt sorry for them.

She spent the next week working ahead in her classes so that when workouts started she could give them her full attention. Every afternoon, Michaela put her classes out of her mind and enjoyed the cheerleading workouts. Within a few days she observed to her satisfaction that she was definitely one of the top candidates. On the first day of tumbling practice, each candidate took a turn on the mat trying a back handspring from a standing position. Most used at least one spotter, and some had spotters on both sides who gave them so much support that the candidate contributed very little to the stunt.

When it was Michaela's turn, she made her eyes wide and anxious as she approached Logan, a graduating senior who seemed to be the unofficial leader of the squad. "I've done this before, but sometimes my knees stick out funny," she told him. "Could you watch and see if I'm doing it right?"

"Sure." Logan planted his feet on the mat, preparing to spot her.

"Is it okay if I try it on the floor, without a spotter?"

He shrugged, looked at the coach for approval, and then told her to go ahead.

Michaela tucked in her T-shirt, made sure she had a clear path, then did a round-off back handspring series that ran the entire length of the gym. When she finished, she returned to the mat, where Logan was grinning and the other candidates were watching her in awe.

"Your knees looked fine," Logan deadpanned with a look that said he knew that she knew that already. "Good job."

"Thanks," Michaela said, flashing him a winning smile as she returned to her place at the end of the line.

The girl in front of her turned around and shook her head in wonder. "That was so great," she said. "You'll definitely make the team."

Michaela feigned modesty and said something about how she didn't have a chance, but the girl in front of her would have none of it. "You'll make it," she said. Then her smile faded. "As for me, I'm probably just wasting my time."

"Don't stress yourself out." Michaela lowered her voice so the others wouldn't overhear. "Trust me, half of these girls will chicken out by the time tryouts arrive."

She giggled. "Maybe we should leave a few banana peels lying around so they'll slip and break their legs."

"That's the spirit," Michaela said, laughing. "Eliminate the competition."

The girl's name was Emma; she was a year ahead of Michaela, and this was her second attempt at tryouts. Michaela was surprised to hear that the previous year she had not made it past first cuts. From what she had seen, Emma was one of Michaela's few real competitors. When it was Emma's turn at the mat, Michaela discovered why. Emma was brave enough to try her back handspring on her own, but the spotters always reached in at the last moment to keep her from falling on her face. Michaela observed Logan shake his head ever so slightly at the coach when Emma couldn't see.

For a week Michaela watched Emma struggle to improve. She noticed, even if Emma didn't, that the senior cheerleaders had dismissed her chances of ever mastering the skill. One evening after the workout ended, she saw Emma alone in a far corner, throwing back handsprings over and over again, each one as awkward and hazardous as the one before. Michaela winced as each time Emma stuck out her hands to catch herself an instant before her face would have smacked the mat. She glanced around the gym. The crowd had thinned, but the coach and the current cheerleaders were standing in a group talking and joking, unaware of Emma's struggle or ignoring it.

Indignant, Michaela went over to the mat where Emma stood with her head bowed, breathing heavily. "You're undercutting," Michaela told her.

Emma turned, and Michaela saw tears of frustration in her eyes. "What?"

"You're undercutting. You aren't getting enough distance. Look down and see where your feet are." Emma did as she was instructed. Michaela motioned for her to try another back handspring, and she obeyed, sticking out her arms at the last minute and landing on her hands and knees as always.

Michaela pointed. "Your hands came down at almost the

exact place where your feet left the ground. See?" When Emma nodded, Michaela removed a bright red ribbon and a barrette from her hair and stood beside Emma on the mat. She set down the ribbon to mark the starting position of her feet. "Now watch me, and put down the barrette where my hands land." She did a back handspring, crisp and swift.

Emma studied the several feet of space between the barrette and the ribbon, then looked up at Michaela, determination in her eyes. "How do I do that?"

Michaela took the spotter's position at her side. "Sit back as if you're going to do the trick." When she did, Michaela supported her so that she wouldn't fall on her bottom. Then she helped Emma to stand, pushed her forward a few steps, and pointed to the two faint impressions in the mat where she had stood. "What's that?"

Glancing over her shoulder, Emma looked from the fading imprints to Michaela, uncertain. "My footprints?"

"Close. They're your *toe* prints. We should be seeing heel prints. If you push off from your toes instead of your heels, you'll go straight up in the air rather than back. It's a wonder you're getting over at all." Michaela took the spotter's position and Emma assumed the starting pose without waiting for instructions. Michaela made her practice sitting back with her weight on her heels until two heel prints were visible each time they checked the mat.

When Michaela was sure Emma was ready to try the stunt again, she adjusted the distance between the hair ribbon and the barrette to account for Emma's additional two inches of height. She told Emma to concentrate on pushing off from her heels and reaching back to place her hands on the other side of the ribbon. Michaela spotted her as she tried. It was the best back handspring Emma had ever done.

She attempted several more, each one better than the last, until Michaela told her to take a rest or she might injure herself. Emma was so thrilled that she threw her arms around Michaela and skipped off to the locker room celebrating.

Amused, Michaela watched her go, and as her eyes followed Emma across the gym, her gaze fell on the coach and the cheerleaders. They were watching her, their expressions inscrutable.

Michaela smiled and waved, and as she left the gym she wondered how long they had been watching—and what they were thinking. She felt vaguely uneasy, but she told herself it was only because they had been watching her without her knowledge.

The weeks of practice and preparation passed swiftly, too swiftly, and then it was the last week in March and tryouts were only days away. On Tuesday a blizzard dumped nearly a foot of snow upon the campus, but Michaela trudged to the gym anyway. Hardly anyone else made it in, so she and Emma withdrew to a corner where they could practice their original routines unobserved. Emma had brought a portable speaker for her iPod, so they took turns performing their routines while the other watched and critiqued. Each told the other that they hoped both would make it, but if only one of them made the team, the other would not be jealous, and the one who was selected would bring the other along to all the cheerleading parties.

Emma worried about her tumbling run, which consisted of only one back handspring from a standing position. Michaela was more concerned with the Hell Dance. On Friday afternoon, the senior women on the team would teach all the female candidates a complex four-minute dance, which they would have to memorize for performance the following day. Michaela had never done anything like that before. When her high school team prepared for a competition, they spent days learning a dance and weeks, sometimes months, perfecting it. She suspected that the coach needed to see who could learn dances quickly and who could maintain their composure when the inevitable mistakes occurred, but she didn't think it was a fair test. If she made the team, she would practice their routines until every movement was recorded in her muscles long before the first performance. No team worth its uniforms threw together a dance the night before a big game, and she knew the Crusaders were no exception.

Then, finally and all too soon, it was tryout eve. There was no workout that day. Michaela called Emma to see if she wanted to come over, but her roommate said she had been throwing up all day.

"Not because of the weigh-in, I hope," Michaela said, alarmed. Unlike in high school, the Crusader Cheerleaders had to meet weight restrictions. Michaela's mother decried the rule as promoting eating disorders and threatened to make Michaela withdraw from tryouts because of it, but she didn't, because she knew it would have broken Michaela's heart to disobey her.

"No," the roommate said. "Emma isn't bulimic, just terrified."

That was a relief, sort of.

The following afternoon, the auxiliary gym buzzed with excitement and fear. A few spectators lined the walls, a pale shadow of the crowds that would come to watch the performances the next day. A photographer and a reporter from the *Tartan Times* circulated through the room as the candidates warmed up and staked out territory on the gym floor with the best view of the place where the senior cheerleaders would stand. Michaela and Emma found each other in the group but were too nervous to speak.

And then the senior cheerleaders took their places, wished them all good luck, and began to teach the dance.

At first Michaela felt pleasantly surprised, even confident. The dance wasn't too complicated and it was set to one of her favorite songs. By the fourth repetition of the second set of eight-counts, however, she was silently cursing the coach for forbidding them to use video cameras. The senior cheerleaders moved along quickly, and by the time Michaela memorized the new movements, the old ones were beginning to fade. Then inspiration struck. When they were granted a five-minute water break, Michaela wiped the sweat from her forehead and spoke directly into Emma's ear.

"Which part do you know better, the first half or the second?"

"The first."

"Then concentrate on memorizing every bit of it," Michaela said. "I'll learn the second half."

A small smile broke through the exhaustion on Emma's face, and she nodded. When the seniors resumed their places, Michaela allowed the first half of the dance to slip away and focused on the second. She made up names for the moves and repeated them to herself like a mantra: "Arms up high, kick and turn, punch punch, left and down."

Three hours later the coach asked if they had any questions.

Not a soul in the room was without one as far as Michaela could tell, but they were too tired to speak and too busy pretending they had memorized the dance more than an hour ago and were just waiting around for their slower friends. The coach warned them to be on time the following evening, led them in a round of applause to thank the senior cheerleaders, and sent them home. "Get a good night's sleep," she advised. Everyone nodded, knowing they had little choice but to ignore her advice.

In pairs and in small groups, the candidates raced off to practice. Michaela and Emma threw on their coats and boots and hurried to Michaela's dorm, where they grabbed a few bottles of water from a vending machine and claimed a vacant study room in the basement. They rehearsed their halves of the dance separately to be sure they remembered, then each taught her half to the other. They practiced until they were too weary to stand, then rested and hydrated, then practiced until they loathed that favorite song and vowed that for the rest of their lives they would change the station whenever that song—no, whenever *any* song by that group came on, ever.

It was very early Saturday morning when Emma headed home to her own dorm across campus. Michaela dragged herself to the shower and off to bed.

She slept in the next morning. When the time came, she put on sweatpants and a sweatshirt and packed her tryout clothes in a gym bag. She changed in the locker room along with several other tense candidates, all ignoring one another as if they were strangers and hadn't spent most of the semester preparing for this day together.

Michaela had chosen her outfit carefully, striking an appropriate balance between dressy and athletic. She put on carefully pressed black shorts, a red polo shirt with collar and cuffs in Crusader Tartan, and white athletic shoes, purchased especially for the occasion. Her makeup was light and natural, and a barrette covered with a bow, also in Crusader Tartan, held her hair away from her face. She tried a practice jump in front of the mirror and watched her blond curls bounce and fall lightly about her shoulders. Perfect.

She signed in at the registration desk in the auxiliary gym, stepped on the scale and waited while the coach recorded her weight on a form, and picked up her number, which she fastened to the left front of her shorts with a safety pin. Emma joined her on the mats, where they warmed up and stretched. All around them, other candidates practiced tumbling runs, stunts, and the Hell Dance. Michaela closed her eyes, stretched, and ran through the dance in her mind.

Then it was time to begin.

The senior cheerleaders led them into the main gymnasium. The bleachers on one side of the gym were nearly full, and when the candidates appeared, the crowd burst into applause. The coach and a few other men and women sat at a long table on the gym floor with their backs to the crowd. The senior cheerleaders directed the candidates to the bleachers on the opposite side. Michaela and Emma chose seats together.

The coach rose and picked up a microphone. When the crowd quieted, she welcomed them to the tryouts and introduced the panel of judges. In addition to the coach, the candidates would be evaluated by the associate director of the athletic department, the director of residence life, the assistant director of public relations, and the president of the associated student government.

A quick jolt of dread shot through Michaela. The last four knew nothing about the sport of cheerleading, and she didn't have enough time to slip them the personal narrative that had enlightened her English professor.

She had no time to dwell on it, for the coach called the first three women and the first three men to the floor to perform the Crusader Cheer. Emma was number three. Michaela gave her hand a quick squeeze as she left to take her place on the floor. Her movements could have been sharper, but she remembered the cheer perfectly. When she finished, Michaela applauded wildly and shouted, "Great job, number three!" The judges might register the praise, if only subliminally.

Michaela was number eight, so one more group went before she was called down. She smiled as if she had never been more delighted in her life as she performed the cheer. In her peripheral vision, she noticed that one candidate was a movement behind the rest of the group. It would make them all seem out of sync even if no one else made a single error.

Other groups followed. Several were comprised of all women since fewer men were trying out.

Stunts followed the Crusader Cheer. They had been taught eight partner stunts, but it was only now that the coach announced which two they would need to perform for the tryout: the Chair and the Angel.

A murmur of anxiety went up from the candidates, as well as from those in the audience who knew what the announcement meant. The Chair was not easy, but most candidates could manage it with at least some degree of success. The Angel was less dangerous but more difficult. The female candidate would take a running start of a few steps toward the guy, who would place his hands on her hips and lift her—head up, legs together and toes pointed, arms outstretched—over his head. If the timing was not perfect, she would get only a few feet off the ground before she crashed into him. The Angel was performed either correctly or not at all.

Since there were more women than men, each man would perform the stunts three or more times, growing more fatigued with each turn. Michaela was thankful that she had heeded the coach's warning to arrive early and had received a low number.

As the first stunt pair was called to the floor, the female candidates tried to figure out who they were paired with. The men's numbers began with fifty-one, which meant that Michaela's partner would be number fifty-eight. She found him and sent up a quick prayer of gratitude. Her partner was a sophomore who had played football in high school. He could easily lift her even if he bungled the timing, as long as Michaela did her part correctly. Besides, they were permitted another attempt if they failed the first time, and they would surely be able to correct any minor errors on the second try.

Then Emma let out a low moan and nodded in the direction of number fifty-three, a junior whom Michaela suspected she herself could best in arm wrestling. He meant well, but he had no upper-body strength to speak of, and he was a good three inches shorter than Emma.

"It's okay," Michaela quickly assured her in a whisper. "The stunt works because of technique, not strength."

Emma nodded, but she looked faint as her number was called. Michaela watched and hoped. The Chair went fine; Fifty-three took a few staggering steps to keep his balance, but Emma held her position and her smile perfectly. The Angel was a disaster. Fifty-three was late on both attempts and although Emma jumped as high as she could, he couldn't straighten his arms. Michaela's heart went out to her as she smiled bravely and left the floor.

When it was Michaela's turn, Fifty-eight waited for her at the bottom of the bleachers so they could take the mat together. "Thank God it's you," he murmured, his relief obvious.

"I get that all the time," she whispered back, smiling.

The tricks went perfectly, as if they had practiced together for years. There was only one slight wobble on the Chair, which her partner immediately corrected. The Angel was so stable that Michaela thought he could hold her up there for an hour. He did hold it longer than was required, just to prove that he could. When they left the floor, he hugged her.

Number Fifty-three had a second chance with a different partner, as all the men did. This time he was paired with a junior from that year's squad who was even smaller than Michaela, and this time he managed to pull off both stunts. Emma applauded along with everyone else and kept her face expressionless, although Michaela knew she was aware that his success the second time around made his earlier failure seem more Emma's fault than his own.

The tumbling runs came next. With each new category the crowd grew more excited and the candidates more determined as they tried to figure out how to compensate for earlier mistakes and tiring muscles. Tumbling was performed alone. The first candidate did a flawless round-off back handspring. The second attempted a back handspring with a spotter but settled for a back walkover. Then it was Emma's turn. She went to the mat, stood for a moment with her arms held in front of her, then sat back in her heels and did a perfect back handspring and then, without pausing, another.

Michaela sprang to her feet with a cry of joy that rang out over the applause. Emma returned to the bleachers, excited and happy. "I had to do something to make up for that Angel," she said. Michaela agreed that it was a smart decision and silently prayed it would work.

When Michaela's turn came, the candidates fell quiet in an expectant hush. She went to the far corner of the gym, faced the corner diagonally opposite, inhaled deeply, and exhaled.

As she entered the round-off and went into her first back handspring, she heard Emma's shout: "One . . ."

And then her stunt partner joined in. "Two, three . . ."

And then everyone in the audience: "Four, five . . ." Together they counted twenty back handsprings, until Michaela reached the opposite corner and finished with a back tuck. The crowd erupted in cheers and applause.

"You're in," Emma shouted when she returned to her seat. "No doubt."

The tumbling runs that had the bad luck to follow hers could not compare, but when the last male candidate finished, Michaela wished there had been more.

It was time for the Hell Dance.

Candidates one through six took the floor, and the music began.

Michaela wondered how the judges could evaluate the dancers when only rarely did two or more of them perform the same moves at the same time. Emma stumbled occasionally, but no more than the others and far less than most, and she was clearly one of the better dancers. As they performed, Michaela went through the dance in her seat, keeping her motions so small as to be unnoticed by the audience. Soon she realized that everyone around her was doing the same thing; some even mouthed the words to the song.

Then it was her turn.

As number eight she was second from the end in line. A position closer to the center would have been better, but she wasn't allowed to choose. The opening bars of the music started, and for the briefest instant Michaela panicked as the entire dance evaporated from her thoughts. Frantic, she turned her head to look at Emma, but as she did she saw the girl on her right standing in a familiar pose. Memory flooded her, and she joined in. She was only two counts late, but it seemed an eternity.

She threw herself into the dance, forcing herself to enjoy it, kicking and leaping higher than she ever had, knowing that the judges were more likely to remember what happened at the end of the dance rather than its first few moments. Her body felt like it was on autopilot, moving to the music as if of its own volition with Michaela's brain a silent passenger along for the ride. Smile, kick, turn and shake. Repeat.

Gradually, through the haze, a thought came to her. She remembered the dance. She remembered every step.

Then the girl beside her spun left when she should have spun right and crashed into Number Ten. As a gasp of dismay went up from the crowd, Nine quickly jumped to her feet and tried to find her place in the dance while Ten sat on the floor clutching her knee and weeping in frustration and rage. Nine faltered and stopped dancing, then pressed her hands to her face and ran from the gym.

Smile, Michaela ordered herself. Arms up high, kick and turn, punch punch, left and down. One more minute and the dance would be through. One more minute. Thirty seconds. The last few bars.

It was over. Michaela held the last pose and plastered a smile on her face until the coach nodded for them to leave the floor. Michaela returned to the bleachers gratefully. She was done for the day.

After the last group completed their turn, the coach made a few announcements. Finalists' names would be posted in the athletic center concourse as soon as they were available, which would be no earlier than eight o'clock that evening. Beside their names, the finalists would find their interview times, and they should be waiting in the chair outside the coach's office at least five minutes early. Candidates would be judged on their original routines beginning tomorrow evening at seven, and then the final selections would be made.

With that, the coach and judges left the gym.

Candidates and audience members spilled from the bleachers and met on the gym floor. Michaela exchanged hugs with fellow candidates and a few friends who had come to watch, but after a while she searched out Emma in the crowd.

"You were wonderful," Michaela said, hugging her.

"Thanks. You were even more wonderful."

"Where should we wait for the scores? It'll be hours until they're ready. Should we get something to eat?"

Emma pressed a hand to her stomach and winced. "I don't think I could."

"Me neither."

They left the gymnasium and went down the hall to wait in

the concourse, where soon nearly all of their competitors and the audience joined them.

At first the atmosphere was loud and animated, as candidates and spectators alike chatted excitedly and some of the candidates began walking through their original routines. As one hour turned into two, then dragged out to three, their enthusiasm waned. Most of the audience had left long ago, and even many of the candidates had headed out, although they soon returned with bags from fast-food restaurants.

Emma was a nervous wreck. "What's taking the judges so long?" she asked. "What's so hard about adding up a few points?"

"Maybe their calculators broke," Michaela suggested. "Maybe there's a tie."

Emma wrung her hands and paced.

At ten o'clock, one of the senior cheerleaders dashed in. The candidates immediately gathered around as she taped two sheets of paper to the wall. "Finalists' names are listed in numerical order," she said, raising her voice to be heard, and then she hurried off before she was mobbed.

Emma and Michaela were at the back of the crowd, and they waited impatiently as people near the front found their names on the lists and shouted with joy or slunk off, dejected.

"What are you worried about?" Number Fifty-eight asked Michaela, grinning as he passed her on his way back from finding his own name on the list. "You know you made it."

Michaela smiled back but kept inching her way forward to see the list for herself.

Finally she pushed her way to the front, close enough to see that one list was for men and the other for women. She went to the latter with Emma close behind. Quickly she ran her eyes over the list. Emma found her own name, shrieked, grabbed Michaela's arm, and jumped up and down. Michaela paused to hug her before Emma ran off to celebrate, and then she turned back to the list.

The gap between six and eleven was still there.

She read the list a third time.

She closed her eyes, took a deep breath, and forced herself to look again at the list, reading each letter of each name to be sure she wasn't mistaken.

She wasn't.

In a daze she returned to her seat. Emma was pulling on her coat. "I can't believe it," she exclaimed. "Isn't this great? Let's go back to your place and practice our original routines."

"I don't have to practice my original routine," Michaela said, numb.

"Well, of course you don't, but I need all the practice I can get. You can help me with mine."

"Okay." Mechanically, Michaela rose and began putting on her coat.

Emma gave her an odd look. "What's wrong?"

"I didn't make the cut," Michaela forced herself to say, still not believing it.

"What? That's impossible."

Michaela shrugged and fumbled with her coat buttons.

"I don't believe it. You're serious."

She nodded.

"I didn't know. I stopped reading at number three." Emma's face was stricken. "Michaela, when I said you didn't need to practice your original routine, I meant—"

"I know." Michaela headed for the door, longing to put the celebration of the better candidates behind her. "I'm sorry, but— I need to go home."

She trudged back to the dorm alone.

As she undressed and climbed into bed, two thoughts kept returning to her. All that hard work for so many months, and nothing to show for it. All that confidence and certainty transformed into profound humiliation.

She'd thought she would make the team. Everyone who had seen her practice had told her she would make it. And she didn't even make it past the first cut.

What had gone wrong?

She fell asleep without figuring out the answer.

The next day she slept until noon, then lay in bed for another hour wondering how to spend the weekend and the rest of her college years now that she no longer had cheerleading. At half past one, her phone sang out Bob Dylan. The times were a-changin', all right.

Michaela rolled onto her side and put her pillow over her head.

Five minutes later, her mother called again, and this time Michaela answered. In a voice like lead, she told her what had happened. "Oh, baby angel," her mother said, sighing. "I'm so sorry."

"Me too."

"I'm sure you did your best."

"I did, but I wasn't flawless."

"I doubt anyone was flawless," her mother said. "You know, there's always next year."

"Oh, please." Michaela flung an arm over her eyes. "I did

the absolute best I could. If I wasn't good enough this year, I won't be good enough next year."

"That's the wrong attitude."

"Oh, really? Then what's the right attitude?"

"Why don't you contact the athletic department and ask to go over your scores? Find out your weaknesses and fix them."

"I didn't think I had any weaknesses." She had remembered the Hell Dance, her tumbling run was perfect, the stunts were solid—she had run through her performance countless times in her mind, and she still couldn't figure out why she hadn't at least made the finals.

"All the more reason to find out why the judges ruled as they did, don't you think? Maybe it was something silly like—I don't know—your music choice, or your tumbling run went out of bounds, or some other technicality."

"Tracking down a technicality won't get me on the team."

"Hiding in bed for the rest of your life won't get you on the team, either."

Maybe her mother had a point. Michaela had done her best, but admittedly, she hadn't given a perfect performance; no one had. By asking the coach to help her improve for next year, she would prove how dedicated and determined she truly was.

"I'll do it." She kicked off the bed covers and put on her robe and slippers, suddenly famished. "I'll call her first thing to-morrow morning before she has a chance to throw out the judging forms. Wait. Maybe I should call and leave a message on her answering machine."

"You could go see her in person tonight at tryouts."

"You're kidding," Michaela said. "You must be completely out of your mind. I can't face them, not after yesterday."

"Why not? You don't have anything to be ashamed of. So you didn't make first cuts. So what? You tried your best and you never gave up. Surely they'll respect that."

"That's not the way it works." Michaela wasn't sure how to explain it to someone who had never been a cheerleader. "They made the cut; I didn't. They're—they're at a different level now. No one who fails first cuts ever goes to the second night of tryouts."

"Not even to sit in the audience and cheer on friends?"

Michaela thought of Emma. "No, not even then."

"Oh, I see," her mother said, exasperated. "No mingling of the classes."

"Exactly," said Michaela, although her mother made the custom sound silly.

"Michaela, honey, you can't let them scare you away. You're just as good as they are, and I'm not talking about cheerleading skills."

"I'm not scared."

"Prove it. Go to the second night of tryouts, if only to see what to expect next year. While you're there, talk to the coach about going over your scores."

Eventually her mother convinced her. That evening, Michaela went to the auxiliary gym to wish Emma good luck and to apologize for not helping her practice the previous night. Emma seemed so happy to see her that Michaela found herself glad she had come, despite the curious glances of the other finalists. She found the coach and, burying her hurt feelings, forced a confident smile onto her face and made arrangements to go over her scores the following day. She was careful to express that she wasn't contesting the outcome; she merely wanted to be better prepared next year. Then Michaela went to the main gym and took a seat in the bleachers with the audience.

Emma performed well, but so did everyone else, and since the scores were cumulative, the previous night's errors still haunted her. It would be close.

Afterward she waited with Emma for the scores to be posted.

"I knew it," Emma said flatly when her name was not on the list.

"You did your best," Michaela said, knowing that it was little comfort. Emma was a junior, and this was her last chance to make the team.

"I know. My best wasn't good enough." Emma hurried off to the locker room, where she had left her things, and Michaela trailed after her. Before going home, they went to a restaurant on campus and consoled themselves with a large pepperoni pizza with extra cheese.

The following afternoon, Michaela met the coach in her office on the second floor of the athletic center. The coach motioned for her to take a seat at a round table in the corner as she dug around in her bag for the score sheets. "I haven't had a chance to go over them yet," she said. "It's been so crazy lately."

"I can imagine," Michaela said politely. She took her binder and pen out of her backpack and prepared to take notes. Whatever the coach told her to fix, she would.

"Here they are." The coach pulled a manila folder from her bag and brought it to the table. When she opened it, Michaela saw two stacks of scoring sheets with rubber bands wrapped around them. These two groups were further subdivided into smaller piles fastened with paper clips. The coach took the smaller of the two rubber-banded piles and set it aside. "These are from the second night," she explained with a little laugh. "We won't be needing these."

Michaela managed a smile. "No, I guess not."

The coach removed the rubber bands from the first pile and took the first paper-clipped stack from the top. The score sheets were organized by event rather than by candidate, so they would have to go through each pile to find Michaela's scores. This would give them a chance to see how Michaela compared with the other candidates.

"First we have the Crusader Cheer." The coach threw Michaela a sympathetic glance as she leafed through the stack. "Most people did pretty well on this, so any mistake would count heavily against you. See here? Out of twenty points, your competitors received a seventeen, a twelve, a fifteen, whoops, here's a five . . ." She flipped through the sheets until she found the average for Number Eight. Then she stopped.

"What is it?" Michaela asked.

"Well, you got a nineteen. So the Crusader Cheer wasn't the problem."

Michaela nodded, not surprised. "Actually, I thought I did well on that." The Hell Dance had to have been her undoing. She was sure of it.

Next they went through the tumbling run scores, which ranged widely. The lowest score Michaela saw for other candidates was a two, and the highest was an eighteen. "Tumbling's difficult," the coach said, still sympathetic. "A back handspring is the absolute minimum for cheerleading at this level."

"I have a back handspring." She had dozens. She found it disconcerting that the coach didn't remember.

The coach found Michaela's sheets, then hesitated and bit her lip. "I gave you a twenty," she murmured, then gave Michaela a quizzical look. "Now I remember you. You're the one who did all those back handsprings across the floor, right?"

Michaela nodded.

The coach pursed her lips and continued through Michaela's tumbling scores. The others were similarly high, except for one. That judge had given her a two and, in the line for comments, had written, "Show-off."

"But you told us to do the best we could," Michaela protested.

"I know I did, and you should have."

Without making eye contact, the coach plowed through the rest of the scores. The pattern repeated itself for both stunts and the Hell Dance, where all the scores were in the high teens except for those from one judge. Even so, Michaela received the highest score overall for tumbling and the second-highest for the Hell Dance. She wasn't a math major, but she was sure that should have been enough to get her through first cuts.

Then the coach came to the last category: appearance. She chewed her lower lip before reluctantly showing Michaela her average.

"A four?" Michaela said, astonished. "I'm a four?"

"Maybe you were marked down for being over the weight limit." She looked Michaela up and down, concealing the score sheets with her arm. "Although . . . that doesn't seem to be a problem."

Michaela rolled her eyes. "Hardly." She leaned forward and peeked at the score sheets, only to discover that one of the judges had given her a zero. "What?" she cried, snatching up the page. She read the comment aloud. " 'Arrogant, should be sweeter.' Are you kidding me? Who wrote that?"

"I can't tell you." The coach shifted uncomfortably in her chair. "But it wasn't me."

"I don't believe this."

"Maybe it was your clothes. What did you wear?"

"Dress shorts and a polo top." Most of the candidates had worn T-shirts and gym shorts.

"Maybe . . ." The coach seemed to fumble for an excuse. "Maybe next time you could dress up a bit more."

Michaela shot her a look of disbelief, picturing herself doing a tumbling run in a sequined evening gown and high heels. "So the verdict is that I'm an ugly show-off."

"Well—"

"So what do you suggest? Plastic surgery? Pretending I can't tumble?"

"I'm very sorry." The coach looked profoundly embarrassed.

Michaela let out a sigh and fell silent. Then she realized she had nothing more to learn from the score sheets. "Thank you for your time," she said, and didn't wait for a reply before showing herself out.

Her outrage had not diminished by the time she met Emma for lunch a few days later. "Can you believe it?" she said after telling Emma about her conference with the coach. "The judges thought I was a four."

"I don't understand that," Emma said. "You're very pretty."

"I know!" Michaela shook her head in disbelief. "I mean, really."

"I'm going to join the pompom squad."

The announcement shocked Michaela out of her self-pity. "Oh, no, Emma. You can't mean that."

Emma held up a hand. "Before you say anything else, just listen. You can try out again next year, but this was my last chance. I don't want to leave St. Andrew's without being a cheerleader here, and if the pompom squad is the closest I can get, then I'll take it. The girls are nice, and I'll be a part of things. That's all I really wanted."

Michaela nodded, not trusting herself to speak.

All that day and the next she mulled over Emma's words. What was it that Michaela really wanted? She wanted to be involved, just as Emma did, but she also wanted the kind of experience that would help her get a coaching job after graduation. She considered joining the pompom squad with Emma but realized she couldn't. She would become so frustrated with their amateurish performances that she would ruin it for everyone else on the team. That wasn't an answer for her, but there was an answer somewhere. There had to be.

Later that week, as she was sorting her laundry, she came across the wide hair ribbon she had worn at tryouts. She held it in front of her, studying the familiar Crusader Tartan pattern and wondering.

Then it came to her.

The next afternoon she returned to the auxiliary gym. A dozen or so men were practicing on the mats, and off to one side, the coach was talking to another four who sat on the floor at her feet. Michaela recognized those with the coach as the men who had tried out for cheerleading but had not made the team.

Steeling herself, Michaela approached the coach, who was distributing handouts to the four men. "These are the rules," she said. "Enrollment status requirements, minimum grade point average, guidelines for designing your costumes, all of it."

"Coach?" Michaela broke in. The men turned around to look at her.

"Oh, hello again," the coach said, wary.

"May I have one of those sheets?"

The coach gave her a curious look but handed her a page. "This is the last day to sign up for mascot tryouts. Tell your friend he has until five o'clock to turn this in, and he should do it in person."

Michaela scanned the requirements. The grammar used "he" and "him" throughout, but according to her College Writing professor, that was a prevalent sexist construction that often was meant to represent both genders. Nowhere in the rules did it specifically state that the mascot had to be male, and even if it had, she doubted that would be legal.

She looked the coach squarely in the eye. "I'm not here for a friend. I'm here for myself. I want to be the next Tartan Crusader."

"But you're a girl," exclaimed one of the four men.

Michaela feigned puzzlement. "A woman, actually, but yes, I know."

"The Tartan Crusader is a man," said another, as if he were speaking to someone not very bright.

"He was this year." Michaela smiled and sat down with the other new candidates. "Maybe next year he'll be a she."

The coached sighed wearily. "Will you excuse me?" she said to the four men. She motioned for Michaela to come with her, so Michaela stood and followed her a few feet away.

"Look, I know you're disappointed about not making the

cheerleading squad," the coach said, keeping her voice low. "I understand that. Come back next year and give it another shot."

"Are you saying I can't try out for Tartan Crusader because I'm a woman?" Michaela's voice became louder with each word. Everyone in the gym was paying attention.

The coach held up her hands. "No, no, that's not what I'm saying."

"I think I would be an excellent Tartan Crusader. For tryouts they have to do the Crusader Cheer, a tumbling run, and an original stunt routine, right?"

The coach winced and nodded as if the admission pained her.

"I can do all that."

"The mascot's stunts are different than the cheerleaders'," the coach called after her as she went to take her place among the other candidates.

"I have a week," said Michaela. "I'll learn them."

That first workout did not go well. The men refused to work with her, and they brushed off her offers to help them with their tumbling. They couldn't prevent her from watching as the male cheerleaders taught stunts to the mascot candidates, though. Unlike the cheerleading partner stunts she already knew, these tricks were performed in groups of three, the mascot and two male cheerleaders. At tryouts each mascot candidate would be paired randomly with two male cheerleaders, but for most of the workouts, the mascot candidates took turns filling the different roles. When it was clear that the men wouldn't let her join in, she looked to the coach for assistance, but each time the coach claimed to be busy helping someone else. Undaunted, Michaela memorized every word of the instructions that passed between the men.

Saturday morning she rose early and drove home to her parents' house, stopping first at the campus bookstore to buy two large wool blankets in Crusader Tartan. Her mother had her sewing machine and patterns spread out on the dining room table when she arrived. Michaela told her what she had in mind for her costume and her mother contributed a few ideas of her own. They worked throughout the weekend, washing the blankets and finding coordinating fabric, experimenting with various designs, fitting the garment, making every last detail perfect. When Michaela returned to her dorm on Sunday evening, she brought with her a Tartan Crusader costume better, she was certain, than had ever been seen.

On Monday afternoon, a few curious students came to the gym to watch the workout. The next day there were twice as many onlookers, including a reporter from the *Tartan Times*. Michaela was accustomed to audiences and didn't mind this one, but the other candidates seemed annoyed by all the attention she was receiving. She made no progress in convincing them to let her practice stunts with them, so she was relieved when the male cheerleaders arrived. When she spotted Number Fifty-eight among them, she felt a surge of hope and searched her memory for his name—Joel. She cornered him when he went to the drinking fountain and pleaded with him to help her. Eventually he weakened, but he pointed out that without a second cheerleader, they couldn't practice anyway.

"Don't go anywhere," she begged, and hurried off to find Logan, the senior cheerleader who had particularly enjoyed her first explosive tumbling run during tryout practices. It took some doing, but she appealed to his sense of honor, their shared loyalty to St. Andrew's—and the fact that he would be graduating in May and wouldn't have to tolerate any potential backlash very long. Eventually she persuaded him to help her.

Her confidence grew once she learned the stunts. At home, she adapted her cheerleading stunt routine to the requirements for Tartan Crusader. She had survived one tryout; she could endure this one. And this time there was no Hell Dance.

When she went to campus Wednesday morning, the stares and whispers were difficult to ignore. When she took her usual seat in Comparative Imperialisms, several students around her stood up and moved a few seats away. As she crossed the campus on her way to lunch, two guys jostled her and knocked her books to the ground. Her heart pounded as she bent down to retrieve them, but she kept her face expressionless. At the entrance to the cafeteria, she picked up a copy of the *Tartan Times* so that she could duck behind it as she ate. After paying for her salad and vitamin water, she found a seat at an empty table and unfolded the paper.

And she almost choked on her cauliflower.

In large bold print, the headline announced, DISGRUNTLED CHEERLEADER WANNABE DEFIES BELOVED TRADITION.

"Oh, no, no, no." Heart pounding, Michaela raced through the article, in which several students and a few members of the alumni association had denounced her blatant disregard for tradition. The university administration said they were powerless to prevent her from indulging herself. The coach was quoted as saying she was at a loss to explain Michaela's actions and that she honestly didn't expect such immature behavior from a college student. On the other hand, the Campus Womyn's Association and several members of the faculty had rallied behind her. As for Michaela herself, she was unavailable for comment before the issue went to press.

"Unavailable?" Michaela exclaimed. "You didn't even try."

Suddenly she realized that the cafeteria was unnaturally quiet. She glanced up, and it seemed everyone in the room was watching her.

She shoved the newspaper aside, grabbed her tray, flung her lunch into the trash bin, and stormed out of the cafeteria.

Before her next class, her French professor met her at the door and took her aside. "I understand you have tryouts on Friday," Madame Fortescue said, ignoring the other students, who were straining to overhear. "If you need an extension on your paper or on any of your assignments, please let me know."

At first Michaela was too astonished to respond. *"Merci beaucoup, Madame,"* she managed to say. *"Cela pourrait me soulager."* I'd appreciate the extra time. This tryout is important to me."

Madame Fortescue looked moved almost to tears. *"On est tous avec toi."*

Bemused, Michaela nodded and took her seat.

Thursday brought more of the same. Everywhere she went, Michaela was the object of both ridicule and unexpected support. The campus chapter of the American Association of University Women took out a full-page ad in the *Tartan Times* wishing her good luck, but the letters-to-the-editor column was filled with students clamoring for her expulsion. Her Educational Methods professor abandoned his syllabus and tried to lead a discussion on Title IX, but the class deteriorated into a shouting match between those who thought that Michaela was a heretic, those who thought she was a heroine, and those who thought she'd look better in a kilt than any previous Tartan Crusader in school history so she ought to be given the role on those grounds alone.

On Friday Michaela was tempted to skip her classes and hide out at home, but she forced herself to go to class. It was all too much—the other candidates hated her, Madame Fortescue worshipped her, and everyone thought she was some kind of radical when all she wanted to do was wear a cute uniform on the sidelines, cheer for the team, and acquire invaluable experience to list on her résumé.

After her last class, she felt so overwhelmed that she took a less traveled, indirect route back to her dorm. There, alone, she dressed for tryouts and admired the uniform she and her mother had made—the pleated skirt in red, black, and white Crusader Tartan, the short black jacket with brass clasps in a Celtic knot-work pattern, and the tartan half cape draped across one shoulder and fastened with a brass pin bearing the university seal. She looked awesome. Definitely very good. Maybe good enough to win over the judges and even the other mascot candidates.

At registration she realized that this was unlikely. The competitive camaraderie of cheerleading tryouts was absent, replaced by a hostility so strong it should have been visible, hovering like coal smoke in the air. Unsettled but refusing to show it, she took her number and joined the rest of the candidates in the main gym.

The noise when she entered almost sent her reeling. The room was packed, filled with twice as many onlookers than at cheerleading tryouts only a week earlier. There was a television crew in the corner and students waving signs of approval and condemnation filled the seats. As if by some prearranged signal, rolls of toilet paper were hurled down from several areas of the bleachers, unrolling into white fluttering streamers as they fell.

The candidate behind her in line muttered something disparaging. She couldn't make out all the words, but from the snorts of laughter it evoked, she knew she didn't want to know.

The first two rounds went by in a blur. Repeatedly the coach had to order the crowd to quiet down, but they erupted into cheers and catcalls whenever Michaela took or left the floor. She performed the Crusader Cheer better than at cheerleading tryouts, and the first round was done. Her turn for her tumbling run came, and when she finished her string of twenty-two back handsprings and a back tuck, the noise was deafening. In a daze she watched the others take their turns. She was halfway through. Only the stunts and the original routines were left, and then she could go home to her dorm, away from the screams and the shouts and the frantic waving of signs and the glaring lights from the television cameras and the dread that something awful was about to happen. It was almost over.

"It's not over yet," a voice behind her muttered, as if reading her thoughts.

It was time for stunts. Michaela watched as one by one the other candidates performed a shoulder press and a basket toss. Then her turn came, and her heart sank. She had prayed and hoped and wished that she would be grouped with Joel and Logan, but two other cheerleaders met her on the mat, their expressions unfriendly.

She smiled and said something. Later she couldn't remember her exact words, but it was flattering and sweet and yet somehow they remained unmoved. They assumed the stance for the shoulder press and waited for her to give the signal. A third cheerleader, the required spotter, joined them on the mat.

Michaela summoned her courage and took her position. "One, two, down, up," she called, and they lifted her smoothly into the air and high above their heads, each foot planted firmly in the hands of one of the two cheerleaders. She raised her arms in a V and smiled.

Then, suddenly, the firm pressure beneath her feet inexplicably vanished. The men took the smallest of steps away from each other, and she was falling into empty air, with no one there to break her fall. She tried to control her landing as if she were dismounting from a cheerleading pyramid, but the height was too great and her descent too unexpected.

She hit the mat, hard, and crumpled to the ground. A shooting pain fired up her right ankle and she felt the strangest tearing sensation around her anklebone.

She heard the crowd cry out. She glimpsed Emma fighting the through the audience, climbing down from the bleachers, trying to get to her. And yet it all seemed as frozen and silent as a photograph, a picture taken at the moment she knew that it was over, that she'd been cheated once again, that it wasn't fair, and that there was nothing she could do about it.

She knew better than to try to stand.

Later, at the hospital, Emma held her hand and tried to comfort her when the doctor showed her the X-rays and explained that her fibula was broken, the ligaments torn. Shortly after her parents arrived, she learned that even after her injury healed, she might need surgery to repair delicate structures in her ankle.

"If I need surgery," Michaela asked carefully, as if choosing the correct words would shape the diagnosis, "when would it be?"

"Not until autumn, so you won't have to wear a cast during the hottest months of summer and miss out on all those sunny days at the pool."

He meant to be encouraging, but Michaela's heart plummeted. "If I have surgery in the fall, how long until I'll be able to do gymnastics again?"

The answer brought tears to her eyes. Eight weeks in a cast, then two months with no physical activity more strenuous than walking, swimming, or biking.

If Michaela had to have surgery, she would not be able to try out for cheerleading next year—and that would be her last opportunity.

Afterward, as she sat in the lobby in a wheelchair waiting for her father to return from the parking garage with the car, she said, "I think this is the worst day of my life."

"I think it's theirs too," said her mother quietly.

Startled out of her sulk, Michaela peered curiously at her mother, then followed her line of sight across the room, where a man and a woman sat near a child in a wheelchair like Michaela's, except that four brightly colored Mylar balloons with HAPPY BIRTHDAY! printed upon them were tied to the armrests. The chair's tiny occupant was a little girl about eight years old, thin and bald and hooked up to an IV. As Michaela watched, a nurse approached with a clipboard, greeted the parents like old friends and the girl like a favorite niece, and proceeded to check them in.

"Thanks, Mom," said Michaela glumly. "Perspective obtained."

Her mother smiled sympathetically, stroked her hair, and kissed her on the cheek.

Michaela endured the rest of the semester on a campus full of people who seemed all too satisfied when they spotted her hobbling across the quad on crutches. Summer break brought a blessed escape from the glares and smirks and obnoxious remarks, but instead of heading off to the Poconos, where, pre-injury, she had landed a job as a counselor at a gymnastics camp, she went home. She spent the first week of her vacation moping, the second moping and looking for work, and the next few weeks helping her mother in the garden. In June the cast came off, and Michaela gladly accepted a job at a tutoring center, working with kids who were struggling through summer school to avoid being held back a year. She figured it would look good on her résumé when she started applying for student teaching positions, and although it wasn't coaching, she found that she enjoyed it much more than she had expected.

As August approached, Michaela considered transferring to another college. Her parents told her they would support her no matter what she decided, but she knew they wanted her to return to St. Andrew's College with her head held high. She didn't want to disappoint them, nor did she want to let Emma down. They had arranged to be roommates, and if Michaela withdrew from the dorm, Emma would get stuck with some random freshman instead. She toyed with the idea of cutting her hair short and dying it red, hoping that without the crutches and the bouncy blond curls, she would be all but unrecognizable to anyone who didn't know her well. Ultimately, she decided to go back rather than let anyone think they had chased her away in shame. She refused to give anyone the satisfaction of thinking she regretted trying out for the Tartan Crusader. In hindsight, she knew she never would have been chosen, even if she had been far and away the best candidate. But she wasn't sorry she had tried. Her only regret was that she had not made a safer landing when the guys dropped her.

September found her back on the St. Andrew's College campus, taking classes in her major and attending physical therapy once a week at the same hospital where she had been treated after her fall. Occasionally, on her way out, she would take the long way past the atrium garden near the children's cancer ward. She often wondered what had become of the little girl she had seen the night of the mascot tryouts. Michaela hoped she had been completely cured and was at that moment playing in her backyard with her parents, and maybe a little sister and a puppy. She hoped never to spot that little girl among the other pale, fragile children working on craft projects with hospital volunteers or reading books or playing computer games in the cancer ward. Sometimes she stopped to watch them in the common room, transfixed by a radiant smile or a burst of joyful laughter. How could she gripe and complain about her stupid ankle when children half her age suffering from far more serious ailments could find reasons to laugh?

One day when she passed by the wall of windows, she noticed a pair of women wearing quilted jackets distributing gifts of brightly colored quilts to an eager group of children, some in wheelchairs, most hooked up to those ubiquitous IV poles. The children embraced their quilts, and snuggled them, and wrapped stuffed animals in their soft folds, and wore them as superhero capes, and altogether behaved as if the quilts were the most wonderful presents they had ever received and the two ladies some magical combination of rock stars and Santa Claus. She lingered, smiling as she observed the happy scene, touched by the new hope and thankfulness she saw in the parents' eyes. When the quilters departed, Michaela caught up to them and asked if they worked for the hospital. They explained that they volunteered for Project Linus, and they made quilts for children at the hospital and many other places.

As soon as she returned to the dorm, Michaela Googled Project Linus, found their website, and made a quick but thorough study of their mission. Every St. Andrew's student was obliged to complete a community service project before graduation, and Michaela's weekly glimpse of the children at the hospital and her memory of the little girl who had celebrated her birthday by checking into the cancer ward made her want to do something to make their hospital stays a little more bearable.

Then she stumbled across a link that took her to the Elm Creek Quilts website, a name she recognized from her mother's week at quilt camp a few summers before. When she read about Quiltsgiving, she knew she couldn't miss it.

Her adviser signed off on the cause, and her professors agreed that she could miss class without penalty as long as she made up the work. Looking forward to Quiltsgiving and making cozy, cheerful quilts for children like those she saw at the hospital brought a rare moment of happiness to her fall semester. The whole mascot debacle had blown over in early October after a cheating scandal erupted in the business school and diverted everyone's attention, but Michaela's doctor had informed her that she would indeed have to have surgery, something her limp and persistent discomfort had already made obvious to her, as much as she hoped she was mistaken.

She had outpatient surgery on the last weekend of October, and a new fiberglass cast became a long-term addition to her fall wardrobe. Back on crutches, she was once again noticed and remembered as the girl who had defied beloved tradition and tried to become the Tartan Crusader. Most people seemed to think she had gotten what she deserved.

Michaela didn't care what they thought. She almost felt sorry for her detractors, that they had nothing more important to worry about. Then it occurred to her that maybe they were the lucky ones, though, to have nothing more important to worry about. It didn't seem fair.

Her brief, failed career as a college cheerleader was over before it had really begun, and the coaching career she had dreamed of and worked for so long seemed suddenly, irrevocably unattainable. Her plans were in disarray, her future uncertain—but she had family and friends who loved her and other skills she could bring to bear. She would figure things out, and in the meantime, the least she could do was make a kid's day a little brighter with the gift of a snuggly quilt.

Michaela figured she owed it to them for their gift of perspective, for reminding her how much she had to be thankful for even on her very worst day.

Chapter Five

✿

Jocelyn

After another delicious supper with her new friends, Jocelyn hurried back to the classroom to finish her Giving Quilt top before the evening program. Since the concert would be held on the dais in the ballroom, campers would not be able to use the sewing machines that evening because the noise would drown out the musicians. "You really should take a break and enjoy the music instead," Sarah had said with a smile. "It's good for you to rest your fingers and your eyes for a while. You'll feel more energized and refreshed when you sit down to sew again."

Jocelyn knew it was sound advice. The back of her neck ached from sitting still for so long, and her wrists were sore from feeding fabric beneath the needle of the sewing machine for hours on end. Even so, she wouldn't let a little discomfort deter her from finishing her quilt top in time for class the next day, and since the alternative was to return to the classroom after the evening program and sew late into the night, she was determined to finish her quilt well before the Waterford College Chamber Ensemble took the stage. When she arrived in the ballroom, she learned that she was not the only student to have made the same resolution. Nearly every sewing machine had a quilter sitting before it, some stitching together rows of Resolution Square blocks, others working on projects they had brought from home.

Her quilt blocks and supplies sat undisturbed where she had left them before breaking for supper, so she quickly settled back down to work. She had been sewing for a few minutes when Karen appeared by her side. "Do you want some help?" she asked, tucking the long strands of her straight, fine chestnut-brown hair behind her ears. "I'm just killing time until the show."

Jocelyn glanced at the clock and gratefully accepted, her original plan to finish the quilt entirely on her own abandoned in the race against time. While Jocelyn sewed, Karen pinned together rows and setting triangles and passed them to her. On the other side of the white partitions came the sounds of folding chairs being arranged on the ballroom floor, increasing the quilters' sense of urgency. In good time Jocelyn attached the last of her block rows, and while Karen pressed the seams, Jocelyn cut long strips for her borders. Adding mitered borders turned out to be more complicated than Gretchen's demonstration earlier that day had led her to believe, but Karen talked her through the process and offered a few clever tips of her own that made her measuring, cutting, and sewing much more accurate.

Thanks to Karen, Jocelyn was able to finish her Giving Quilt top and put away her supplies with plenty of time to spare. She made a quick stop back at her room to freshen up and call home to speak with her daughters and her parents, who were staying with the girls in Jocelyn's absence. As she hurried back downstairs, it occurred to her that Elm Creek Quilts had missed out on an opportunity to add a wonderful teacher to the faculty when they had decided not to hire Karen all those years ago. As a teacher herself, she recognized that Karen had a gift. The Elm Creek Quilters' loss was surely the String Theory Quilt Shop's gain.

Michaela had saved Jocelyn a seat, so she quietly slipped into the audience while the musicians were warming up. She always felt a thrill of expectation at that moment of cacophony, a jumble of instruments calling out trills and runs and arpeggios like birds in a rain forest. Whenever brief motifs from the concert pieces suddenly stood out from the random notes, Jocelyn felt as if she recognized the voices of friends amidst a crowd of strangers. Then came the moment an oboe played an A, sonorous and strong, rising above the din, and all the other instruments would tune to it until the many voices became one beautiful and perfect note. Jocelyn loved that moment of anticipation before the music began, when anything was possible, mediocrity or transcendent brilliance, and no one knew but everyone hoped.

Jocelyn took her seat just as the oboist sounded the tuning note. "Did you finish your top?" Michaela asked in a whisper. When Jocelyn nodded in reply, Michaela beamed, bounced in her seat, and made wild motions of applause so comically that Jocelyn had to stifle laughter. Michaela seemed to be one of those rare people who were genuinely happy for the good fortune and blessings others received. She too would make a wonderful teacher.

Jocelyn settled back into her folding chair and let the music envelop her, drinking in the beautiful, familiar Christmas carols she had loved longer than she could remember. Tears filled her eyes when the first haunting notes of "O Holy Night" played, and as the music swelled they spilled over upon her cheeks and she made no move to wipe them away.

This would be her second Christmas without Noah, and it already felt lonelier than the first.

When Jocelyn arrived at the classroom the next morning, every ironing station was occupied and two quilters were seated at sewing machines feverishly putting the last stitches into their mitered borders. Michaela, Pauline, Linnea, and Mona were sitting in the front, their finished quilt tops neatly folded on the table before them. Karen's Giving Quilt top hung upon the design wall, where she and Gretchen were engrossed in conversation. They both took turns tracing designs on the surface of the sample quilt with their fingers as if they were debating patterns for quilting stitches.

Gretchen soon called the class to order, but although the two stragglers had finished sewing, they were still hastily pressing the seams. "There's no need to rush," Gretchen assured them. "We have to take turns with the longarm, so if you're not quite ready, you can simply sign up for a later time slot."

"Thank goodness," one of the quilters declared, unplugging the iron and heaving a sigh of relief.

"Why didn't you tell us that yesterday?" grumbled the other, blinking as if she were running on too little sleep and too much caffeine.

"If I had," replied Gretchen mildly, addressing the entire class, "how many of you would have procrastinated instead of trying your best to finish your top by this morning?"

Laughing, more than two-thirds of the students raised their hands, Jocelyn among them. Karen merely smiled and folded her arms over her chest, and Pauline shook her head as if scandalized by the very thought of not finishing by the deadline on the syllabus. Last of all, the grumbling quilter sheepishly put her hand in the air too, and then she offered Gretchen a rueful, apologetic grin.

"Ready or not, the time has come," said Gretchen cheerfully. She invited the students to gather their quilt tops and backing fabrics and to follow her to the opposite side of the ballroom, where more moveable partitions created a separate workspace for the longarm quilting machine. As they followed Gretchen into the nook, some of the quilters pushed to the front eagerly, while others, including Jocelyn, hung back. The quilting machine resembled a greatly oversized, aluminum sewing machine, longer and narrower than the standard machines the campers had used to piece their quilt tops. Two black handles curved away from the head of the machine above the needle, and two more jutted out from the base. The machine sat upon a rectangular table that looked to be about fourteen feet long, partially concealed beneath what appeared to be a modified quilt frame. Completing the scene were tall cones of thread, a long piece of white plastic that resembled a stencil, and other gadgets whose purpose Jocelyn could not discern.

"I'm officially intimidated," Mona said under her breath, taking a step backward.

"You're not the only one," Jocelyn murmured. She thought

wistfully of the lap hoop she had brought from home, purchased at the recommendation of the clerk who had buzzed around her quilt shop excitedly helping Jocelyn gather the items from the supplies list the Elm Creek Quilters had mailed her a few weeks before Quiltsgiving. Hand-quilting supplies were included only as "optional" items, not as required items for the Giving Quilt class, but the eager clerk had insisted, much as Karen had, that if Jocelyn wanted to learn hand quilting, Elm Creek Manor was the place to do it, and she ought to be prepared.

"Let's hang out in the back and try not to draw attention to ourselves," said Mona. "Maybe she'll call on someone else."

"I'm not so sure. Those are the students I always call on first," Jocelyn warned her, but she couldn't think of a better idea.

Just then Gretchen asked everyone to gather around the table, spacing themselves so everyone had a good view. "I'll demonstrate how to put your quilt top, batting, and backing onto the rollers," she said, "but when it's time for your session, we don't expect you to go it alone. An Elm Creek Quilter will be here to assist throughout the day."

Jocelyn was not the only student to sigh with relief at the news.

"Have any of you used a longarm machine before?" asked Gretchen.

Karen, Pauline, and a very few others raised their hands. When Gretchen asked Karen if she would be willing to go first, Karen brought her quilt top and backing to the long edge of the roller bars opposite the machine, and as Gretchen narrated and assisted her, she demonstrated the steps. First they placed the fabric Karen had selected for the back of her quilt onto the rollers, the wrong side facing up; then the fluffy inner layer of batting; and last of all, the quilt top, right side up. When the quilt was perfectly in place on the frame, straight and square and smooth, Karen grasped the handles on the head of the quilting machine and made one long, straight basting stitch along the edge of her quilt top, not only to secure the three layers but also to get a feel for the machine.

"When you stitch with a standard sewing machine, the needle remains stationary and you move the fabric beneath it," Gretchen explained as Karen demonstrated. "With a longarm quilting machine, it's the opposite. The quilt layers stay in one place and you move the needle over the surface. To me, it feels like drawing upon the quilt."

Nodding and craning their necks to see better, the students watched while Karen created a delicate stippling pattern as she quilted the outer border. Gretchen described freehand quilting, and quilting in the ditch, and allover patterns that could be drawn by following a template—the item that resembled a stencil—by tracing the pattern with a device like a laser pointer built into the machine. The machine clattered loudly as Karen steered the handles in loops and swirls and scrolls, the needle speeding up or slowing down in time with her movements.

"Okay," Mona remarked as Karen deftly quilted a twining vine in the inner border. "I'm feeling significantly less intimidated now."

Jocelyn too felt much more confident after seeing the machine in action—and it helped to know that an Elm Creek Quilter would be there to guide her when her turn came. Even so, when the clipboard holding the sign-up sheet came her way, she chose a session after lunch, hoping that Karen wouldn't mind if she stuck around to watch her work and perhaps pick up a few more tricks of the trade.

She was at long last learning to quilt, although this was not at all how she had imagined her lessons would be when her interest in traditional art forms had been sparked by her love of history and her wish to share them with her students.

She knew all too well how drastically life could change in a moment.

Eighteen years earlier and a lifetime ago, Jocelyn and Noah had met as students in the School of Education at the University of Michigan. Jocelyn, born in Pontiac and raised in Lake Orion, had been class secretary and editor of the school paper for all four of her years at Pontiac Catholic High School; Noah, a Detroit native, had been the valedictorian of his public high school class and a two-time state champion in the four-hundred-meter dash. Jocelyn's parents and maternal grandfather were Michigan alumni, and from a very early age she had planned to follow in their footsteps. Noah was the first person in his family to attend college, thanks to a combination of athletic and academic scholarships.

They first became acquainted at a Black Student Union mixer in Noah's junior and Jocelyn's sophomore year, but they were both dating other people at the time and were content to become very good friends. As they spent more time together—in classes, at church, through campus activities—the other relationships fell away, their mutual respect and admiration deepened, and they fell in love.

After graduation, two years with Teach for America for

Noah and graduate school for Jocelyn kept them apart for a time, but with hard work, faith, and a healthy dose of good luck, they managed to find jobs in the same city, and then, shortly after their marriage, in the same metro Detroit middle school.

Noah had often remarked that Westfield Middle School reminded him of every school he had attended until college—overcrowded, underfunded, staffed by dedicated teachers fighting to do the seemingly impossible with very limited resources. Like so many other communities throughout Michigan, Westfield had been devastated by the collapse of the American auto industry and had never quite recovered. Students—and their parents—ran the gamut from indifferent to intensely focused on acquiring the best education they possibly could and making something of themselves.

Although Jocelyn hoped to inspire and motivate all of her students, she found herself drawn to the most determined among them, those who worked hard to learn whether they were considered gifted, average, or learning disabled. As the adviser for the school paper, she encouraged her students to observe the world and write about it, to shine the light of truth upon injustice and inequity, and to never ignore an opportunity to make their community and the world a better place. In the classroom, she tried to bring history alive by inviting veterans and civil rights activists as guest speakers to talk about their experiences during those crucial eras in American history, and she assigned oral history projects in which her students interviewed elderly family members or neighbors. She played recordings of music from the historical periods they studied and scheduled time in the Family Consumer Education lab—once known as the Home Ec kitchen—so her students could prepare and taste traditional foods. She encouraged her most promising students to take the Advanced Placement exam in history and led an after-school study hall to help them prepare. Sometimes she felt as if she were making little headway, but she persisted, finding hope in her students' progress, however small the increments.

Noah, who appreciated a challenge and saw himself in many of the young people slouched behind the battered, graffiti-strewn biology lab tables, gravitated to the students who fell on the lower end of the academic spectrum. He set high standards for students who had been dismissed as incorrigible by other teachers and kindled school pride in even the most apathetic by encouraging them to go out for track and field. He had a rare ability to find the smallest spark of talent within even the least-athletic children and matching them to a distance or an event in which they could excel. In addition to coaching, he directed the annual science fair, organized field trips to science museums, and helped place his most promising students into summer enrichment programs where they could meet actual scientists, work in labs or in the field, and discover career options they had not known existed. Twice he was named Michigan Teacher of the Year, and he was well-known even beyond their school district as a demanding but beloved educator who changed lives.

Jocelyn was enormously proud of him. He was the sort of teacher she aspired to be, patient and tireless and smart, refusing to give up on even the most unmotivated, belligerent, exasperating students. He couldn't save them all, although she loved him for trying. Some kids dropped out and disappeared; some got into trouble so serious it was beyond the power of the schools to help them. But some discovered dormant academic interests that flourished with Noah's mentoring, and some enrolled in college against all odds. Others learned what it meant to be a part of a team, to work with others toward a common goal, to see that sometimes a group was stronger and more powerful than the sum of its parts. Years after they graduated, former students returned to tell him all that they had achieved and to thank him for setting them upon the right path and insisting they go forward.

Jocelyn had success stories of her own too, but she was no Noah. She lacked his charisma, his relentless optimism. There were days she wanted to give up, days she wanted to throw up her hands in despair and kick troublesome students out of her classroom so they could be someone else's problem. But Noah inspired her just as he inspired the kids, and so even in her lowest moments, she knew, deep down, that she would not quit, and that even when she felt exhausted and frustrated and was sure she had given all she could, she could still find deep within herself untapped wells of strength and ingenuity.

Noah was her rock and her second wind, and as the years went by, he proved to be as wonderful a father as he was a teacher. Every night before she went to sleep, and every Sunday at church, she thanked God for her husband. He and their beautiful daughters were proof, if ever she needed it, that God was good and loving and merciful.

They lived in the same district where they taught, and Jocelyn and Noah were perhaps more excited than their eldest daughter, Anisa, when she started sixth grade at Westfield Middle School. Naturally Noah encouraged Anisa to go out for cross-country in the fall and track in the spring, and if she rolled her eyes as they pulled into the faculty parking lot in their Ford every morning and hurried ahead of them on the sidewalk so she didn't have to enter the school flanked by her parents, she seemed glad to have two capable tutors at home and two protective advocates watching her back as she learned to navigate the complex social hierarchy of her new school. Her sister, Rahma, two years younger, thought Anisa didn't appreciate her good fortune. Rahma couldn't wait to drive to WMS with the rest of the family and have her parents as her teachers and her dad as her coach. Anisa thought that Rahma was too young to understand how embarrassing parents could be in public, even when they were otherwise very good parents.

When Anisa was in seventh grade and Rahma in fifth, Noah and the assistant coaches took a group of eighth-grade runners on an overnight trip to Ann Arbor to participate in the Blue and Gold Invitational track and field championships on the University of Michigan campus. Anisa, an exceptionally swift half miler, had wanted to participate, but the competition was open only to students aged fourteen to eighteen. "Next year, baby," Noah promised Anisa when they dropped him off at school. He swept the girls up a hug, gave Jocelyn a quick kiss, slung his duffel bag over his shoulder, and grinned and waved as he climbed aboard the orange school bus with the rest of the coaches and athletes.

He called home later that evening to report that his runners had made him proud in the first day of competition, putting forth their best efforts and demonstrating good sportsmanship both in victory and defeat. Several runners had performed well enough in the preliminaries to make it to the next day's finals, two had set personal-best times, and based upon what he had seen, the relay teams stood a good chance to place in several events. Jocelyn congratulated him and passed the phone on to the girls so Noah could wish them good night. She missed him, but he sounded so proud and happy that she was glad he had made the trip.

The next day they expected him home in time for supper, but at four o'clock, he called to explain that the meet was running late and they hadn't left Ann Arbor yet. "Go ahead and have dinner without me," he said.

"Of course we will," Jocelyn teased him. "Dinner will be ready in an hour. We're not going to go hungry just because you lost track of time."

"Don't blame me," he protested, laughing along. "I'm not running this show."

If he had been, everything would have been on time to the minute. "When do you think you'll head home?"

"It's hard to say. They're just about to start the three hundred hurdles and we have three more events after that." He sighed, mildly exasperated. "It's a good thing they have lights in this stadium. I think it'll be dark before we get to the sixteen hundred relay."

"Oh, baby, really? At that rate you won't get back to school until close to ten."

"I know. I don't like it either. Don't worry about picking me up. I'll get a ride home with one of the other coaches."

"Are you sure?"

"Of course. It'll be way past the girls' bedtime and they need their sleep. When are you planning to set out tomorrow morning?"

"Seven o'clock sharp." Jocelyn had been looking forward to the Traditional Arts and Crafts program at Greenfield Village in

Dearborn for months. The weekend seminar was designed to give secondary teachers an opportunity to observe artisans such as glassblowers, blacksmiths, and weavers creating authentic period crafts using techniques of the seventeenth and eighteenth centuries. Jocelyn was especially looking forward to the quilting workshop on Saturday afternoon. Her grandmothers had quilted but her mother had not, so Jocelyn had never been taught how, and she was eager to learn. Unlike glassblowing and making horseshoes, quilting was a traditional craft she could easily work into her American history curriculum. For several years in a row she had applied to the school district for a grant to pay for her tuition, room, and board, and at last they had come through with sufficient funding. Her suitcase had been packed for days, the gas tank filled, the road maps neatly arranged on the front passenger seat.

"Seven o'clock, huh?" said Noah. "Then you should be sure to get to bed on time too."

"Don't be silly. I'll wait up for you."

"You really don't have to."

"I know I don't have to, but I want to. It's all right. I have papers to grade." She missed him and wanted to greet him at the door the moment he arrived, but he knew that, and she didn't need to say it.

"I wish I were there to make you a cup of tea."

She smiled. "Me too." It was their usual evening routine. After they put the girls to bed, Noah would fix them each a cup of tea—or glasses of iced tea in summertime—and she would make them a little snack, cookies on a plate or slices of banana bread. They would push their books and ungraded tests aside, sit on the sofa under the same quilt, and talk about their day.

They didn't have the budget, babysitters, or time to go out at night much anymore, but those quiet moments together at the close of the day meant more to Jocelyn than dinner at a fancy restaurant or dancing at a club.

She felt compelled, suddenly, to tell him so, but before she could, he said he had to go. The runners were lining up for the start of the next race and he didn't want to miss it. "See you soon, baby," he said, and hung up.

She and the girls had dinner and cleaned up the kitchen. The girls did their homework, practiced piano, and played outside in the yard while she folded laundry and made a few phone calls to parents whose children had not turned in assignments or had missed so many classes they were in danger of receiving failing grades for the quarter. The sun was still rosy pink in the west when she sent the girls upstairs to bed, but it had set by the time she tucked them in.

Downstairs alone in the quiet house, she made herself a cup of tea and curled up on the living room sofa with a quilt, a stack of student essays, and a red pen. Every so often she glanced out the front window or at the clock, wishing that she had asked Noah to phone her when the bus left Ann Arbor so she would know when to expect him. She hoped his silence meant that it had not occurred to him to call and not that the meet still hadn't finished.

She must have drifted off to sleep, because she woke to the sound of the teakettle whistling. Groggy, she sat up, scattering essays about the Continental Congress on the hardwood floor. "Noah?" she murmured. Blinking and stumbling, she made her way to the kitchen and flipped on the light switch, only to find the kitchen silent and empty, the kettle on the back burner, the stovetop cold.

Yawning, she studied the kettle for as long as it took her to come fully awake, and then, just to be sure, she touched the handle. It was cold; she must have been dreaming. She glanced at the clock—it was a few minutes after nine, and Noah was surely on his way home by now.

She returned to the living room, gathered the scattered essays, and settled back down upon the sofa, snuggling up in the tattered Michigan Beauty quilt her grandmother had made years before. Every time headlights shone through the picture window, she glanced up from her work and waited to see if the car would pull into their driveway, but they always continued down the block. By ten thirty, she had finished the last of the essays, recorded the grades on the family computer, and packed the papers into her satchel. She called Noah's cell phone, but when he didn't pick up, she left a message asking him to call her back.

He must have fallen asleep on the bus or his phone charge had run out, she told herself, although it wasn't like him to neglect simple things that would keep her from worrying. She was just turning away from the window to go upstairs and put on her pajamas when a police car, lights flashing blue and red but siren silent, pulled into the driveway.

Her heart thumped. She waited for the officer to realize he had the wrong address, for the car to back out of the driveway and pull onto the street.

The flashing lights went dark. The front doors on either side opened and two shadowed figures emerged.

Her heart pounded in her chest but she could not move. They had the wrong address and they were coming to ask for directions, she told herself silently. That was all they wanted.

The men came up the front walk, and stood on the porch, and rang the doorbell.

She did not answer.

One of the men knocked on the door. The other glanced through the front window and his eyes held hers. She held her breath and waited for him to go away, but he had seen her, and even as she stood there praying for them to recognize their mistake and leave, he spoke to his partner and they both looked at her, waiting for her to let them in and say whatever they had come to say.

She forced herself to go to the door and let them in.

They did not tell her Noah had died instantly and had not felt any pain, perhaps because they knew she would eventually discover they had lied.

The track meet had ended at twilight. The parking lot had been jammed with school buses and cars, drivers and passengers alike weary and eager to get home. Noah was standing outside the school bus door checking off the names of his athletes as they boarded when he suddenly remembered a duffel bag of equipment he had left in the bleachers. He handed his clipboard to an assistant coach, told the driver he would be right back, and jogged around the front of the bus on his way back to the track—directly into the path of a car driven by a seventeen-year-old boy who had taken second in the eight hundred meter earlier that day.

More than a dozen witnesses called 911, and coaches and parents rushed to his aid, but the ambulance had difficulty getting to him because of the throng of vehicles trying to leave the lot. Although they did all they could for him and the surgeons at the U of M hospital fought valiantly for his life, he had suffered massive internal injuries. Ultimately there was nothing they could do.

Noah had died at 9:03 P.M., while his daughters slept peacefully in their beds, while his wife dozed on the sofa with a student paper in her hands and a cup of tea cooling on the table beside her, while his horrified students waited for news in the darkened bus in the lot in front of the stadium.

"Is there anyone you would like us to call?" the older of the two officers asked Jocelyn gently. She shook her head. "Are you sure? A neighbor, a pastor?"

"No, thank you." Her voice sounded very faraway, very still. "It's late. You'd wake them."

The officers exchanged a look. "Ma'am, I don't think they'd mind," the younger officer said.

She should probably call someone. She was probably in shock and should not be left alone. Oh, Lord in heaven, she was going to have to call Noah's parents. How could she tell them?

How would she tell the girls?

She pressed a hand to her mouth to muffle a scream. The room grew blurry around the edges and a roaring filled her ears. The doorbell rang; a moment later the wife of one of the assistant coaches was sitting beside her, taking her in her arms, telling her in a choked voice that she was sorry, so terribly sorry. They all were. They were all so shocked and sorry and devastated.

Jocelyn clung to her and tried to remember how to breathe.

The district offered counseling to the students who had witnessed the accident and soon thereafter extended it to the rest of the school. An investigation found that the driver was not at fault and would not be prosecuted, although he was so traumatized by the accident that he left school for the semester.

Someone—fortunately for them Jocelyn later could not remember who—gave her the business card of a lawyer brother-in-law and told her she could still sue the driver's family for damages in civil court. Jocelyn had been too stunned to reply. Why would she put herself or that poor young man through such an ordeal? It wasn't his fault that Noah had carelessly, heedlessly ignored the one simple rule they had both endlessly, emphatically repeated to their daughters as soon as they learned to walk: Look both ways before crossing the street. Noah had not, and now he was gone, and sometimes it was difficult not to be angry, shaking with grief and fury at him for making such a stupid, senseless, fatal mistake, but she could not take her anger out on this boy. He was exactly the sort of young person Noah had dedicated his life to helping. It would bring Jocelyn no comfort to punish him.

The memorial service was moving, touching her even in the fog of her grief. On the day of his funeral, hundreds of students, former students, parents, and educators filled the church. On that day Noah belonged to all of them, and she felt their grief as keenly as her own.

In the weeks that followed her return to work, students Jocelyn had never taught approached her as she drifted numbly through the halls. They stammered out a few broken phrases and fell into her arms, sobbing. The track team circulated a petition asking the school to be renamed after him, but the school board offered them the stadium instead. The eighth graders dedicated their graduation ceremony to Noah, but Jocelyn could not bring herself to attend. Later, someone mailed her the program, which included a reverent biography and a poem written by one of his honors biology students. It was probably lovely, but Jocelyn quickly put it away in a drawer unread, awaiting a time when she could bear to see his wonderful life, which should have stretched on decades longer, condensed to fit within the empty margins of a single page.

As soon as the school year ended, Jocelyn packed the girls' suitcases, put the mail and newspapers on hold, and arranged for a neighbor to mow the lawn and keep an eye on the house for the summer. Her own suitcase had sat forgotten on the floor at the foot of her bed, packed for the Traditional Arts and Crafts weekend at Greenfield Village she had not attended. She emptied the suitcase and filled it again with clothing more suitable for the season.

It was a relief to lock up the house and drive away.

Jocelyn and her daughters spent the summer on a small island in North Carolina in the house that had once belonged to her maternal grandparents, and before that her great-grandparents, who had tried to grow cotton in the rocky soil but had eventually abandoned farming in favor of fishing and crabbing. The forests had reclaimed the tilled fields ages ago, and now the cottage and its seventeen acres belonged to the whole family, to be enjoyed as a vacation retreat and site for reunions. Noah had never been one for the outdoors other than the hammock and grill in his own backyard and the perfect oval of a cinder track, so he and Jocelyn had never spent time at the ancestral homestead except when the entire clan gathered for significant occasions. Thus the cottage held few memories of the husband and father they missed and mourned so desperately, which made it the perfect place for them to spend the long, lonely summer months.

August waned. They returned to Michigan and a house that

seemed smaller and emptier than Jocelyn remembered. Rahma enrolled in sixth grade at Westfield Middle School, but the day before classes, she panicked and begged Jocelyn to send her to another school—any other school, anywhere, she didn't care. Rahma had looked forward to middle school for so long that her meltdown bewildered her overwhelmed mother. It wasn't until later that night that Jocelyn realized that the middle school of Rahma's fond imaginings didn't exist anymore. Of course she didn't want to go to a place that echoed with her father's absence. It was hard enough to walk through the front door of their own house, to sit at the dinner table where his chair was conspicuously empty. Jocelyn didn't want to return to school either.

But return all three of them did. On that first day, Rahma held her mother's hand as they walked from the car and did not let go until they reached her first-period classroom. Friends on the faculty hugged Jocelyn and urged her to let them know if there was anything they could do. For days, students and staff stopped her in the halls to tell her how much they missed Noah, what a good man he had been, what a wonderful teacher. At the first faculty meeting of the semester, the new track coach hesitantly introduced himself, an apology in his eyes as if he feared Jocelyn blamed him for the circumstances that had led to his hiring. She made an effort to smile and be kind to him, because it was obvious how much he needed her to do so.

In mid-September, Noah's name went up in huge letters on the side of the stadium. The rededication ceremony took place during a school assembly on a bright, sunny autumn day that reminded Jocelyn too much of his memorial service. At the conclusion, the wives of the assistant coaches presented Jocelyn and her daughters with a patchwork quilt sewn from emblems cut from track team uniforms and T-shirts from the most significant meets of his coaching career, with sashing and borders in the WMS colors of blue and orange. Each image carried a memory of triumphs and defeats, of student athletes who had demonstrated grace under pressure that belied their years, of the man they admired and whose respect they strove to earn and whose approval they cherished.

It was a beautiful, heartfelt memorial, more tender and precious to her than the renamed stadium. Jocelyn wished she could have created such a tribute to him herself.

One day after school at the end of September, Jocelyn was chatting with the mother of one of Anisa's classmates about an upcoming eighth-grade field trip when the friend's mother said, "I suppose we won't be doing Imagination Quest this year. It's really too bad. The team did so well in the state finals last spring that we all hoped they might place at nationals this time, or maybe even win."

Jocelyn took a deep, shaky breath. "I hadn't even thought about it." As the faculty adviser, Noah had always taken on the responsibility of registering the school's team. All Jocelyn had been obliged to do was make sure she kept the family calendar clear for their weekly meetings and charged up the video camera battery before the tournament. "Maybe one of the other parents would be willing to take over."

The other mother shook her head wryly. "Maybe, but Noah is a hard act to follow. I can't think of many people brave enough to try."

You're talking to one, Jocelyn almost said as a hot surge of desperate anger rose up within her. Noah had left voids all over the place that she struggled every day to fill—for her daughters, for his students, for herself. But some of the roles he had abandoned she simply could not take on—she could not teach science, she could not coach track, and she could not manage the Imagination Quest team.

Ironically, it was Jocelyn who had first learned about Imagination Quest at a teachers' convention, she who had been intrigued enough to collect pages and pages of information, she who had returned home and eagerly made a case to Noah for organizing a team at their school. Imagination Quest was a national, nonprofit educational organization dedicated to promoting creativity, problem solving, and teamwork beyond the classroom. Teams of five to eight students would work together over the course of several months to choose one of five challenges, solve it, and present their solution at a regional competition. Depending upon the challenge the team selected, the students might be required to build a device that could perform specific tasks within a certain time frame, write and perform a skit, or—most often—a combination of the two. Although each team had a parent or teacher acting as adviser, the work was explicitly required to be the students' own. Parents could teach their children how to hammer a nail and join two boards together, for example, but they could not build any part of any device used in the competition. They could drive the team to the hardware store and pay for supplies within the team's $150 budget, but they could not tell the students what to purchase. They could schedule a meeting with an English teacher to discuss how to write a skit, but the English teacher could not tell them how to write that particular skit, nor could the parents contribute a single scene or line of dialogue.

Noah embraced the idea with as much enthusiasm as Jocelyn had known he would. The very next day, he successfully persuaded the principal to let him form a team, although the cash-strapped PTA could not provide any funding and the students had to hold a car wash and bake sale to raise money for their entrance fee and supplies. In that first year, six students signed up, all seventh-grade boys, and after a few weeks of ice-breakers and team-building exercises, they chose a challenge titled Construction Junction. They were required to design and build two identical structures capable of holding up to twenty golf balls, as well as some sort of transportation system for transferring the golf balls one at a time from one of the structures, around a course of traffic cones arranged at random by the judges, and into the other structure ten feet away. They also had to incorporate their creations into an original skit that addressed a real-world transportation problem. The boys attached a small aquarium net to a remote-controlled toy car and made up a story about transporting food and water to victims of Hurricane Katrina through a hazardous landscape of broken levees and washed-out roads. At the tournament, they managed to transport only four of the twenty golf balls and came in second to last. They were disappointed, but Noah insisted that it was a fine showing for their first venture. He was proud of them and declared that they should be proud of themselves.

The following year, all but one of the now eighth-grade boys signed up again, a seventh-grade girl joined the team, and they finished tenth out of fourteen in a challenge involving solar energy. A year later, they filled the roster with eight boys and girls from all three middle school grades and took third place in a challenge that required them to spend the preparation months studying the history, culture, and mythical creatures of six different civilizations; at the tournament, they were required to perform an improv skit about one of the civilizations that was drawn from a hat as well as an "unexpected problem" assigned by the judges ten minutes before their performance. That was the first time the WMS team made it to the state finals, where they were one of the few teams comprised almost entirely of minorities. They finished third from last, but Noah refused to let his heartbroken students wallow in disappointment. He praised their achievements and reminded them that their first trip to the state competition had been a valuable learning experience. "Someday," he promised, "the WMS Wildcats are going to win state and go on to nationals. And someday, we're going to win nationals. Maybe none of us here today will be on that team, but we're breaking ground for those who come after us. They're going to benefit from what we learn, from the traditions we establish, and on the day they bring that trophy home to our school, we can all say we did our part."

But that would never happen without Noah to lead them. The team would stall, and Jocelyn couldn't imagine anyone starting it back up again once the momentum Noah had worked so hard to sustain ran down. And Imagination Quest truly had been a marvelous learning experience, giving the students invaluable practice brainstorming and working with a team and solving problems. In an era when teachers were pressured to teach to a standardized test, Imagination Quest celebrated creativity and innovation. Jocelyn's only criticism was that due to the lack of parent volunteers to lead teams, it offered those lessons to far too few of their bright, deserving pupils.

And if no one took over Noah's team, even fewer WMS students would benefit from the program. Anisa had learned so much from her two years in Imagination Quest, but Rahma—Rahma would never have the opportunity at all.

She wouldn't, unless someone took over the team. And as the days passed, it looked more and more like that someone would be Jocelyn.

First she asked her daughters if they even wanted to participate in Imagination Quest that year. If they didn't, she would not lead the team, because she couldn't take on anything that would oblige her to spend more time away from them. As much as Anisa had enjoyed her previous two years in the program, and as much as Rahma had looked forward to joining the team as soon as she was old enough, it was possible that Imagination Quest, like so many other things they had once reveled in, would have become unbearable without their father. To her surprise and relief, when she broached the subject, the girls shrieked with delight and flung their arms around her, jumping up and down in their eagerness. "Thank you, Mama," Rahma said. "I thought we couldn't, without Daddy."

Jocelyn's throat constricted with grief when she thought of the great many things they would have no choice but to do without him in the years to come. "We can do anything we put our minds to," she reminded them firmly. "Sometimes it all comes down to deciding to begin."

Tears filled Jocelyn's eyes and she sensed, somehow, that they were moving forward, that they were at last choosing to brave a future without the man they all adored so much. They had no choice. They had to move on. The only way to do it, the only right way, the only way that would have made him proud, was with courage.

Three members of the previous year's team had graduated in June, but when Jocelyn contacted the parents of the remaining members, their outpouring of enthusiasm and support overwhelmed her. Rahma and two other sixth graders filled the empty places on the roster, and after taking a deep breath and murmuring a prayer, Jocelyn officially registered the team and scheduled the first meeting.

She had observed enough meetings through the years to know how Noah ran things, and she saw no reason to fix what wasn't broken. For the first few weeks, she guided the seven students through a series of team-building exercises that gave them opportunities to solve puzzles together—and to learn to speak up as well as to listen to their teammates, and to resolve the disputes that inevitably arose. The more experienced team members quickly remembered the skills they had learned in years past, and the newer, younger members followed their lead. Other parents pitched in to help when and how they could, and by early November, Jocelyn thought they were ready to choose one of the five official challenges.

After careful consideration and debate, the students chose a challenge entitled Direct Delivery, a whimsical name that belied its difficulty. Teams were instructed to design and build equipment to deliver objects by mechanical means from a start zone; over an opaque barrier ten feet long, two feet wide, and six feet high; to a set of targets located on a grid in a "landing zone" on the other side. The team would make their own targets, which could be either one foot square or two feet square; larger targets would be easier to hit, but smaller targets were worth more points. The team would also need to develop a "targeting system," a method to aim the delivery equipment at the targets on the other side of the barrier. The team would also supply the objects, which were required to be "items with a pliable cover that contain some type of loose fill material." The description took the team quite some time to decipher until a soccer player, with a sudden burst of insight, said, "Oh, I know. Something like a hacky sack." The teammates eventually decided that any sort of beanbag would do, even something they made themselves.

At the tournament, one member of the team would be responsible for placing the targets in the "landing zone" behind the barrier according to a grid-based diagram provided by the judges at the start of the presentation. After arranging the targets, that teammate would have to stand aside, forbidden to help aim the delivery system or to tell the other members where the targets were. Last of all, while attempting to deliver as many objects as possible to the targets, the team had to perform an original skit tying all the elements together and explaining their solution to the problem—all within eight minutes.

In Jocelyn's opinion, they had chosen the most interesting and the most difficult of the five challenges offered that year.

Some of the kids wanted to jump right in and begin designing their targets, but Jocelyn encouraged them to think of possible delivery systems first. The following week, she arranged for the team to meet after school in the gym, where she and another parent stacked folded gymnastic mats in a rough approximation of the barrier they would face in the tournament. She also taped pieces of paper together to show the size of both the large and small targets. Standing on the start-zone side of the barrier, she said, "You have to get your objects from here"— she strode to the barrier and held her hand up, measuring its height—"over this"—next she walked behind the barrier and pointed to the two paper targets on the floor—"so that they land directly on top of the targets, somewhere around here."

The size of the barrier and the distance their objects had to travel gave the students pause, and Jocelyn could almost see the wheels turning in their minds as they studied the course.

"Can't we just throw the beanbags over the wall?" asked one sixth-grade boy.

Tashia, an eighth-grade veteran of two previous tournaments and Anisa's best friend, shook her head. "It says in the rules that the delivery has to be by mechanical means."

"We could make a robot arm to throw them. That would be mechanical," an eighth-grade boy named Niko ventured, and the conversation took off from there. A slingshot, a beanbag-hurling cannon, a magnet on the end of a fishing line, a trampoline—the ideas came fast and furious. Rahma scrambled to write them all down, and when the barrage of suggestions slowed, she wondered aloud how they could aim at targets they couldn't see.

"We could make one of those things like on a submarine," another boy said. "Or maybe even two or three of them."

"A periscope?" said Anisa.

"Yeah, that's it. A periscope."

As the team began to discuss how to build a periscope, Jocelyn exchanged proud, amused glances with the other parents. It was always a joy to see the children coming up with solutions on their own, however implausible or outlandish, rather than looking to adults for ideas they could simply parrot back.

By the end of that meeting, the teammates had settled upon

a combination of periscopes and mirrors placed on the floor for their targeting system, but a delivery method and a theme for their skit eluded them—not only that day but the next meeting and the one after that, which they devoted to discussions and building periscopes out of cardboard boxes and inexpensive mirrors from the dollar store. Jocelyn resisted the urge to suggest options. The whole point was for the students to use their imaginations to solve the problem, and if she stepped in with her own solutions, she would defeat the entire purpose of the program. That principle was enough to restrain her, but even if it hadn't, her word would have. She and all the other parents had been required to sign a pledge that they would not interfere and that the work would be entirely the students' own. The students had signed a similar pledge attesting to the team's independence.

One evening nearly three weeks after they had chosen their challenge, Jocelyn was in the kitchen loading the dishwasher after supper when Anisa came running in carrying a heavy book. "Mom," she exclaimed, setting the book open on the counter and tapping a page. "I've got it! I know what we should do!"

"What is it, baby girl?" Jocelyn recognized the book as the world history text used in the eighth grade—battered and badly in need of replacement. The department chair had assured the history faculty that they were next in line for updated editions, just as soon as the school district could fit new books into the budget.

"We could build a catapult," Anisa said. "Just like the siege engines used in medieval times."

Jocelyn drew closer, studying the illustration. "That could work."

The commotion brought Rahma running downstairs, and after Anisa described her idea, the two sisters ran off to the computer in the family room to look up catapults on the Internet. They found illustrations and plans on a variety of websites, including a Cub Scouts activities page and something from the Society for Creative Anachronism. When Anisa presented her solution at the next team meeting, it was chosen by an enthusiastic and unanimous show of hands.

"But that's what I said the day we chose our challenge and you all laughed," Niko protested, grinning. "Remember? I said we should build a mechanical robot arm to throw things."

Everyone laughed, but in a way, he was right.

The father of another team member was a carpenter, and he allowed the team to use his basement workshop—with adult supervision—to begin designing and building their catapult. "Sometimes I just want to pick up the screwdriver and say, 'No, do it this way,' you know?" Isaiah confided to Jocelyn when the children were too busy to overhear. "It's hard to keep from stepping in and solving the problem for them."

Jocelyn knew exactly what he meant. The team still hadn't come up with a theme for their skit, whereas Jocelyn thought of a new idea every other day without even trying. On more than one occasion, she forced herself to leave the room during their brainstorming sessions rather than blurt out her own ideas. She had never appreciated how difficult it had been for Noah not to do the children's work for them. "It's not about winning," Noah had said once, a remarkable admission from a born competitor. "It's about the process. It's about proving I trust them by letting them make their own mistakes—and their own successes."

Jocelyn had come to truly understand what he had meant.

A week later, she was delighted that she had not given in to the temptation to influence the skit, because the students came up with a brilliant idea on their own.

Niko wanted to attend the Air Force Academy and become an astronaut when he grew up, and whenever an article about NASA or astronomy appeared in the newspaper, his mother would circle it in pencil and leave it by his cereal bowl at breakfast. One evening, he came to the meeting at the Ames residence triumphantly clutching a rolled-up newspaper, just as Jocelyn had seen many a newly minted graduate hold a hard-won diploma. "I've got it," he declared, shrugging off his coat inside the Ames's front door and tugging off his shoes. "This is our skit. Right here. It's genius."

Anisa, who had something of a love-hate relationship with her closest academic rival, folded her arms over her chest and regarded him skeptically. "Genius, huh?"

Niko grinned back. As far as he was concerned, hate hadn't figured in the equation regarding Anisa since the fifth grade. "Pure genius. You'll wish you'd thought of it first."

Jocelyn was as curious as her daughters to hear Niko's idea, but he refused to show them the newspaper until the rest of the team arrived. Only then did he read aloud an article about NASA's plans to launch a new rover to search for water on Mars. Astrogeologists had determined that craters in certain regions offered the greatest likelihood of finding ice on the planet's surface, so mission specialists were hoping to land the rover safely near one of those promising craters.

"Our catapult can be the rocket launching the rovers into space," Niko said.

"But they're sending only one rover," said Rahma. "We want to launch as many beanbags as we can so we can get more points."

"That's in real life. Our skit can be fiction." Niko turned to Jocelyn. "Can't it?"

Fortunately, team managers were permitted to answer technical questions of this sort. "They don't specify that it has to be fiction or nonfiction. And you know the rule—if the requirements don't expressly forbid something, it's allowed."

"Our targets can be craters," Tashia said. "We can make them out of paper bags, you know, like grocery bags. We can crumple them up to make them look like rocky ground and roll down the tops and kind of mold them into a circle."

The rest of the team chimed in their agreement.

"What about the barrier?" asked another member. "If the catapult's supposed to be a rocket on Earth, and the landing zone is the surface of Mars, what's the barrier going to be?"

Niko hesitated. "I guess . . . it could be a mountain range on Mars."

"We don't have to be so literal," Anisa said. "The barrier can represent . . . the depths of space. That's a real challenge the NASA scientists have to deal with, right? They can't really look directly at their targets when they launch that rocket. They have to use their computers and stuff to figure out where things are."

"Maybe we could use a computer to find *our* targets," burst out one of the sixth graders.

"I'm afraid that would be well over your budget," said Jocelyn.

"Besides, we already made the periscopes," Rahma pointed out.

"Niko, I hate to admit this," said Anisa, her smile indicating otherwise, "but you're right. Your idea is genius."

Niko puffed out his chest. "And *I'm* a genius."

"I wouldn't go that far."

Everyone laughed, and then everyone began talking at once, throwing out ideas for characters and costumes and punch lines and plot twists. Jocelyn stood back and watched them proudly, her gaze lingering on her daughters—especially Rahma, who had waited impatiently for years to join Imagination Quest and was clearly enjoying every moment, especially moments like this one, when everyone in the room felt their ideas and plans snapping into place like the pieces of a jigsaw puzzle, each new addition revealing more of the whole and leading to even better discoveries.

Her heart ached with longing for Noah to be there to watch it unfold.

Over the next few weeks, the team split up into three groups to concentrate on the most important elements of their solution: building the catapult and making the targets, writing the skit, and organizing props and costumes. Several members belonged to more than one group, which helped the team complete the work more quickly and communicate more efficiently. They were obliged to take two weeks off for the holidays and winter break, but as soon as school resumed in January, they threw themselves into their work even more diligently. March had seemed so far away when they had held their first meeting in September, but the start of the New Year brought with it a greater sense of urgency.

The students finished their skit, assigned roles, learned their lines, rehearsed, critiqued, and rewrote. They completed the catapult, tested it, and tinkered with the design to improve its accuracy. They practiced with the homemade periscopes and the pile of folded gym mats and figured out where to place the mirrors on the floor and how to prop them up so they would reveal as much of the landing zone as possible. All this the students did in addition to their usual class work, homework, sports, music, and responsibilities at home and in church and within the neighborhood.

January sped by, with February following swiftly after. Two weeks before the tournament, Jocelyn received their official team T-shirts from the Imagination Quest national headquarters, the cost of which was included in their registration fees. Although every team's shirt bore the Imagination Quest logo and the year, teams were allowed to choose their own colors. As Jocelyn distributed the blue shirts with orange lettering to the team—and to those parents, including herself, who had purchased adult sizes for themselves—she thought of the tribute quilt Noah's coaching staff had made from team uniforms and track meet T-shirts. Perhaps, if she continued to coach the WMS Imagination Quest team, someday she would accumulate enough T-shirts to make a quilt—if she ever found time to learn how.

The day of the tournament arrived. Early that morning, students and parents met at the Ames residence to take inventory of their equipment and carpool to Grosse Pointe South High School, twenty miles and a world away from Westfield. Jocelyn silently rehearsed her pep talk as she drove Anisa, Rahma, Niko, and Niko's mother in her car, the children's excited chatter in the backseat doing little to ease her own nervousness. She hoped the new members of the team wouldn't be intimidated when they entered the impressive school building and caught their first glimpse of their opponents, most of whom would inevitably hail from wealthier neighborhoods and more desirable school districts. Not for the first time, Jocelyn was thankful for the Imagination Quest team T-shirts and the mandatory $150 budget that provided some measure of fairness. Some of their competitors could indeed have afforded a computerized targeting system if the rules had not restrained them.

Each team was assigned a holding area in the hallway outside the gymnasium where the tournament would take place. Jocelyn went into the school first to locate theirs, after which she returned to the parking lot to help carry equipment and lead the others to their home base. While Niko's mother and Tashia's aunt watched their belongings, Jocelyn led the team to a relatively quiet spot near the cafeteria to rehearse their skit. Other teams in Imagination Quest T-shirts in a rainbow of hues occasionally passed, searching for their own rehearsal spaces. Jocelyn watched the competitors sizing up one another and was relieved when her daughters and their teammates continued practicing, calm and focused.

The Direct Delivery challenge was third on the schedule, so when the team believed they had prepared as much as they could, Jocelyn led them quietly into the gymnasium so they could watch from the bleachers as other teams presented their solutions to alternate challenges. They observed the other performances intently, occasionally nudging a teammate and whispering in an ear. When the second challenge was half over, Jocelyn waited for a break between teams and led her students to their holding area in the hall outside.

"What did you learn from watching the other teams just now?" she asked them.

"Talk loud during the skit," said Rahma. "Half the time I couldn't understand what anyone was saying."

Her teammates nodded. It was true that the acoustics in the gym were less than ideal, and only the tournament announcer had a microphone. "Excellent point," said Jocelyn. "What else?"

"If you mess up, pretend you didn't and just keep going," Niko said. "Maybe the judges won't notice."

Other teammates chimed in with more ideas, and when they had finished, Jocelyn said, "I think you left out something very important."

"What's that?" asked Anisa.

She smiled. She was so proud of each and every one of them. "Have fun out there."

They all grinned back at her, and she saw them exchange amused, tolerant glances. Adults were always saying stuff like that, when kids knew the point was to do their best and to win.

An announcement rang out over the PA system summoning the Direct Delivery competitors to move their equipment from their holding areas to designated staging areas along the walls of the gym. As the students pulled on their scientist costumes—long white coats borrowed from the WMS chemistry lab—Niko's mother clapped her hands for their attention. "Before we go in," she said, looking around at the group, students and parents alike, "I think we should have a round of applause for Coach Ames, without whose leadership, patience, and dedication we wouldn't have made it this far."

Jocelyn felt a familiar pang of wistful longing. "I know Coach Ames would have wanted to be here with you," she said, managing a tremulous smile. "You've all worked so hard and you've accomplished so much. I know when you go out there, you'll do him proud."

She raised her hands to applaud her husband in absentia, only to stop short when she realized the students were looking up at her in puzzlement, the parents with sympathy and compassion.

"Mama," said Anisa softly, "*you're* Coach Ames."

Jocelyn's hands fell slowly to her sides as their applause filled the hallway. Blinking back tears, she smiled, murmured her thanks, and led them into the gym.

Managers and parents were permitted to help their teams transport materials from the holding areas in the hallway to the staging areas in the gymnasium, but only members of the team could carry items needed for the competition into the "arena" in the center of the gym. Fortunately, the catapult, mirrors, targets, and beanbags were light enough for the team to manage easily, although it took Niko and Anisa working together to carry the catapult. In the center of the arena, a barrier had been constructed of milk crates draped in olive-green tarps, narrower and slightly higher than the pile of folded gym mats they had practiced with had been. To Jocelyn's relief, Tashia noticed the difference and pointed it out to her teammates responsible for firing the catapult and setting the floor mirrors in place so they could adjust accordingly.

When the announcer gave a five-minute warning, the parents hugged their children, wished them good luck, and found seats in the bleachers. As team manager, Jocelyn was permitted to remain in the staging area. Quietly, she helped the kids check and double-check their materials, and when they were confident that everything was in order, she offered them a few last-minute reminders and lots of encouragement, keeping their nervousness at bay with little jokes and teasing. Glancing around, she noticed other coaches doing the same—and some of them looked more apprehensive than their students. Jocelyn supposed she might too, but she tried to maintain a serene, confident façade. Noah had always made everything look so easy. He had never mentioned heart-thumping trepidation as the minutes counted down.

And then the last one ticked away, and their session of the tournament began.

They were the fourth of nine teams to perform, so they sat on the floor and watched their first three rivals present their solutions. The first team had configured a network of long cardboard tubes that they extended over the top of the barrier and raised or lowered as needed to roll hacky sacks through to the landing zone. They too used mirrors to find the targets, but they had chosen small mirrors held by team members standing at opposite ends of the barrier rather than the longer, full-length mirrors propped up against boxes the WMS team had devised. They hit only three large targets, but their skit was amusing and had the audience laughing, which could compensate for the loss of points if the judges scored them generously.

The second team's skit impressed Jocelyn even more, appealing to her love of history and mythology by taking inspiration from the siege of Troy. They used a slingshot contraption that turned out to be surprisingly accurate, perhaps because their targeting system was a wooden ladder concealed by cardboard cutouts designed to resemble the Trojan Horse. One team member merely climbed the ladder, peered over the barrier, and told the slingshot operator where the targets were.

The third team had constructed a precarious scaffold out of PVC pipe, which the smallest member of the team carefully scaled with a fishing rod and reel clasped in one hand. The scaffold shook whenever its young occupant moved, and Jocelyn could not follow the plot of their skit because their dialogue was frequently drowned out by gasps of alarm from the audience. After striking their targets a remarkable fifteen out of twenty times, they managed to complete their presentation without injury or major structural collapse, but they ran almost thirty seconds over the allotted time, which would reduce their final score.

The team carried their rickety structure from the arena, and as the judges completed and turned in their scoring sheets, Jocelyn had time for one more quick word of encouragement for her students before they took the stage.

Jocelyn felt as if she held her breath for the entire seven minutes and twenty seconds of their performance. The catapult worked better than it ever had in rehearsals, striking large targets eight times and small targets six. The youngest member of the team forgot a crucial line in the skit, but Anisa and Niko covered for her so smoothly Jocelyn had good reason to hope the omission had escaped the judges' notice.

Almost before she knew it, the last beanbag was hurled over the barrier and struck the last target dead center, and the last line of dialogue was spoken. Anisa, as team captain, called out, "Time!" to signal the end of their presentation to the IQ official operating the stopwatch. Applause thundered down from the bleachers as the judges jotted notes on scoring forms on clip-boards. Swiftly, calmly, the teammates cleared their materials from the arena and returned them to the staging area, where

Jocelyn waited, their bright eyes and broad grins revealing that they knew they had done well. They managed to contain themselves until the last entry in the Direct Delivery round was complete, but as soon as they finished returning their materials to their holding area in the adjacent hall, they broke into cheers and high-fives and enormous sighs of relief.

They were ravenous from the stress and activity of the long morning, so Jocelyn and Tashia's aunt led them off to the cafeteria, where they celebrated with burgers and fries. They went over their performance note by note, critiquing themselves, teasing one another over small mistakes, and exultantly recapping their best moments. Eventually, however, the adrenaline wore off and they quieted down, realizing that it would be several hours before the final results were announced.

The news was worth the wait. They had taken first in their division, outscoring the second-place team by twenty points out of one hundred. They would take home a marvelous trophy and move on to the state tournament the following month.

Jocelyn gave the team two weeks off to rest and recuperate before calling a meeting to prepare for the state tournament. Over pizza and soda around the Ames's kitchen table, Jocelyn read the official rules and guidelines for the state competition, which were almost identical to those for the regional level except for the locations and dates. "You're allowed to make whatever changes you'd like to any part of your presentation," she told them. "You have to stick to the same challenge, but you could come up with a completely different solution if you want."

"We don't want to," Anisa and Niko said in unison, and to Jocelyn's relief, the others promptly agreed. They wanted to practice with the catapult some more, and they thought they should revise some parts of their skit—a few lines that were supposed to be jokes didn't get a laugh at regionals—but otherwise they wanted to stick with what had worked so well for them the first time.

Over the next two weeks, they practiced their revised skit until they knew every line by heart. They painted the boxes that propped up their mirrors a reddish brown to resemble Mars rocks and fine-tuned the catapult. And then, ready or not, the day of the state tournament arrived.

Once again the students and parents met at the Ames home early on a Saturday morning to load their equipment and carpool to the tournament venue at Michigan State, a ninety-minute drive away. The students riding along in Jocelyn's car seemed confident and full of anticipation, showing none of the jittery nerves Jocelyn felt. She hoped they would perform as well as they had at regionals, and she thought it quite likely that they would do even better since they'd had additional time to prepare. But then again, so had every other team. She knew, and had tried to warn her students, that the competition would be much tougher this time around. They could not afford to go into the tournament overconfident, expecting to win or to offer anything but their very best effort. She wished Noah were there to advise them.

But no, she suddenly realized, she didn't want that. She didn't want to relinquish her coach's position, which over the past few months had transformed from a job she had undertaken only because no one else would to a role she enjoyed and treasured. She wished Noah were there—as she always, daily, minute by minute, wished he were there—not to take over for her, but to advise her, to encourage her, so she could be the Coach Ames the children needed.

She would have to do the best she could on her own.

The state tournament was the previous competition magnified in every respect—the beautiful campus, the scale of the venue, the skill of their rivals, the stakes. None of the children had mentioned nationals on the drive to East Lansing, nor did the subject come up as they located their holding area in the Intramural Sports Circle building, but everyone, even the youngest sixth grader in the tournament, knew a spot in the nationals awaited the teams that earned the highest scores in each division. And every one of them wanted to go on to nationals. They had all worked too hard to have their journey end any other way.

As before, the Direct Delivery competition was scheduled third out of the five rounds, but the venue was too crowded with parents—and the teams too determined to fit in as much last-minute strategizing and rehearsing as they could—to watch the other challenges from the bleachers. Jocelyn and the other parents tried to keep the team focused and relaxed, but tension and excitement permeated the entire building, and their nervous anticipation steadily increased as the morning passed.

At last the second session ended and the Direct Delivery competitors were permitted to move their equipment to their staging areas. Jocelyn and the other parents quickly helped the team gather their materials and haul them into the gymnasium, a vast space at least half again as large as the regionals venue, with twice as many bleachers, filled with spectators in school colors holding banners and waving signs. With a pang, Jocelyn realized that she should have tried to organize a contingent from their school, but now it was too late. Next year, she vowed. Next year she would arrange for a school bus to bring as many students and chaperones as were willing to make the trip. It would be good for the team to have a cheering section, and it would be great for the students to visit a university campus. Perhaps the trip would plant the seed of possibility in the imaginations of children who had not previously included college in their dreams of the future.

As the teammates pulled their white lab coats over their blue-and-orange Imagination Quest T-shirts, they surreptitiously looked around the gym, checking out the competition. Jocelyn could not resist doing the same, and she observed several variations on themes she had seen at regionals, as well as a few entirely new devices. No one else had made a catapult as far as she could discern from a quick glance around, which could possibly help the team score additional points for originality. One team had constructed an elaborate yet elegant system of pulleys and levers, while another had built a scale model of the Statue of Liberty. Whatever its purpose, delivery device or targeting system, Jocelyn couldn't wait to see that team's skit. She glimpsed structures with mirrors and bungee cords, ladders and stomp rockets, amazing in their diversity, creativity, and whimsy.

Then she felt a hand on her shoulder, and a low voice said close to her ear, "What the hell is that?"

It was Isaiah, the carpenter and father of one of the seventh graders, and he was glaring across the arena at a team gathered beneath a large piece of equipment inconveniently left in their staging area. "I don't know," she replied, studying it, trying to figure out what purpose it served. It resembled an L rotated ninety degrees clockwise, at least ten feet tall and twenty feet long, with a diagonal brace at the juncture and a heavy square base to keep it from toppling over. She had spent a fair amount of time in school gyms but had never seen anything like it. She was about to remark that the building custodians should have taken greater care to move university equipment out of the way before the tournament when a man in a red-and-gold Imagination Quest T-shirt led two similarly clad children to it. As if demonstrating how to move it out of their way, he placed his hands on the vertical post and feigned pushing it. When the two children, a brown-haired boy and girl who looked enough alike to be siblings, did as he had shown them, the structure glided smoothly forward, and Jocelyn realized two important facts simultaneously: The structure was on wheels, and it was the red-and-gold team's delivery device.

Jocelyn gaped.

"Unbelievable," Isaiah muttered, shaking his head. "We all signed the same Code of Conduct. They knew the rules."

"Children could not possibly have built that," said Jocelyn, unable to tear her gaze away.

"Build it?" Isaiah's voice rose in contempt. "Those kids couldn't even lift the pieces."

Jocelyn's heart sank as she realized he was absolutely right. Around the base of the enormous gallows—for that's what it resembled, with all the symbolic implications for her own team that it entailed—red-and-gold-clad children kicked hacky sacks back and forth, squealing with laughter when one rolled away and a child had to go racing after it. Nearby, adults Jocelyn assumed were the team parents chatted and snapped photos and checked the battery charges on their camcorders, perfectly at ease. Not one shot a furtive glance to any of the other teams; not one winced with embarrassment at the obvious, enormous disparity between their children's equipment and that of every other team present.

Suddenly Rahma was at Jocelyn's side, staring across the gym, awestruck. "Theirs is so much better than ours," she breathed.

Jocelyn put her arm around her younger daughter's shoulders. "We don't know that for sure. It's big. That's all we know."

The rest of the team had gathered around. "I can't believe kids made that," said Tashia, wide-eyed.

"They didn't," said Anisa flatly, turning her back upon the red-and-gold team and the anomaly too large to be contained within the boundaries of their staging area.

"What can we do?" Tashia's aunt asked Jocelyn.

She didn't know. "It's the judges' concern, not ours." She turned to the students, who had gathered in a circle around her. "Listen carefully. Don't let that contraption intimidate you—that, or anything else any other team brings into the arena. Don't worry about what anyone else is doing. You have a brilliant solution to this challenge. Focus on presenting it as well as you can. Everything else will take care of itself."

"But that thing . . ." Tashia's voice trailed off as she gestured across the gym. Niko quickly pushed her hand back down by her side before the other team noticed, but she was too upset to glare at him.

"We don't know what that thing can do," said Jocelyn. "It might not work. Put it out of your mind."

A parent spoke up. "She's right. They'll probably be disqualified anyway."

For a moment the students brightened, but then Niko's

mother pointed out that the red-and-gold team obviously hadn't been disqualified at regionals. The children's smiles faded. "There's an entirely different panel of judges here," said Jocelyn, wishing the concept of disqualification hadn't been mentioned. She didn't want their victory to be awarded on a technicality; she wanted them to win on their own merits. "Put it out of your mind," she repeated. "You can't control what anyone else does. You can only control how you react. Ignore them. Concentrate on what you've come here to do."

Some of the students nodded, and she was glad to see that their gazes were fixed on her instead of the contraption across the way. Their faces were determined and serious, and at that moment she knew they would present their solution better than they ever had before.

And so they did. Their skit drew laughter and applause from the audience, no small feat considering that it was comprised almost entirely of people who had come to support their rivals. The catapult worked beautifully; they struck ten large paper bag craters and eight small, and if not for a minor targeting error, which they promptly corrected, they might have hit all twenty. When they left the arena, they were obviously, and rightly, pleased with their performance. They had risen to the occasion and had shown extraordinary grace under pressure, and Jocelyn could not have been happier for them or more proud.

Two other teams performed, and then the red-and-gold group's turn arrived.

They needed almost every member of their team to wheel the contraption into place; the base and the vertical post were on the launching-zone side of the barrier, which the long arm extended over, covering the entire length of the landing zone on the other side. Even from a distance their costumes appeared to have been expertly sewn. As they finished setting up, Jocelyn put on a mask of polite interest and clenched her hands together, preparing herself for the worst, but her jaw dropped when one of the team members entered the arena carrying a leaf blower. The audience murmured with expectation and Jocelyn quickly regained her composure. She exchanged looks with Isaiah and the other parents, enough to see her own consternation reflected in their eyes. Then she took a deep breath and steeled herself for their presentation.

It was astonishing to behold.

The way Isaiah explained it afterward, the gallows contraption must have contained various PVC tubes of different lengths, each measuring a particular distance from the barrier. The team members with the periscopes noted the location of the targets on the grid and called out that information to the brown-haired brother and sister operating the delivery system, who moved it along the barrier accordingly. When one of the pipe openings in the long horizontal arm was aligned with a target, the boy inserted a hacky sack into an opening in the vertical post, held the end of the leaf blower firmly against the opening, and, with a mechanical roar and a rush of air, shot the hacky sack through the tubes and out the other side, where it fell neatly, dead center upon the target. The leaf blower occasionally drowned out the actors performing the skit, which appeared to be something about bees and pollination, but the judges stood much closer and might not have had any difficulty hearing. Not that such a small flaw would have affected their score in any significant manner; they hit all twenty of their targets well within the time allotted.

The outcome was all but certain, but afterward, as they picked at the sack lunches they had brought from home, loaded their cars, and waited for the judges' verdict, Jocelyn urged her team not to lose hope. They would know for certain soon enough. She wouldn't admit it aloud, but it seemed impossible that they could win unless the red-and-gold team was disqualified—as they ought to be. Surely the administrators would see what was obvious to everyone else. Those children could not possibly have built that delivery system without adult assistance—but even supposing they were a team of engineering prodigies who had designed every feature and cut each plastic pipe and driven every last screw on their own, they could not have done so within the $150 budget. The leaf blower alone would have guaranteed that.

The wait seemed interminable. As the team's gloom deepened and speculations grew wilder, Jocelyn waited for a break between presentations and led her students back into the gym, where they founds seats high up in the bleachers and watched the last session, the fifth and final challenge, called Stop the Presses. Using only newspaper and glue, teams were required to build a bridge capable of supporting weight in the center. Points were awarded for the length of the bridge and the amount of weight that could be stacked upon it before it collapsed. Jocelyn remembered her team considering that challenge the previous autumn. Although they ultimately rejected that challenge in favor of Direct Delivery, they had considered it seriously enough to have already figured out that it would be necessary to find a perfect balance between a longer, weaker bridge and a shorter, stronger one.

Jocelyn could well imagine what the red-and-gold team parents would have done had they chosen Stop the Presses instead. Perhaps they would have created a replica of the Golden Gate Bridge, capable of sustaining not only dozens of chrome scale-calibration weights placed in the center but gale force winds and earthquakes. Their skit would have been a re-enactment of the 1906 San Francisco earthquake, complete with period costumes that would put an average community theater group to shame.

Jocelyn watched the final groups perform and waited for it to be over.

The first session's runners-up were announced, and then the first-place team was called down to the arena to claim their trophy and a certificate of honor announcing that they had qualified for the nationals to be held in Washington, DC, in June. Then the second challenge's awards were presented. And then, at last, the Direct Deposit results were revealed: The West-field Middle School Wildcats took second, outscored by the red-and-gold team by eighty points.

Jocelyn's students were crushed but not surprised.

"I knew it," said Tashia with a sigh, leaning back against Anisa, who sat behind her on the bleachers.

"I can't believe it," said Isaiah, his eyes glinting with disgust and anger. "This isn't right."

"Should we take it up with the judges?" asked Tashia's aunt.

Jocelyn searched her memory for the proper protocol, and when the specific details eluded her, she withdrew the rules packet from her purse. "'All judges' decisions are final,'" she read aloud. " 'Participants desiring a more detailed explanation of the results may contact the national IQ office forty-eight hours after the conclusion of the tournament.' "

"This is bull," muttered Isaiah, shaking his head. Abruptly he stood, made his way past the people sitting in the row between him and the stairs, and climbed down from the bleachers. His son looked from Isaiah to Jocelyn and back, his brow furrowed anxiously, but when Niko put an arm around his shoulders, he stayed put, watching worriedly as his father stalked out of the gym. Through the open doors, Jocelyn spotted him pacing back and forth, shaking his head, thoroughly disgusted.

The parents briefly and quietly conferred, and they decided to leave without waiting to hear the results of the final two sessions. Isaiah joined them as they left the building, but he said not a word.

Driving home, Jocelyn wondered if they should have stayed to discuss their concerns with the officials anyway, regardless of the policy listed in the rules packet. Deep down, she doubted it would have done any good, and she was too weary and heartsick for a fight. All the way back to Westfield, her young passengers discussed the day, and the consensus was that they'd had a great time, they'd done their best, they'd given an awesome performance, and they'd been robbed—of first place, and of a trip to nationals.

"I hope those parents are proud of themselves," said Anisa. "Big accomplishment, beating a bunch of middle school kids."

That got a laugh, but then Niko said what they were all thinking: "It's just not fair. It's not right."

"I know, baby," his mother replied quietly from the front passenger seat.

Niko wasn't finished. "Everyone knows they didn't do their own work. *They* know they didn't do their own work. How could the judges let them win? How can they take that trophy home knowing that they cheated? How can they not feel bad about that?"

Jocelyn and his mother exchanged a look. Neither of them had a good answer for him, for any of the children in the backseat, for the rest of the team members, who were probably having similar conversations in the other cars. All Jocelyn could promise was that she would contact Imagination Quest in two days and request the detailed scores. That might give them some answers, although it wouldn't change the outcome.

She wondered what Noah would have done.

Two days later, she steeled herself and called the national office for the detailed scores. The IQ representative immediately e-mailed them to her so she could review them as they talked. "Your team did exceptionally well," the representative said. "They should be very proud of themselves."

"They are," said Jocelyn, more defiantly than she had intended. And indeed the judges had been effusive in their praise for the team's innovative design, their stage presence, and their clever scenario. If not for the red-and-gold team, or rather, their parents . . . "However, I have to say that they were disappointed that the first-place team didn't appear to have followed the rules."

"Ah." The woman conveyed so much in that single syllable that Jocelyn knew she was not the first to broach the subject.

When the representative said nothing more, Jocelyn prompted, "What's going to be done about it?"

"We're aware of the controversy, but I'm afraid the judges' decision is final."

"But that's not right. What message does that send to the kids—not just my team, but every team that competed last Saturday? What does that tell the kids who were awarded first place?"

The woman sighed, regretful. "Much of what we do is on the honor system. The team members and their parents or guardians all signed a pledge stating that the work was the students' own. The judges are instructed to take them at their word. We can't ask them to police what is or isn't truly the team's work. They really have no way of knowing that. I'm sorry, but with respect, neither do you, not unless you witnessed a parent or coach doing some of the work."

Jocelyn hated to admit it, but the woman was right. "What about the budget issue?" she persisted. "I'm not sure if you've seen pictures of the session—"

"I saw some video."

"Then you can understand why I don't see how they stayed within the budget. That leaf blower, all that lumber, the PVC pipe—one of our parents works construction, and he estimates that they spent well over five hundred dollars."

"The team submitted receipts, as required." Jocelyn heard the shuffling of paper in the background. "They indicated that most of their equipment was purchased used or was donated."

"We were supposed to list a fair market value for anything that was donated or lent." Jocelyn had been obliged to do so for the lab coats they had borrowed from the chemistry department.

"They did that, and again, it's on the honor system." The woman sounded genuinely sorry. "We can't put our judges in the position of auditing the budgets submitted by the coaches. The judges are volunteers, typically local educators or scientists.

We can't ask them to confront coaches when something doesn't look like the students' work. What if they're wrong? I'm sure you know that there are exceptional young people out there creating exceptional work. We want children to excel. We don't want to create a precedent for encouraging them to dumb down their solutions so we won't accuse them of cheating."

Jocelyn understood that, and yet it all felt very wrong.

She ended the call better informed but still entirely unsatisfied. The question she had posed to the representative nagged at her: What message did it send when a team could cheat, take home first prize, and move on to nationals while everyone with the authority to ensure fairness insisted there was nothing they could do?

Her heart sank when she realized that this was surely the end of the WMS Imagination Quest team. They had worked so hard and had done their best. They had followed the rules—but children who had broken them had been rewarded. They wouldn't ever want to put themselves through such disappointment again.

She couldn't blame them.

Two weeks later, she was pleasantly surprised to receive an invitation from Isaiah for an end-of-season team party and barbecue at his family's apartment complex. Isaiah grilled ribs and chicken and burgers, all the other families brought dishes to pass, and the children laughed and played as if they had entirely forgotten their disappointment in the outcome of the tournament. The resilience of youth, Jocelyn thought wistfully, wondering when she had lost it.

She had already passed along the information from the IQ representative, so she was less surprised than relieved that the subject didn't come up at the party. Why spoil a beautiful, sunny afternoon with bitterness and disappointment better left in the past? Jocelyn had come to terms with her own outrage and disappointment, but one regret lingered—that it was all over. Despite the way the season had ended, she had loved coaching the team. She had hoped to lead the WMS Wildcats for years to come, until her own daughters had moved on to high school and college, until she had accumulated an entire quilt's worth of colorful IQ T-shirts. But it was not to be.

Life wasn't fair, as the children had learned, and as Noah's untimely death had taught her all too well. Life wasn't fair, and sometimes goodness wasn't rewarded, and sometimes the wrong people won. It was a hard lesson to learn, but Jocelyn found hope in thinking of all that her daughters and their teammates had gained over the course of the year. They had learned how to bring individuals together as a team and how to find creative solutions to difficult problems. They had faced down stage fright and deadlines. They had made friends and had fun. By those criteria, that year's Imagination Quest had been an overwhelming success. By those criteria, which were far and away more important than a trophy, the Wildcats had won and the red-and-gold team had fallen short. What pride of accomplishment could those other children take in work that their parents had completed? What problem-solving skills had they nurtured that would serve them later in life? What would happen to them the next time they cheated—in school or on the playing field or on their taxes or on the job? Not all judges would be so tolerant and forgiving.

The more she considered what all of the children had truly won and lost, Jocelyn actually, remarkably, felt sorry for the red-and-gold team—and tremendously proud of the young people gathered around her, seated at picnic tables and on blankets, eating burgers and chips and celebrating a job well done.

They had won much more than they had lost, and so had she.

At the end of the day, Anisa and Niko, the team's cocaptains, called everyone together for a few parting words. They thanked their families for their support and patience throughout the year—and in one rare allusion to the tournament, they added that they were glad the adults in their lives trusted them and believed in them enough to let them do their own work. Then they presented Jocelyn with a framed team photograph, she and the children on the front steps of Grosse Pointe South High School clad in their IQ T-shirts. The children had signed the mat with messages of thanks and appreciation that touched her heart and made her laugh. Jocelyn told them it was one of the finest gifts she had ever received and that she intended to hang it in her classroom by her desk as an inspiration to other WMS students. And to their teacher, she added silently. She would never forget the lessons she too had learned that year.

The families and students applauded Jocelyn's brief speech, but when Anisa held up her hands, everyone else promptly quieted as if, unlike Jocelyn, they had known Anisa had more to say. "I think we all wish the state tournament had turned out different," she said, evoking a chorus of affirmation. "And, Mama, we know you wanted to make things right for us."

There were no words for how much Jocelyn regretted that she had been unable to fix everything.

"We thought about asking all you guys to make a petition or something and complain," Niko said, "but if there's anything we've learned this year, it's that we can solve problems ourselves."

"Or at least we can try." Anisa beckoned to her sister, and Rahma promptly darted to her side carrying a few sheets of white paper. "We've been working on a letter to send to the IQ national office. We're not just, like, complaining. We described what happened at the state tournament, and how it made us feel, and what we think they should do different next year."

"We've been passing around a rough draft for a while and now it's ready to send," said Niko. "We're all going to sign it—"

"But we want you to hear it first," Anisa finished for him.

As her daughter read the letter aloud, Jocelyn's heart swelled with pride and amazement. Their summary of the tournament fiasco was rational, objective, and accurate, but it still made their disappointment and unhappiness clear. Their solutions were reasonable, and although Jocelyn knew they were not quite the panacea the children believed them to be, they did offer the judges steps to take to help ensure that the children on each team had done the work themselves. One of their proposals—that immediately following a presentation, the judges should interview the team and have them describe how they had come up with their ideas, how they had built their equipment, and how exactly everything worked—was so simple and brilliant it was remarkable that the Imagination Quest administrators hadn't thought of it first.

When they finished, the parents applauded. Jocelyn too praised the team, but not without some misgivings. "Kids," she said hesitantly, "you do realize that this won't change anything regarding nationals, right?"

"Not for this year," said Niko. "But next year, maybe."

"Next year?"

"Well, sure," said Anisa, puzzled. "I mean, Niko, Tashia, and I won't get to participate, but maybe this'll help the younger kids. Remember what Daddy used to say about paving the way for the people who follow after us?"

Tears sprang into Jocelyn's eyes. "Yes, I remember." She took a deep breath and looked around the circle at the younger children and then their parents. "Does this mean you'll want to continue on next year?"

"Of course," exclaimed Rahma.

"If you'll coach us," said one seventh-grade boy, studying her worriedly. "You will, won't you?"

Before Jocelyn could assure him that she most definitely would, Anisa broke in. "We know you're worn out, but before you decide—well, we're going to make sure you get a vacation before the next tournament so you can rest up for it."

Tashia's aunt rose and joined the three children at the head of the circle. "We wanted to thank you for all you've done for our children, so we asked your girls what you would especially like."

"Anisa told us that you've always wanted to learn to quilt," said Niko's mother. "We found a wonderful place for you to take lessons."

They went on to describe a beautiful retreat in rural central Pennsylvania where Jocelyn could attend a weeklong quilt camp led by some of the most respected and admired teachers in the quilting community. Since she would be making quilts for children in need—something they knew she would appreciate—tuition, room, and board were complimentary, and they had all pitched in for her airfare. When they had told her fellow WMS teachers about the plan, several of her colleagues had volunteered to sub for her classes so she would not have to sacrifice her vacation days or a week's pay.

"And Grandma and Grandpa are coming to stay with us while you're gone," said Rahma, fairly bouncing up and down with excitement as she had when she was a much younger child. "We already asked them and they said yes. Do you like your present, Mama? Isn't it the best present you ever got?"

"It is," Jocelyn assured her, laughing as she embraced her daughters and smiled for everyone else. "Thank you all so very much. You don't know what this means to me."

In truth, the week at Elm Creek Quilt Camp was only the second-best present she had received that day. Knowing that the team wanted to continue despite their disappointment and that they wanted her to stay on as their coach—that was the best gift of all.

As Jocelyn quilted her Giving Quilt on the longarm machine in the ballroom of Elm Creek Manor, she thought of the generous, thoughtful people who had made her Quiltsgiving week possible and her heart overflowed with love and gratitude. Thanks to them, she was learning to quilt at last.

Soon she would be able to share what she had learned about the traditions and art of quilting with her students, shedding light upon the hard business of ordinary life woven into the fabric of their common American history.

And someday, years from now, she would make herself an Imagination Quest T-shirt quilt as a tribute to the students who had taught her so much that difficult year—invaluable, unforgettable lessons about determination, integrity, and overcoming loss with grace.

Chapter Six

Karen

Since Gretchen had chosen Karen to demonstrate how to use the longarm machine, she was the first to finish quilting her Giving Quilt top. With Gretchen's help, she removed the quilted top from the rollers and carried it back to the classroom to trim the excess batting and backing even with the pieced top. If she had been at home working upon one of her own quilts or at the String Theory Quilt Shop whipping up a store sample, she would have spent the rest of the afternoon preparing the bias binding and sewing it in place to cover the raw edges of the quilt. But since Gretchen intended to cover that topic the next morning, Karen decided to wait and keep pace with her classmates. She was confident she could finish her quilt in time for the Farewell Breakfast even without a head start, and she didn't want to look like a show-off. Instead she spent an hour or so cutting pieces for a second Giving Quilt to complete at home and donate to her local chapter of Project Linus, and then she passed the rest of the day helping classmates with the longarm. Her husband would be amused—and her coworkers, who thought she worked too hard and had practically insisted she take a vacation, would be exasperated—to see her falling into the familiar role of teacher rather than relaxing with a good book by the fire or working in solitude on a quilt for herself. "You're a natural quilt teacher," Nate would say as he had before, placing his hands on her shoulders and drawing her close for a kiss. "I'm sorry it took me so long to understand."

It was true that Nate had needed some time to learn how important quilting was to her and how sharing her love and knowledge of the art was as meaningful and fulfilling as teaching undergraduate business courses and working in the university's Department of Development had once been. It was fair to say that Nate had learned the hard way. But once he had learned, he had never forgotten the lesson, and he had become her most ardent supporter. It was Nate who had surprised her with a gift of a week at Elm Creek Quilt Camp when she was expecting their first child, and it was Nate who had encouraged her to quash her nervousness, jettison any lingering embarrassment, and return to the manor for Quiltsgiving. "You have no reason to be shy," he insisted. "So they didn't hire you. That's nothing to be ashamed of. I've been turned down for lots of jobs. It happens. You shouldn't take it personally and you shouldn't let it keep you from attending an event you know you'd enjoy."

Karen knew he was right, but her rejection from the faculty of Elm Creek Quilts still pained her from time to time—the pangs becoming sharper and more frequent since her return to the beautiful estate—and it still felt very personal.

It didn't help that since her arrival, she had discovered that out of the five finalists, she was the only one who had not eventually found a place within the circle of quilters at Elm Creek Manor.

In the winter following her ill-fated interview, she had learned that Gretchen Hartley and Maggie Flynn had joined the faculty when their photos and biographies appeared on the Elm Creek Quilts website. Reading the lengthy lists of their credentials, Karen had ruefully admitted to herself that Sylvia, Sarah, and the others had made the reasonable choice. It was not until the first day of Quiltsgiving, however, that she had learned that Anna, the Cookie Lady, had been hired as their chef. Even that wasn't too hard to accept; Anna had been so friendly and helpful with the boys as they waited in the hallway outside the parlor for their interviews that Karen couldn't begrudge her any good fortune. But to discover in a casual conversation with Maggie at the Welcome Banquet that the last remaining finalist, renowned art quilter Russell McIntyre, was frequently invited back as a visiting instructor—that was too much. That meant that the Elm Creek Quilters had found all of the finalists worthy of inclusion in their celebrated circle of quilters—all except Karen.

It was a humbling realization at a time when she didn't think she could feel any worse about her precarious position in the quilting world.

But what could she do? Leave early? Hide out in her suite, sew in solitude, and hasten away home as soon as she donated her finished Giving Quilt to Project Linus at the Farewell Breakfast?

She couldn't imagine Sylvia, Sarah, or any of the Elm Creek Quilters resorting to such cowardly measures.

Thus on her first full day of Quiltsgiving, upon waking in

her cozy suite in Elm Creek Manor, she set her injured feelings aside; fixed her thoughts upon all she stood to gain from spending an entire inspiring week among such talented, giving quilters; and resolved to do more than merely make the best of the situation.

Before long, she was very happy that she had. In a week that was passing all too swiftly, she had learned a charming new quilt pattern, she'd had an enlightening conversation with Gretchen about establishing a chapter of Project Linus through the quilt shop, and she had made some wonderful new friends. There was nothing, really, to regret. Any experience that sparked even a single new friendship was inherently good, and Quiltsgiving had blessed Karen with five—six if she counted Gretchen, and why shouldn't she? After all, they were no longer rivals. Gretchen had won the coveted post, and rightly so, and Karen had followed another path.

Helping her classmates master the longarm machine granted Karen time to get to know her new friends even better. Quilters had always shared conversation and confidences around the quilting frame, and regardless of the changes in tools and technology, the desire to share, to be heard, and to listen endured.

Michaela had signed up for the quilting session immediately after lunch, so Karen offered to help her carry her quilt top and backing from the classroom to the longarm machine nook, since lugging them even the short distance across the ballroom would be difficult on crutches. Once there, the usually eager young woman studied the machine dubiously until Karen offered to help her master the controls. Before long Michaela was cheerfully quilting away unassisted, but Karen lingered just in case she needed help removing the quilted top from the rollers, and also to keep her company.

It couldn't have been easy or comfortable for Michaela to steer the handles of the longarm while supporting her weight on the crutches, but she didn't complain, nor did the quality of her stitches suffer. "You manage quite well on those things," remarked Karen over the clatter of the machine.

"That's because I've had lots of practice," said Michaela. "Too much. This is the second time I've had a cast on my leg this year."

"You injured yourself twice?"

"Not exactly. My first time in a cast was for the injury. This time is for surgery to repair the injury."

"How exactly did you hurt your ankle?" asked Karen. "You've been a little . . . vague. We're not sure if you injured yourself or if someone hurt you."

Michaela's eyebrows rose. " 'We'? You mean everyone's been talking about me?"

"I don't know about everyone, but our circle has been, a bit. Forgive us. You haven't let many details slip, and we're curious."

Michaela laughed. "I guess I would be too in your place." Her smile faded. "The truth is, I got hurt trying out for mascot at school last spring, and if I've been unclear, it's because I'm not really sure whether it was an accident."

Karen hung on every word of the story of Michaela's ill-fated tryouts for cheerleader and mascot. The young woman's focus and determination in the pursuit of her goal impressed her, even though things hadn't worked out as Michaela had planned. If Karen had analyzed the Elm Creek Quilters as thoroughly as Michaela had studied the St. Andrew's College cheerleading squad, she might have sailed through the interview and won a place on the faculty despite her inexperience. Michaela's disappointment after being cut in the first round and her inspired decision to try out for mascot reminded Karen of her own failed attempt to join the circle of quilters at Elm Creek Manor and subsequent employment at the String Theory Quilt Shop. But Michaela had shown far more grace and courage than had Karen, who had not faced ridicule and hostility from an entire campus, just a little bemused resistance from a well-meaning husband.

"So what do you think?" Michaela asked. "You've heard everything. You know everything I know. Did they drop me on purpose or was it just a stupid, freak accident?"

"I don't know." Karen mulled it over. "Not knowing the guys involved, not witnessing it myself—any conclusion I could make would be nothing more than a guess. I'd hate to believe that they'd intentionally drop you, but even if they had, they might not have meant to hurt you. Maybe they just wanted you to lose points on the stunt so you wouldn't win."

"I thought of that too," said Michaela, and she sighed. "I know that ultimately it doesn't matter. The damage is done. I won't be mascot or cheerleader now, and without that experience on my résumé, I'll never get to be a cheerleading coach."

"You don't know that for sure," protested Karen. "Don't rule it out. Granted, this is a setback, but your chances can't be completely ruined. Another opportunity will come along, unless you give up. If this is your dream, you'll just have to find another path toward it."

Karen fell silent, struck by the echoes of the encouraging speeches Nate had given her when she was stuck in the doldrums after her rejection from Elm Creek Quilts. She had listened, and she had believed him, but five years had passed and she wasn't any closer to joining the faculty. Was she wrong to give Michaela what could turn out to be false hope?

"I know. I get it," said Michaela plaintively, oblivious to Karen's sudden uncertainty. "I don't want this to be the end of my dream. I don't want to give up, but I don't know what to do next. What am I supposed to do—wander around aimlessly until I trip over this other path?"

"Not aimlessly, but otherwise, yes," said Karen. "That's essentially what you have to do."

Michaela looked dubious, but when she declared that she intended to give it her best try, Karen didn't have the heart to caution her that she might stumble around lost for a while before a new path appeared. Nor did she warn her that sometimes even a clear route led to an unanticipated destination rather than to the threshold of a long-cherished dream.

Karen and Michaela parted ways after Michaela finished quilting her top and trimming off the excess batting and backing. Karen remained in the classroom to cut more pieces for her second Giving Quilt, and she had just finished crosscutting the last of her square pairs when Linnea and Mona appeared in the doorway. "Michaela said we might find you here," said Linnea. "She said you helped her 'huge tons' with the longarm, and we were hoping you might do the same for us."

"I'd be happy to," said Karen, setting her work aside and following them back to the longarm nook. They found Gretchen tidying up after the previous camper's session, but she gratefully accepted their offer to take a much-needed break, since Karen would be there to assist the sisters. Mindful of their limited time, they promptly set themselves to work, with Linnea evoking an elder sister's privilege to go first, something to which the less experienced Mona was more than willing to accede.

While they worked, the conversation flowed as easily with the sisters as it had with Michaela. While Linnea quilted her top, she told Karen about Mona's struggles with her precarious employment situation and her governor's crackdown on unions, and while Mona worked on hers, she described Linnea's valiant battle to keep her town's public library open. Each sister seemed to consider the other's struggle more challenging and her efforts more impressive, revealing a mutual bond of admiration and support that made Karen, an only child, wish for a sister of her own.

Mona had nearly finished quilting her top when Linnea's cell phone rang—her husband, Kevin, calling from California with apologies for interrupting her vacation. Linnea cheerfully assured him she didn't mind, but her sunny expression swiftly darkened as Kevin apparently delivered unexpected news. Mona let the longarm machine clatter to a stop, and she threw Karen an anxious look as they listened in on Linnea's end of the conversation.

"You're kidding," Linnea said after listening in shocked silence for a long moment. "They can't be serious," she said a bit later. Another lengthy silence, and then, "Do you think anyone will come? I mean, anyone other than those crackpots from Close the Book, California?" Another pause, a sharp frown, and then, "Oh, no. No. A live broadcast? If I ever had any doubts that he was a ratings whore—" She listened, nodding vigorously. "I think Alicia's right. The sight of flames and smoke rising in the air will probably harm their cause more than it will help." A short, helpless laugh. "Okay, I'll try. You have a good day too." She told him she loved him, hung up, and threw her companions a bleak, stricken, angry look.

"What's wrong?" asked Karen, alarmed.

"Did you say flames and smoke?" asked Mona. "Is the library on fire?"

Linnea shook her head grimly. "Not yet."

"Not yet?" echoed Karen. "You mean it might be later?"

"If they thought they could get away with it, I wouldn't be surprised if they tried." Linnea closed her eyes, raised her palms, and inhaled deeply to calm herself. "Sorry, but I'm just so upset about this I can't think straight. Our delightful local chapter of Close the Book, California has decided to host a get-out-the-vote book-burning party in the park by the library on the evening before the millage goes to the polls."

"A book-burning party?" said Karen, incredulous. "Is that even legal?"

"Oh, sure. They've already obtained a permit for a bonfire, and they're planning to burn their own books—not books they love and cherish, mind you, but copies of the so-called 'bad books' they'll buy especially for the occasion." Linnea shook her head. "And they have a sponsor with deep pockets. Ezra McNulty promised to match listener contributions up to fifty thousand dollars to purchase fuel for the fire. He's been on the air for days crowing about how together they'll clear out every used book store in Los Angeles County of every last copy of the books on the ALA's 'One Hundred Most Frequently Challenged' list."

"I can't believe it," said Karen.

"I can believe it, considering the parties involved," said

Mona. "Let me guess: The entire spectacle will be broadcast live over the radio?"

"You're almost right," said Linnea. "This time he's taking that three-ring circus he calls a news program to television. I guess book burnings are more entertaining in a visual medium."

Astonishment and dismay struck Karen speechless. Book burnings conjured up memories of black-and-white, grainy film images from far-off nations in the early throes of emerging fascism, a frenetic precursor of far worse violence yet to come. They were relics from an ugly, violent past, not elements of rational debate in a healthy, modern democracy. It seemed impossible to believe that anyone would consider the destruction of property to be a reasonable means of peaceful protest, or that it could contribute productively to a thoughtful discussion of contentious issues. Then again, the players involved didn't seem particularly interested in peaceful demonstrations or civil debate.

"Why would someone like Ezra McNulty want to get involved in a local millage vote that will have absolutely no impact whatsoever on his life?" Karen wondered aloud. "Never mind. I know the reason. Publicity. Higher ratings. Both of which translate into more money and attention for him and his show."

"I'm sure you're right," said Mona. "Call me cynical, but I bet he doesn't even care whether the millage passes. He'll wring as much publicity out of the situation as he can and then move on to something else the day after the vote, once the damage is done."

"If he can," said Linnea darkly. "He has a history of stirring up more trouble than he can control. Remember what happened in Indianapolis before the last presidential election?"

"Oh, my goodness, that's right," said Karen, recalling the

notorious event of a few years past. One of the vice presidential candidates, a senator and longtime proponent of strict gun-control legislation, had been scheduled to make a campaign appearance at a community college a few days after voting in favor of a Senate bill requiring more extensive background checks before firearms could be purchased. In the interim between the passage of the measure and the campus appearance, Ezra McNulty had repeatedly denounced the candidate's vote. The day before the campaign stop, McNulty mentioned a gun show taking place at the Indiana State Fairgrounds at the same time and dared the senator to show up there to explain himself. "He won't do it," McNulty predicted scathingly. "He won't do it because he's a coward. He won't do it because he knows he can't justify taking away the rights of the American people. He won't do it because he knows he'll get what he's got coming. It's just too bad we can't take the gun show to him."

Later McNulty insisted he never could have imagined that hundreds of his loyal listeners would attempt to do exactly that. Within an hour of the doors opening, attendance at the gun show swelled beyond capacity, with firearm sales—and thefts by people too impatient or incensed to wait in line to pay—soaring past all previous records. Armed, angry protestors marched from the show to the campus, where forewarned security forces blocked their way. Only a handful of marchers made it to the auditorium, where they were promptly apprehended by the Secret Service, but clashes between campus security, demonstrators, and students supporting the candidate led to several arrests, a few minor injuries, and thousands of dollars' worth of damage to college property. When the ensuing investigation shone a spotlight on McNulty's role in the melee, he repeatedly denied any responsibility and emphasized that he had specifically stated that his listeners *couldn't* take the gun show to the senator. His longtime fans rallied to support him, but his show's corporate sponsors were more mindful of sudden shifts in public opinion. When it was leaked that several wary sponsors intended to cancel their advertising, McNulty first urged his listeners to boycott them, but then, in a surprising reversal that hinted at contentious behind-the-scenes discussions with teams of lawyers, he began one morning's broadcast by praising his sponsors for their staunch loyalty and announcing that he would personally pay for the damage done to the college campus. After that, he refused to discuss the matter publicly, and the furor eventually subsided.

Either McNulty had forgotten the incident entirely or he had learned nothing from it, because he seemed oblivious to the potential disaster in the making. A bonfire—a terrible idea no matter what the instigators were burning, given Southern California's arid conditions—could easily spread from the park beside the library to the library itself, the real target of their fury.

From the worry and outrage in Linnea's eyes, Karen knew that she too was imagining the swarming crowds, the lighting of torches, the library and all its precious books engulfed.

"Has anyone thought to appeal to McNulty?" asked Karen. "Maybe if someone pointed out the possible consequences, he'd withdraw his support. Or maybe it would be worthwhile to appeal to Close the Book and ask them not to burn books, or at least to move their protest to another location."

"Vote Yes for Libraries has already tried that," said Linnea. "Close the Book flatly refused and McNulty hasn't responded at all."

"What about the city council?" asked Mona. "Surely they'd consider it prudent to revoke their bonfire permit."

"They're on that too, but so far the only official response has been a few feeble arguments about protecting citizens' rights to free speech and so forth."

"What about citizens' rights to avoid unnecessary wildfires?" countered Karen. "Close the Book could protest all they want without burning books."

"Not according to them. They insist the book burning is a crucial part of their statement. But we're not giving up. At this very moment, Kevin and Alicia—she's the president of the Friends of the Library—are drafting an emergency request to the county fire marshal to step in and revoke the bonfire permit. They don't usually intervene when an event is held on city rather than county property, but it's not unheard of."

"You're absolutely right to go over the city council's heads," declared Mona. "They were incredibly stupid to issue the permit in the first place, just as Close the Book was stupid to request one. Yes, a book burning will get them a lot of attention—"

"The announcement alone already has," Linnea broke in.

"Yes, but as a means of protest it's shortsighted and probably ineffective," said Karen. "As you told your husband, the sight of books going up in flames is just as likely to rally their opponents as it is to encourage their supporters."

"That's true." Linnea sank into a chair with a sigh. "But what good will it do us to win the millage vote if the library burns down before election day?"

Karen and Mona exchanged a look, dismayed and helpless. Linnea was absolutely right, and nothing would change that.

"It'll be okay, Linnea," said Karen. "You'll think of something.

They'll see reason and cancel the book burning, or the county will force them to, or the fire department will make sure the flames don't spread beyond the bonfire. The library won't be harmed. You'll see."

Linnea thanked her with a wan smile, but to Karen, the words of encouragement sounded empty and flat. She wished she had something more to offer.

Later, before they reunited with their other friends in the banquet hall for supper, Linnea told Mona and Karen that she had checked in with Kevin, who had reported some new developments. The county supervisor and the fire marshal were considering their request to revoke the bonfire permit, and they promised to respond within a few days. An acquaintance within the supervisor's office had confided to Kevin that the supervisor was reluctant to engender more controversy by overruling the official decision of a city council, so he intended to proceed with utmost caution and diplomacy. With their own elections approaching, officials throughout the city and county were wary of taking action that could appear politically motivated. Unless the fire marshal concluded beyond question that the book burning posed a threat to the surrounding community, it would go on as planned. Meanwhile, Close the Book, California had been informed of the challenge to their permit, and they were at that moment feverishly composing a "fire containment safety plan" to explain how they would conduct their protest safely.

"What are they going to do," Mona asked, "pass out fire extinguishers to their members?"

"Sure, why not?" said Linnea wearily. "That would work great, until someone gets the bright idea to bash a counter-protestor over the head with a fire extinguisher."

"So you think there'll be a counter-protest?" asked Karen.

"I'm certain of it," said Linnea, "even if it's only me, my husband, and my coworkers carrying signs and chanting slogans."

Linnea seemed eager to abandon the subject and join in the more cheerful conversation going on around the table, so Karen kept the rest of her questions to herself. If Kevin called with any new developments, she hoped Linnea would pass them on.

For dessert the campers were offered warm gingerbread with pear–vanilla bean sauce, and as they savored every spicy morsel, Karen and her new friends chatted about how they had spent the day. Linnea, Mona, and Michaela embarrassed Karen with excessive praise for her help with the longarm machine. "I didn't do much," she protested. "Gretchen showed us every-thing we needed to know in class this morning."

"Maybe, but it's so much easier to learn working one-on-one," said Michaela. "The Elm Creek Quilters totally should have hired you."

Karen felt a pang of regret, but she hid it behind a smile. "I find myself utterly unable to disagree."

"So," mused Jocelyn, "what are your plans for after supper?"

This time Karen's smile was genuine. "If I'm not mistaken, I think I'm going to be helping you with the longarm."

"Oh, okay," said Jocelyn, all innocence. "If you insist."

"I do," said Karen, laughing.

Later, as they worked together, Karen learned the tragic story of how Jocelyn had lost her husband, and how Jocelyn and her daughters had grieved and struggled to cope without him in the months since. Karen's heart went out to her new friend. The thought of losing Nate to some terrible, senseless accident, of their sons growing up without the father they adored, was too unbearable to contemplate.

"I don't know how you do it," Karen told her frankly. "In your place, I don't think I'd manage."

"You'd find a way," said Jocelyn somberly. "You have to. What's the alternative, especially when you have children relying on you?"

The longarm machine had fallen silent, and Jocelyn stood with her hands loosely grasping the handles, staring into space. "It's been more than a year and a half, and most of the time, I think I'm holding it together pretty well." She inhaled deeply, shakily. "And then something will happen and I'll feel the loss and heartbreak as sharply as if it happened only yesterday."

"I'm so sorry." Karen didn't know what else to say.

"It comes out of nowhere too, so unexpectedly that I can't take any measures to protect myself." Jocelyn gestured to her Giving Quilt top and then around the room as if to indicate the whole manor, perhaps the entire week of quilt camp. "Even here, a place Noah never visited, a place that holds no memories of him. The simple act of learning to quilt reminds me of the night he died."

"But—why would it?" asked Karen gently. The manor had surely witnessed its share of sorrows, but it should have been a welcoming, comforting, safe place for its guests. Why would Jocelyn find pain rather than solace there?

"I was supposed to take my first quilting lesson the day after the track meet. I had signed up for a special program about traditional handicrafts for teachers at Greenfield Village—it's a historical museum complex in Michigan—" Jocelyn gestured impatiently as if to wave off the digression. "Anyway. My suitcase was packed, the car had a full tank of gas—I was all ready to go. And then Noah—" Her voice faltered. She paused, pressed her lips together, cleared her throat, and continued. "So now, as I'm finally learning to quilt, I can't help thinking of how I was supposed to learn back then, and why I didn't."

"Oh, Jocelyn."

"I know I probably seem ridiculous—"

"Not at all."

Jocelyn uttered a small, bleak laugh. "To make matters worse, I feel guilty for not enjoying Quiltsgiving more, considering that the kids and their parents went to so much trouble to arrange this week for me . . ."

Karen's bewilderment must have been evident, because Jocelyn went on to explain how her visit to Elm Creek Manor had come to be. As she recounted her adventures with her daughters' Imagination Quest team, the distress gradually left her face and her voice became warmer, more animated, even when she described the rival team's undeserved win.

"They cheated," Karen said, astonished. "Or rather, their parents cheated. How could the officials let them get away with it?"

Jocelyn shook her head as she guided the longarm needle over her last unquilted Resolution Square block. "I guess they decided that confronting the other team wouldn't be worth the trouble."

"Since when is it appropriate to do what's easy instead of what's right?"

"Since never." Jocelyn sighed, but then she lifted her chin— in pride or perhaps defiance. "I have to say, though, I was very impressed by my team's response. They were enormously disappointed, but instead of crying or whining about the unfairness of it all, they wrote that letter recommending changes—not to benefit themselves, because it was too late for that, but to help future teams, to improve the entire program."

"That was very mature of them," said Karen. "Knowing you brought them up right has to be a better reward than any trophy."

"Of course it is, for me and the other parents," said Jocelyn, "but that's our reward. The kids were denied theirs. They deserved to go on to the national tournament, and that was taken from them."

"Something very important was taken from the team that won too."

Jocelyn nodded. "I believe that absolutely. Sooner or later, there will be consequences for the parents and students alike."

"Will you see them at next year's tournament?"

"If they sign up. We'll definitely be there. Despite everything, my team never even considered disbanding. We've already chosen a challenge. The kids aren't giving up and I didn't let them down."

"Of course you didn't," said Karen. "Were you really worried that you might?"

Jocelyn hesitated, emotions warring in her expression. "Noah left big shoes to fill."

"Who said you had to fill his shoes?" said Karen. "Wear your own shoes. They're bound to fit better. Walk your own path your own way and you'll be more likely to get to where you need to be."

Jocelyn considered that, and then she nodded thoughtfully, a slow smile dawning on her face.

So engrossed were they in their conversation that the longarm sewing machine had occasionally sat idle. With only five minutes left in her session, Jocelyn raced to put the last stitches into the outermost border, but she and Karen were still hastily removing the quilted top from the rollers when Pauline arrived, carrying her two Giving Quilt tops.

"I'm almost finished," said Jocelyn. "Sorry I ran over time."

"That's all right," said Pauline.

"Blame me," said Karen. "I distracted her with conversation."

"Oh," said Pauline a little forlornly, as if she wished she had been similarly distracted. Then she shrugged and took a seat in a folding chair against the side wall, holding her quilt tops on her lap. "Take your time. I signed up for the last session of the day so I can work as long as I want without getting in anyone else's way. Not that you're getting in my way. It doesn't matter if I start a little late."

Jocelyn thanked her, and as soon as the quilted top was free, she rolled it up loosely and carried it off to the classroom to trim away the excess batting and backing with her rotary cutter. Karen began to follow her, but Pauline's crestfallen expression brought her to an abrupt halt. "See you later?" said Karen tentatively from the doorway.

"Okay," said Pauline, forcing a smile. "Sure. Tomorrow at breakfast?"

"Sure, see you then." But Karen lingered, watching Pauline unfold the first of her two quilt tops, the one she had made in red and purple hues like Gretchen's sample.

Of all her new friends, Pauline was the one Karen felt she knew the least. They had not spent any time alone together and had never shared a solitary conversation, although of course they had chatted as part of the larger group. Karen's impression was that Pauline was perfectly nice, and funny, and impressively knowledgeable about quilting, but she also possessed a competitive streak that seemed to embarrass her and that she fought mightily to conceal. It seemed to Karen that Pauline wanted to be the best, and yet she didn't want to be the kind of person who wanted to be the best, or cared about who or what was the best. Karen, who thought a little healthy competition could bring out the best in people, suspected that Pauline saw her as her nearest rival, and considering Pauline's status as a Cherokee Rose Quilter, Karen found the assessment rather flattering. Unfortunately, however, that same regard had kept Pauline at a distance, which Karen thought was a shame.

She glanced out the doorway in time to see Jocelyn disappearing behind the partitions on the other side of the ballroom, and then she turned back to Pauline. "Do you need some—" Not help; Pauline would not need help and would not admit to needing it if she did. "Would you like some company?"

Pauline straightened, hesitating. "Um, sure. That would be nice. I mean, if you don't have anything else to do."

"I have some pieces to cut for a new quilt," Karen replied, "but I can do that while we chat."

"That would be nice," said Pauline, almost shyly.

Karen helped Pauline layer her quilt top, batting, and backing upon the rollers before leaving for a moment to retrieve her supplies from the classroom. Pauline was quilting merrily away by the time Karen returned, deftly creating intricate free-motion swirls and scallops in variegated thread. Karen was so impressed with Pauline's skill that she often paused in her work to watch. "You really know your way around a longarm," she said, coming closer for a better look.

Pauline beamed, but her hands never paused. "Thank you," she said. "I took an excellent workshop at a Cherokee Rose Quilters retreat—before I was a Cherokee Rose Quilter myself—and I practice whenever I can. I'd love to have one of these babies in my sewing room, but A, it's half again as large as the room and B, that's about two years' worth of college tuition and I think my husband's head would explode."

Karen laughed. "I think my husband would have the same reaction. I'm lucky we have one at the quilt shop."

Unexpectedly, Pauline allowed the longarm to clatter to a halt. "That must be a dream job, working in a quilt shop."

Karen wasn't quite willing to say that; her real dream job had eluded her and the quilt shop position sufficed as a second choice. "It's a lot of fun and I enjoy it. Of course, no job is perfect. You can't please every customer every day, and we've been hit hard by the downturn in the economy. But I absolutely adore my coworkers and it's inspiring to be surrounded by fabric, patterns, books, and creative people all day."

"I can only imagine." Pauline sighed wistfully. "I'm surrounded by ringing phones and tension and frantic calls from people in danger. Sometimes I think I'd like to chuck it all and just quilt all day."

"No one at the String Theory Quilt Shop gets to quilt all day," said Karen, smiling. "Don't I wish. It's a retail shop like any other. We order products and take inventory and pay the bills and pray for customers to choose us over some chain superstore or the Internet. There's a lot of stress in my line of work too—not like yours, not life-and-death stress—but it's not lying on a beach in Hawaii either."

"Quilting on a beach in Hawaii," mused Pauline. "Now that would be just about the perfect job."

"Nice work if you can get it," Karen agreed, and they laughed together.

Pauline started up the longarm again, and after she had quilted a few more blocks, Karen said hesitantly, "Do you mind if I ask you a question?"

"Be my guest."

"As wonderful as Elm Creek Manor is, I can't help wondering why you're here instead of at your own quilt guild's retreat."

Pauline grimaced, but she continued steering the longarm over the surface of her quilt top without missing a beat. "It's kind of a long story."

Karen smiled, pulled up a stool, and sat down. "I've got nothing but time."

"It's also probably kind of boring."

"I doubt that very much, but if it is, I'll let you know."

Pauline eyed her. "All right, but don't blame me if you fall asleep from sheer boredom, tumble off that stool, and break something."

With a heavy sigh, Pauline launched her tale, her expression varying from glum to hurt to embarrassed as it unfolded.

"You memorized that whole horrible, spiteful note?" Karen asked after Pauline recited Brenda's first e-mail.

Pauline nodded miserably. "Word for word. I couldn't help it. It's a sickness. If she had written something as sweet as peach cobbler with ice cream on top, I probably wouldn't remember a single line."

"I'm the same way," Karen admitted. "It seems that the hateful things people say linger in my thoughts forever while their kindness and encouragement too often drift right through."

"I wish I wasn't like that," said Pauline.

"Me too."

As Pauline continued her story, which culminated in her husband's insistence that she attend Quiltsgiving rather than deny herself the fun of a quilting retreat all because of outside influences and less-than-ideal circumstances, Karen realized that she and Pauline had more in common than she had suspected. In Pauline's place, she would have felt just as astonished and hurt by Brenda's e-mails. She would have been just as disappointed by her friends' inexplicable failure to hold Brenda to account. Karen might have made the same decision to leave the Cherokee Rose Quilters rather than risk a schism that would destroy the guild—but since she had not gone through what Pauline had, she could be empathetic without losing her objectivity.

"Have you really left the guild for good?" she asked.

Pauline shrugged. "I suppose so. They've started interviewing for my successor, so it's not like I have any choice."

"Of course you do. Maybe not for much longer, but at least until they offer your spot to someone else."

Pauline regarded her quizzically. "Do you really think I should go back?"

"I don't think you should let one crabby, self-absorbed, irresponsible, immature woman force you out of a group that has meant so much to you. You've done so much good as a part of that guild."

"Who says I'm planning to stop doing good?" Pauline gestured to her Giving Quilt tops, one nearly quilted, the other folded upon a chair nearby. "I wouldn't let Brenda or anyone else keep me from giving."

"And yet you'd let her stop you from enjoying the company of your friends?"

"That's different."

"Only in one significant way—the first involves giving to others, the second giving to yourself. Why would you deny yourself the kindness and generosity you so eagerly give to others?"

"Well, because—" Pauline hesitated, and the longarm machine fell silent. "I guess I don't know."

"Think about it," Karen urged her. "Would it really be that difficult to return, even if it meant facing Brenda again?"

Pauline studied her. "Not any more difficult than it must be to face the Elm Creek Quilters after they turned you down for a job."

"And yet here I am," said Karen. "If I can do this, surely you can go to your next guild meeting, where you know your friends in the group will be thrilled to see you."

Pauline nodded, thinking it over, and Karen hid a smile. Perhaps it wasn't fair to appeal to Pauline's competitive nature, but if it set her upon a path to greater happiness, then Karen figured she would be forgiven.

"You know something I can't figure out?" said Pauline later as they removed her first quilt from the longarm machine and began layering the second.

"What's that?"

Pauline shook her head in fond puzzlement. "How the Elm Creek Quilters could have let you get away."

Karen felt a pang of regret. "I don't think they see it that way."

"If they knew you better," said Pauline firmly, "they would."

Karen wasn't so sure. Gretchen and Maggie were talented quilters and exceptional teachers. Sylvia, Sarah, and the other original Elm Creek Quilters were surely well pleased with their choice. If they ever reflected upon Karen's effort to join the faculty, it was probably only to wonder why she had bothered to try.

Sometimes Karen wondered that herself.

Two weeks after her disastrous interview, Karen had been in the kitchen fixing the boys a snack of soy nut butter and strawberry jam sandwiches when the phone rang. Sylvia kindly and regretfully delivered the bad news Karen had expected since leaving Elm Creek Manor.

"I'm very sorry," Sylvia said.

"That's all right." Or it would have been, if Karen thrived on disappointment and rejection. "I expected as much when I couldn't find a babysitter and the interview turned into a debate on the merits of prolonged breastfeeding."

"That wasn't the reason at all," said Sylvia. "We appreciate a rousing discussion as much as anyone. We simply found that some of our other candidates had more teaching experience. Perhaps if you teach at your local quilt shop, the next time we hire, you'll be among the most qualified."

"Thank you for the suggestion," said Karen, although she doubted there would be a next time. Yet even in the depths of her disappointment, she couldn't help but find inspiration in Sylvia's parting words.

And so it happened that a week and a day after Sylvia's phone call, Karen visited the String Theory Quilt Shop in Summit Pass, a quaint village halfway between State College and Waterford. Founded by a retired physics professor and her mathematician partner, the String Theory Quilt Shop boasted a marvelous inventory of fabric, thread, notions, books, patterns, and gadgets that, in Karen's opinion, made it well worth the half-hour drive along Pennsylvania's winding rural roads. Its unique setting, a hundred-and-fifty-year-old restored carriage house on a street of quirky shops, bed-and-breakfasts, and cafés similarly converted from historic buildings, enhanced its charm. Karen had taken a few workshops in the spacious, sunny classroom they had created in the old hayloft and had come to think of the owners, Elspeth and Margot, as cordial acquaintances, if not yet friends. The shop was usually bustling with customers, but even when Karen was the only quilter browsing the aisles, Elspeth, Margot, and their single teenage part-time employee seemed constantly busy.

Karen chose a few yards of brightly colored fabrics to make matching quilts for the boys, and then, as Margot was ringing up her purchases, she impulsively asked if they were hiring. Taken aback, Margot first said that they weren't, but then she seemed to reconsider. "Maybe we could use some help around here," she said. "Colleen's going off to college in the fall, but we figured we'd manage without her somehow."

"If you decide you'd rather not do without a third pair of

hands, I'm interested," said Karen, smiling. "Full time, part time, whatever you need."

Margot promised to consult Elspeth, so Karen left her phone number and hoped for the best. A few days later, Elspeth called to invite her to join them for lunch at a cozy teahouse down the street from the shop. It was a casual, friendly meeting that felt nothing like a job interview, so Karen was pleasantly surprised when, as they lingered over their vanilla rooibos, Margot asked if she could start the following week.

Delighted, Karen immediately accepted.

Back at home, Karen, Nate, and the boys celebrated her good news with a family pizza party—but almost as soon as Karen cleared the table, she set herself to the task of making all the practical arrangements necessary for her return to the workforce. Ethan would be starting full-day kindergarten in the fall, and they managed to place Lucas in a wonderful day care program offered by the College of Health and Human Development right on the Penn State campus.

And then Karen was suddenly a working mother rather than a stay-at-home mom.

In her first year with String Theory, she worked as a clerk and assistant, replenishing stock, cutting fabric, ringing up purchases, and making sample projects for display. One of her favorite tasks was to help Margot, Elspeth, or visiting instructors as they led workshops in the hayloft classroom. She observed them carefully, noting what the students seemed to enjoy and what they didn't, which teaching strategies seemed effective and which fell short. A week shy of her first anniversary with the shop, she asked Margot and Elspeth if she might teach a foundation paper-piecing class. It was a technique she knew particularly well—in fact, even at her ill-fated interview, the Elm Creek Quilters had praised her handiwork. The success of that class led to another, and within another year, Karen had become a regular instructor, adding other courses to her repertoire and garnering praise from her employers and students alike.

In all that time, the shop weathered a stormy economic climate fairly well. The Fabric Warehouse, a crafting superstore in Waterford, was too far away to siphon off many of their customers, and although shopkeepers and restaurants all along their street noted that customers were spending less, considering their purchases more carefully, and buying online in ever-increasing numbers, String Theory's loyal quilters kept them in the black.

"We have an advantage over other brick-and-mortar shops," said Margot one afternoon as she, Elspeth, and Karen crowded into the tiny office in the back of the store to discuss their quarterly revenue projections. "People might feel perfectly comfortable buying books or appliances over the Internet after viewing a low-res photo and reading a blurb, but when it comes to fabric, quilters want to see it in person, and touch it, and compare the colors to other fabrics. That's something you can't do online."

Elspeth and Karen agreed. "No computer algorithm can equal our experience and knowledge, either," Karen added. "Even the most experienced quilters seek our opinion on matching colors or assembling blocks from time to time—and beginners rely on us even more. That kind of customer service can only happen in real life, in a real, not virtual, store."

"We need to make sure our customers are aware of that,"

said Elspeth, the most cautious of the three. "I've seen far too many perfectly lovely shops and restaurants close because they assumed everyone knew how wonderful they were, what services they offered, and everything they contributed to the community. We can't become complacent."

It was a sobering but necessary reminder. Karen knew that the teahouse where Margot and Elspeth had held her interview lunch was struggling, and the children's bookstore down the block was barely hanging on. She also understood that their remote location was a disadvantage to busy shoppers, who often had to choose convenience over rural beauty and historic charm. Customers who traveled out of their way to visit a particular favorite business usually strolled up and down the picturesque streets, window shopping, making purchases at other shops, reading the history of the buildings off brass placards affixed to their brick or stone walls, and enjoying a bite to eat or a cup of coffee before heading home. If any one of those businesses were to close, their customers would no longer make the drive to Summit Pass, and those lucrative, impromptu visits would inevitably decline.

They were all in this together, Karen realized. Just as one empty storefront hurt its neighboring shops, one thriving business would help others to prosper. None of them could match the low prices offered by online retailers that sometimes didn't have to collect sales tax and received huge wholesale discounts due to their bulk orders, but the small business owners of Summit Pass could offer a better, more engaging, more enjoyable shopping experience, especially if they worked together.

Karen spent every spare moment pondering the matter. She brainstormed with Elspeth and Margot and hashed out ideas with Nate as they lingered at the supper table after the boys finished eating and ran off to play. When she was confident that she had devised a sound plan, she made arrangements with the owner of the Wise Owl Teahouse and invited the owners of all the independent, small businesses on their street to a meeting where they could discuss their collective fate.

It was a sunny, bright, auspicious October afternoon when nearly three-quarters of the invited guests crowded into the teahouse to hear Karen's proposal that they band together for mutual support. The mission of her proposed new organization, Explore Summit Pass, would be to sustain the village's economic viability by educating residents and visitors about the importance of supporting local small businesses. "They need to know it's not merely for our sake," Karen said. "One very important reason I doubt most shoppers consider is that their sales tax provides important revenues for our schools, fire department, police force, emergency medical assistance, snowplows— services we all use, or at least ones we want around in case we need them someday."

As nearly everyone nodded in agreement, the shopkeepers, restaurateurs, baristas, and others chimed in with other important reasons: Shopping local created local jobs. It helped ensure better, more knowledgeable, more personal customer service. It was better for the environment, because local products required less travel time and thereby reduced carbon emissions. It invested in the long-term stability of the community, since local business owners typically lived near their businesses and cared about the region's future. It increased consumer choices, promoting innovation, competition, and lower prices over the long term. It promoted entrepreneurship, helping local residents move up the economic ladder. It increased support to local non-profits, since local businesses were more inclined than huge chains with administrative offices hundreds of miles away to give to community organizations and charities.

So many sensible, pragmatic, and inspiring ideas were thrown out that Karen, newly energized, had to scramble to write them all down. "This is exactly what we need our customers to know," she declared. "They may believe they're merely shopping or dining out or enjoying a relaxing getaway when they patronize one of our businesses, but they're also investing in the future of their community."

In addition to educating the public about the benefits of shopping local, Karen explained that they also needed to introduce them to the other shops and services just down the block from their favorites. To encourage loyal customers of one establishment to consider trying a neighboring business, they should actively promote one another and cohost special events designed to draw shoppers to the village. "The Wise Owl Teahouse could set up a tea table in the String Theory Quilt Shop, arranging teahouse menus and business cards there too," she suggested. "We'll benefit from having refreshments for our customers, and the samples will encourage our customers to make their way down the block to the Wise Owl. We can display some of our sample quilts on the walls of the Oasis Day Spa and Salon. Oasis staff and customers will enjoy an ongoing art exhibit, regularly updated, and their clients may be tempted to cross the street and see what else we have to offer."

"We could produce a street map marking all the participating businesses," suggested the owner of the Centerpiece Art Gallery. "We can divide up the printing costs. I know an exceptionally talented artist who might be convinced to design something absolutely gorgeous for us in exchange for a nice lunch at the Summit Pass Café and a few books from Wild Things for his nieces."

"Throw in a citrus–green tea detox facial from Oasis and you've got a deal," said the art gallery owner's partner, who everyone had already guessed was the artist he'd had in mind.

"The back of the map should list all the reasons to shop local we've mentioned here today," said the proprietor of the Woodpoppy Inn. "And any more we can possibly think of."

As everyone chimed in their agreement, Karen threw Margot and Elspeth a look of triumph. Explore Summit Pass was officially under way.

The map was, as promised, a work of art suitable for framing. Even before the boxes of maps were delivered from the printer, individual businesses began arranging cross-promotions among themselves—a tea party at the Wise Owl to celebrate a bestselling author's appearance at Wild Things Children's Bookshop, discounts on massages at Oasis for guests of the Woodpoppy Inn. A few days before Thanksgiving, Karen, as the de facto leader of Explore Summit Pass, held a press conference on the village green to announce the organization's official launch and to urge neighbors far and near to buy local for the holidays. To her delight—and immeasurable relief—Black Friday in Summit Pass turned out a deeper shade of midnight than it had been in years. Sales at the String Theory Quilt Shop were up; classes were at full enrollment. Help Wanted signs appeared in storefronts up and down the street, and everywhere the air hummed with a new spirit of cooperation and optimism.

In January, when the last receipts were counted, nearly

every business that had joined Explore Summit Pass reported dramatic improvements in holiday profits compared to the previous year. Even those merchants who had not come aboard benefited, but not as much as they might have had they been more involved. By spring, it was necessary to order a reprint of the village map—revised to include several shops whose initial skepticism had been quelled by the organization's quick success. A third printing was ordered just in time for the height of the summer tourism season, and as summer waned and the holidays approached again, Karen organized the creation of a special coupon book and punch card, which gave shoppers the opportunity to earn Summit Pass Points and win prizes for shopping at a variety of local businesses.

Month after month, the shops and restaurants of Summit Pass reported stable profits despite the rocky economy. Elspeth and Margot often told Karen that hiring her was the best decision they had ever made in the history of the String Theory Quilt Shop. Nate was tremendously proud of her, and once, abashed, he apologized for forgetting that he had married a genius. And above and beyond her success with Explore Summit Pass, Karen enjoyed every hour she worked at the quilt shop, whether she was teaching, sorting bolts of fabric, or ringing up purchases on the cash register.

And yet, every so often, she felt a small, almost imperceptible twinge of wistfulness. A customer would remark that she was purchasing supplies for a week at Elm Creek Quilt Camp, or Karen would read a profile of an Elm Creek Quilter in a quilting magazine, and she would feel the sad sting of rejection anew. She would recall each painful, embarrassing moment of her disastrous interview and wonder if anything she could have said or done would have made a difference. She would imagine how different her life might have been if only Nate had come home from work to watch the boys as he had promised. Then she would look around the quilt shop, shake off her melancholy, and remind herself that things had turned out rather well for her. She was necessary and appreciated, and she had made a difference not only for String Theory, but also for businesses throughout Summit Pass. She could not regret anything that had led her to that point. She was happy. Her friends, coworkers, and family were happy.

She had no regrets—only rare, ephemeral misgivings that swiftly dispersed.

The astonishing success of Explore Summit Pass eventually leveled off. As the economy worsened, and as Internet commerce surged, a few shops on the street closed their doors after melancholy going-out-of-business sales. Other storekeepers chose retirement over the endless uphill slog to remain viable. The String Theory Quilt Shop suffered a minor dip in sales as new online quilting retailers like ifabricshop.com and virtualmaterial.biz popped up almost weekly, but as Margot reminded them whenever the outlook turned bleak, certain bulwarks protected them against the threat of competition from the Internet: Quilting classes were much more fun in person, and quilters still preferred to see fabric with their own eyes in natural light, to touch it and evaluate the drape and quality before they purchased a single yard. "They can't do that with a grainy image on a computer screen," Margot would say confidently, even as book and pattern sales dwindled.

In mid-October, at the same time Karen was debating whether to attend Quiltsgiving, she began to notice a strange trend in the shop. Quilters would browse through the aisles of fabric, compare one bolt to another, take what appeared to be detailed notes as if they were planning complex projects, but then leave without purchasing so much as a spool of thread. Within weeks, Elspeth worriedly reported an unexpected decline in fabric sales. Karen did not correlate the two curious occurrences until one morning at breakfast when she happened to mention both. "What exactly are all these scribbling quilters writing down?" asked Nate, immediately wary.

"I'm not sure," Karen replied.

"Maybe you should find out."

Her suspicions heightened, Karen became more observant. She soon realized that the browsers who spent hours examining fabric and not a single minute buying any were writing down information from the ends of the bolt cardboards—the manufacturer, the designer, the name of the collection, and the SKU number. Having gathered those details, they could purchase the fabric at any retailer, be it another small, independent shop like their own, a big box chain store such as Fabric Warehouse in Waterford, or an online shop anywhere in the world.

"They're using our shop as a showroom," said Margot when Karen shared her jarring suspicions. "I can't believe the audacity. Have they no consciences? To make use of our services, our products, and then to shop somewhere else—it's positively unethical."

"It was inevitable," said Elspeth grimly. "The question is, what can we do about it? What they're doing is morally wrong but it's not illegal, and we can't prove anything anyway. If we accuse someone of using our inventory to help them make purchases elsewhere, they'll simply say they were only browsing but didn't find what they wanted. What exactly could we do to stop this?"

Neither Karen nor Margot had a good answer for her.

The following week, they raised their concerns at the bi-monthly meeting of Explore Summit Pass, only to learn that other shopkeepers had observed the same startling practice at their stores. The manager of Wild Things Children's Bookshop conceded that it had been going on at their store for years, and the customers were becoming bolder and less embarrassed with each passing week. "They don't bother to discreetly write down authors and titles on the backs of old receipts anymore," he said, shaking his head in disgust. "They just pull out their cell phones and snap a photo or scan a bar code."

"That's shameful," declared the owner of the Wood-poppy Inn.

"It's more than that," said the bookstore manager flatly. "The challenge used to be getting customers into the store. Now even that's not enough. If more and more people go to the trouble to come into the store and still buy online—well, that could be the last word in the final chapter of our history."

The admission sent a chill through the room. Wild Things had been a cornerstone of Summit Pass for more than fifty years. If parents no longer brought their children to the village, if neighbors no longer came to buy charming board books for expectant friends and stayed for lunch, if grandparents and aunts and uncles no longer made their annual pilgrimages to satisfy eager younger readers' birthday wishes, if publishers no longer sent popular children's authors to town on their publicity tours—every business in Summit Pass would suffer.

"We still have our quilt classes," Margot said after the

meeting broke up and she, Karen, and Elspeth walked somberly down the block to their cherished quilt shop. "We still have better customer service than any computer algorithm could ever attempt to imitate. Our loyal customers won't let us down."

"Of course they won't," said Karen, but Elspeth remained silent.

Perhaps even then she suspected the worst was yet to come, although none of them could have imagined the form it would take.

Although it seemed like a terribly inconvenient time to go on vacation, Margot, Elspeth, and Nate joined forces to convince Karen that she needed and deserved a respite, so on the last possible day, she made her reservation for Quiltsgiving and began looking forward to her return to Elm Creek Manor with a dizzying mixture of excitement and apprehension. On the Sunday before Thanksgiving, a week before her trip, Karen had woken early to fix Nate and the boys blueberry pancakes for breakfast when she glanced at her cell phone and discovered that Elspeth had called and left a message at five o'clock. She never phoned Karen at home so early, especially not on her day off.

"Please come in as soon as you can," Elspeth said in her voice mail. "They've really gone too far this time. We need to strategize."

They? Who were they, and what had they done? Quickly Karen called the shop, but the phone rang and rang and went unanswered. She left a message promising to be in by nine, and then she scrambled to get her family fed and herself showered and dressed. Worried, Nate kissed her good-bye and asked her to call him as soon as she found out what was going on.

She drove as quickly as she dared, and when she finally arrived at the quilt shop, she found Margot and Elspeth huddled in the back office, eyes fixed upon the computer screen, their expressions a mixture of anger and worry.

"What's going on?" Karen asked breathlessly, unwinding her scarf and slipping out of her coat.

"iFabricShop has declared war on brick-and-mortar quilt stores," said Elspeth grimly. "Overnight they've gone from being a competitor to being an outright predator."

Bewildered, Karen turned to Margot and was alarmed to find the more optimistic of her two employers nodding. "What exactly have they done?"

They had designed a price-check-and-purchase smartphone application, the two women explained, sometimes interrupting each other in their haste to get the story out. Users could scan the bar code on the end of a bolt of fabric by snapping a photo. The image would automatically be sent to the iFabricShop database, which would within moments respond with all the relevant information about the fabric as well as iFabricShop's price per yard. With the touch of a few keys, the user could then purchase yardage from the website via their existing user account.

"We don't pay for inventory, rent, utilities, and wages so that iFabricShop can use us as a showroom," said Elspeth, pushing back her chair and pacing around the cramped office. "It's wrong. It's not just comparison shopping. It's using our shop, our products, and our people without investing a single cent into any of it."

"It's unconscionable," said Karen, faint from disbelief.

"It gets worse," said Margot, a shocking admission from their resident optimist. "To kick off the holiday shopping season in a big way, they're offering five dollars off any purchases made through the new app."

"It's bad enough that we can't compete with them on price," said Elspeth. "How can we compete when they use us to acquire all the benefits of a brick-and-mortar store without any of the expenses?"

"And when they bribe our potential customers to aid and abet them," added Margot, her voice rising in anger.

"We'll have to circumvent them somehow." Karen thought quickly. "Can we ask people not to use their cell phones in the store?"

"Not without alienating them," said Elspeth.

"Can we cover up the bar codes?"

Elspeth and Margot exchanged a look. "That might work," said Margot, nodding. "They can still write down the information, but at least we're making it a little more difficult for iFabricShop to steal our customers."

Karen didn't think their usual, loyal customers would want any part of iFabricShop's scheme. It was more likely that iFabricShop's usual customers would visit String Theory for the first time, browse, scan bar codes, make their online purchases, and leave. The shop might become more crowded than usual, but as threatening as the new app seemed to be, String Theory might not suffer any loss of sales.

She would have said so aloud, except that her employers seemed in no mood to hear about a possible silver lining in what looked like an entirely overcast sky. Margot rummaged through a desk drawer searching for thick black markers to obscure the bar codes, while Elspeth produced a box of address labels from a cabinet. The three spent the rest of the morning racing to conceal bar codes beneath adhesive labels or opaque black ink, pausing only to open the shop at noon. Whenever customers were present, they labored more discreetly, unwilling to pique their interest and give iFabricShop free advertising for their app.

If any of their customers used the application in the shop that day, Karen, Margot, and Elspeth were too busy and preoccupied to notice.

There were more than a thousand bolts of fabric on the shelves of String Theory, and with all of their other Black Friday preparations still needing attention, they did not finish defending themselves against iFabricShop until Wednesday afternoon, minutes before they were scheduled to close early for the Thanksgiving holiday. They kept their tradition of joining several other local merchants at the Summit Pass Café for a pre-holiday-shopping-season lunch, but the mood was far from celebratory. Earlier that day, Karen had observed several unfamiliar browsers roaming the aisles with their cell phones in hand, and later Margot had discovered crumpled adhesive labels littering the floor beneath bolts of fabric whose bar codes had been newly exposed.

Evidently, their precautions were not enough.

Karen tried to put the unsettling developments out of her mind as she celebrated Thanksgiving, playing host to her mother and her in-laws. The next day, Black Friday, Nate kept everyone entertained and well-fed with leftovers as Karen worked a busy shift at the quilt shop. On Saturday, sales were as brisk as in previous years, but Karen had arranged to leave at noon so she could prepare for her trip to Elm Creek Manor.

"This is the worst possible time for me to be away," she said, lingering behind the register five minutes after Nate and the others had expected her home. "I should cancel my trip."

"You most certainly should not," called Margot from the

cutting table, where customers waited in a line three deep. "You deserve a vacation. You'll come back rested, refreshed, and ready, and we'll have plenty of work waiting for you, never fear. Now go, before Nate calls asking where you are."

With a sigh, Karen left the register and went to retrieve her coat and purse from the office, where she found Elspeth working at the computer. Elspeth glanced up and smiled fondly when Karen entered, but she was obviously exhausted. "Heading out?"

"I'd better. I promised Nate I'd be home for one last family dinner before our relatives leave, and after that, I have to finish packing."

Elspeth's smile deepened. "I don't think you ever leave work on time. You should."

"You and Margot never do."

"Hmm. You have me there." Elspeth's gaze shifted, became distant. "Years ago, we took early retirement from the university so we could open this lovely shop, our home away from home. We expected to work here until we retired for good, and recently—well, I suppose it won't surprise you if I confess we were hoping you would eventually take it over."

In truth, the confession surprised Karen utterly. "I'm honored that you'd place so much trust in me."

"You've earned it. I only wish we could reward you accordingly. You deserve so much more than a week's vacation." Elspeth rose from her chair and gave Karen a hug that seemed somehow both affectionate and sorrowful. Then Elspeth released her, took a step back, and hesitated. "You once mentioned that you were a finalist for a faculty position at Elm Creek Quilts a few years ago, but they didn't offer you the job because you lacked teaching experience."

"That's what they told me," said Karen. "I'd taught introductory business courses when I was an MBA student at the University of Nebraska, but I'd never taught quilting."

Elspeth regarded her steadily. "I think it would be a good idea if you let the Elm Creek Quilters know that you've filled in that gap in your credentials."

"Why?" Karen studied her, worry stirring. "Why should I do that?"

"I think perhaps you need to—" Elspeth shrugged and shook her head, and if Karen didn't know better, she would have thought she spotted tears glistening in her eyes. "Just be sure to let them know how qualified you are. You're a wonderful quilting teacher. They ought to know that."

Speechless, Karen nodded.

On the long drive home, Karen mulled over Elspeth's words and came to one unmistakable conclusion: Elspeth believed that this time, the shop wouldn't survive. She wanted Karen to keep her eyes open for a lifeboat rather than go down with the ship alongside her and Margot.

Karen blinked back tears and swallowed hard as she pulled the car into the garage.

She couldn't bear the thought of String Theory going under. After all she had learned there, the friendships she had forged, the students she had inspired with her passion for quilting—the end couldn't have come so soon. There had to be a way to keep the shop open, despite unfair competition and a lackluster economy. They had all worked too hard to revitalize Summit Pass for the place Karen loved best to shut its doors.

But what if Elspeth was trying to tell her that it was already too late?

It could not be too late, Karen told herself firmly as she helped Pauline remove her second quilt from the longarm frame. Together they rolled up the quilts and carried them back to the classroom, where they draped them over the table where Pauline usually sat.

"Are you all right?" Pauline queried as they climbed the grand oak staircase on their way to bed. It was nearly midnight, and although a few sewing machines still hummed industriously in the ballroom and a few campers remained chatting by the fireplace, the rest of the manor had fallen into a quiet and restful slumber.

"Just tired," Karen replied. "Preoccupied with thoughts of home."

They reached the landing, and as they parted ways, Pauline said, "Whatever it is, you'll work it out. I have faith in you."

Karen smiled. "You've only just met me."

"Even so. I know." Impulsively, Pauline hugged her. "Thanks for your help. Now, get some sleep. You'll feel better in the morning."

Karen hoped she was right.

As it turned out, Pauline was right, at least a little.

Margot and Elspeth had forbidden Karen to call the shop during her vacation, so upon waking, instead of picking up her phone, she stared up at the ceiling and wondered what the day would bring to all those she loved. Would more new visitors prowl the aisles, selecting fabrics to purchase from iFabricShop? Would Elspeth examine their accounts and find them dangerously close to empty? Would Margot believe that everything would be fine, even as they hung Going Out of Business signs in the window?

Not if Karen had anything to say about it.

She waited until she was fairly sure the boys would be awake before calling home. Nate sounded cheerful but harried, so she gave them all her love and bade them good-bye so he could get the boys to school and head off to campus. She showered and dressed and met her friends for breakfast—Belgian waffles with real whipped cream and cranberry-apple compote, sheer heaven.

And then she and the other students gathered in the classroom for their final Giving Quilt lesson.

After confirming that everyone in the class had finished quilting her Giving Quilt top—or tops, in Pauline's case—Gretchen walked them through the process of creating the binding. First she instructed them to cut a large square of the same fabric they had used for their outer border. "Unless you want a contrasting binding," she added after giving them the proper measurements and borrowing a piece of fabric from Pauline, who had volunteered one of her quilts for the demonstration. "That's perfectly fine too. It's an artistic choice you're each free to make on your own." She then demonstrated how to cut the square in half diagonally from corner to corner to make two identical triangles, which she sewed together to form an offset tube. Karen had made so many bindings in her brief, precious career at String Theory that she could whip one up almost without measuring, and she easily kept pace with Gretchen as she showed how to cut the asymmetrical tube into a long, narrow, bias binding strip.

Moving to an ironing station, Gretchen folded the long binding strip in half, wrong sides facing inward, and pressed it to fix the crease. "Doubling over the strip increases its durability," she explained. "That's important because the edges of a quilt—especially a quilt made for a child—experience so much wear and tear."

She then carried the binding to the front sewing machine, where one of Pauline's quilts waited, and as the students watched in the overhead mirror, she sewed the binding strip to the top of the quilt all around the edges, mitering the binding at the corners. Eagerly the students followed suit, invigorated by the sense that they were nearly finished, that they had accomplished so much that nothing short of a total power outage could prevent them from meeting their deadline.

Gretchen strolled through the classroom, lending a helping hand where needed, offering praise everywhere. When every student had completed the step, she returned to the front of the room. "Now you have a choice to finish binding your quilt either by hand or by machine," she said. "I'll teach you both methods, and you can use the one you like best."

The first step was the same for both styles, she explained, showing them how to fold the binding strip over the raw edges of the quilt and pin it in place. "If you prefer to sew by hand," she continued, "you can pin a few inches of binding at a time, blind-stitch or whipstitch the binding to the back of the quilt, and move the pins ahead of you as you go along." She taught them both stitches, using thread that matched the binding fabric. Her needle moved slowly and meticulously through the bias strip and quilt backing without poking through to the top, and when she drew the thread all the way through, the binding lay flat and smooth against the quilt backing, the stitches nearly invisible.

"I personally prefer to sew my bindings to the back of the quilt by hand." Gretchen sewed a few more inches before tying a knot, trimming off the trailing threads, and poking her needle into a pincushion. "If time is of the essence, however, you can also complete the binding by machine."

Taking a full box of pins from her basket, Gretchen folded the bias strip over the raw edges of the quilt the entire length of one side and pinned them in place, mitering the strip when she reached the corner. "You should pin the binding in place on all four sides," she said. "I'm doing only one because this is only a demonstration, and I think Pauline would like to finish her quilt herself."

"No, that's okay," said Pauline. "Feel free to do as much as you like. For demonstration purposes, of course. Not because I'm lazy."

Gretchen laughed along with the rest of the class as she slipped the edge of the quilt beneath the presser foot of her sewing machine. She aligned the needle with the "ditch" between the quilt top and the seam where the bias strip was attached to the front of the quilt, and sewed down the entire length of the quilt, removing the pins before they went beneath the needle. When she reached the corner, she backstitched, tied off the thread, and removed the quilt from the sewing machine. "If you've prepared your binding, pinned, and sewed properly," she said, showing them the back of the quilt, "you'll find that you've sewed through all of the layers and caught the edge of the binding on the back. If you've missed any small sections— and we've all made that mistake at one time or another—you can simply repin and resew those places."

A murmur of excitement passed through the classroom, making Karen suspect that the binding-by-machine technique was new to even the more experienced quilters present. Several of her classmates were obviously eager to give it a try, judging by how quickly they dug into their tote bags and sewing baskets for their pins. Others, including Jocelyn, took out needles for hand sewing and carefully chose threads that best matched their bias strip fabric. The class was already dividing, Gretchen noted wistfully, an early herald of the end of Quiltsgiving, when they would all go their separate ways.

Like Gretchen, Karen too preferred to sew her bindings by hand, but instead of joining Jocelyn's group around the back table, she carried her Giving Quilt to the seat in the front row beside Pauline, smiling at her new friend as she sat down and got to work.

She would finish binding her quilt more quickly if she used the sewing machine, and that would give her more time to help her classmates.

She couldn't fix everything wrong in the world—for that matter, she could barely keep her own life sorted out—but she would help where she could, knowing that every stitch made a difference.

Chapter Seven

🌱

The Giving Quilters

On Saturday morning, Sylvia, Sarah, Maggie, and Gretchen woke early to prepare a special Farewell Breakfast for their guests, choosing one of their favorite menus from the recipe binder Anna had compiled for them before she moved away. The other Elm Creek Quilters arrived in time to help arrange the buffet table with platters of eggs baked in ham cups, raspberry-mocha crêpes, blintzes topped with smoked salmon and crème fraiche, Greek yogurt parfaits with almonds and dried cherries, whole wheat sunflower-seed bread, maple-cured bacon, and broiled grapefruit with vanilla-ginger sauce, as well as carafes of coffee, tea, and a variety of juices. The Quiltsgiving campers seemed to savor every bite and every last precious moment spent in the company of new friends.

After breakfast, Sylvia invited everyone to accompany her to the ballroom, where they had spent so many pleasant, industrious hours together. They gathered around the fireplace for another Elm Creek Quilts tradition, show-and-tell. Their mood was quiet and nostalgic, and Sylvia could read their thoughts on their faces: They missed their families back home, but Quilts-giving had fulfilled their fondest wishes and exceeded every ex-pectation, and they couldn't bear to see the week come to an end. They were surely wondering whether they would ever enjoy another time such as this, another week full of perfect mo-ments. Sylvia hoped they understood that they could return next Quiltsgiving, next summer, and every year thereafter if they wished, to find inspiration, respite, and opportunities for giving within the strong, gray stone walls of Elm Creek Manor.

After everyone settled down before the crackling fire, each quilter displayed the quilts she had made for Project Linus and shared her favorite memory of Quiltsgiving. Even their newest quilters proudly showed off the Giving Quilts they had created in Gretchen's class and received well-deserved praise and en-couragement. The stories each quilter shared of the moments she would cherish when their week together was but a memory sent the campers into gales of laughter and sometimes made them blink away tears.

"My favorite memory is reuniting with my sister, of course," said Linnea after she held up a perfectly lovely Giving Quilt made in shades of blue, yellow, and very light cream, as well as a Girl's Joy quilt in pretty pink-and-green florals.

"Mine too," her sister Mona chimed in, showing off a Giving Quilt in adorable pastels—her very first quilt, if Sylvia was not mistaken, and a fine one at that.

Next the youngest quilter in the circle, the pretty blond student named Michaela, held up a Giving Quilt made in red, black, and white, which seemed to be her favorite color combination judging by her apparel and luggage. "My favorite part of this week, in addition to sewing quilts for the kids and making new friends, was starting my Giving Journal," Michaela said. "I don't think I've given enough thought to how I give to others throughout the day and how grateful I am for the people in my life. I've been keeping the journal for only a few days, but it's already encouraged me to be more aware. I'm going to make it a lifelong habit."

Sylvia caught Gretchen's eye and gave her an approving nod. The Giving Journals were Gretchen's idea, and they had caught on so well that Sylvia had considered making one of her own. Perhaps she should not wait until next Quiltsgiving to begin.

Pauline, the dark-haired quilter from Georgia, held up two beautiful quilts she had made in Gretchen's class. "I fell far short of my goal of five quilts for the week, but I'm very happy with these two," she said. "As for my favorite memory of Quiltsgiving, I'm going to copy Michaela"—the two exchanged a look and a laugh as if sharing an inside joke—"and say that making new friends is right up there. I also want to especially single out a particularly enlightening conversation I had with my new friend Karen."

Sylvia gave Sarah a significant look across the circle, and Sarah returned a thoughtful nod. Throughout the week, they had overheard campers praising Karen's helpfulness and generosity. The Elm Creek Quilters had compared notes as they prepared breakfast that morning, and all had agreed that Sylvia should speak with her alone before she departed. Pauline's remark only strengthened Sylvia's conviction that she and Karen ought to have a little chat.

Karen herself spoke next. "I'm very glad I returned to Elm Creek Manor to celebrate Quiltsgiving. I didn't realize how much I needed a getaway. Now I feel rested, refreshed, and ready to go home and face the challenges awaiting me there." She held up her Giving Quilt, a delightful, scrappy confection of primary colors. "As for my favorite memory, it has to be getting to know so many of you as we worked together. It reminded me anew of how much I love teaching, and collaborating, and spending time in the company of creative people working together for a common purpose. We can do so much more together than we can alone."

All around the circle, her companions nodded, some regarding her thoughtfully, others turning their gazes inward, as if contemplating challenges in their own lives.

"This is my first quilt," Jocelyn began, holding up a lovely Giving Quilt pieced from blue, orange, and light tan reproduction fabrics. "I have so many wonderful memories of this week that it's almost impossible to single out one. For me, what's more important than memories are the other things I'll take home with me—new friendships and lessons learned."

Sylvia knew from the warmth in Jocelyn's voice that she meant something even more significant than what she had learned in Gretchen's quilting classes.

As each quilter took her turn displaying her handiwork and sharing her memories, Sylvia and the Elm Creek Quilters looked on proudly from outside the circle, honored by the guiding roles they had played in each woman's journey.

After the last quilter had spoken, the Elm Creek Quilters gathered up the more than thirty quilts their guests had made that week. "On behalf of Project Linus, please accept my heartfelt thanks for your donations," said Gretchen, smiling at everyone in the circle. "I promise you, all of your quilts will find loving homes."

"And on behalf of all the Elm Creek Quilters, I thank each and every one of you for joining us for Quiltsgiving," Sylvia added. "I trust that you'll continue to experience the joys of giving in this holiday season and throughout the New Year—and I hope you'll visit us again soon."

With those closing words, a hush fell over the circle, and someone sighed. Every quilter had taken her turn to share her handiwork and her memories. Quiltsgiving was over, and it was time to say good-bye.

As the campers reluctantly rose from their chairs and left the fireside, Sylvia approached Karen and touched her on the arm. "I beg your pardon, dear," she said. "May I have a word?"

When Karen nodded, Sylvia took her aside and waited until the other campers had moved out of earshot. "I understand that since we last met, you've taken a job at a quilt shop."

"That's right," Karen replied, visibly surprised that Sylvia knew. "I've been working at the String Theory Quilt Shop in Summit Pass for several years now."

"Oh, yes, I know the place. Such a charming little town. Have you ever been to the Wise Owl Teahouse?"

Karen smiled. "Many times. There's a table by the window I think of as my very own. I have you to thank for my new career, you know."

"Is that so?"

"Don't you remember? You explained that the reason I wasn't hired here was that I didn't have any experience teaching quilting." Suddenly Karen looked pained. "Unless that was just a polite excuse."

"No, no, dear, of course not," Sylvia assured her, patting her on the arm. "That was the real reason. Your understanding of the spirit of Elm Creek Quilts surpassed that of all our other candidates. I certainly don't mean this as any slight against the ladies we did hire, but if you had taught even a single quilting class, you would have been at the top of my list. Am I correct to assume that you've acquired teaching experience since you've been working at String Theory?"

"Yes," said Karen, a strange hesitancy in her voice. "I teach quite a lot, actually, and I love it."

"I wonder, then, if you'd be interested in providing me with an updated résumé?" When Karen's eyes went wide, Sylvia continued, "Do you remember Bonnie Markham? She's a founding Elm Creek Quilter, and she was present at your interview."

"Yes, I remember her. Short, dark hair, loved folk art and homespuns?"

Sylvia nodded. "That's our Bonnie. A few years ago she helped launch a new quilters' retreat on Maui, and since then, she's been spending her winters teaching at Aloha Quilt Camp in Lahaina."

"How wonderful," said Karen. "Wait until I tell Pauline that quilting on the beach isn't just a dream job but a viable career option."

"I beg your pardon?"

"It's a long story. Never mind."

"If you say so," Sylvia said with a laugh. "Well, along the way Bonnie fell in love with a perfectly wonderful Hawaiian gentleman. They're going to be married next month, and after that, she plans to live on Maui year round rather than returning to teach for us in the spring and summer."

"I suppose you can hardly blame her," said Karen. "Pennsylvania is lovely, and Elm Creek Manor is especially so, but Hawaii is—well, Hawaii."

"It is difficult to compete with paradise," Sylvia agreed, "especially when it's your sweetheart's childhood home. We'll miss Bonnie terribly. Her absence leaves an empty place in our hearts—and on our faculty. I don't suppose you'd be interested in giving us another try?"

Karen stared at her for a long, silent moment. "Did someone put you up to this?"

"Goodness, no."

"I don't mean as a joke. I mean, did someone ask you to offer me a job?"

"Of course not. Who would do such a thing?"

Instead of answering, Karen shook her head. "I—I'm thrilled and flattered—and I admit, a little stunned—"

"More than a little, it would seem," said Sylvia, amused. "But do send me an updated résumé when you get home, won't you, dear? My friends and I are very interested in what you've accomplished since your previous visit to Elm Creek Manor. We do hope to welcome you—and your sons—back soon."

Karen nodded, speechless.

Sylvia thanked her and patted her arm again for good measure, hoping she hadn't dumbfounded the younger woman so much that it would be unsafe for her to drive home.

The ballroom had all but emptied by then, as the campers returned to their suites to finish packing and to bid their newfound friends sad good-byes. They carried suitcases and tote bags downstairs, Sarah collected room keys, and Matt loaded luggage into the Elm Creek Quilts minivan for the first shuttle ride to the bus station and airport. Sylvia made sure to bid everyone a fond farewell and to thank them for coming. The twins joined her, when they weren't busy playing, and Sylvia saw James give Linnea a picture he had drawn of a library with towers of books piled up to the ceiling. Linnea thanked him and assured him she would hang it in a place of honor above her desk in the library where she worked.

Gradually the upstairs halls fell silent, the back parking lot emptied.

The Elm Creek Quilters collected linens, emptied trash, discovered forgotten items under beds or in drawers. They broke for a simple lunch of soup and sandwiches, which they enjoyed in the cozy warmth of the kitchen, reminiscing about the week and Quiltsgivings past, sharing amusing stories about their favorite campers and unexpected mishaps. Afterward, they resumed their work until the manor was restored to order, closed for the season until quilt camp resumed in the spring.

Weary but satisfied with a job well done, the Elm Creek Quilters returned cleaning supplies to storage closets and washed the dust from their hands and faces, and congratulated one another on another successful Quiltsgiving come and gone.

And then they returned one last time to the ballroom to admire the quilts their guests had made that week—charming and whimsical, soft and bright, warm and comforting— precious gifts from the heart, one and all.

·   ·   ·

The moment Pauline arrived in baggage claim, Ray swept her up in a bear hug. "I missed you so much, sugar."

"I missed you too," she said, laughing as her toes skimmed the floor. "Now please put me down before one of us gets hurt."

On the drive home, Ray updated her on all the news—amusing stories of the kids, the house, the neighborhood, the workplace. It was astonishing how much had gone on in her absence, what a difference a week made.

"Jeanette stopped by this morning," Ray said as they pulled onto their tree-lined street. "She thought you'd be home already. She'd like you to call her as soon as possible."

"She probably wants to tell me about the Cherokee Rose retreat," said Pauline. "She knows I'm craving every detail."

Ray glanced at her as he pulled the car into their driveway. "Are you sorry you missed it?"

"A little," she admitted, "but I'm not sorry I attended Quiltsgiving instead. Not at all."

In fact, her stay at Elm Creek Manor had been exactly what she'd needed.

She was so busy working her way through the pile of small tasks and obligations that had accumulated during her week away that she couldn't find a moment to call Jeanette until a few days later. They chatted about the retreat—the successes and mishaps, the grand total their fund-raiser had earned—and Jeanette assured her that everyone in the guild had missed her.

Pauline was skeptical. "Everyone?"

"Almost everyone," Jeanette amended. "Speaking of Brenda, I have shocking news."

For a moment Pauline held her breath. "She's quit the guild and joined a Tibetan monastery?"

"No, silly. She and her husband have separated."

Pauline's first response was an utter lack of surprise—she wouldn't want to be married to Brenda either. Then, a moment later, it occurred to her how she would feel if her own marriage fell apart, and empathy won out. "Oh, that's a shame. When did this happen?"

"They decided a few days before the retreat and he moved out while she was at the Château Élan."

"Bless her heart. And their poor kids! They're probably devastated."

"I don't know about that," said Jeanette. "Apparently Brenda and her husband haven't been getting along well for years. A divorce might actually come as a huge relief."

Pauline wasn't so sure. From what she had observed of neighbors and friends—and the occasional 911 call—children usually wanted their parents to stay together and learn to get along, except when abuse figured into it. "I had no idea things were so bad for Brenda at home," she said, unsettled by the peculiar sensation of feeling sorry for the one person who had made her so miserable. "She never talked about it, at least not in front of me. Not that I was ever her most cherished confidante."

"She never talked about it with anyone, no more than a few negative comments now and then that only make sense in hindsight." Jeanette sighed. "Brenda dreaded going home from the retreat. Her husband had the kids, and he'd cleared out his stuff, so she would be going home to a quiet, half-empty house—"

"Well, sure. Who'd be eager to go home to that?"

"Daria and I are taking her out to lunch today, just to see how she's doing."

Pauline almost told Jeanette to give Brenda her best, but it occurred to her that her sympathies might not be welcome. "I hope she's doing okay. Let me know, won't you?"

"Of course." Jeanette paused. "And how are *you* doing?"

Compared to Brenda? Peachy. "I'm doing fine. Really. Don't worry about me."

"You know, we all really do miss you."

"I miss you all too."

She missed her friends, the guild, and that sense of purpose, of belonging to something bigger than herself. After Karen's pep talk, Pauline had made up her mind to attend the next guild meeting and not to let one unpleasant, selfish person keep her from doing good works and enjoying the company of her friends. But now, the broad, distinct lines of what she had viewed as a clearly defined battle between good and evil had blurred, leaving her less certain that she understood the whole story. Perhaps Brenda was not the heartless, cruel villain of the tale Pauline had spun for herself. Perhaps Brenda was simply desperately unhappy. Every day, Pauline went home to a husband who was absolutely crazy about her and teenage children who did well in school, never got into any serious trouble, and thought she was pretty cool for a mom, if a little strict. She went home to a house full of love and happiness and laughter. What had Brenda gone home to all these years?

Pauline didn't know, and she certainly was in no position to ask. What she did realize was that Brenda clearly needed the Cherokee Rose Quilters more than she did.

Pauline could give her that.

The following week, when the Cherokee Rose Quilters met for their annual holiday party, Pauline stayed home.

The next morning, Jeanette sent her a text saying they had

missed her. She followed that up with an e-mail asking when Pauline's next day off was, because she and Daria wanted to take her to lunch. When Pauline didn't write back promptly enough, Jeanette called, brushed off Pauline's feeble excuses, and would not relent until Pauline chose a date, time, and restaurant for them to meet.

Pauline had not seen Daria in ages and never saw enough of Jeanette, so they had a lot of catching up to do. They chatted and laughed through lunch, as well as dessert and two cups of coffee apiece afterward, to prolong their time together. It was not until after they paid the bill that Jeanette said, "As you know, we've been interviewing candidates to take your place in the guild."

Pauline tried to smile. "Well, I figured. It's about time."

"We met a lot of fabulous quilters, but we all agreed that there's only one person we want." Daria took a red file folder from her purse and slid it across the table to Pauline. "It was unanimous."

Pauline looked from the folder to Daria to Jeanette, dubious. "And you want my opinion?" When they nodded, she muffled a sigh, quashed the stirrings of envy in her heart, and opened the folder.

Her own face smiled up at her from a photo paper-clipped to the portfolio she had submitted several years before.

Quickly she closed the folder and forced a laugh. "I can't look at that hair. What was I thinking?"

Jeanette reached for her hand. "Pauline, honey, we want you back."

"The vote was unanimous, you say?"

Jeanette and Daria exchanged a guilty glance. "Yes, it was," said Daria. "Brenda happened to be absent the day we voted."

"Really." Pauline regarded them skeptically. "The woman who skipped opening night of her son's senior class play rather than miss a guild meeting happened to be absent on that particular night."

"We called an emergency meeting and didn't invite her," Jeanette admitted. "Look. We've all agreed. What Brenda did was completely out of line, and allowing you to walk away rather than holding her accountable is not in the spirit of the Cherokee Rose Quilters."

"If you don't feel comfortable returning to the guild as long as Brenda's around, that won't be an issue," Daria said. "If you come back, we're going to ask her to leave."

Pauline stared at them. "You're going to do what? Now?"

"Not right this minute," Daria said. "We'll meet her in person some time before the next meeting."

"No, I mean now, as in mere days after her husband moved out. The timing"—Pauline gestured, searching for the words—"really stinks."

Jeanette sighed. "It does. That can't be helped."

"You can't kick her out now," Pauline insisted. "That would be cruel. She needs the guild now more than ever. She needs friends."

"You need friends too," Daria pointed out. "Don't you?"

Pauline felt a catch in her throat. "Doesn't everyone?"

"You left for the good of the guild. We get that." Jeanette leaned forward and rested her elbows on the table. "We let you. That was our mistake."

Daria nodded. "For the good of the guild, we want you back, and we want the person who caused the whole ugly incident to step aside. It's the only fair way to resolve the situation."

Pauline shook her head in disbelief. Her friends were at last standing up for her, speaking up for her, the way she had wished they would, but instead of feeling vindicated, she felt appalled and unhappy.

"That's not the only way to resolve the situation," Pauline said firmly. "I want to come back. Really, I do. And I will, under one condition."

Daria brightened, and Jeanette asked, "What's that?"

"That you don't ask Brenda to leave." Pauline raised a hand to silence their astonished protests. "Surely even a small guild like ours is big enough for both of us. Brenda's your friend, and she's going through a lot right now. If it's up to me, I say we should choose mercy over justice. Let's give her another chance."

Daria beamed, and Jeanette smiled, and both agreed to her condition.

Pauline knew it wouldn't be easy to work with Brenda after so much ugliness had passed between them. She knew that Brenda might slap the olive branch out of her outstretched hand.

Giving could often be as difficult as it was necessary, and gifts of the heart were sometimes rebuffed. But Pauline knew she had to try.

Maybe, in the spirit of the season, Brenda would decide to give Pauline a second chance too.

After leaving Elm Creek Manor, Michaela drove home to Pheasant Branch to do her laundry—for free and with appliances that didn't shrink her clothes, unlike those at school—and to have dinner with her parents. Her mother hung on every detail of her Quiltsgiving week, and she especially admired Michaela's Giving Journal and the handouts Gretchen had distributed in class.

Michaela had so much to share that she started back to St. Andrew's College later than she had intended. The snow-covered campus was dark and quiet by the time she parked in the student lot and pulled her wheeled suitcase across campus, planting her crutches carefully on the sidewalk wherever the sprinkling of rock salt had failed to do its job.

"Stupid ankle," she muttered as she struggled through the doors into the lobby of her dorm. *Stupid guys who dropped me*, she thought as she punched the button to summon the elevator. She was so sick of cast and crutches that when she was finally through with them, she thought she might either hurl them out of her dorm room window or set them on fire, or perhaps both.

She spent the next week catching up in her classes and writing a report on her Quiltsgiving experience in order to earn her community service credit. When she dropped off the paper at her adviser's office, she spoke so enthusiastically about Elm Creek Quilts and Project Linus that her adviser, a longtime quilter herself, declared that she intended to sign up for the next Quiltsgiving.

"You totally should," said Michaela. "You'll be glad you did."

On Friday afternoon, she and Emma met at the library to study for their English final. Emma had taken such meticulous notes during Michaela's absence that she didn't feel like she had missed out on anything, although she wouldn't be foolish enough to tell their professor that.

After a few hours, they took a break and went downstairs to the basement café for coffee and a warm, gooey chocolate chip cookie, which they shared while bemoaning the number of miles they would have to run to work it off. "I won't be running anywhere any time soon," said Michaela. "How many calories do you suppose hobbling burns off? More or less than running?"

"More, definitely," said Emma, licking chocolate off her fingertips. "Hobbling uses more of your upper body."

Michaela mulled that over. "You could be right. When I finally get this thing off of my foot, maybe I'll be able to do even more back handsprings in a row."

"They'd have to build you a bigger gym first."

Michaela giggled, but her mirth swiftly faded. "I wish my tumbling had been enough to get me on the cheerleading squad. It's not just that I wanted to cheer, which of course I really, really did. It's also that I know it would have helped me get a coaching job after graduation. But without having that on my résumé . . . I don't know. I'll just have to figure out something else."

"Well, actually," said Emma, "I kind of wanted to talk to you about that." She wiped her fingertips on her napkin, stalling for time, and then she spoke in a rush. "Pompom practices have been going really well. The girls are so sweet. I know you'd really like them."

Michaela held up a hand. "Emma, you know I don't want to join the pompom squad. And even if I wanted to . . ." She gestured to her injured ankle.

"I know. I didn't mean for you to become a pompom girl." Emma grimaced ruefully. "Listen, we know we aren't very good. We know people laugh at us, and it hurts. But we aren't

going to let other people's opinions keep us from doing something we enjoy."

"That's absolutely the right attitude," said Michaela, immediately regretting her dismissive attitude. "You'll show them."

"I hope so. We want to be good, and if we can't be good, we
at least want to be better." Emma drew herself up and regarded
Michaela with anxious hope. "We want to know if maybe you'd
consider joining the squad—as our coach."

"Your coach?"

"We couldn't pay you, but don't you think it would be fun?
Everyone's really nice and you'd get great experience for your
résumé, don't you think?"

Michaela considered. She pictured herself directing rigorous
workouts, choreographing routines, standing on the sidelines
as the girls put on a spectacular performance, smiling in satisfaction as the cheerleaders turned various shades of green
with envy when they realized they weren't the best show in town
anymore.

"Tell the girls they have a new coach," she said.

Emma let out a shriek of delight and hugged her.

Jocelyn returned home to Westfield refreshed, invigorated, and
thankful.

It took her no time at all to get back into the rhythm of
school and family. Rahma and Anisa begged her for quilting
lessons, so every night after they finished their homework, she
showed them what she had learned at Elm Creek Manor. She
also purchased several books on hand piecing and quilting
from her local quilt shop. Now that she understood the basics of

assembling a patchwork block, she was confident she could make the transition from machine to hand work on her own, guided by the books' photos and step-by-step instructions. She couldn't wait to introduce her history students to the traditional handicraft. Perhaps they could even make a quilt or two to donate to Project Linus as a class project.

One evening a week after Quiltsgiving, Jocelyn returned to Grosse Pointe South High School to attend an Imagination Quest managers' meeting. Nearly forty managers, some of whom Jocelyn recognized from the previous season's tournament, gathered in the auditorium for a presentation by IQ officials and a question-and-answer session. The state director spoke first, welcoming them to another exciting year of creativity, teamwork, and problem solving, and providing them with an overview of the IQ mission and the program rules. The regional director followed with a description of that year's challenges and logistical details about the venue and procedures for the upcoming tournament.

It was fortunate that most of the information covered that evening also appeared in the manager's handbook Jocelyn had received when she registered the team, because she could hardly follow a word of the question-and-answer session, so stunned was she by a change in the rules the directors had announced.

After each team presented its challenge solution, the judges would interview the children and have them describe in their own words how they had come up with their ideas, how they had built their equipment, and how everything functioned. It was an almost verbatim statement of the changes Jocelyn's team had suggested in the letter they had sent to Imagination Quest headquarters the previous spring.

She couldn't wait to tell Rahma, Anisa, and the rest of the team, past and present, that their letter had made a difference.

In her haste to depart as soon as the meeting concluded, Jocelyn was in her coat, out of the auditorium, and halfway to the exit before she realized someone with a deep voice was calling her name. "Mrs. Ames," she heard again, and turned around to find a man jogging toward her, a briefcase in one hand and a long wool coat draped over his other arm. "You're Mrs. Ames, from Westfield Middle School, aren't you?"

"Yes, I am." She surreptitiously glanced at her watch and waited for him to catch up. He looked vaguely familiar, near her age with a sprinkling of gray in his curly black hair, and dressed as if he had come to the meeting directly from his job as an actuary or insurance agent, complete with glasses on the bridge of his nose and pens in his breast pocket.

"I'm Miles McKinney," he said, setting down his briefcase and extending his hand for her to shake. "I'm the manager of the Bloomfield Hills Middle School team."

"Oh, yes." Jocelyn thought back. There were, regrettably, few people of color among the coaches, making Miles easy to place. "Your team wore the green-and-white shirts last spring, right? If I remember correctly, you took first place in the Stop the Presses challenge and went on to nationals."

"That's right." He smiled, visibly pleased that she remembered. Suddenly his smile faded and his expression grew sympathetic. She knew at once what he was about to say, and she braced herself. "Please accept my belated condolences for your loss. I knew your husband—not well, but enough to know he was a good man."

She felt a catch in her throat. "Thank you. You're right. He was a very good man."

"I'm glad to see your team is carrying on."

"I'm glad the kids still want to," she heard herself say. When Miles peered questioningly back at her, she added, "Last year didn't go well for us."

His brow furrowed and he shook his head. "I was in the bleachers with my team during your session. I thought your kids did fantastic."

"If you were watching, you must remember the team who won our challenge." Jocelyn had a sudden thought, and she glanced around at the managers filing past them on their way to the exit just to be sure. "I didn't see their manager here tonight."

"No?" Miles looked around too, then turned back to Jocelyn, folded his arms over his broad chest, and shrugged. "I wouldn't be surprised if they didn't sign up this year."

"Really? Why?" Perhaps they didn't have enough room in their trophy case, Jocelyn thought tartly, but she managed to refrain from saying so.

"Are you kidding? After they crashed and burned at nationals?"

"After they . . ." Jocelyn stared at him. "What happened?"

"You didn't hear?"

Jocelyn shook her head. She hadn't even checked the Imagination Quest website to see if the red-and-gold team had won, so certain had she been that they would, and so reluctant was she to subject herself and the girls to photos of their celebration, their proud parents beaming in the background.

"You know the new rule they implemented for this year's tournament, the team interviews?" asked Miles. Jocelyn nodded. "They actually started that at nationals last spring. All of us— the managers, I mean—were notified by phone a week before the tournament. That was enough time for middle schoolers to practice talking about something they had done and under- stood well, but not enough time to fake it if someone else had done the work."

Jocelyn nodded, and although she tried to look only moder- ately, objectively interested, she couldn't help it—she felt her smile growing.

"Of course those kids couldn't tell the judges how their de- livery device worked or how they had managed to build it given that none of them was a licensed carpenter capable of dead- lifting eighty pounds, so they got a zero for that portion of their score. They came in second to last."

Jocelyn strangled out a laugh. "How did they manage to beat anyone at all?"

"Another team went hugely over budget and didn't hit a single target." Miles grinned down at her, curious. "You really didn't know any of this?"

"Not a bit."

"I admire that," he said. "You didn't care who won or lost. You really are all about the quality of the experience. I care maybe a little too much about winning."

"I care more about winning than I'll ever admit to my team," Jocelyn said dryly. "I feel bad for those kids, though. They must have been so embarrassed."

"They shouldn't have cheated, and they shouldn't have lied," said Miles bluntly. "I don't doubt that they were following their parents' lead, but come on, they're old enough to know right from wrong."

"They are, but I still feel sorry for them."

"Don't feel too sorry for them. They learned a valuable lesson at a time when they're old enough to benefit from it and young enough that it won't jeopardize their futures."

"I hope so." Jocelyn would be very sorry indeed if no good at all came of the debacle. And yet some good already had come of it. The rules had been changed, and her team would have the satisfaction of knowing that their concerns had been heard and addressed. They would learn that some adults did care about justice and fairness after all.

"Well—" Miles glanced at the door, turned back to her, and smiled, looking as if he were not quite ready to go. "I guess I'll see you at the tournament in the spring."

"I guess so," she agreed, smiling back.

"Unless . . ."

"Unless what?"

"The thing is, I have almost an entirely new team this year. All of my students from last year except one moved on to high school. I was thinking, since our teams didn't choose the same challenge—"

"How do you know that?"

"I saw you raise your hand when the director polled the group." He winced comically as if embarrassed to admit that he had been watching her. "Maybe we can get our teams together a few weeks before the tournament for a dress rehearsal."

"That's a wonderful idea," said Jocelyn. "The practice will be good for all of them, and it would be nice to have another team to cheer for at the competition."

"My thoughts exactly. Let me give you my number." He pulled a pen and a business card from his shirt pocket and jotted something on the back. "My work number and cell are on the front, and I wrote my home number on the back. My work number isn't usually a good place to reach me, though."

Jocelyn accepted the card. "I imagine not. Your employer probably wouldn't like you to take calls while you're"—she glanced at the card and managed not to do a double take—"while you're performing surgery. But the home number is okay?"

"Sure. It's just me and my son." He grimaced, rueful. "Two weekdays and alternate weekends, anyway. The rest of the time my son's with my ex-wife."

"I see." And Jocelyn did see.

Miles prompted her for her number, so she wrote it on an extra piece of loose-leaf paper from her IQ binder. He folded it in eighths, tucked it into his chest pocket, and patted it, smiling.

They were leaving the building at the same time, and heading to the same parking lot, so it was only natural for him to escort her to her car.

"I'll call you," he said.

She nodded. She had no doubt that he would.

He waited until she was behind the wheel and had started the engine before he waved and walked away. Suddenly she thought of something she had neglected to ask. Quickly she lowered the window. "Miles?"

He stopped and turned around. "Yes?"

"How did your team do at nationals?"

"They took third in their division, and they got a perfect score in the interview."

Jocelyn smiled, pleased. It was the perfect answer, revealing more about him than he probably realized. "Congratulations."

"Thanks," he called back, grinning as he tucked his hands into his coat pockets and braced himself against the winter wind. "This year we're aiming for first."

She laughed. "So are we."

He waited until she raised the window and pulled out of her parking space before he turned and made his way across the lot to his own car.

On the morning of the book burning, the day before the millage vote, Linnea received encouraging e-mails from her sister, the new friends she had made at Quiltsgiving, and at least half the members of her California Librarians' Collective mailing list. Her phone began ringing before she was quite ready to speak to anyone other than her family, calls from eager reporters hoping to score a pithy quote about the value of libraries or a scathing rebuke of Ezra McNulty. Linnea accepted a call from Renee Montagne because she was a big fan of NPR's *Morning Edition*, but she let the answering machine take the rest.

The kids hugged her and wished her good luck before they set out for school. Soon thereafter, Linnea and Kevin kissed and parted ways, Linnea for the library, Kevin for the coffee shop and a last-minute strategy meeting with the other leaders of Vote Yes for Libraries before their final get-out-the-vote effort. "I'll see you soon," Kevin promised as he climbed into his car. She nodded, blew him a kiss, and watched him drive off before setting out alone, apprehension forming a dull knot in the pit of her stomach.

A few members of the media had staked out the library's front entrance, probably seeking patron comments on the protest being set up in the adjacent park, but only one intrepid reporter and a cameraman had thought to wait by the employee entrance at the rear. "Of course I'm disappointed that the county didn't revoke the bonfire permit," Linnea replied to the reporter's entirely unnecessary question, hurrying past him and inside, breathing a sigh of relief when the heavy door swung shut between her and the microphone he had thrust in her face.

Behind the scenes, the staff area was abuzz with anxious pages and solemn librarians following the developments outside via radio, television, and Internet. In the public area, staff and patrons alike strove to keep the atmosphere one of business as usual, but a frisson of nervous tension ran through the entire library. From the children's department, Linnea watched as patrons set down their books and newspapers and left their laptops unguarded in study carrels and watched from the east windows as a veritable fleet of fire engines drove past on their way to the park, their sirens muted but lights flashing. The fire chief intended to station some fire trucks at the scene of the bonfire, one in the library parking lot, and two in the fields in between. If something did go drastically wrong, they would be prepared to douse the flames.

But Linnea had a plan, and if all went as she hoped, the bonfire would amount to nothing.

She left the children's department in the care of a library assistant and summoned a few pages to help her set up the meeting room. One of her favorite artists from a previous "Saturday with the Artists" program, a papermaker and bookbinder, arrived an hour early, a bit jittery but eager to do his part. Distantly she heard loudspeakers and bullhorns, and her stomach fluttered nervously. The protest was about to begin.

She steeled herself and went to the lobby, where she found the president of the Friends of the Library Foundation and the library director already waiting. "Good luck," the director told her and Alicia, hugging each of them quickly. "If things turn ugly, promise me you'll get out of there. I don't want either of you to get hurt."

"At the first sign of trouble, we'll run for the fire engines," Alicia replied.

"With any luck, we'll be back soon," said Linnea. "And not alone."

The library director managed a tight smile and nodded.

Side by side, Linnea and Alicia walked along the pedestrian trail through the stand of live oaks and over the creek to the park. They saw the television lights and heard classic rock blasting from loudspeakers from a quarter of a mile away, and the sounds of voices grew as they approached. When they reached the site of the protest, a stone patio on the shore of a pond, Linnea estimated the gathered crowd to number at least a hundred protesters, each carrying a book or two, and a few dozen members of the media. A stage had been erected, and upon it strode a stocky man in khaki pants and a light blue shirt with the sleeves rolled up to the elbows—Ezra McNulty, older and less attractive than the photo on his website, but unmistakably the same man. A wreath of curly brown hair encircled a bald pate, and even from a distance Linnea could see that he was smiling, cheerful, and completely at ease, as if the agitated crowd milling at the foot of the stage were a handful of good friends gathered for a backyard barbecue. Nearby stood a pile of

artificial fireplace logs on the edge of the playground surrounded by pea gravel; a young man with a red can of lighter
fluid stood beside it chatting happily with a young, blond reporter from a right-wing television network that prided itself,
entirely without justification, on its fairness and impartiality.

Linnea took a deep breath. "Okay," she said. "Here we go.
All they can do is send us away, right?"

"Wrong," retorted Alicia, falling in step beside her as she
headed for the stage. "How fast can you run?"

Linnea laughed bleakly as they made their way through the
crowd. At the foot of the stage, they picked out Ezra McNulty's
producer by his headset, his clipboard, and the number of assistants scurrying back and forth carrying out his directives.
"Mr. Fielding?" Linnea asked, raising her voice to be heard over
the crowd. "May I have a moment?"

"Sorry," he said, not even glancing her way. He spoke a few
commands into his headset and gave Ezra McNulty a thumbs-up.
Ezra grinned back and made an elaborate show of cracking his
knuckles, preparing for battle. "Kind of busy here."

"I'm Linnea Nelson from the Conejo Hills Public Library."

His head jerked up and he spun to face her. "You're the one
who set up the display of trashy books in the children's department."

Linnea smiled thinly. "That's not how I would characterize
it, but yes, I'm the one. I understand that you're allowing a few
members of the public to address the crowd, and I'd like to be
the first."

Fielding brushed off an assistant and beckoned Linnea and
Alicia closer. "Are you here to offer an explanation? An
apology?"

Linnea shook her head. "An invitation."

His eyes narrowed as he regarded her speculatively. "Okay," he said. "I'm game, but don't blame me if McNulty tears you a new one." Into the microphone he added, "Add this to the crawler. 'Contrite librarian to address crowd at protest.' Now."

"She's not contrite," Alicia began, but Linnea shot her a warning look. Alicia bit back her complaints, shaking her head in disapproval.

The producer instructed an assistant to show them to a waiting area behind the stairs while he hurried onstage to inform Ezra McNulty about the change to the program. McNulty fixed Linnea and Alicia with a level stare as the producer spoke close to his ear, but suddenly his face broke out in a bright grin and he waved merrily. The women waved uncertainly back. Linnea caught a chemical whiff of smoke as someone lit the artificial logs, and the crowd broke out in cheers of anticipation.

Over the loudspeakers, the music swelled and a rich baritone voice announced Ezra McNulty. He approached the downstage microphone stand like a prizefighter, throwing punches and waving to the crowd. Linnea's heart was pounding so hard that she couldn't focus on his opening remarks, a slanted account of the events that had led to the protest, designed to stir his listeners into a frenzy.

Just when Linnea began to worry that he would move ahead to the burning of books without allowing her to speak, he took a step back, bowed his head, and raised a hand to the crowd, who gradually quieted. "Don't let anyone say that I'm not willing to listen to the other side," he said. A few scattered boos rang out, and McNulty raised his hand again and shook his head to silence them. "No, no, we're all about freedom of speech. We're willing to let them speak their piece. Of course, when they do, they usually just prove themselves a bunch of idiots—" A roar of laughter interrupted him. "But if that's what they want to do, fine by me. We have an unexpected guest who's asked to speak to you. We're gonna let her talk, and I'm gonna ask you to be polite and respectful, no matter how much you disagree with her. Folks, I give you Linnea Nelson of the Conejo Hills Public Library, or as she's better known, Linnea the Lascivious Librarian!"

Linnea's heart sank as the crowd roared back with laughter and jeers. Alicia squeezed her hand encouragingly and accompanied her to the foot of the stairs. On trembling legs, Linnea met a grinning McNulty downstage. She nodded to him and took the microphone. "Thank you for letting me speak," she said to the crowd, but their shouts drowned her out until McNulty gestured with outstretched arms for them to quiet down.

She took a deep breath and tried again. "I know there are many subjects on which we disagree," she said, raising her voice to be heard, "but I hope that before you destroy these books—books that have meant so much to generations of readers—I hope that we might find some common ground."

She spoke briefly, mindful of their impatience, their animosity. She talked about her love of reading and how it had inspired her to become a librarian. She spoke of how she witnessed every day the good libraries did and the services they provided to the community. She shared her belief that even a book whose merits were in dispute could be a catalyst for discussion, for healthy, vigorous debate that could lead to greater understanding on both sides.

"The very books you want to burn today, the books you believe are some of the worst ever written, have been considered some of the greatest works in the English language," she said, ignoring a stream of catcalls. "How can two sides be so completely opposed?"

"We're right and you're wrong," someone shouted, evoking jeering laughter from those around him.

"Maybe you're right," Linnea countered, "but you won't convince me unless you talk to me. Let's talk together, not shout at each other from opposite sides of a bonfire. Let's create, not destroy." She drew courage from the few faces in the crowd turned to her in thoughtful curiosity. "I'd like to invite you to come with me to the library. I know that for some of you, it would be your first visit. Our librarians and friends would like to talk with you about these books—why we think they're worthwhile and why you think they aren't. We also have an artist waiting, a bookbinder, who's eager to teach us all how to make our own books. You can make your own book for whatever you want to write— your memoirs, your argument in favor of this book burning, your secret recipes, a novel written the way you wish the books you want to burn had been written. It's up to you. It's your book. All we ask is that instead of tossing the books you're holding into the fire, you instead put them into our donations bin." She forced a smile. "And if conversation and handicrafts don't tempt you, we also have coffee, tea, and cookies." To her everlasting gratitude, someone actually laughed. "We have room enough for everyone, so please, think about it. My friend and I will be waiting over there by that bench." She pointed across the pond to a spot near the start of the pedestrian trail. "We sincerely hope that you'll join us. Thank you."

She replaced the microphone in the stand and left the stage. Suddenly the music surged and Ezra McNulty bounded back onstage, grinning and waving to the crowd. From the way he studiously ignored her as they passed on the stairs, she knew he was furious.

Only eight people, five women and three men, tore themselves free from the crowd and met Linnea and Alicia by the bench. "Should we wait in case anyone else is coming?" Linnea asked, her eyes fixed on the protest as Ezra McNulty paced the stage shouting his diatribe into the microphone.

"I think this is it," Alicia said. "Let's go. I don't want to be here when they start tossing books on the pyre."

So Linnea and Alicia led eight skeptical protestors to the library, where they placed copies of *The Grapes of Wrath*, *The Adventures of Huckleberry Finn*, *The Origin of Species*, and *Are You There God? It's Me, Margaret*, among others, into the donations bin. They chatted with the librarians and Friends of the Library and politely watched the artist demonstrate how to bind a book. A few even tried to make books of their own. All the while the demonstration raged outside, barely audible, not very far away.

Eventually their guests thanked them and departed. Linnea wondered whether they intended to go home or return to the protest, but she couldn't bring herself to ask.

Linnea observed the little she could bear of the book burning on CNN during her lunch hour and breaks. Kevin called twice to let her know how the get-out-the-vote effort was going and to offer her encouragement. She needed some. "Only eight people came," she told him. "Out of more than one hundred protestors, only eight were willing to talk to us. Only eight chose conversation rather than argument, creation instead of destruction."

"But that's eight more than would have if you hadn't tried," he reminded her. "Sometimes changing minds happens a little at a time."

Linnea knew he was right. She wondered how those eight people would vote the next day.

The protest wrapped up before Linnea left work for the day. The scent of smoke lingered in the air as she exited the library, but the cameras, loudspeakers, fire engines, and crowds were gone. She contemplated walking to the park to see what they had left behind, but the thought of seeing a pile of ashes where some of her most beloved books had met their end was unbearable.

Instead she drove home. Kevin greeted her with a kiss and a wordless hug. She clung to him and felt some of the stress of the day leave her.

The next morning, Linnea and Kevin walked down the street to the elementary school that was their polling place. She overheard a poll worker remark that they were expecting a record turnout. Though Kevin had been a leader of the movement to support the millage, he could not tell her whether a high turnout would most likely work in their favor or against.

They stayed up late that night awaiting the results.

Shortly after midnight, the late local news team interrupted the syndicated programming to announce that with 98 percent of the votes counted, they were declaring that the measure had passed. Fifty-two percent of the voters cast their ballots in favor of the millage, versus 48 percent against.

Kevin thrust his fists in the air and cheered, but Linnea

didn't feel like celebrating. Although she was relieved that the library would be, for the immediate future anyway, safe from closure, it pained her to realize that 48 percent of her neighbors and fellow citizens of Conejo Hills did not want to save the library.

"They're not necessarily against the library," Kevin told her when she confessed that she was relieved but not happy. "They just don't want to raise taxes to pay for it." He gave her an encouraging smile and brushed her hair out of her face. "But well over half of the town did agree to chip in to keep the library open for everyone. They bought you time to convince the other forty-eight percent that the library is worth it."

Linnea supposed he was right.

In the days that followed, the mood at the library was more cheerful and optimistic than it had been in months. The patrons were delighted that their literary haven would remain open, and the members of the library staff were greatly relieved that their jobs had been spared. Vote Yes for Libraries disbanded, but not before they threw a farewell party at Kevin's favorite Thai restaurant downtown. They all promised to keep in touch and to reunite whenever intolerance or injustice threatened their town.

Kevin's jovial mood diminished as they drove home. Linnea knew that his unemployment weighed heavily upon him, and working with Vote Yes for Libraries had filled his idle hours. Now, with his job prospects no better than they had been before the library was threatened, he would be thrust back into long, dull, empty days of searching for work and attending to household chores.

And life returned to normal, or something close to it.

Two days later, as Linnea and Kevin were enjoying a leisurely Sunday breakfast on the patio while their two resident teenagers slept in, Kevin went inside for another cup of coffee and returned with something on his mind. "You know, I've been thinking."

"That usually leads to trouble," Linnea remarked, setting the newspaper aside.

"And it might this time too." Kevin took a sip of coffee and sat down. "Working with Vote Yes for Libraries was the most rewarding experience I've had since I lost my job. I'm glad the battle's over but I'm sorry my work is done. Do you know what I mean?"

Linnea took his hand. "I understand completely."

"It occurred to me that there are probably other worthy causes out there, causes I believe in, that could use someone with expertise in marketing."

"Probably? I would say definitely."

Kevin clasped his other hand around hers. "Then maybe, in the meantime, I could contact a few nonprofits and see if they could use me. I don't mean that I'm going to volunteer forever. I want to find paying work—believe me, I do, and I'm going to keep looking."

"I know," she said quietly, giving his hand a gentle squeeze. "You'll find something."

"But until I do, I'd like to lend my skills to worthy causes that need my help," said Kevin. "I want to give back. And who knows? Maybe I'll make some contacts. Maybe volunteering will lead to a job. But even if it doesn't, I know I'll be happier if I'm making a difference."

Linnea's heart swelled with pride. "I think that's a wonderful idea," she said, and she rose out of her chair to kiss him tenderly across the table.

Linnea's e-mail about the results of the millage vote and her husband's decision to continue to give back to his community through pro bono work was the best news Karen had heard in a long time. She quickly wrote back to congratulate Linnea and to wish her continued good luck on the library front. "Perhaps we should all plan to reunite at Elm Creek Quilt Camp this summer," she suggested. "If not then, then perhaps next Quiltsgiving."

She had already decided that when she next returned to Elm Creek Manor, it would be as a camper, not as a member of the faculty.

In the weeks that had followed Quiltsgiving, Karen had updated her résumé as Sylvia had requested, but something had held her back from submitting it. She still admired the Elm Creek Quilters and liked them more the better she knew them. She still believed that working at Elm Creek Quilt Camp would be enriching, inspiring, and rewarding—but so was working at the String Theory Quilt Shop, and they needed her so much more.

It was enough to know that the Elm Creek Quilters wanted to welcome her into their circle. That knowledge, that acceptance, was a gift that filled her heart with peace and gratitude. She told Sylvia so when she called to explain why she wouldn't be applying for the vacant position on the faculty.

"I understand completely, dear," Sylvia had replied. "However, if you ever change your mind, please do let us know. You'll always be at the top of my list."

Karen had thanked her and promised to keep that in mind.

She quit her e-mail and hurried downstairs to fix Nate and the boys a hearty breakfast before they set off for work and school in the blustery cold. Heavy snow was forecast for the evening, but by then the family would be reunited at home, content to let the storm rage outside while they kept safe and snug indoors, in the company of the people they loved best.

After seeing her family off, Karen set out for Summit Pass. She stopped for a cup of Christmas Chai to go at the Wise Owl Teahouse and greeted fellow merchants sweeping the sidewalks clear of snow in front of their shops as she walked down the block, her collar turned up, her chin buried in the scarf Margot had knitted her for her last birthday.

Margot and Elspeth were working at the cutting table when she arrived, cutting fat quarters from bolt ends to make into ribbon-tied bundles.

"I've been thinking," Karen greeted them, setting her tea on the checkout counter long enough to shrug out of her coat, scarf, and mittens. "This iFabricShop app doesn't have to be a harbinger of doom. We could turn it to our advantage."

Elspeth's eyebrows rose. "How so?"

"Getting customers into the store is half the battle, isn't it?" Karen carried her cup to the cutting table and pulled up a stool. "This app, as annoying and invasive as it may be, could be doing us a favor. It's sending new customers through our doors. It's up to us to win them over."

"We can't beat the big box stores and the Internet juggernauts on price," Margot reminded her.

"Then we'll beat them another way," Karen countered. "Fabulous customer service. An inviting atmosphere. Complimentary tea and scones. A more engaging shopping experience. And let's not forget immediate delivery." She sipped her tea, her thoughts racing, her optimism rising. "These potential customers are here in our charming shop, where they're treated like valued friends, not some account number. They're holding the fabric they want in their hands. Why on earth wouldn't they buy it from us and take it home as soon as they ring up their purchase, rather than go home, order it online without interacting with a single human being, and wait a few days for it to arrive in their mailbox?"

Margot and Elspeth exchanged a look. "She has a point," Margot said, and Elspeth didn't disagree. Instead she sat back, regarded Karen thoughtfully, and waited for her to say more.

And Karen, who intended to be a part of String Theory until her own retirement many years hence, when she would pass the beloved, thriving shop on to a younger apprentice who would cherish it as much as she did, had much more to say.

ACKNOWLEDGMENTS

I am very grateful to the friends, family, and colleagues who offered the gifts of their time and talents to *The Giving Quilt*, especially Denise Roy, Maria Massie, Liza Cassity, Christine Ball, Brian Tart, Kate Napolitano, Melanie Marder Parks, and Janet Miller. I especially wish to thank Geraldine Neidenbach, Marty Chiaverini, and Brian Grover for reading early drafts of the manuscript and offering invaluable critiques and encouragement. *Merci beaucoup* to my friend Valerie Langue for the French dialogue. *Bisous!*

Most of all, I thank my husband and my sons for their steadfast love and support. You are life's greatest gifts to me.